WI

By: Christina Vlahos

ACKNOWLEDGEMENTS

There are several people in my life to which I owe great thanks. To my family and great friends, thank you for the unconditional love and support – rehab has nothing on y'all. To the people that inspired this book, you shall forever remain nameless, but shall forever remain entrenched in my mind. To my editor, Artimis Vlahos, thank you for pushing Bridget to the brink, and for making it all a little more wicked. To the person who told me to pick up a pen and just *write*, well what can I say Uncle Bill, we did it. Without you Bridget would never have come to life, and a hopeless girl would have remained sitting in an Athens apartment. Thank you for guiding me, encouraging me, and yelling at me, *it worked.*

'There will always be a reason why we meet people. Either you need them to change your life, or you're the one that will change theirs."

Madeline Sheehan.

Dedicated to anyone that's ever been on the verge of a nervous breakdown on course to finding true love.

GLOSSARY

Mr. Big: A recurring fictional character in the HBO series *Sex and the City*. He is the primary on-and-off love interest of Carrie Bradshaw and the protagonist of her columns & books, which focus is understanding men & relationships and finding love.

Mr. Grey: A young businessman and male protagonist in the 2011 erotic romance novel by British author E. L. James.

Bridget: an Irish name derived from '*brígh*', meaning 'power, strength, vigor, virtue'.

Vivian: From the Latin name *Vivianus* that was derived from Latin *vivus* 'alive'.

Lea: The American & Greek meaning of the name Lea is 'bringer of good news'.

Bobby: Deriving from the name Robert, meaning 'fame, & glory'.

Theron: An ancient Greek name meaning 'hunter'.

Leonidas: Greek for 'Lion Like'; Leonidas was an ancient Spartan King.

Hermia: An ancient Greek name meaning 'of the Earth'.

Melina: Greek name for honey (Meli); meaning of sweet.

Lane: Gaelic for 'descendent of Luan,' a given name meaning 'warrior'.

Jacob: A name whose Greek origin means 'may God protect'.

Faaris: An Arabic male name meaning Knight, and an English name meaning iron strong.

1

"Penelope Cruz and Javier Bardem are here! I'm going to scope out the lobby!" Stargazing was right up Vivian's alley – it was all she could do to prevent herself from leaping atop Pat Sajek at the Ivy on a girls' trip to LA last summer. 35 and single, Vivian stood 5 foot 3 inches tall with a chubby frame, ivory skin, and a dark mane like Chaka Khan, and she was the life of the party.

We'd grown up together in the not so trendy suburbs of Chicago, Niles, Illinois, to be exact, and being a few years older, she watched out for me – and always had good advice – even if she never took it herself. "Bridget OMG I'm going to blind them with this flash," she gasped pointing at her bright blue Cannon Powershot. I turned to her chuckling, with my usual look of disapproval. I needed no more entertainment to amuse me then that of my two best friends, my only friends actually – Vivian and Lea, and that's just the way I liked it. "Oh stop being so shy Bridget, get up in front," she insisted poking me in the back. God only knew I wasn't up for it tonight, but I saddled up like a good friend and tried to push myself through the crowded lobby of the Toronto International film festival party.

Above average height, I had no problem excusing myself and pushing through the sea of sharply scented, over-sprayed bodies waiting to catch a little glimpse of Hollywood. Broke, from yet another late payment on a crappy PR gig, I wore a $10 mini black skirt from Forever 21, and a peach colored short sleeve top that hung loosely from my shoulders. For most of my life I felt gawky and unbeautiful. Luckily I had grown out of the ugly duckling stage at a decent age, and survived with minimal childhood damage. Being a late bloomer may have had its benefits after all, at the very least (and very best) I'd never have to wear big red glasses, cotton frilly dresses (that were two sizes too small) or black Chinese slippers, *ever again*. All of course exceptional choices for a chubby, awkward, adolescent, courtesy of an overbearing Greek mother and Irish-American father, whose passion had brought them together to produce *yours truly*. Naturally their ever-present hot tempers had prohibited them from passing a day without a heated argument, which according to my mother was even evident at the scene of my birth. As the story goes, they each wanted a name from their own heritage; my mother a Greek name honoring her mother, and my father a strapping Irish name; consequently they had decided on both; Bridget Elizabeth; my father using his trusty double headed coin to win first position.

Some thirty years later I had managed to sustain a medium sized, (alright *voluptuous body*), golden-ish wavy hair, and green Irish eyes under clear contact lenses. In a city like Chicago, I didn't really stand out, unless of course my overly developed bust was seeping out of a top a few sizes too small – something that happened on rare occasion. I suppose I was happy to be noticed and complimented like any girl, when it happened, but I was definitely not enthused about fitting into wanna-be crowds, of any sort, including those looking for the picture perfect mate. In fact I had only ever had one – one long drawn out adolescent relationship that had probably done more damage than I cared to admit. Every other so-called relationship never lasted more than a couple of months. I never really examined why, but assumed it was a combination of my modest experiences and dating choices; wannabe musicians, actors, and bona fide pro-athletes, *who by the way* made for the worst mates. Meeting a guy in one of the above categories typically occurred while on a PR gig or, in a nightclub after taking three hours to put on four layers of make-up, a variety of attire I couldn't sit in, and designer shoes I could barely walk to the elevator in. Needless to say, the illusive outcome attracted exactly the wrong men; particularly because they assumed I actually looked like that; *all the time.* Furthermore, it would appear that showing up in jeans and a t-shirt for a date wasn't exactly what *that type* of guy expected. Unfortunately by the time I enlightened the exceptionally egotistical play boys I was just a normal girl who swapped glasses for contacts, had crumbs in her pockets and didn't wear pleather jumpsuits to the movies, it was, well, *all over.*

My pre-disposition was simple; I was in PR and knew what people wanted to see. Illusions were a wonderful concept. I had even grown fond of watching guys gawk over an overflowing rack. It was enough to reel them in, and maybe even have a first date, but after realizing I was a workaholic, a no-nonsense house cat, and most certainly not an effortless slam-dunk, the gig was up. I for one was not on a 5-week root hair color program or 6 am work out regiment, and I ate when I was hungry, which typically included daily quantities of chocolate – naturally, I never fit their superlative expectations.

I assumed this evening out with the girls would be no different than all the others. I had almost forgotten where I was when I spotted Vivian making her way to the front of the crowd practically guarding the service elevator while chatting up the security guard. I slipped through the crowd of trendy VIP wannabe's, casually stopping to pull my hair to the side avoiding cigars and long flames of silver-plated lighters. I couldn't fathom the pain of my throbbing feet getting any worse, and more importantly I couldn't believe I was 30 and still doing this.

Single, with decent skin and good hair, I was doing what I vouched I'd never do again. I had given up on parties of all kinds when I retired from the nightclub PR world a few years back, but I couldn't let my other bestee, Lea; spend her 33rd birthday wallowing over an ashtray of Marlborough Lights in her parents' basement. So here I was.

Lea was a natural beauty. A pretty, petite brunette with Bambi-like brown eyes and a slender build, and she was my rock. Forever down to earth, she was there for me through every anxiety attack, cheating boyfriend, and emergency room visit, so I was going to be there for her on her birthday. Her boyfriend Giovanni was a less than consistent figure in her life; a successful textile entrepreneur, he travelled a lot on business and their three year relationship seemed to take a rather large back seat, so this trip to Toronto was a well-needed distraction. I planned on networking for my dream projects – my own indie films - and having the girls along would make the dreadful, *'interesting idea, but we're sorry we can't invest,'* speech assimilate much easier.

I had one more meeting to go, and couldn't dread to meet over another Perrier in an over-crowded star gazing filled café. Instead I had invited the former Wall Street financier I'd been pitching yet another ground breaking film idea, to join us for a drink in the hotel's lobby bar where we'd be celebrating Lea's birthday. I'd never met Martin before, but he was all I imagined, and more. A polite, well-mannered finance wizard, who stood 5 foot 6 inches tall, wore square framed black glasses and a perfectly tailored navy suit. He wasn't as brash as the other financiers I was pitching, and mentioned inviting me, and my friends for a weekend to his Malibu mansion. I liked him already and knew he'd be harmless. I also knew I'd get a good laugh from watching him take a shot with Lea; and that wasn't too far from reality. Lea on the other hand seemed less then amused; an exchange Vivian and I took great pleasure in watching.

11

"Actually I have a boyfriend, we're practically engaged," I could hear Lea's stern response through the misty crowd of the lobby bar. "Oh well that's great, a little more work for me to do then," Martin replied chuckling, his perfectly hemmed pants moving up along his leather Prada loafers.

Just as Martin was going into another New York investment recovery story, the shiny doors of the west side elevator slid open and out walked Penelope Cruz and Javier Bardem. Dressed in a creamsicle floor length gown, her hair parted to the side held up by a diamond-studded pin, Penelope was the epitome of glamour, a 1960's Hollywood starlet. Javier held her around the waist, and didn't flinch at the flashing bulbs, screaming fans, or scantily clad women. Accompanied by three other Spaniards and two security guards, they walked right through the crowd into the garden café set alongside the Toronto skyline.

"I'm gonna go talk to them – this is my chance Bridge." "Ok Vivian, if you get past security make sure to snap a couple photos for proof, oh and tell Penelope that her hubby is hot." Just like that, off she went, her Kardashian-like booty swaying from side to side as she strolled into the garden café.

Meanwhile Martin continued to smother Lea with attention and potent Cosmopolitans, and I found myself alone. My eyes swept the room for something interesting amongst the mix of star gazing visitors, party hopping locals, and bored looking business men, when a screeching voice pounded my left eardrum. "Bridge! Bridge! OMG! I met them; him, her, whatever… you know what I mean!" Breathless and sweaty, Vivian sashayed her way through the half empty lounge, towards us. "Well who'd you meet?" asked an intrigued Martin, maintaining his conservative demeanor.

"Martin I know we just met, and you don't know me, but I am inclined to tell you, that I just approached Penelope Cruz!" Martin smiled broadly, shifting his glasses towards the upper bridge of his nose. "Wow, and what did you tell her?" he asked with enthusiasm. "Well I said… I'm sorry to disturb you but I just had to tell you, you, and that man look amazing. The way he carried himself; I mean I will never date another loser again!" "You said what?" Martin asked confused.

I let out a gasp and a simultaneous uncontrollable laugh. "That's amazing Viv! You did it for the team – here's to no more losers!" I said raising my glass to cheers Vivian on a job well done.

"So what was her response, Viv?!"

"You mean Penelope's, Bridge?"

"Yes, of course," I replied anxious to hear what a Hollywood starlet thought about the dreary single life of an ordinary American girl.

"Well she turned to me and said, *yes he is amazing!*"

"I can't believe you were talking to Penelope Cruz about her hubby Viv! Even more mortifying, about the losers we date," I responded taking a sip from my cosmopolitan.

"Well I'll drink to that," Martin said calling over the waitress for another round of drinks at the table. *Well at least he had that down pat.* After receiving our drinks we decided to move over to the comfy hotel lobby area. I couldn't have been more pleased to remove one half of my Michaels Kors strappy sandals and sink back into the cushioned armchairs the lobby offered.

Lea and Martin continued an intensely pointless conversation on a couch across my eyes view, while Vivian circled the area with her digital camera for any leftover celebs. As I reached down placing my foot back into the strappy culprits of my swollen feet, I looked up to catch a glimpse of a chubby olive skinned young man bopping his way towards the overcrowded party. *Oh God that's Oliver*, and without thinking about it, my lips parted and a soft hello fluttered out of mouth. "Hi," he answered back walking briskly passed the lounge with a driven yet confused look on his face. *Now that was weird.* I had met Oliver in College, he was originally from a Greek Island I couldn't remember the name of, and in Chicago studying economics and learning how to expand the family business. He was 37 years old, rather short, and overweight, and wore his curly hair as a fuzzy dark afro.

From what I recalled he ran a less than successful family Tea business he had been trying to implement into the United States. He came off as an arrogant, know it all, with a proficiency in ancient Greco-Roman thinking. In short, he was a pervert who couldn't keep his hands to himself, and had a competitive and egotistic disposition, especially towards women. Needless to say we did not get along. As odd as it may seem, it wasn't due to my lack of trying. Oliver had a compassionate, funny side I found alluring, and it was this that led me to the back of his motorbike, one summer evening after an off-campus group-drink. It was also this barely thought out, dreadful idea, that led me to jump off his partially moving motorcycle at a yellow traffic light. Who would have thought a few tainted slanders out of Oliver would have exasperated me to that extreme? Evidently, there were some things I just couldn't handle – and a chauvinist pig was most definitely one of them. Some four years later he looks weathered, heavier and more confrontational than ever in his stretched out Ed Hardy T-shirt. As I sorted through old memories, I inhaled deeply, knowing I had just deflected a less than pleasant encounter.

My thoughts were interrupted by Vivian's proverbial screeching voice, "Bridge! We need to go! Lea's totally bombed!" Selfishly, I felt a sigh of relief; I needed a good excuse to make an early exit. Lea didn't drink much but when she did she certainly didn't hold back. My mind was always racing around work, and I wondered if Martin would ever consider financing one of my projects. This was quite the norm for me - a somewhat quirky impression, a friendly contact, and an unsigned deal memo.

I smiled at Martin, gathering our things, while helping Lea up off the sunken purple couch. "She doesn't get out much," I explained as Martin gathered Lea's pink ruffled clutch. "Well you could have fooled me girls! It was a real pleasure Bridget and I hope we can do this again some time, please do let me know when you're in LA or the Big Apple, and feel free to bring your friends." *Oh God the kiss of death, sealed with neon lipstick.* There was no point in addressing my dream film, or investment, or the next meeting, it was exceedingly clear, Martin was a lovesick puppy, with a patented lock over his bank accounts. "Alright Martin, well thanks for your time, lovely to meet you and safe travels back to the Big Apple." "Allow me to at least get you ladies a cab," he replied, in an endearing Pee-Wee Herman style voice. "That's not necessary," I countered half holding up Lea. "Oh I see," he chuckled in his nerdy Wall Street style, grabbing Lea and heading for the taxi stand.

Piled up safely in a yellow cab a few moments later, I pondered how long Lea would be able to hold her liquor. "I wonder if we gotta pay double if she pukes?" I inquired looking over at Vivian. "Shh!" she urged – "Canadians are nice, but I'm sure they don't take well to drunk and vomit stricken American girls in their cabs!" A suspicious looking Asian cabbie, peered through his bottled glasses a few times in the rear view mirror, but asides from that, seemed unconcerned, getting us back to the hotel in just a few minutes.

Arriving at the Sheraton, I felt a sense of relief gush over me once more. "Vivian get her out and I'll pay." Squeezing her behind out of the half open cab door, Vivian peeled Lea off the back seat and half held her up on the curb. "It'll be fine," I said slamming the yellow door behind me. "Once she pukes or passes out we can have a drink, a cigarette, and relax."

Staggering though the corridor of the 12th floor, we finally made it to the hotel room – puke free. "Let's get her clothes off and onto the bed she goes," I urged exhausted. I was glad I had opted for the sleeping bag Vivian had wisely asked the concierge to bring up; "just in case," she had said, and this was indeed *a case*. Vivian glanced over at me sending disapproving looks over her cat shaped eyeglasses, as I unrolled the sleeping bag giggling.

After laying out the sleeping bag and comforter, I pulled out a face cloth wiping what felt like the night's woes off my face. Tossing it aside, I thought about how different my life had become since quitting my job, how much I had grown to hate routine, and how the structured life I once loved had become my nemesis. My thoughts were interrupted by the room's balcony door sliding open. "Night Viv," I called out softly before snuggling under the quilt. "What happened to the drink and Cigarette Bridge?" "Reign check Viv, you're on your own tonight," I mumbled closing my eyes to the sounds of pouring liquid, breaking glass, and the word "crap!"

I pulled my cotton socks up over my knees and pressed my face into the cold pillow; dozing off to thoughts of summer nights, motorbikes, and *losers* I'd never date again.

2

"Hold her hair back Bridge!" "I'm trying Vivian!" I yelled out tightening my grasp on Lea's shiny brown ponytail. Who would have thought that the dead weight of such a tiny girl would feel like pounds of cement! "I'm doing my best, considering I slept for two hours in a second-hand sleeping bag." "Hey, you opted for that Bridget, I took the risk of sleeping in the same bed as a vomit ridden drunken girl! Wait Bridge, I need to take my watch off, it was a graduation present from my folks, and the only decent thing they've ever given me; there's no way its going down the toilet with Lea's vomit!" "Vivian your sentimental side is making me teary eyed, and by the way, I can't believe you're this alert in the morning before coffee!" "Well I do have a few years on you Bridge, it's an acquired trait! I mean who barfs the morning after?!" "Well technically it's just a few hours after Viv!" "All done Lea? All better?" I asked in my best motherly, 'I'm not the least annoyed' voice. "Oh yes!" Lea responded exhausted and thankful.

"Didn't this happen in an episode of Sex & the City?" she added holding a cold compress to her forehead. "Oh yeah," I said stretching my tired torso, "only Carrie wasn't drinking away her birthday blues, she was dumped by Mr. Big who had reappeared with his 26 year old fiancée!" "Glad you clarified that Bridget," Lea responded sinking her body on the bathroom floor. "Girls do you think everyone has a *Mr. Big*?" I asked placing my loose pink sweatshirt over my customary beige bra. "Well that depends how you define Mr. Big," Vivian responded popping open a can of Pringles. "You know, the guy you are enamored by; he's not the guy who writes you poems and calls you when he should, but the one who keeps you waiting, finally decides he loves you, than leaves you for something better; but of course eventually reappears." "Sounds like a vicious cycle," Lea said brushing back her hair into a ballerina bun. It was a cycle she was all too familiar with, but would never admit. "But why do we, *I mean girls*, want to be with a guy like that?" she added. "It's not a matter of *want* at that point Lea, your head doesn't always have control of your heart," Vivian said polishing off the can of Pringles.

"Regardless of the case," I interrupted, "I think it's true, we all have one – whether we've met him yet or not, and for the record I hope I never meet mine." "How about if he's your true love?" Lea asked raising her eyebrows in optimism, causing the thin folds in her forehead to appear. "He can't be – he just can't be," I said, "oh yes he can," Vivian joined in, her mouth full of crunchy Pringles, "Carrie wound up with Big." "That took 10 years!" I scowled, "and I'm not sure anyone should have to go through that to get to their true love. I'd just much rather be swooned by *a Mr. Grey*." "The fictional character in the erotic romance, *Mr. Grey*?" Lea asked perplexed. "The one and only, ladies; he loved only one woman and fought for her! There are way too many Mr. Bigs' out there," I continued. "Commitment phobes, egotistical, insecure maniacs leading us on, not knowing at all what they want!" "You and Mr. Grey, Bridget, really? Enough already!" Lea rang out in a less than approving manner. "Well actually Lea, it's me, Mr. grey and most of the women on this half of the hemisphere. Probably more than this half, the book's been translated into 27 languages." "Bridget, Mr. Grey is not exactly an iconic representation of men and relationships; in fact hoping he is, is like walking down a dead-end street, with armed killers waiting at the end of it!" "So much for subtlety Vivian!" "I'm just saying it's pure fiction, Bridge." "Note taken Viv, but he's still set the bar very high." "As far as Mr. Big goes Bridget, yes, I think everyone's probably got one," Lea said looking at herself skeptically in the full-length mirror. "He's the guy who comes into your life by sweeping you off your feet. Says all the right things, is perfect on paper, than wins you over and…" "And then what?" I demanded. "Well, then he disappears without just cause, and re-enters your life when he sees fit; consistently exiting and returning at his will, with no consideration of you, or your feelings. Of course as he leaves you incessantly hanging on, you are too smitten to date another guy - who could never of course meet your new standards - and too emotionally involved to break it off permanently." As if Lea's sorrowed expression didn't say enough, there it was in perfect pitch as only Lea could deliver it, the tale she had lived for years, and the same one I was petrified to experience.

"Anything else we need to know?!" Vivian said adjusting her glasses, taking a bite out of her chocolate chip cookie. "There's one more thing actually," I added. "Mr. Big types always know when to return, it happens when you're moving on; they seem to miraculously appear when you're with a new guy you actually like." "Come on guys, it can't be that formulated," Vivian said chomping on another bite of her cookie. "I mean *I don't have a Mr. Big*, and neither does Bridget for that matter." The girls looked at one another, and than me, "there's still a lot of time," they rang in unison.

Vivian may have been in denial but I surely was not. Having just finished the *50 Shades of Grey* trilogy, I had developed a new outlook on what I thought romance, love, and dating should be, and oh yes, sex. My lack of experience certainly didn't resonate for a lack of imagination, even though I was in the midst of a drought, a long, long drought. I wasn't sure if I was subconsciously waiting for a *'grey'* meteor to hit Niles; but I was sure of one thing; there was no way I was going to get tangled with *a Mr. Big*. I had watched every episode of all six seasons of Sex & the City (countless times) and had learned a thing or two from Carrie Bradshaw's attempt at finding, and keeping love. There was no way I was going to get tangled with someone who used me for his amusement, put me second, and came back only as I moved on. Needless to say, avoiding *a Mr. Big* was at the top of my list.

*

A few large cups of coffee, espressos, and cappuccinos later, and we had settled into our United Airline seats, on the way back to Chicago. I leaned my head against the cold beige windowpane peering into the marshmallow clouds floating on the baby blue sky.

"What's up Bridge?" Vivian nudged sleepily.

"Just thinking."

"What about? And please don't tell me another *get rich quick scheme*. I'm all out of booty-luscious skirts for another one of your events."

"No dear." I smiled, admiring Vivian's willingness to join me on yet another pointless pursuit. "I was just thinking about stuff," I said gazing into the clouds. "Isn't it odd that I would see that clown, you know that troublemaking womanizer Oliver after all these years? The fact that he zoomed right by me, and turned away; I mean he definitely is one for a confrontation." "Well, yeah Bridge, but you have been outta the loop for a while, and you also jumped off the back of his moving motorcycle the last time you saw each other." I chuckled at the irony of the despondent memory. "I guess you're right - I totally dodged a bullet, I should be happy." "Yes – stay clear of assholes

Bridget – it's no doubt you attract them – and maybe you can't control that – but you can control your own actions. They aren't good for you, in any capacity," she said pointing her short chubby finger my way, a shiny Tiffany silver ring dangling from her middle finger. Between my parents' divorce, my one juvenile boyfriend, and countless attempts at dating the wrong guys, Vivian knew how hurtful love had been for me in the past, and saw my raw outer shell for exactly what it was. She knew me well, sometimes I thought better than myself. "Roger that Viv," I responded kissing her soft pudgy cheek. I eventually drifted off, the Gravel keeping me un-alert, until the plane's squeaky wheels landed on the wet tarmac of the windy city's airport.

*

Lea and Vivian headed to the closest Starbucks the Chicago O'Hare airport had to offer. I followed after hauling as many overweight bags off the luggage carousel as I could carry. "Double espresso!" Lea yelled over the airport announcer's vibrant voice – "I'm on it," called back Vivian strutting in her overstuffed yoga pants. Vivian had a knack for making herself noticed and of course creating some drama. "Ouch! This is way too hot! At what temperature did you steam this milk? Is it non-fat? I'm on a strict diet you know!" I smiled at Vivian's unconventional, overbearing, yet lovable self. "I'm sure it's fine Viv, complaining to the college kid running the counter isn't going to get you anywhere right now! Throw it in another cup and lets grab a cab." "You know I could complain to the manager about this shitty service and get us some free gift cards," she said pouting. I laughed, knowing it was one of Vivian's specialties – and I for one had enough Dunkin Donuts 'we're sorry' gift cards to last me for the next two years. "Let's go Viv – save it for next time."

We shuffled into one of the yellow taxis in the lineup outside the arrivals gate, and were on the expressway a few minutes later. "I'm the first stop," Lea called out softly to the cabbie. Her parents lived in an original, three-storey semi detached town house in a quiet suburb outside Chicago's downtown core. Lea had furnished the basement and created a semi-private entrance a few years back when things with Giovanni just weren't going anywhere. With an entry level position at Burberry not paying close to anything enough to live off of, she was too uneasy with her off again on again relationship to cohabitate, yet too in love to leave him altogether. "I'll call you tomorrow," she rang out, scrambling for her vintage bag and used coffee cup.

"City center next Sir," Vivian commanded, "and don't take the Kennedy expressway – it'll be crazy this time of night. Get off on Ohio – we're going to River North." Vivian and I had been roommates for the last two years. She had moved into my apartment while the pre-fab condo unit she had purchased was being built. I could use the roommate since quitting my PR job, and following my admittedly ludicrous, film dreams.

"That will be $65 dollar ladies, that is the remaining fair," the driver said in a thick Indian accent. "What?! That's highway robbery!" replied Vivian. "Hey lady we go by the meter here! The airport tolls are extra – it's the law! Not to mention your luggage weighed enough to have five dead cats in 'em." The driver was in no mood for negotiations, or for Vivian's uncharismatic attempt at a pointless argument.

"Oh yeah, well just one moment while I take down your registration number and plates." I rolled my eyes as the Indian cabbie unloaded the rest of the bags. "Honestly, I'm starting to think it's the espresso Vivian, your energy is really outta whack." Barely standing on my cognac colored wedges, my eyelids fluttered as I daydreamed of soapy bubbles, hot running water, wine and chocolate, in any order I could obtain them.

"We'll pay you now sir, but don't think I won't have this investigated," Vivian huffed. "Bridget, can you believe these rates?! I mean I'd have to go from the art department to the Vice President of the Ad Agency to start paying for prices like this in Chicago! Where's a man when you need him?! This weekend has cost me an arm and a leg!" "Viv, first off, with our luck, the man would make us go dutch, or make us pay for it all together, and secondly, no one forced you to buy those neon pink Louboutins. Now that was a couple weeks salary, not the cab ride!" "They were a steal – last pair at Marshall's is a sign from above Bridget!" she expressed proudly pointing both arms upwards. I looked beyond Vivian's shiny glasses into her warm eyes starring back at me for approval. Those heels pinched her chubby feet and made her feel like she walked on freshly shaved maple wood, *but she loved them,* so like any good friend, I told her the truth. "Ok you're right Viv, you never know who you're gonna meet in neon pink Louboutins…"

3

I sunk into the Epson salt filled tub, my toes, the only exposed skin floating above the soapy suds. As I rose to the surface for air, I pushed my dirty blonde locks against the back of my head, slicking the wet hair away from my rosy cheeks. Vivian had cranked Gloria Gaynor and was bopping around in the kitchen. She had an endless library of soulful hits – something I would never buy or even download, but loved listening to *with her*, just the same.

As the track changed to Marvin Gaye's *"Let's Get It On,"* heavy water pounded against the plethora of bubbles almost overflowing the tub, and I found myself in a daze; I was alone, *again*. The scars from my last real effort at a relationship had healed, and thoughts of past flings, and attempts at dating nonsensical crushes, rushed through my mind. No matter how ridiculously disappointing or hurtful those experiences had been, I missed the passion, or possibly the excitement that came with them. The pain always healed with time, leaving just enough scar tissue to remind me what I had endured; but the mundane mediocrity of what my life had become, had taken its toll on me. Since quitting my PR job to find myself, I was constantly hustling; a single, thirty year old freelancer, chasing her dreams in a fast paced city that waited for nobody. I figured Vivian was too preoccupied in her own world to notice, but I know Lea had. She had asked me where was I running to, on more than one occasion, perhaps more importantly, what I was running from. I interpreted it as a rhetorical question and whined about the boredom I felt in the only city I'd ever called home. I imagined what it'd be like, to jump on a plane to Paris, walk down the streets in thigh boots, a trench coat and a beret, eating a croissant and pondering where I'd go for dinner. I'd accidently meet a single handsome stranger on the Champs d'Elysee; next, lust, passion, and excitement would follow my illicit fantasy. What the heck was going to happen in my life, sitting in this Chicago apartment working on clients' barely paying projects?! Was a handsome, single heir going to walk through the condo lobby while I checked for mail in my ice cream cone covered jammies? The thought made me gasp – and thoughts of my Parisian fantasy raced through my head. *Was there nothing more for me? Is this all my life would be?* My heart began to pound, beating heavy on my aroused chest; my hands swept softly up and down my wet legs, and I began to sink deeper into the tub, and … "Bridget! Your Skype is ringing – come get it – it could be a gig!" Startled I burst from under the bubbles, stumbling to the bathroom door. "Jesus Vivian, you could give someone a heart attack with that pitch! Fuck it, who ever it is I'll call them back." Disappointed at having my fantasy interrupted, I reluctantly washed up, releasing the hot soapy water from the tub, and towel drying my soaking hair. In the distance I could hear Skype pop up messages. Who ever was looking for me wanted to correspond with me now- not necessarily a bad thing for freelancers. I wrapped my mini robe around my soaked body and let my hair down wet, falling just past my shoulders.

"Alright so let's see who just has to speak to me this late, Viv." "You think it could be a guy from the party?" "Really, Viv? You think one of the extremely interesting financiers fell in love with my movie script and are offering me $5 million to produce it, right now?! I think I have better odds of getting hit by lighting, but I do appreciate the faith you have in me," I smiled peering past Vivian's glasses into her mothering brown eyes. "Well it's their loss Bridget; it will come, you will make your films; for now just look who it is!"

I tilted the screen back, entering my password. The screen went from black to grey, revealing a silver tie as the screensaver. I clicked the red colored number one that hung above the blue Skype symbol on the dock of icons to reveal the message:

Was that you at the party last night?

The message was from Oliver.

I felt knots made of heavy rope doused in turpentine sinking to the pit of my stomach. I thought about deleting the message for a moment, forgetting I still had him on my Skype contact list. Oliver was bad news – a nuisance at the very least – and I knew what ever his intentions were, they were not genuine. "Well who was it Bridget?!" Vivian yelled over the blaring music. "That guy Oliver I told you about… he asked if it was me at the party, apparently I now look like a cross between a young Jerry Hall and old Blake Lively, and possibly a girl he used to date." "Wow he sounds like a real charmer Bridge." I glanced at her through my peripheral vision, rolling my eyes at the thought of Oliver, "you do not know the depths of this guy's evil Viv."

Ironically enough, I was curious to find out what he wanted, so I began to type on my pink covered keyboard.

Bridget: Yes Oliver it was.

His response was immediate.

Oliver: Nice. I just stopped off to see some friends who invited me. I was at the Madonna concert earlier – the concert of the year actually, I had floor seats!

Oliver was still the same boasting, egotistical show off, I had sworn off years' prior. "Oh God I wanna gag Viv – he hasn't changed one bit." "Well don't talk to him, if you don't want to, but maybe he's got a lead on a gig – you're always saying freelance is a hustler's game. I'm beat, going to bed, let me know how it goes tomorrow over morning coffee." Skeptical at Vivian's optimism, I smiled, and blew her a kiss, "Ok Viv – night."

Turning back to the light blue text box, I began some shoptalk with the butter-balled villain I had persistently disliked. Apparently his family's Herbal Tea business had grown substantially over the years, and he had finally achieved national distribution. Evidently, his family processed flowers and herbs into natural teas from the plantations they had inherited on the Greek island of Paros for generations.

Bridget: That's cool, Oliver, wishing you the best.

Biting my tongue, I hoped it'd be the end of the painful conversation when he began to type in a furry.

Oliver: Actually Bridget, I got a quote for a commercial for my new tea line. Can you take a look at it?

My intuition told me this had to be a ploy. He'd lure me in with business, lock me in herbal pressing tea boiler room of sorts, and try to assault me! *Get a grip Bridget– he makes tea for Christ sake! He's lost and needs help… but why should I help him?* I wondered what he was digging for, so I held my breath and typed:

Bridget: What do you need exactly Oliver?

Apparently Oliver's business was booming and he was going to get a chance to sell on QVC.

Oliver: I need a promo spot, or a commercial or something like that – and you know show biz. I can't get a trustworthy production company to do it for under 35 grand.

Oliver continued his pitch, and I grew more annoyed by the minute – until of course he asked me for a quote.

Bridget: What do you mean, you want me to shoot the spots? You want me to go to a desolate Greek Island I've never been too, work with a crew I don't know, and bring back a stellar concept and produced television commercial for your Herbal Tea Business?!

Oliver: Pretty much Bridget, if you're up for it! Send me a quote I'm busy. Goodbye.

What a prick. Who signs off like that?! Womanizing pig. I slammed the cover of the black Mac book and tossed my soaked hair over an oversized burgundy pillow. *Oliver, what a character, why do I even bother?!* I propped my feet on the off-white ottoman, shut my eyes, and dozed off.

4

The sweet sounds of Maxwell filled the air of the condo *"Get To Know Ya,"* was softly playing over Vivian's I-pod speakers. The light of the early morning weighed on my tired eyelids, as I slowly lifted them to see Vivian's backside swaying side to side to Maxwell's lyrics over the hot stove. "That smells amazing Viv," I said propping myself up off the same spot I had laid down some eight hours earlier. "Hey Bridge you're up! You slept on the couch?!" "Yeah I must have dozed off after my conversation with that imbecile, Oliver." I fussed my hands through my damp hair and began to explain the conversation I had had with my old nemesis. "God he sounds like such a savage Bridget. I don't know how you deal with these clients," she exhaled pouring some more batter into the pancake-maker.

"So he wants you to come up with an awesome marketing concept for his herbal tea business, write the commercial and produce it in a foreign country? On a Greek island you've never been to, with people you don't know no less?!" "Well in the butterball's own words Viv – pretty much." *"You* doing a stellar job is not the issue here Bridge – we all know you could knock this outta the park, it's that perv that has me concerned – do you really think he's shed his stripes?! On the other hand, I suppose you could ask some of your cousins from your mom's side of the family if they have any contacts in Greece to help you prepare and film, perhaps it's time to use the half Greek Goddess in you! You know what to do – just get a damn deposit this time! I can't stand by and watch you get screwed over by yet another wanna-be business guy who convinces you to take him on as a client! Once you have your cappuccino and are fully awake call Lea, she'll have something to say about this as well."

Vivian's sermon wasn't entirely uncalled for; in fact it was her no-nonsense approach at life that had gotten me out of an abundance of unforeseen disasters. "Ok," I muttered hopping up on the bar stool digging into Vivian's breakfast. After feasting on some blueberry pancakes, I decided to call my mom before trying Lea. Mother was a Greek ex-pat born and raised on a small yet extraordinarily beautiful Greek island in the northwest Aegean Sea called Skiathos. She had barely finished high school when she began working at a local bed & breakfast, a tourist favorite, *which she says* changed her life forever. It was there that she met my dad on a boy's trip to Greece. Dad was originally from Ireland but had migrated to the US from Dublin with my grandparents, years' prior after granddad had began running a few Irish pubs in Chicago for a family friend. He eventually inherited them and he and Dad opened a few more throughout the greater Chicago area. According to Dad, mom stole his heart in Skiathos and he couldn't live without her, so he convinced her to come to America; well actually he convinced her parents he'd provide her with a better life in the land of grand opportunity. Mom eventually moved to Chicago and they married shortly after. I came along before her 24th birthday and that was it as far as kids would go for my parents. Although they divorced while I was still an adolescent, I never heard them fighting, and really only noticed a change when my dad moved out. Our relationship was never really strained, as it had never really gotten close enough for real conflict. Dad was always busy running the pubs, and Mom took on the combat of raising a teenage girl solo, while Dad paid the bills. She was definitely not someone to be reckoned with, after all Dad called her a vixen for most of their marriage, and I knew she'd have something to say about Oliver's proposition.

"Hunny that sounds exciting, and you do need to spread your wings, but this character seems questionable - and I do recall the motorbike incident. Maybe you should speak to your uncle Dimitri in Greece, he should be able to set you up with some folks in production over there. Your father was just visiting with him last summer, and he mentioned he wanted to see you." Uncle Dimitri was Mom's cousin, and a fun loving long distance family member. He was a talented music composer who had remained a bachelor way too long. Having met him when I was 12 on my one and only family trip to Greece, we had managed to maintain a great relationship – phone calls, pictures in the mail, and most recently social media. "I think he has Skype now too Bridget, you should definitely connect with him. Ask your father for the details, I've lost touch with him. This may be a great opportunity for you to get back to some of your Greek roots." "Mom, please, my roots are firmly planted in Niles, Chicago." Although unintentional, my tone must have rung condescending in my mother's ears, because she swung back with a fiery tongue-lashing.

"Well young lady, if I'm not mistaken your DNA is not! It is Greek and Irish, and need not I remind you that your temperament is quite demonstrative of this. I'm not telling you to trace our family ancestry but your father and I have some fond memories in Greece, it's a beautiful, magical place, but you'll have to discover that on your own." "Got it mom, I'll remember that, and try to control myself," I answered sarcastically. "Let me know how it goes and remember hunny, you create your own destiny. I'm off to yoga sending you love and light."

*

"So does your mom want you to venture into the Aegean and meet a Greek Casanova Bridget?! I knew she had become an eccentric yogi maybe, but not nearly that avant-garde!" Dad's sarcasm was at an all time high. "No Dad, she thinks I should examine the opportunity and discover some of my Greek roots," I replied as non-sarcastically as my brain allowed.

"Greece is a magical place Bridget," *oh here we go again,* "so I heard Dad." "It may sound cliché but it's true, how do you think your mother wheeled me in and got that ring on her finger?! Greeks are passionate in every sense of the word and before you know it you're selling your soul for another taste. It may have its wonders," he continued to preach, "but it's not what you're accustom to…" "Dad I haven't even decided if I'm going yet," I interrupted. "Ok fine, just be careful, *you're a Lane,* and that ain't no joke in Ireland; there's a reason the Gaelic named us after warriors you know!" "Yes Dad, I know, I'm a tough cookie remember?" "Ok enough babble Bridget, I'm sure you get plenty of that from your mother. Just beware if you do end up there, you'll be in the land of great passion, love & lust, and although all this, *including love,* can feel like magic, magic can sometimes be just be an illusion." His words were profound and should have resonated further into my thick skull, but I brushed them off and sorted through the information he had given me about Uncle Dmitri's whereabouts. Dad had reminded me that Greece was in a time zone eight hours ahead, and also that Uncle Dimitri was usually up at odd hours writing and rehearsing his music. I jotted down the info and tucked it away in the pocket of my soft cotton robe.

Across the kitchen counter Vivian was chomping away on her homemade pancakes and fruit and mumbling something. I could barely

29

hear her over the tall table and stools when she yelled out: "Lea thinks you should call your uncle ASAP!" "Thanks Viv, but remember to swallow I barely remember the Heimlich maneuver." She took a swig of her freshly squeeze orange juice and gulped loudly. "Thanks for the reminder, I forget to chew slowly sometimes. Listen, get all the info you need to get a quote, write a kick ass commercial, and send it to the spineless bastard. You have nothing to lose," she concluded nonchalantly cleaning her plate. "Why thanks for that resolution Vivian, and Lea, but I don't have all the time in the world so technically I do have something to lose – you know, time, brain power, my youth!" "Why?! Are you getting any younger sitting in your ice cream coned jammies waiting for your life to change? We all want you to make your movies, meet your prince charming, and live happily ever after, but none of that is going to happen from inside this 750 sq foot space. Got it?" "Yes!" I replied, eagerly waiting for the punch line that would grant me an answer to dilemma. "Before you say I'm being mean and bossy, let me verify that it's called tough love!" I smiled an annoyed familiar tightlipped smile, knowing Vivian was right. She reciprocated a smile before gathering a few things together, "I've got a date with Youssef, off to get a blow dry darling!"

*

That night I sat in front of my beloved, scratched up black Mac Book and began to write about wild flowers growing over mountainous, sea-side hill tops, ancient herbal remedies & medicinal benefits. By 3 am, I had come up with a first draft for a 60 second TV spot. Unwilling to lose another night's sleep on my tattered sofa, I forced myself to my feet, and crashed under my Roadrunner duvet. What felt like minutes later, I was tossing and turning at a vision of myself in a large straw hat covering most of my face, creating a large shadow in front my body. I was climbing amongst small hilltops, under a hot sun, pulling dandelions and fresh herbs out from the roots, placing them in a large wicker hand basket. A little girl with bright blue eyes held my hand, as we began to run through endless rows of tall wild flowers. The air was warm and soft against my face. "You want to keep searching for some more?!" I asked happily caressing the snow-white like face of the toddler. The bright-eyed girl looked up at me smiling, "yes mommy, let's keep looking." "You got it hunny," I walked slowly ripping a variety of long stems from the muddled earth. "There, now that should be plenty my love, or do you want some more?!" But when I turned to her again, the little girl had disappeared, and the word 'yes' had gotten louder, albeit from a very different high-pitched voice. "More yes, more, yes!" I jumped up from under my covers to hear an aroused Vivian screaming out from inside the living room. "Yes Youssef, more, more!" I reached for my old blackberry, 4:47 am. Well at least one of us would go to bed happy. I shuffled searching for an old sleep mask that spelled out PRINCESS in pink diamonds, and a pair of airplane ear buds. Yo soy, tu eres, el es, ella es… If conjugating verbs in Spanish worked as a blocking and isolation mechanism in College, it surely wouldn't fail me now.

5

I opened my eyes to the sun streaming past my light grey blinds. I had actually managed to get in a few hours of sleep. There was something to be said about those airplane earplugs after all. The apartment was quiet, and the only evidence that a lust brawl had taken place here last night were a couple of half empty wine glasses, a bowl of dried up strawberries, and a large silver hoop earring that had landed on the kitchen counter.

I opened up my laptop, letting the messages download while I made my skinny cappuccino. A few dings went off as I began to scroll through the messages. An email from Uncle Dimitri:

My dearest Bridget, your father said you'd be in touch. Waiting to hear from you. I have entered the 21st century and use Skype. Please add me to your contact list. Love Uncle D.

As I continued to scroll down I noticed an email from Oliver with no subject heading. My stomach ached at the feeling of the proverbial knots as I opened it up.

Where is my quote Bridget?! I have money to make you know, and QVC is waiting.

I immediately slammed the Apple cover and began to dial Lea's number. "Can you believe this guy Lea?! What an ass! How am I supposed to work with someone like this?!" Lea had an instant way of calming me down. She rang out to her mother in Italian before answering; "No, non hai fame adesso mama!" Turning to look my way, she changed her demeanor, "Bridget, we all know this guy is a jerk. No mystery there to solve. You work with pricks you call 'clients,' all of the time. Send him your work, attach a price list, and let it sit. If he wants you to do it, you don't move without a deposit - easy." A good pep talk and an hour later, I had re-opened my trusty Mac computer and began working on revisions. It was good enough for a first version and I knew I could get a quote on it. I opened up the blue 'S' icon on my screen and searched for Uncle D. There he was, a photo of him on a baby grand, in his living room. I added him onto my contact list and sent him a message. His response was immediate, and his 'Gringlish' quite impressive; and even though my Greek was not, the conversation managed to flow nicely. "I have the perfect director for you. He is a friend of your cousin's, and he will round up the crew. This will be a spectacular job for you young lady! My niece! The Hollywood producer!" "Well uh, not exactly Uncle D – trying to get there you know." "Oh have some faith Bridget, this commercial will open gateways for you – and it wouldn't hurt to find you a nice Greek boy while you're at it." Uncle Dmitri's voice was full of enthusiasm and anticipation, and although it was endearing to hear, I knew better – much, much better.

"Ah Uncle D, I'm not exactly good at the dating thing." It was another sharp reminder of my sorry social habits, and lame sexual experiences. Perhaps all the signs were pointing to a flight out of the US. "Well where is the Mediterranean Goddess in you, young lady?! You must have taken after your Irish father – never did have any game – that man!" Uncle D, as overzealous and obnoxious as he was, did always have the best intentions. He gave me a name and number and told me not to worry about a thing – words of wisdom, as he called them.

*

Leonidis Papadopoulos. Well there was nothing conspicuous about that name. It was as Greek as they came, and he would be my star director and savoir. I dialed into my Skype minutes and waited for the odd beeping noise they called a ring. On the third beep a soft male voice answered, "Parakalo?" My Greek was minimal, but I knew enough to get by, the gentlemen on the phone was answering hello politely. "Um yes, hello, I'm looking for Leonidis – I'm calling from Chicago," before I could finish my sentence, the voice on the other line answered, "oh yes you must be Bridget, I've been expecting your call. Thank you for reaching out. Your cousin and uncle speak very highly of you." He was kind, easy to talk to, and professional - we exchanged Skype info and scheduled a call for later that evening.

"Hey girl, what cha up to?!" Vivian had entered the living room in a blue romper, her glasses were tilted to the right, and hair propped up in a side ponytail with a metallic silver hair scrunchy. "Did you sleep in your glasses Viv?!" "Uh not exactly but I needed them to get a little closer to the patient last night if you know what I mean," she said chuckling in her best deep throttle laugh. "Well I definitely think you did some healing last night. Is he all cured or what?" "He's in recovery actually, sleeping away." "Enough shop-talk, I found a director Viv – I mean he's a friend of my cousin's in Greece, but a real director. We spoke briefly, he seems really nice and professional." "Is he cute?" she asked adjusting her specs. "There we go, I don't know and I don't care – and anyhow he has a girlfriend, I could hear her frolicking over him in the background." "Does that count for Greek guys? You know having a girlfriend – after all they are synonymous – Greek lovers…" "Once again I don't know and I don't care Viv!" "We have a Skype call scheduled in a little bit and I need to prepare!" "Oh great I'll do your hair and make up!" "I meant prepare for the creative work Viv!" "Oh God how boring. As you like Bridget, I'm going back to bed. Knock 'em dead girl – and wear something low cut, and definitely not those glasses!" Typically unpleased with my passive attitude, Vivian walked away, leaving me alone to ponder in my thoughts.

An hour later, I was propped in front of my Mac waiting for Leo's call. I had showered, tied up my hair in a bun, wore a plain white t-shirt and my silver framed glasses. I didn't want this guy getting the wrong impression of me. A few minutes later, and just on time, a Skype call was coming in. I answered straight away, revealing myself in the laptop's camera. Leo reciprocated. Although he sat perched on a black leather chair, I could tell he was tall and thin. He had dark hair, covered in some grey patches particularly in the front. He wore a thin dark scarf draped around his neck over a lose button down, a fuzzy grey cat sprawled over his lap. He looked just as I had imagined, and thank heavens wasn't my type. With my luck in love, that would potentially have been a recipe for disaster.

We spent the next hour exchanging ideas on concepts, pricing and crew members. His girlfriend popped up in the background from time to time, bringing him water or chips, or perhaps pissing around him, I wasn't sure, and I didn't care. There was something about Leo that made me feel confident and at ease, unaware if it was regarding the gig, or just my sanity, for the first time, I knew I could make this commercial work, and Leo was the man for the job.

Satisfied with the information I had received, I worked on budgeting, proposals, and a final quote for the rest of the evening, stopping for a cigarette and glass of wine in between. Finally, I was ready to send off an email to Oliver.

Dear Oliver:

Thanks for this opportunity. Attached you will find a concept idea for your product, as well as a quote for producing an awesome commercial.

Yours truly,

Bridget.

I put my laptop to sleep just as Youssef was coming out of Vivian's bedroom. "Oh hi Bridget. Congrats on the gig. Viv tells me you're off to the Aegean. Be careful out there the men are nuts and I think you're just their type," he mumbled approaching the kitchen. "Thanks Youssef, but all I did was pitch the client. It's always a nightmare negotiating." "Just get a deposit Bridget and keep the material and you'll be fine."

Vivian's on-and-off again lover, Youssef was a little older and wiser, even if the lessons had came from a few shady business deals and run ins with organized crime groups. Youssef was in his mid 40's, with a medium build and good set of salt and pepper hair, and of course had a proud hairy chest peeping out of his button down to match. "You know real estate isn't as easy as it looks Bridget." I nodded and smiled politely, knowing his money had come from less than legal deals infiltrated by his father's nightclub consortium in his hometown of Beirut. He did however have good intentions, and I appreciated Vivian's lover offering me well-needed advice. I watched as Vivian fussed over him, making sure he was primped and perfect, then handing him a paper bag full of snacks for the road. "I'm gonna walk Youssef down to the lobby Bridge. "Thanks for the advice Youssef" I called out waving. "Bye bella," he replied waiving and blowing a kiss my way – "good luck with the commercial."

The sound of the heavy door shutting behind them awoke my senses. It had been a sluggish day and although I had made some good progress on a new gig, I worried about what, and who would come next, and of course what the fuck I was doing with my life. Something

I heard time and time again from my less than present father, regardless of his current support. I walked toward the crisp Chicago skyline glaring back at me through the large bay window. Failure was not an option. There was no way I was going to bail on another month's rent. I marched over to the sunken beige couch, prying open my laptop.

As the grey tie appeared on my screen - the Skype icon bounced up displaying a bright red number 1. I clicked on the blue icon to reveal a chat message.

Oliver: You think I'm made of money? The budget's gotta come down – way down. I want a modern concept. Yours will work. Cut the budget and send me a new one. I don't have time to waste.

Before I could digest the Skype message, my attention was swayed by a loud voice and persistent knocking. "I forgot my keys Bridge!" Vivian's voice blared from the other side of the door. "Coming!" I leaped off the couch opening the door to a disheveled looking Vivian. "So are you still working Bridge?" "Well actually I sent my quote to Oliver and he just responded," I said showing the screen to Vivian. "What a savage! Bridget I can't believe the crap you have to go through to get a gig. Girl let me write the response," she said grabbing my laptop and placing it on her lap.

Bridge: Hey Oliver, savages belong at the bottom of the deep blue sea! Or perhaps in the zoo next to the lions den. Oh and take your tea bags and shove them up your …

"Vivian! Stop – do not press enter. Jesus!" I grabbed the laptop deleting Vivian's rant. "I'll handle him – you catch more bees with honey, and right now I need enough to fill a hector of hives." "Point taken, but even if you get the gig, how can you work with this guy?! Since when do you use hectors by the way, Bridge?" "European parents remember?! Besides I think it's some old proverb. Can we forget about hectors for a moment please?" I snarled annoyed.

Vivian's words resonated in my head. A bright red flag was waving in a gust of wind on a large cement pole, but I chose to ignore it. *No, I can do this.* "Don't worry, the director seems great, and it's his crew. I'll write the spot, we'll shoot and edit it together and I'll be back in three weeks. Producing it will be a breeze, I got it all set out in my head." "Ok well at least promise me you won't send him one of your sweet

'I'll fix-everything answers' – he doesn't deserve it! Or you for that matter! I'm showering and going back to bed." "You mean to bed period. I don't imagine you got any sleep last night or this morning...." "Of course I didn't – there are some things more important than work Bridge, and my libido is one of them!" "Perhaps that's true Viv, but considering I'm completely loveless and single, please don't rub it in." Vivian shuffled off in her pale blue romper, and I envied every inch of that self-confidence that followed her into that bathroom. I wondered if I would ever get there. One lover, and numerous failed dating attempts certainly didn't do much for a girl's ego. I reached for my computer tugging at the frayed cord held together by black hockey tape. I began formulating a response to Oliver.

Dear Oliver,

Thank you for the feedback. In order for me to tighten the budget, we will need to shoot a longer day and a shorter week. Moreover, I will have to reduce the amount of technical crew, not allowing for a steady cam. Lastly, I will not be able to produce the diverse ending I had written, as that requires an extra day in an editing suite with 2 editors.

Therefore, I will meet your budget requirements with a simplified version of my concept. When should I schedule the shoot?

Yours Truly,

Bridget.

I copied and pasted the email into the Skype text box and hit enter.

6

For the next few days I revised, re-edited the concept again and again, then the script and corresponding budget. When I felt it was just right I sent it off to Oliver in an email and waited patiently for his response. The weeks to follow were quiet. I had heard nothing from Oliver and had almost forgotten about the herbal tea business and a presumptuously precarious venture.

"It's Saturday night Bridge, come on let's go out!" Lea's voice on the other end of the telephone was clear and upbeat. Her parents were renovating the basement, and there was no way she was going to spend the night in her primitive, Italian style, childhood bedroom. "Alright fine" I responded, "but I better not end up holding back your hair over a toilet at the end of the night! When are the renovations done anyway?" Well they decided to put down some new maple wood flooring now, so it'll be a week more at the least. It's bad enough I have to eat pasta twice a day, and listen to Gigi D'Alessio, but now my Nona Lucia has moved in and I have to listen to the *I can't believe you're not married yet speech.*"

I giggled under my breath, secretly admiring Lea's family dynamic. I wondered what it would feel like to have a warm nest to come to, a family that got involved in all my decisions, and a nosey Nona that was forever on the lookout for a good Italian boy. I hit the red end key on my phone's dial pad and headed for the swarming armoire I called a closet. My thoughts were interrupted by Vivian's voice, "the cab will be here in 20 minutes Bridge." I decided on a black slinky dress and canary yellow pumps. Vivian wore her customary style maxi dress with a thick brown belt wound tightly just under her protruding bust. We strutted through the condo lobby just as the cab was pulling up. "Your cab is here - have a great night ladies," called out the concierge. "Thanks Cecil, we plan on making it a good one!" replied Vivian. Cecil chuckled a deep baritone laugh and waved goodbye. Cecil was a strikingly handsome 47 year-old, with caramel colored skin and a German accent. Originally from Tunisia, he had moved to Dusseldorf as a young boy and lived there until his mid thirties. He had joined the condo concierge team about a year prior, and had most of the women swarming over him. "I would love a romp in the hay with him" whispered Vivian. "Now there's a great idea Viv; sleeping with the concierge you'd have to see every single day for as long as we both shall live in this condo." "Ok you have a point Bridge, but that only counts for as long as I live here, because after that, it's a whole new ball game," she said smiling and waving back at Cecil. Twenty-five minutes later we pulled up to in front of little Italy to see Lea waiting on her front porch putting out a Marlborough Light in a boot shaped ashtray. "Bonne note Nona!" "Ciao Lea, baci!" a distant voice called back. Lea was casually chic as per usual in her low-rise diesel denim and a white draped cotton long sleeved blouse cut at the mid-drift revealing her white diamond belly ring. "Giovanni's back in town," she said as she kissed us both on the cheek and shuffled into the back seat. "Oh perfect," answered Vivian, "Youssef will be out tonight too, and we can double." Fixated on sending any Chicago bachelor my way, I reiterated what had become oh too familiar to my two best friends, "stop giving me those looks girls, I'm perfectly fine on my own, please tell them no single tag-alongs!"

*

The smoke filled patio was full and Giovanni and Youssef were huddled over a pair of Molson Canadians. "How fitting guys – Toronto was so much fun!" I boasted walking towards the high top tables. "We're sure that smile means trouble," Youssef said smiling and greeting Vivian. "Did Lea hold her liquor?" Giovanni added grabbing Lea and placing her on his lap. "Of course Gio," I responded winking at Lea, grabbing a stool at the end of the table. I knew deep down Gio didn't trust us, and even though he adored Lea, he himself was far from faithful. To Lea, he was irresistible, actually to most women he was. Tall, dark, and strikingly handsome, Gio had a characteristic Italian style, and a wondering eye to match. Unsurprisingly all of which left Lea forever chasing after his attention. He was as Italian textile executive with a factory in Italy and an office in Shanghai. Although he treated Lea well when he was around, he just wasn't around *enough*, and there was no way of knowing what he was doing when he wasn't.

"You guys ok if I leave early, I have a splitting headache," I said. "Oh come on Bridget, the night is young," Giovanni responded taking a swig of his beer. "Plus there's a bunch of guys that would love to buy you a drink in here." "That's the least of my worries Gio," I said standing to adjust my dress, and the truth was, it really was. "It really is a waste of a hot black dress Bridget," added Youssef. "It's not a waste if no-one sees me in it and I can repeat the outfit Youssef." I flashed a sarcastic smile and kissed everyone goodbye. "What ever happened to that commercial Bridge? Are you leaving us for the mystic Mediterranean?" Youssef said in his inquisitive Lebanese accent. "Who knows Youssef – who knows!" I responded waving and running towards a bright yellow taxi.

Maybe it was a waste, I thought starring at my yellow pumps shining against the car mat of the taxi's back seat. "You seem skeptical if I do say so Madame…" "Oh yes, I suppose I am," I muttered under my breath. The cab driver had caught me off guard; even he had noticed I was in the wrong place. "I don't mean to pry Madame, but is it a boyfriend issue?" "No, no, just life I guess," exhaling. Peering through the rearview mirror the driver continued, "struggles, Madame, are difficult, but they are a part of life. It is these things that shape us, and make us stronger. You must take the plunge. In the end we only regret the chances we didn't take. I know this from experience," he concluded placing his stare back towards the cab's large windshield. Although unfamiliar, his voice was genuine. I knew his prolific words had come from a wound of his own; perhaps one he was still trying to heal. He flashed a warm smile through the rear view mirror, told me a few Middle Eastern hometown stories, and safely dropped me off back home.

Flashing somewhat of a disappointed wave to Cecil, I walked swiftly towards through the condo's foyer, entering the shiny elevator. Needless to say I was unexcitedly anticipating my return to the familiar dwelling that was my home, office, and whole life. After peeling my pumps off my tired feet I threw my dress onto the reupholstered leather chair that sat faithfully by my bedside, and housed my trusted nightly attire; ice cream coned jammies and a white tank top. I slipped them on, added a hooded sweater, and headed for the familiar sunken spot on my beige couch.

I flipped open my laptop, waiting for all the email messages to download. Yoga Class Updates, LinkedIn job searches, zip recruiters and … *God please, let there be a human message in here.* The last email had a subject line that read HELLO! The name alongside the email was Jack Nichols. Jack was an amazingly loyal friend I had met 6 years earlier on a spontaneous Italian vacation with Lea, who (before Giovanni's time) had had a summer fling with Jack's cousin who was visiting Florence on an architectural retreat. I had tagged along with them one night, and there was Jack, a thirty year-old year old distinguished Brit from London, in Italy for a few days on business.

He had instantly taken an interest in showing me the most beautiful sights the city had to offer. He asked me out time and time again, but being 24, confused, and distraught from yet another failed attempt at love, I was less than interested in seeing Jack's genuine goodness and more importantly, his sincere interest in me. Jack was a successful financial executive from London, with an uncharacteristic gentle disposition, kind, smart, and true gentlemen. I recalled him holding my hand crossing busy Italian roads, and shielding me from speedy drivers on desolate streets with non-existing traffic lights. He was easy to speak to, and from what I had discovered, selfless, consoling me during endless self-indulging conversations. He matched my height in my highest heels, wore his dark hair short, and had pale skin and big blue eyes completing his thin frame. He was not my usual *bad boy* type; of course a *good thing*, but I was none the wiser. On paper he was worryingly perfect, but unfortunately his timing was not. It seemed he was on the receiving end of a broken and bitter Bridget – something oblivious to me at the time. We spent a few beautiful days in Florence, but that was it. There was never a hot steamy night, a tender moment, or even a kiss. Jack and I had done the unthinkable, and developed a platonic relationship, *all thanks to me.*

Jack continued to befriend me from a far. I suppose someone with decent male radar would call it 'pursue me'; and he did this, for years with no avail, even proposing I come to London for work when I became disgruntled with Chicago and the world of PR. However, I had placed him in the unflattering friend category and in my mind that was where he was going to stay. He stayed up late with me on Skype, listening to pathetic dating story upon story, even coaching me through difficult clients, and was always the first one to call me on my birthday. There was no looking further for a Prince Charming, but being accustomed to chasing the unattainable, I found Jack oddly polite, even labeling him boring. Instead of reciprocating his wonderfully kind gestures, I turned him down time after time, deciding to remain in Chicago and date unfaithful jocks, musicians and womanizers, who made me work for my worth.

Needless to say, all attempts ended up in disaster, each one damaging me a little more than the one before. The only time Jack and I ever lost touch was during one of my so-called two-month relationships – which of course Jack heard about in *great* detail days after its demise. Our conversations had since lightened up and I was excited to hear from him again. As usual Jack's messages were short and to the point:

Bridget, I'm checking up on you. How are you, are you working, and more importantly are you staying out of trouble? J.N.

I smiled, knowing Jack actually cared about me. I loved him. I recognized this now. I bit on the edges of my chipped nail polish, hit the reply button, and began to type:

J! How do you just always know…? How is London? I'm working on confirming a gig overseas. I'll keep you posted - if I make it I'll be close by.

Luv, Bridget.

I hit send and checked for messages one more time. Waiting for the send/receive to complete, I peeled my drugstore lashes off my heavy eyelids and tossed them by the wastebasket. The download had completed; there were no more messages. That would call it a night. Before I could place my Apple computer to sleep, I laid my head on the oversized burgundy pillow that had become my refuge, allowing the thoughts in my head to subside. By the time I could get past the first Spanish conjugation I was in dreamland. This time I was running. It was a foreign airport. "Miss please take your passport and run – you are going to miss the flight." I grabbed the passport and began running through the airport, with each stride my legs grew heavier, making the destination harder to get to. My loyal Puma handbag hung from my shoulder as I ran through various terminals searching for the right gate.

The sounds of Skype call buzzed through my ears like sirens. Soaked in a cold sweat, I opened my eyes to find the loud ringing noise coming from my computer. *Shit I had forgotten to log off.* Still disoriented from my sleep and intense dream, I scrambled in the dark, attempting to type in my password, but the grey tie was not appearing. By the third attempt I had managed to use my blackberry backlight for some guidance and had successfully unlocked the keyboard. I clicked on the proverbial Skype icon to reveal two missed calls and a chat message. The calls were from Oliver, and I suspected the message would be as well; and alas there it was, in bold Arial font.

Oliver: We are on. Pack your things and book your flight. I am sending you a 50% deposit. I want to shoot in 3 days, and don't be late I'm on a tight schedule. Yes or no?!

A warm rush of blood filled my body. I sat starring at the screen when the heavy apartment door flung open disclosing a partially drunken Vivian. "You're still up! Don't tell me you're working?" I smiled thinking of the night that had passed, the cab driver, Jack's message; and watched as my fingers stroked across two letters on the keyboard. I pressed the two keys softly. "Bridge?" Vivian plopped down beside me on the sunken sofa, her eyes peering onto my computer screen. "Good girl Bridge, you're doing the right thing." She gave me a hug and retired to her room. I relaxed back on the couch, closing my eyes and exhaling; never suspecting such a tiny word would have such a large impact on my life. I hit enter allowing *"OK"* to bounce out of my text box.

7

"Ladies and gentlemen British Airways Flight 790 to London is ready for boarding. We now welcome persons travelling with small children to come forward." The Chicago O'Hare airport was buzzing as usual, only the chaos in the international gate was more than I was accustomed to. Travelers were bustling through the terminal racing for the stretched out gates, while I sat on my overstuffed handbag munching on salted corn chips. In three days I had managed to ransack the shelves of Zara & H&M, stuffing my luggage with European appropriate attire for my filming days, and editing filled weekends. I had arrived early anticipating any luggage weight issues, but luckily, the British Airways agent was kind enough to let a few extra pounds slide. I sat patiently listening to my I-pod, waiting for row 33 to be called. A variety of pop tunes blared through my be-jeweled earphones. I hummed to the sounds of my latest obsession, Canadian R&B artist *The Weeknd*. His sultry track *Wicked Games* had debuted during the Toronto Film Festival and I had become fixated with it ever since I heard it blaring trough the speakers of the hotel lobby.

"All remaining passengers may now board Miss," a friendly BA representative said lightly tapping me on my shoulder. She stood over me, in her blue and white uniform, a red scarf wrapped around her neck, and neatly applied lipstick of the same color outlined her thin lips. "You must have some good stuff on there," she chuckled in her poignant British accent, pointing to my scratched-up I-pod. I smiled and thanked her, quickly getting up to join the line.

"Welcome to your non-stop flight to London England's Heathrow Airport. Ladies and Gentlemen this is your captain speaking, James Mitchell." I was happy to be making a stop in London on my way to Greece to break up the flight, plus I thought it'd be a great opportunity to see Jack, even if it was just for a few hours. "We will be flying at 35,000 feet and expect to be placing down in London in approximately seven hours & forty minutes; approximately 19:35 local time." Military time always threw me off; I had forgotten it was standard in Europe, but never bothered to figure out an easy conversion method. Jack had my itinerary and he'd be there waiting for me, so I had nothing to worry about. I looked at my watch reaching for the pill bottle I had shoved in my overstuffed coat pocket. Half an Adavan should do the trick. I'd keep the Gravol handy too, in case we hit some turbulence somewhere over the Atlantic. The crew started the emergency exit speeches, and by the time they were into the safety procedures I was securely in my first REM cycle, having started conjugating variations of Spanish 'like terms'… a mi me gusta tu…

*

"Excuse me, Miss please place your set in the upright position, we're preparing for landing." I couldn't believe I had slept right through the flight. "Welcome to Heathrow International Airport, London, England. The temperature is 10 degrees Celsius and the local time is 19:30." I felt relaxed and eager to get off the plane and freshen up. By the time I made it through British customs, my bladder had become a relentless inferno burning against my tight blue jeans. I had found the ladies room just in time to use the bathroom and moisturize my make-up less face. I applied a coat of black as blackest Mascara, some wing tipped eyeliner to match, and very berry lip-gloss. I tossed my messy hair into a low ponytail and zipped up my Canada Goose jacket, exposing only a third of my leg between my tall riding boots and three-quarter-length jacket. Impressed at my quick overhaul – I felt moderately pretty after the long flight. Jack wasn't one for compliments, and since our relationship was purely platonic I felt no pressure to be super attractive or anything other than barely noticeable.

The busiest airport in the UK was extremely organized with well-mannered staff and easily comprehendible signs. I liked London already. As I turned to look for an arrow pointing to the Heathrow Train, I felt my blackberry buzzing in my coat pocket:

Jack: Welcome to London Bridge! I'll be waiting for you at Paddington Station. The train station is on the North side of the airport. Buy a ticket from the currency exchange booth. Jack. P.S. North probably means behind where you're standing at the moment. ☺

I immediately made a quarter turn to my left and low and behold, there hung a large sign that read HEATHROW EXPRESS. After buying an overpriced one-way ticket for 20 pounds I ran towards the glass doors that lead the way to the train. "Next train in 2 minutes." I read the digital sign aloud, racing for the train doors. "This way Miss!" called out a platform attendant dressed in a crisp conductor's outfit. The doors shut closed behind me as I fell into a cushioned purple seat. Jack would be waiting for me on the Paddington station platform – he said the train ride would be about 20 minutes away. Knowing his exquisitely precise disposition, I expected I'd arrive right at the twenty-minute mark, and I was right.

"Paddington Station, the next stop is Paddington Station," the announcer's sharp British accent rang over the speaker as I stumbled for my dilapidated Puma bag. Rumblings filled the pit of my stomach, as I grew exceedingly nervous. Asides from the odd video Skype call, I had barely seen Jack in the last six years. I wondered what his style would be like. Certainly not far from country club preppy – cotton slacks and a Polo button down, perhaps a cashmere sweater thrown over his shoulders. More importantly how would he act towards me…? After all *he had* told me he loved me once. Although according to Vivian, 'I love you's' during crying fits didn't count, and considering Jack's words came after one of my sobbing hysterics over bad- boys, I figured she was right.

Regardless, I did love Jack. He genuinely cared about me, and was always there to bail me out of trouble. There was just no chemistry. I mean I wasn't attracted to him. Before I could further rationalize why I wasn't with Jack, married to him, and living a blissful life in London, the next announcement rang, "Paddington Station, arriving at Paddington Station." The doors slid open and I walked onto the platform holding on to my luggage. I looked around and decided to walk towards my left, searching for Jack. I grabbed my phone to look for a text message; but there was nothing. Maybe he was late, or maybe he'd given up on me. Maybe six years of 'no' and a broken heart had sealed my fate. I was alone in a strange city and needed Jack to rescue me. Shoved by large crowds of strangers, I felt panicked, my sweaty palms causing my phone to fall from my hands onto the concrete platform. I immediately stretched down to retrieve it, examining all the pieces were in tact. With my Blackberry in the palm of my hand, I lifted my head to see a familiar face in the distance. He was dressed in torn blue jeans, red Adidas, a crisp white shirt, and black leather jacket. Leaning on a pole by the escalator, he was typing into his phone and had yet to look up. Fully standing now with my phone and luggage intact, I approached closer, as Jack tilted his head up and flashed a large white smile. *"Jack!"* I called out, running into his arms. "Bridget you're here!" There he was, the guy I had rejected for the past six years, and he never looked better.

8

"That's Big Ben. It's the major tourist attraction in this area," Jack said proudly, pointing to the impressive structure across the metro stop. He had handed me a prepaid underground pass back at Paddington Station and we had ridden a few stops west, and were now standing outside the Westminster Tube station. The station was next to the River Thames that ran through London making the wind chilly, and the air crisp. Across the great bell of the clock, a bride and groom stood taking pictures. The knot that had been sitting in my stomach for five metro stops had begun to twist and turn again causing butterflies to rumble under my Canada goose feathers, "how sweet Jack." "It's a weekly occurrence here Bridge, nothing too special," he blurted sharply, shutting down any romantic inclinations surging through my tired torso. There was nothing quixotic written on Jack's pale face; in fact he was as frosty as a snowman, and dead set on his mission; being my London tour guide for the night.

Ninety minutes into the tour, my jetlag had begun to sink in, and my legs were starting to give way, causing my riding boots to drag against the cold pavement. "Jack, do you think I could buy you that coffee now?" "Sure Bridge, you getting tired? I told you about the shoes!" his eyes rolling in sheer disappointment. "We've barely scratched the surface Bridget." Unbeknownst to Jack, the only surface I was thinking about was the grey concrete I was about to hit face first, but I tried to keep on a brave face. "Um, I'm sorry Jack I'm so excited to be here, I just need a time out – perhaps a juice or something and then we'll get back at it. Soho, China town, Piccadilly…" "You got it Bridge." Knowing my budget was non-existent Jack led me to a Java House bordering Soho. Seven pounds and a couple of teas later, Jack and I had gone through the latest highlights of our lives – particularly mine – I spoke, and he listened – most of the time laughing or looking perplexed.

"Are you sure you're ok to film in Greece Bridget?" Jack's furrowed brow spoke volumes. "It'll be an adventure Jack. I found a great crew, and we will film for a week or so then edit in Athens, and I'll be back to my life in the windy city in three weeks." Jack looked at me with a less then approving expression, "Bridget, I want you to rock this, so I'm not going to say I'm waiting for the rescue call, but just be careful,

promise ok?" his enlarged blue eyes starring straight at me. "Yes ok."
My response placed a wide smile on Jack's face, perhaps even the first
of its kind I'd seen since we'd met in Italy. "Come on we've got a lot
more of London to see."

*

Jack led the way through several other British districts, each time
stopping to explain the significance of each structure, or blocking me
from being side swiped from oncoming traffic. "Bridge you gotta
watch out for the moving traffic; its opposite the U.S. remember?"
"Oh yeah, I must be more jetlagged than I thought." The truth was I
wanted to call it a night a few hours ago, check out Jack's flat, and sleep
on a comfy bed before my flight in the morning. However, Jack had
mentioned nothing about letting me crash at his place. In fact, he had
down right avoided the topic of conversation. Maybe he had a
girlfriend after all. His private demeanor sure didn't give away much;
perhaps she'd be waiting up for him, or waiting for him at her place –
or he's really just pissed at me for putting him through years of
unprecedented begging, and really had no feelings left for me at all.
Whatever the reality was, the mental torture, along with pain in my cold
feet were getting the better of me. "Jack I'm tired," I muttered. "Let
me call you a cab Bridget, I'll grab a black taxi." My heart sank. He was
dead serious, ordering a cab from his I-phone app. "You know you
really should get one of these," he said pointing to his I-phone, I can't
live without it, it really does everything – it's all you need." "Well I
guess I'm just used to my blackberry, I don't really need..." "It will be
65 pounds Bridget," he said interrupting my lame attempt to explain
why I was using a decade old mobile. Great, another heart sink, and by
this time, my heart was swimming somewhere between my liver and
kidneys. "Ahh ok sure no problem Jack," I replied trying to recall the
amount of pounds remaining in my dated Diesel wallet. "So where will
you sleep Bridget? You have several hours before your flight. You
know, you really should have gotten a hotel room to rest."

Jesus Christ, was he being serious, I was waiting for the punch line to
set in, but nothing remotely close to a joke came out of Jack's precise
pink lips. "I'll be fine Jack, I'll crash for a few hours on the airport
lounge chairs – they aren't that bad." "The cab will be here in 8

minutes." His answer ran through my ears like a cold stream of wind in the brisk London night. As disenchanted as I through I could ever feel around my Prince charming, I leaned over giving him a big hug and light kiss on the cheek, "thanks Jack."

The cab arrived sooner than expected and I crawled into the back seat, confused and exhausted. Trying not to look back I placed my hands in my warm jacket pockets, when I felt a hard card, and pulled out the cold underground day pass. "Jack!" I called out as the taxi was pulling away. As the taxi came to a screeching halt, I turned over my left shoulder to see Jack walking back. "What is it Bridge?!" he called out from a few steps away. Sticking my hand out the window I waved the tube pass and yelled back "your underground pass!" Jack walked briskly towards the cab, "you could have kept it you know?!" "No, no, take it you might need it," I replied, a wave of disappointment ringing through my tired voice. I had given up on souvenirs years back, and I knew the constant reminder of this evening would not be healthy for my mental state later on. I could hear Vivian's voice echoing in my head – *just let it go Bridge, it's not meant to be;* and so I did. Jack placed his arm through the open window reluctantly reaching for the blue and red card, his cold hands barely touching my fingertips. I smiled and waved goodbye again. "Ready to go now Sir," I said fastening my seatbelt. "Where are you headed Miss?" "Heathrow Airport please, oh and Sir, take your time, I'm in no hurry."

*

"British Airways flight 867 to Eleftherios Venezelos Airport will be landing in Athens in approximately 17 minutes. Ladies and gentlemen please place your seats in the upright positions and ensure your hand luggage is stowed neatly under the seat in front of you." After the night I had spent on two metal chairs in the Heathrow departures lounge, the flight to Athens felt like a night's sleep in a four seasons suite; my neck a soar reminder of the disappointing night before. Jack was my friend, a good friend, and nothing more. Still unsure as to why I was confused and annoyed, I needed to get over the fact that I had rejected the perfect guy for years, and he had come to respect the fact that we were friends. *Just friends.* I was the one to declare I never felt any chemistry other than friendship. It was time to move on, and face yet another decision that would mould my life in a less then desirable way. I took a deep breath, tightened the seatbelt around my waist, and prepared for landing.

After quickly obtaining my luggage, I exited the impressive Athens airport and headed for the Sofitel Hotel directly across the street. I was happy I had earned enough air miles to secure myself a safe and comfy night's rest before flying to the island the next morning. The airport and surrounding area was surprisingly beautifully kept – immaculate actually, although I had no expectations what so ever. I had feared a scary place where the English language was scarce and people were abrupt but I was pleasantly surprised at the gentle demeanor of the locals, and the frequency of good English. Greece had evolved into another world since I was 12, and I couldn't wait to rediscover it. After settling into the cozy Sofitel room, I sunk under the fluffy duvet with the book I had picked up during my night in the Heathrow Airport.

By the time I managed to turn the page pass the prologue, the hotel room phone rang, loud and clear to the right side of the bed. I must have dozed off while reading, and reached for the phone wondering whom it could be. "This is your morning waking up call Miss." "What?!" I answered, but I just fell asleep. "It's 8 am Miss Lane." Oh God, Leo would be meeting me in the lobby in 20 minutes and I barely had time to shower, find wrinkle-free clothing, and put some makeup on my tired skin. Confused and panicked, I scrambled and managed to make it out of the room some 40 minutes later. I gathered my overstuffed luggage and pulled my way through the heavy hotel room door; the clean white sheets remaining in a twist of layers over the bed. Oblivious to me, and perhaps an omen for things to come, my book lay in between, barely stirred from the night before; an African American man stood smiling in a suit on the front cover, *"Think like a man, act like a lady: What Men really think about love, relationships, Intimacy and Commitment."*

9

Leo was just as he appeared on Skype, perhaps even a little thinner and gawkier. "I'm terribly sorry for the delay Leo," I breathed heavily embarrassed with my tardiness and disheveled first impression. "It's no problem at all Bridget, I was late in fact, as well, the traffic in Athens can never be foreseen." His accent was slightly British, and his command on the English language was striking. "Shall we make our way to the airport, then?" he asked wrapping a thin grey and white scarf around his neck. Leo was easy to speak to, and quite professional. I knew he was the right man for the job, and more importantly, the right man to handle Oliver. About a half hour later, I still hadn't heard from Oliver, so Leo and I decided to check in our luggage at the counter and were exchanging some small talk with the airline attendant, when I heard my name being called out from a scruffy breathless voice across the departure doors. What an entrance, of course it was Oliver. "Quite the dramatic entrance Oliver. Have you ever considered making an understated appearance?" My face hung low with revulsion at what I knew would be an arrogant response, "ha-ha, not this business tycoon Bridget! He knows how to make things happen!" I had forgotten how annoying Oliver was – *all the time*. "Leo this is Oliver, we will be shooting his company's amazing Herbal Tea products." "Pleased to meet you Oliver," replied Leo reaching out his hand. Oliver returned the gesture, and seemed to thankfully take a liking to Leo. After checking in and paying an overage fee for overweight luggage, we passed customs and sat waiting in a small departure lounge. "You seem quite relaxed Bridget! Are you ready to work your ass off and produce amazing commercials?! That's why I brought you here you know! It's not a vacation!" Oh my goodness, he had already started his nonsense and we weren't even on set. As I sat allowing the blood to rush down from my flustered face, Leo looked at me with a paternal concern whispering, "I know his type -don't take it personally, or seriously, we will do a great job." Leo was a God-sent, and I smiled in response to his endearing sentiment, "well you just might have to referee Leo –it could get ugly." "Don't worry, I got you," he laughed pointing to the machines that were stationed in the corners of the departure area. "See those machines Bridget? They are high tech, vending machines installed with state of the art lighting and sound systems. I brought them here from China," he explained proudly. "Wow, you do that as well Leo?" I asked impressed with his additional business venture. "Well my partner and I did, many years ago. I tried to be a business man once, but it wasn't for me." "What happened?" I asked noting the intense look on Leo's face. "Well Bridget, my partner was a snake. We were best friends for many years. We actually met in the nightclubs where we worked together. Back in the day, I was actually a tech geek and amateur Disc Jockey." Actually I *could* believe it; it matched Leo's profile quite well. And your partner?" "He was the lightning expert, you know lasers, and all that stuff." "Let me guess," I said cynically, "you started off an innocent, wide –eyed young man, and left a lion." Leo laughed at my assessment, "so you've worked in nightclubs as well?" he asked, his head almost dropping in shame. "PR girl at your service," I replied smiling, "so I've got some idea," I said with a wink. "I, I – it wasn't really my style," Leo stuttered. "I mean the nightclub scene and all, but it's very alluring. I got caught up, well followed his lead actually, and…" "Allow me," clearing my throat and sitting up tall, I yearned to assist Leo in his lame attempt at explaining his X-rated experiences. "You became a master at picking up chicks, including trading them off amongst yourselves, and got an abundance of experience in the art of one-night stands." Leo chuckled shyly, "well I guess I should take responsibility for my own actions, but he definitely introduced me to a new world." "It's not uncommon Leo, it comes with the territory," I said feeling a need to console him. "Sure, but it just wasn't me, I was sort of under the influence, and did a lot of things I'm not proud of," his face displaying much more than I assumed his words ever could. "I should have known someone like that would never make a good business partner," he continued, "but I trusted him. We eventually created a company together and began importing those vending machines into the clubs we worked at, then made our way into airports." "Well that seems like a great venture Leo…" "We were making money," he interrupted, "but you see Bridget, I'm not a businessman and I wasn't watching our finances or expenses. He, on the other hand, was, and knowing he was always money hungry, I should have known better." "What do you mean?" I asked fearing Leo's story would end up in some ghastly mob-driven drama. "To make a long story short Bridget, he told me the company was going bust and so we needed to close it down, and leave with the little we had. I signed off on the paperwork for my exit, but he stayed on and followed through with several pending contracts and made a whole bunch of money" he concluded, shuffling through the contents of his carry-on. "Wow Leo, I don't know what to say." "I'm no business man Bridget – I will die a starving artist, but I will do so with dignity" now burying his head into the baggage. Silence filled the space between us as I awaited Leo to glance up; and when he eventually did I could see the hurt in his eyes. It was a pain I was sure had resonated more so from the moral and unethical betrayal rather than the financial defeat. "You know we even went to jail together; I think you call it the slammer in America?" "Yes," I replied with a giggle, uninterested about the circumstances surrounding the experience. "It was just an over-nighter but we definitely bonded. The mighty dollar – well the Euro in our case, can turn even the best man into the devil." "You think it was only about the money Leo?" "I don't know Bridget, until this day, I actually still don't know. He was a powerful guy, very connected, and I think it was more about control, he had this issue with his women." "Women?" I asked inquisitively, wondering if it was customary to refer to women in plural on this side of the Atlantic. "He didn't have a harem Bridget, but he was a womanizing pig, and I stood by him with every cheating scandal. He had a girlfriend, but that didn't stop him from having nightly conquests and gloating about them. Not that she was a gem or anything; actually she was a neurotic bimbo and I could barely stand her; I still don't know why he kept her around. Girls flocked to his charm, and they'd call me when he didn't pick up the phone after a one-night stand. I'm ashamed of being an ally for someone like that. That's not who I am, and I was disappointed with myself for a long time, but now I have simply deleted him from my life."

It was a long drawn out story, to which I cared to hear no more details, and besides, I wanted to lighten the mood, and eradicate the pain from Leo's eyes. "Ok, well when were done with the commercials I'll buy the drinks and you can tell me about how the heck you ended up in jail for the night!" He laughed retrieving his things, preparing for the mini bus that would be taking us to the small plane at the end of the runway. "Done," he said placing his arm around me.

*

Oliver had been unapparent visible throughout my conversation with Leo, an omen I know I owed to his hidden with his flying anxiety – a

55

little tidbit he had let known during College. He sat uncharacteristically quiet, across the gate's lounge, stuffing his face with Greek chocolate filled croissants and a small box of local fresh milk. "Well at least he can't complain while his mouth is full," I said whispering into Leo's ear. "I heard that Bridget – don't you think for one minute, this is going to be a free ride! And by the way, I'm taking the aisle seat, I'll never squeeze into that tiny space they call a window seat." "I guess its referee time for me" Leo said looking my way, "you can have my seat Oliver," he offered politely. Oliver thanked him taking no time at all to jump into the pre assigned seat. Before I could finish my freshly squeezed Orange Juice and chocolate chip cookie, we were preparing for landing. After a quick descent and luggage claim, we were sitting on the tarmac of one of the most beautiful sights I'd ever seen. The Cycladic island of Paros was truly breathtaking. Images of white sugar cubes and blue fixtures piled up in blocks filling the distant space with residences and businesses. "Welcome to Paros!" called out Oliver as he waved over a bright red pick up truck. "This is my Mom, Mom meet the director and producer, Bridget and Leo." "Pleased to meet you," we said in unison. "Are you hungry, it's dinner time!" she rang out jumping back into the pick-up truck.

Unlike Oliver, his mother was a sweet humble 60-something year old widow – who only always wore black. The dinner consisted of traditional Greek cuisine and the best part, traditional island liquor. The house was as Oliver had explained – a large ranch style main house with small bachelor type apartments surrounding the main quarters. I would be sleeping in the main house and the rest of the crew would have separate rooms adjacent to the main info structure. After a few shots of the homemade liquor, I was all warm and fuzzy and ready to report to my quarters; a pretty pink, colored girls' room filled with family photos and a few stuffed animals. The room was uncharacteristically chilly and I soon figured out there was no central heating anywhere in this complex, and with that, my warm fuzziness began to disappear in the frigid cold of the small room.

I stayed dressed in my down filled jacket trying to maintain some warmth but there'd be no getting used to sleeping like this. I decided to search the room for some kind of electrical heater and stubbed my toe on what looked like a jumbo sunbeam plug in heating lamp. Luckily my toes were partially frozen to numb the throbbing pain. Ecstatic, I plugged it in, immediately feeling some heat – *success!* The fan turned clockwise creating large beaming winds of heat. Next all I had to do was weaken the light rays, but of course it was too good to be true; the batman like light was part of the heat mechanism and where there was no light, there was no heat. Exhausted I fumbled for my sleep mask trying to block out some of the light; buried under three blankets I fell fast asleep; *an hour before call time.*

*

"BRIDGET! BRIDGET!" The sound of Oliver's voice in the crisp island morning pounded against my head like a college hangover. "It's 8 am – call time is 8:30 am Oliver! Don't you dare think I slept in for one second!" I wasn't about to let on I had barely slept and was a walking zombie; I washed my face with freezing cold water, brushed my teeth using the airline's mini brush and cheap toothpaste, and pulled my hair back into a tight ponytail. With the adrenaline running through my frigid body, I ran down out of the main house through the chicken coop in the backyard to find Leo and meet the remaining production crew. They were a rough edgy group of guys from Athens; clearly experienced and noticeably cool. I liked them instantly, and more importantly I knew they wouldn't be taking any crap from Oliver.

*

The filming days to follow went rather smoothly. There were hitches along the way of course, Oliver's wining, Oliver's over-eating than vomiting, Oliver's objections about which tea mountains and natural herbs to shoot, where to eat lunch, and which local girls he would bring on set for hair and makeup and of course as his personal assistant. Thankfully after day four, Leo and I had all the material we needed to edit a few promotional spots and a television commercial, so we sent the crew back to Athens and would spend one last day on the island filming some extra landscape.

"Bridget you need to come meet my grandfather, he is expecting you, and just got released from the hospital." Oliver's voice penetrated my eardrums like a bat across the head. I had been polite and cordial with his family the entire time, as manners were a big deal to Europeans, my

57

mother had been strict about this, *but what in the world did I owe Oliver?!*
"Ok fine Oliver," I replied promising to visit him later that night. After
my last cold shower, I packed up my things and checked into my flight
online. Leo had left the island about an hour earlier, having to be back
in Athens for a wedding gig by nightfall, so I was alone. Pulling up my
socks and zipping my knee-high riding boots, I felt elated at the
thought of leaving the island on a decent note and was looking forward
to staying with my cousin in Athens and editing all the materials for the
next few weeks. As I dragged the luggage down the stairs I could hear
echoes of loud female voices – my inadequate command of the Greek
language wasn't helping, but I did make out the words 'help, help!
Father!' I ran down the stairs following the sounds, to see Oliver's
mother and another woman of about the same age standing over an
elderly man in light blue pyjamas; Oliver's grandfather.

"Bridget call the ambulance," yelled out Oliver. "Oh my God, my
Greek isn't that good, how the fuck am I going to do this!" I screeched
in panic, "well my sister then Bridget, there's no time to lose, run!"
Good God, I had only seen her once feeding the chickens in the
backyard; she seemed polite and friendly and resembled a younger
version of Oliver.

"Elena, call the ambulance it's your grandfather!" I called out.

"They're already on their way Bridget – but we need to go meet them!"
she replied, her voice bouncing off the hallway's thin walls.

*Huh?! Go meet the ambulance? Was this some kind of cruel joke Oliver has
devised?!* "Ah, excuse me, Elena, are you there?" I called out beyond the
long hallway.

"Yes, Bridget, what is it, we don't have much time!"

"Don't they come to you in this part of the world?!"

"Not really, not when it's a secluded area," she answered running
towards me than grabbing her car keys.

A few moments later we were riding in her pick-up truck towards a
local supermarket. A long 20 minutes later in the supermarket's parking
lot, the ambulance and local police arrived and followed us to the main
house where they managed to revive Oliver's grandfather quickly. This
was heavy. I needed a break, a drink, a Greek cigarette, or something to
take the edge off.

"Aren't you gonna miss your flight Bridget?" Elena turned to me coolly.

"Shit what time is it?!" I countered in pure terror. "Forget it Elena, I'm not waiting for a ride I'm calling a cab."

"No I'll take you!" she responded taking a drag from her cigarette.

"Thanks but don't worry," I reassured, recalling a local cab number from the production itinerary, and grabbing my packed bags, "I'll call a taxi!"

*

Twenty-five minutes, a few prayers and Greek cigarettes later, I was in a cab on my way to the national airport of Paros. In all the commotion, I didn't even recall greeting Oliver or his mother goodbye, but was sure I'd be hearing from Oliver enough in Athens. I had arrived on time, but for the small island – it was quite early. I grabbed a box of cream crackers from the canteen and sat in the departures lounge while my racing heart recovered from the night's events. "The next flight to Athens will be boarding momentarily," a female voice in a thick Greek accent called over the PA system; the announcement couldn't have come sooner. After lining up amongst the families, students, and black dressed grannies heading towards the gate, I handed my passport to the attendant. Just like that, I was out of Paros and off to Athens. A sigh of relief ran through my body. I had made it, and even though I was drained and weary, I couldn't wait to see what was going to happen next.

10

Mikey's apartment was pretty big for a bachelor pad. Red fluffy carpets covered the large living space and beige curtains masked the sliding doors to the wrap around balcony. "This is huge for downtown Athens by the way, Bridget." Mikey was my first cousin from my mom's side of course, and although we hadn't seen one another since I was 12 years old, we had tried to keep in touch over the years, and he made me feel right at home. Tall with short brown hair, and large bug-like brown eyes, Mikey had grown up to be quite attractive, and as a bonus was a great cook and listener, and I knew he'd be a great roommate while I was editing in Athens.

"Thanks so much for taking me in Mikey." "It's my pleasure Bridget – we're family and I love the company, and since Mary-Anne is away at College, you can have her room. It's all set up – pink curtains and all."

He was right Mary-Anne's room was painted violet, fuchsia pink curtains hiding the balcony door, with fraternity photos, and college stickers covering the walls. "Mary-Anne's studying literature, so don't be surprised if you see poetry stuffed in the desk drawers. She's also in love every other week with a new Casanova. You may see some Shakespeare lying around here too," he smirked as what I assumed any older brother would. "I love it Mikey!" And that I did; it was sweet and comforting and my new abode, perhaps my new start. "Well maybe my little cousin could give me some advice someday – God knows I'm completely hopeless in that department." "Still single then I take it?" "Yep. I definitely haven't been anyone's plus one in a long while." "Well this is Greece – that will change cousin." I must have looked at Mikey with some kind of grand confusion because he dragged me to the kitchen, pulled up a couple chairs, two glasses, and a large bottle of unlabeled liquor. "This is homemade wine. Now we drink, I talk, and you listen ok cuz?" His tone was serious for a change, and I sat attentively, curious about what he was about to convey.

"Sure Mikey, but you should know that I can't hold my liquor." "It's ok cuz, you'll be walking 15 feet to the left for the toilet and five feet back to your bed." Mikey had a way of making me feel safe and at home, even in a city where I was a complete stranger. "So, listen up. The men here are not like any you've ever met before. *Take a drink,*" he ordered lifting my glass-holding hand towards my lips. "They love foreigners, blondes, the accent, the sweet naïve demeanor; the whole package. So that means you need to be extra careful here." I laughed remembering mom and dad's comparable lectures while Mikey placed some fresh tobacco into thin rolling paper, handing me a beautifully wrapped cigarette. "Its no laughing matter Bridge. You need to know what you're getting into here with men." "I understand what your saying Mikey, but I came to work; shoot, edit, get paid and return home," I explained methodically. "Now you're thinking like an American. The Aegean carries with it a lot of mystery Bridget. The air here is different, and you'll be carried away by the strong current if you're not careful. Don't get me wrong, you do need to loosen up, go with the flow and enjoy all the Mediterranean has to offer; and for your information, the sun, sea and sex are at the top of that list!" "But its January," I interrupted perplexed. "Exactly why the latter is so dangerous. You'll get it sooner rather than later cousin. Actually tomorrow night will be a good start." Why what's happening tomorrow?" I inquired taking another sip of the homemade concoction. "Isn't your friend spinning at the Cheetah club? You had mentioned something to me on Skype about a childhood friend who is a DJ here now?" "Oh yes." I had totally forgotten. Theron was a childhood friend who had moved to Greece when he was 15. We had lost touch for years, but then reconnected on social networks years ago. He was a rising DJ and I had promised I'd go see him spin when I arrived. "I almost forgot Mikey, yes, tomorrow night it is." "Alright then cousin, cheers, stin iyea mas (to our health)!" "Cheers!" I called out tossing the gold colored liquid down my throat. "To your adventure Bridget! *Welcome to Greece.*"

11

"Mikey if you weren't coming with me I wouldn't go you know!" "You need to go cuz, it's your friend – and you need to get out and taste some of the nightlife here – I promise it's nothing like in the U.S., we don't really go by last-call here," he added with a grin.

It was Friday night; I was exhausted from a long day of editing and the commute back and forth into the city, and my innate housecat was reappearing. I would have much preferred to cuddle up in a blanket and sweats and watch a movie, but instead I grabbed a pair of skinny jeans and a loose blouse and made my way to the kitchen. "Come on Bridge, put on something else, this is Europe; you must have some sexy clothes in that American closet, that's way too casual." Sluggish and uninspired, I knew Mikey was right. I walked back into the violet painted bedroom reaching for my new camel colored pleather tights; a low cut black top and my favorite Michael Kors pumps. There that should do it. I grabbed my Marciano Faux fur making my way to the door. "Now that's the cousin I know – you look hot Bridget!" "Really, its not too much?" "Are you kidding, what man could resist a blonde in leather and fur?!" I smiled, feeling a little embarrassed and unaware of whom I'd be trying to impress in a city where I knew barely anybody.

*

It was a little chilly in the ancient city, and the sidewalks were romantically lit with dim streetlights & soaring lampposts hovering over the cobblestone streets. It was like nothing I had ever seen, charming, classical, and antique.

Apparently Athenians didn't head to nightspots until after late dinners and drinks, making midnight a very early arrival time. The nightclub was pretty empty, excluding the staff preparing their bars, and what seemed like the bar's managers. I scanned the naked room looking for Theron and finally spotted the familiar face by the DJ booth. We had spoken on Skype quite often as of late, and I knew exactly what to expect, his baby face had remained just that, reminiscent of our adolescent friendship. He waved me over smiling a big full smile, his cheeks falling and rising. "Theron!" I called out walking briskly towards him to give him a big hug. He leaned forward and gave me double kisses. "Wow you're all grown up Bridget, and much prettier in person!" he said, flashing a beautiful, welcoming smile. His words were simple and few, yet they injected me with a confidence that made me feel more alive than I had in years. "Theron, this is my cousin Mikey, I'm staying with him while I'm editing the commercial." Theron was an untraditional Mediterranean looking man, or at least defied my expectation of one. Now 32 years old, he was tall with a chubby frame, fair-haired, with a thick beard, heavy-set eyebrows, and had somewhat of potbelly, perhaps from excess partying and drinking. He wore a bright red cap, a symbol of his favorite football club, and was well mannered and I could tell brought up with small town good values. He offered Mikey and I some traditional island liquor and fresh tobacco. We sipped while discussing music, life, and Athens, rolling cigarettes in between. Theron was a talented DJ and Producer who loved to play classic house music. I was happy to take a listen and perhaps help him book some gigs in the US, especially since I had been away from any nightlife for the past three years and missed the excitement that came with it.

"Cuz I hate to leave you but I really gotta go."

"But it's just barely into the night Mikey, and you said there's no last call – at least none as long as people can be seen!"

"You're a quicker learner Bridge, you're right, but duty calls bright and early tomorrow morning," he responded with tired eyes nudging my shoulder. "Are you alright with taking a cab home?" Although I was disappointed with Mikey's early departure, I wasn't ready to retire from my first European night out after only a few hours.

"I'll be fine Mikey, get some rest."

"I'll take good care of her!" called out one of Theron's cousins.

"I'm sure you will – keep her safe away from the goons will ya? Her Greek isn't good enough to scare them off yet" Mikey responded sarcastically. Thomas was one of Theron's many (many) cousins that supported all his gigs in Athens. He was in his early twenty's undeniably sweet, and a few inches below average height, with big googly blue eyes and a large crooked nose. He was harmless enough company; most his small talk consisting of the half naked oriental go-

go dancer that swung her legs over the shiny pole across Theron's DJ booth. Thomas kept me company for the next hour or so until he received what seemed like an urgent text. "Well now it's my turn to make my exit Bridget," he said placing his drink down. "I must leave now in order to be at work by dawn." He kissed me on both cheeks and gave me his number for safety, or as he put it, 'emergency keeping'. A few more shots of homemade liquor later, I glanced up to see the club packed and quite rocking; it had filled up nicely. Guys mostly, had filled the VIP area, Theron introducing me to each one that entered the space. All sweet and polite, their line of questioning had become somewhat of a reoccurring phenomenon. "Where are you from? Why are you here? Do you like Greek men…?!" By the time I had met most everyone in the club and satisfied their probing questions, it was time for the headlining DJ's to take the decks. The stars of the show were a duo of Spaniards who were travelling around Greece playing a few gigs during their world tour. One was tall and limber, while the other was short and somewhat cuter. They smoked excessively and drank out of Vodka bottles, continuously trying to pump up the mixed crowd. The club eventually began roaring, and I felt content and excited to be back in a familiar element, even if it was in a place I vouched I'd never enter again.

After another hour had flown by, I had met what seemed to me most of the men in the club, all of whom were friends or acquaintances of Theron's, all except one. Most likely he had just arrived, and I had caught him looking my way then quickly turning to the crowd. Up and down the VIP aisle he went; I wondered if he was pacing or bothered or had a medical problem. After Theron retook the decks I decided to chat it up with the headlining DJs brushing up on my College Spanish. After a few flirtatious exchanges, a short chat about music, and a slight boost in my self-esteem, I looked up to find an unfamiliar face starring back at me.

He was dressed in a black waffle shirt and slim fitting blue jeans; his face was long with a square chiseled chin; his eyes dark and mysterious. The unforgiving nightclub lighting gave away an unsmooth surface on his face, perhaps years of harsh experience. I looked away allowing him to become lost in the thickness of the dry ice.

Feeling uneasy I turned towards Theron who was coincidentally leaning towards me. "Bridget this is Bobby, my best friend." It would appear

Bobby was the mystery man standing by the VIP railing making his rounds up and down the isle for the latter part of the evening. He leaned right into me giving me a stern handshake. "Hello, it's nice to meet you Bobby." "It's a pleasure, Bridget," he responded in a deep voice and heavy Greek accent. Satisfied with the introduction, I turned away forcing him to stand back by the VIP area's railing.

A few moments later Bobby took a seat beside me on the leather sectional, placing his hands through his dark thick hair. "So where are you from?" he said in a deep tone. "Chicago, I'm here filming a commercial. I'm actually in editing now," I explained proudly, reminiscing the survival of Oliver's heinous behavior and family drama.

"Nice," he said turning away reaching for the mobile phone in his pocket. Bobby was a 33 year-old successful entrepreneur, who looked much older than his age. He was around 5'11 with a good lock of groomed brown hair, light brown eyes, and an untypical button nose. His lips centered out his square jaw line and he smiled to reveal a large set of teeth, protruding canines and all.

He was the founder of a modern technology & lighting company, something to do with holograms and graphics I believe, much of which he tried to explain to me in detail, but most of which was unfortunately lost in translation. Needless to say he seemed to enjoy going on about himself and his endeavors. Within an hour, I had learned about his last two relationships, his father's passing, his pursuit of success, and clashes with ex business partners. I don't recall another question coming my way. In fact, I'm sure it didn't. Naturally I was elated to be joined by one of the Dj's during their next set break; this time a little about his daughter and the art of dj'ing, drinking and travelling; all of which was much more welcoming than Bobby's self indulgent babble.

The break was short however, and once again Bobby took the seat beside me, continuing to fill me in on every crevice of his life, lastly turning to his musical preferences. I managed to get in my two cents on this subject, telling him that Theron needed to remix my latest favorite track, 'Wicked Games' by *The Weeknd*. "He can't seem to find the 'a capella' version to do it properly," I explained adjusting my black top over my pleather tights. "Write me all the details here," Bobby said sternly, holding out an empty memo page on his Samsung Galaxy S III. I grabbed the phone, annoyed at his persistence. Although it was obvious he was trying hard, I was unclear for what purpose, and my inexperience was not aiding my plight. "So take a look at some of my work," he said, showing off some photos of colorful odd shaped machinery. "Those look familiar. Hold on let me take a closer look," expanding the photos on the shiny screen. "Yeah, those look just like the machines my director installed in the airport a few years back." "Not possible, I have these babies patented," he countered confidently. "Well they look just like them Bobby," returning his device with a careless shrug. "Well as you Americans say, I don't think the world is quite that small Bridget." "Ah the mantra is *it's a small world after all* Bobby." He looked almost annoyed, or maybe a bit like a sore loser; he wasn't the only person in the world with a unique concept and innovative business after all. I chalked it up to male competition and took another sip of the unmarked liquor. I didn't know anything more about his business and God only knew I didn't want to. Instead I smiled politely, concealing the pain my heels were starting to administer on my tired feet. "A few more minutes and I will take you home Bridget," Bobby said turning to me. Taken back by Bobby's statement, I was ready to decline the offer, when I realized it wasn't an offer at all. Bobby was taking me home, and that was the end of it. Instead I opted for a simple nod, figuring by this time my tired disposition was displayed all over my face. Bobby had an assertive and domineering way of speaking and I could tell, accustomed to getting what he wanted. He left no room for nonsense. At the very least happy to avoid annoying late night cabbies and the half cracked sidewalks that I may have otherwise encountered. I would be breaking my general rule and taking a ride home from a stranger, but it was Theron's best friend, and I felt surprisingly tranquil. I hugged my new DJ buddies goodbye and exchanged information – accepting one of their cards. "You're welcome to come back to our hotel," one of them said in a sweet voice. "Don't worry we will take care of you," the other added. *There it was in broken English, the familiar 'end of the night' DJ proposal, something I never thought I'd hear again.* Thoughts of Chicago nightclubs, scantily clad groupies, and drunken artists I'd have to take the airport in the morning, flooded my memory. "Thanks guys but I have to go I'm beat" I smiled, my face flushed and torso warm with stimulation.

Flattered by the attention, part of me wanted to explore their proposition – but I knew, oh too well, it would only end badly. Besides that, I didn't want to leave that type of impression with Theron, *or bossy Bobby* for that matter. I hugged Theron goodnight and turned to find

Bobby hovering over us. His stare might as well have been laced with kryptonite, and although I barely knew him, I dreaded being on the other side of it. Strutting towards the exit, I walked carefully focusing on the 4-inch heels under my feet, when Bobby interrupted my concentration. "Ah Bridget, the exit is this way – you're entering the washroom." As serious as he was explaining his beloved business, Bobby pointed me into the right direction and stood by the front entrance pending my arrival.

"Oops," I giggled changing directions and following him through the dark double doors. He seemed to know everyone at the club, and walked swiftly ahead, greeting each one goodbye. "I'm parked close by," he said pointing to a black Audi parked under a broken street lamp. Thank God, if I had to walk another block I'd be doing it bare foot. I smiled at the sight of a comfy car – an Audi no less – how 50 shades of him! He put on his seat belt, turned on the radio, and began to drive away slowly. "Oh it's broken, courtesy of the DJ," he said as I reached for my seat belt. "You know DJs." "Yes I'm familiar, and those two look like a feisty duo." Bobby smiled but never turned to look at me, then drove off without asking for directions.

I wondered if Theron had informed him where Mikey's apartment was. "I live somewhere behind that hill top" I said pointing to the large mountain behind the plethora of short rise apartment complexes. "It's not too far" I added, waiting for some type of response, while continuing to point, this time to the left side of a major road guarded with a large number of police officers. "Don't worry about a thing," he replied, "I know this place like the back of my hand," he sounded off with confidence. I wasn't sure what was worse, his conversational or navigational skills, regardless, his attempt to impress me was endearing; it may have even been charming if I was remotely interested in him. Once again, Bobby took control of the conversation, speaking about his life, his business, his ex girlfriend, and then his ex-girlfriend some more, and I listened as carefully as my pounding head and sore eardrums permitted; even throwing in the odd comment to stay alert, *and awake*.

Some 30 minutes and several Bobby-centric stories later, we were circling the mountain *he knew like the back of his hand*. On the third protracted drive by, I had slouched into the right corner supple leather seat, while Bobby discussed his hobbies, working out, eating in, providing for his family, and lastly his brother's daughter. "Oh, I have a niece, she's only two and understands three languages, she may be a genius, or at least advanced," he said. He continued to offer details in a rumbling tangent that I could no longer take. "I cook and bake and I run!" I blurted, hoping to cut him off in random thought. "I guess you could count hot yoga in too," I continued, but before I could complete my sentence he had of course interjected. "Would you like to race sometime Bridget?!" "What? No thanks," I replied immediately. My effort to cut off his rambling was not an attempt at landing a date. I reciprocated with a quick explanation thinking he'd gotten the picture by now. "I have bad knees now, so I wouldn't be much of a competitor." I wondered why Bobby Siteros would even want to see me again. I chalked it up to male ego and the need for a rebound girl; perhaps a few months alone still required a bounce back – I of course was clueless. Finally reaching the right neighborhood, I forwarded Bobby directions to the top of hill, and finally Mikey's humble flat.

"Here we are," he said proudly pulling the car to one side of the dark street and lifting up the emergency break. I don't think I'd ever been as relieved to reach a final destination. "Thanks so much for the ride Bobby." "How about cheesecake Bridget." "Huh?" I replied perplexed with his question. "Can you make a cheesecake?" he repeated. Ok this guy was not taking a hint, that, or he wanted to win some type of competition very badly, so I decided to humor him. "Well I've got a recipe for New York style but I don't know if you'd like it," I said "I'm not that good so I wouldn't want to disappoint you." The girls would be so proud of my sarcasm, I thought, showcasing a slight smile. "Theron is playing again tomorrow," he said quickly changing the subject. "I will pick you up at 11 pm. But you need to meet me at the bottom of this hill. I'll never find my way up here again" he smiled, uncharacteristically lightening up for the first time that night. I was impressed at his relentless attempt to convince me he was great, or at the least worthy of a date. I chalked it up to being a real Greek Casanova, and now accustom to his overbearing manner, giggled under my breath. "I'll wear smaller heels and meet you at the supermarket at the bottom of the hill" I assured him. "I'll get your number from Theron," he replied. "No it's ok," I replied un-phased by his attempt to be gentleman-like. "I'll give it to you now." "Please take mine he said, and ring me, I'll wait." Bobby left little room for hesitation, and no room for options. Albeit rare for me, I followed his instructions. He called out his number patiently and I typed it into my dated blackberry. "I've got you now" he said. *Oh no you don't, far from it buddy, I am not falling for this game!* "Well thanks again for the ride Bobby, it was nice of you," I said reaching out my hand. "No need to say that again Bridget," he replied reaching out his hand into mine. I sat still until he leaned forward to kiss me on both cheeks. "Goodnight Bobby, drive safe," I said softly, holding onto my faux fur tightly, making sure my leather tights didn't slip further down my hips. Opening the passenger side of the four-door Audi, I ran across the road into the foyer of the apartment, and climbed up the short staircase towards the elevator. I managed not to turn around, but figured Bobby might be the type to watch me settle in. I waited a few minutes for the elevator to appear; moments later the sound of its arrival was swept under the noise of a car driving off into the distance. A soft smile brushed my face as I exhaled entering the lift, never thinking for a moment that I had just met *my Mr. Big.*

12

The morning sun in the ancient city was intense. It poured through the glass windows filtering through the fuchsia curtains and directly into my eyes; the light awakening me much earlier than my body was willing to get up. Regardless of my late night, too much homegrown tobacco, and homemade alcohol, I felt good. Mikey was right about the Mediterranean air, there certainly was something extraordinary about it. In fact, nothing compared to waking up under this strapping sun in the dead of winter, which by the way, felt like spring. It had absolutely nothing in common with slamming an alarm clock under countless layers of blankets and comforters in the dead-of-a-*Chicago*-winter.

Mikey had left early for work, leaving his 3-bedroom apartment vacant and soundless. It was perfect timing for ramping up his pulsating stereo system. Dancing around in my boxers holding a frothy cappuccino never felt so free. I reached for my frizzy bun, releasing the elastic band that held it up, unleashing a main of multicolored gold locks that fell past my shoulders. There was no Skype call ringing, no email inbox beeping, and no urgent text message to be answered from a demanding client. Most importantly, there was no exhausting regret from another failed attempt at a relationship or phone call that would never come. I felt so liberated that I hadn't noticed Mikey's neighbor across the apartment complex standing shirtless on his balcony in his underwear. He looked to be in his mid-50's his face aged from the sun, his reseeding hair curly and dark, and his dominant potbelly hanging well over his knee length boxers. I laughed aloud as I jumped off the couch, pulling the dangling drapes all the way to one side hiding me, and it seemed to have been just in the knick of time…

"What are you doing out there – what are you looking at?! Get in here and set the table!" The Greek words came from beyond the neighbor's balcony in a fiery female voice. I laughed aloud throwing on a light blue pair of jeans, white t-shirt, and short leather jacket; I was off for a day of window-shopping in the south suburbs.

*

The area of Glyfada in Athens was once home to an American Army base and had a large population of what Greeks referred to as 'foreigners' – non-Greeks who had relocated there for either marriage or work. The main street, fittingly named Metaxa, was filled with endless cafes, bars, and clothing boutiques. The sidewalks were wide and clean, and the local tram ran right through the middle of the street. It wasn't the Champs d'Elysee but it was cozy, quaint, and comfortable. After walking around for a few hours, stopping for a decadent Greek dessert & Turkish coffee, I decided to hop back on the tram and make my way towards the metro station. I squeezed in between a middle-aged woman decked in a leopard blouse, and slinky animal-print leggings to match, and a heavily pierced teenaged skate border. I could hear echoes of dance music blaring from the I-pod of my seated neighbor, reminding me of Theron, the night before, and of course, Athens' most eligible bachelor, Bobby Siteros. The thought prompted me to reach for my trusty blackberry. Ensuring it was in working order, I clicked on the home screen, and just then it began to buzz and then ring in my hand – the caller I.D. reading Bobby Siteros.

"You must be psychic," I said laughingly pressing the green button on the chipped keypad. "Hello, Bridget?" a deep serious voice answered in a thick accent. "Yes, hi Bobby, it's me. You have ironic timing." I wasn't sure if he had understood what I said, but nevertheless he exuded a deep sexy laugh. "What are you doing?" he asked inquisitively. "I'm just on the tram, returning from a day of shopping," I replied, trying to make it seem as mysterious and interesting as possible. He was out for a walk with his dog Nunka, and apparently looking forward to going out tonight. "I'll pick you up at 11 pm, I'll call you when I'm close by and meet you at the bottom of the hill-top, at the supermarket I showed you yesterday Bridget." He was quite militant with his instructions, and I could tell was used to being in control. "Sounds good Bobby," I answered in my most nonchalant voice. "Filia Bridget." Europeans always sent kisses as sentiments at the end of conversations. From besos in Spain, to baci and bisous in Italy and France; the Greeks apparently used the same technique. It was a simple verbal affection that I found endearing – it sucked me in actually, making me feel all warm and fuzzy inside – and for no apparent reason at all. "Kisses Bobby," I replied softly clicking the red button on my blackberry.

By the time I returned to Mikey's apartment the day had turned to night and the moon hung like a golden beach ball in the dark sky. The sight from Mikey's apartment was picturesque. Starring out the living room glass doors, I had a clear view of Mount Lycabettus, the highest point in the city. The hill was a popular tourist destination that had a funicular railway climbing the hill. It was nothing short of magnificent. "We can climb the mountain on the weekend for a workout Bridge," a voice called out from way behind me. "Hey Mikey! I didn't know you were home." "I was asleep, I just got up, going to start cooking soon. How does beef stew and fresh greens sound?" The truth was it sounded like home, felt like Mom's cooking, and an unusual warm feeling I had only attributed to my childhood.

"Ah delicious of course, and after some dessert, we actually need to climb that mountain this weekend." "Ok deal – I'm gonna get cooking. Are you going out tonight?" he asked strapping on a half apron.

"Actually yes, Theron is spinning again in a little bar called The Mouse." "Oh yeah, I've heard of it. Are you going alone, cause I got plans tonight and can't tag along."

"Actually Theron's friend is going to pick me up. We're going together." "Who is this guy? Was he at the Animal Club last night?" Mikey asked concerned.

"Yes, he was the guy dressed in black by the DJ booth, tall, dark – you know typical looking…"

"Ok I see," Mikey interrupted. "Just be careful, you're not used to Mediterranean men, and…"

"I know, I know, I'm a sheltered American," I interrupted.

"Well I don't know how sheltered you are, but you sure aren't used to the guys here – this I can guarantee. They don't like to take 'no' for an answer, and will tell you anything *they think you want* to hear to get the 'yes'. Oh and they work fast, and make sure he knows your smart, and cultured and picky and …"

"I got it Mikey!" I responded chuckling grabbing a celery stick to munch on. "I'll stay in lit areas and won't let him hold my hand, touch my face or feed me drinks," I said sarcastically. "Sure mock me cuz, but I don't want to see you hurt – it's fierce out here; we are ancient thinkers. It takes one to know one, and you just aren't one; not yet anyways," he continued in a stern voice. It was undeniably sound advice, but unfortunately I wasn't taking any of it too seriously. It wasn't even a date, I mean, he was obnoxious, overbearing and just giving me a ride to the bar because I was a friend of Theron's.

Sitting in the aftermath of Mikey's sermon, surrounded by the kitchen's dated green tiles, I thought about how excited I was to see Theron again; he had an energy that lit up a room, and was so attentive and sweet. After we had reconnected several years after he moved back to Greece, I thought our friendship had potential to turn into a hot love affair; quite laughable when I think of it now. He was a giant teddy bear, and no one I'd ever date; he also had a long-term girlfriend who, I was told, adored him. I suppose my radar had been slightly off back then, but then again when had it been fully 'on'? Vivian always said my biggest issue was not reeling them in, but keeping them on the line.

"Bridge, come and eat while it's hot!" My walk down memory lane had come to a halt with the sound of Mikey's voice, and it wasn't a minute to soon, I was famished. "That smells just like Mom's" I said excitedly. "Yeah I've been told I have that effect; Mom's cooking…" he responded laughingly. We ate and drank homemade wine until the kitchen clock rang a soft 10 pm. I had lost track of time and had an hour to get on full makeup and try to match up a somewhat sexy outfit. "Bridge I'm only letting you off the hook for the dishes because I know it takes you forever to find an outfit," Mikey explained removing the dishes from the table. "That and you know I'll bake you some brownies tomorrow," I responded. "That too," he said.

*

Fifteen minutes later my makeup was complete. Deep brown shadow ran across my eyelids, bringing out the green in my eyes and every lash was covered in two coasts of black mascara. Satisfied with my makeup, I glossed my lips with some cotton candy lip balm & searched for my favorite dark blue jeans. They fit a little better than I remembered; snug against my gluts; a booty bump I had grown proud of. I searched for a top to match; a good thing about having a limited selection was *having a limited selection*. I sorted through a few colored tank tops and settled on a double layer. Navy blue and then skin color, I through them over my lace bustier and was ready to go. I chose a pair of black over- the knee boots, with a medium sized heel to get me safely downhill and splashed on some Sugar based perfume. I decided to check over emails to waste some time until Bobby arrived, particularly those that Vivian and Lea had sent over the past few days. There wasn't much of anything new to discuss, particularly because I hadn't told the girls about London, or Jack, or any of the happenings in the Mediterranean thus far. I suppose I didn't feel like being lectured about any potentially bad choices, so I decided to refrain from telling them anything about my visit with Jack, and further, anything that was happening thousands of miles away from them. The truth was I was fearful of the 'I told you so' lectures, and didn't want to ruin my newly found Mediterranean vibe, so I wrote a couple of generic messages avoiding any details.

Before I knew it, it was 11 pm, then 11:15, and no word from Bobby. I wondered if I should call, or if promptness was as prevalent out here as it was in the US. By 11 30 pm I had reached for Mikey's homemade wine. A few drinks later, my phone began to vibrate, than ring. I grabbed it, answering hello in the softest voice I could muster up. "Bridget, it's Bobby. I'm so sorry I slept in, I took a nap and my alarm didn't go off." Bobby's voice was deeper than before and I could tell scruffy from a recent awakening. "I will be there in 45 minutes, don't worry it's a small bar that won't get busy until later – Athens is like that." Bobby knew what he was talking about and although I was a little disappointed over waiting all dressed up, and not having extra time with Theron, I felt reassured the night would turn out just fine. "Ok, I've worn smaller heels so I'll walk down the hill top." "Oh no, I like high heels," he replied in a sultry tone. *He loved heels?! Just who the heck did this guy think he was?! Why didn't I just ask him what lingerie to slip into later as well! He was going to pick me up over an hour late and was suggesting I wear high heels to walk down a potentially hazardous hilltop for his enjoyment?!* "I'll see you in front of the supermarket in my two-inch-heels," I replied, hanging up the phone. I was content with myself for sticking to my guns, yet annoyed with Bobby's pretentious behavior, so I decided to pour myself another drink before my descent. Two more drinks and 30 minutes later, I grabbed my faux fur, deciding to start the trek down and take my chances with Bobby's arrival. I could also hail a cab, I thought, if Bobby didn't arrive in a timely manner.

The walk down the hilltop might as well have been a crawl. I dug the small wooden heal of my boots into any crack in the road that would hold my weight from tumbling forward or sliding back like a third grader on thin ice. Remembering how that felt from personal experience, I was going to avoid it at all costs, even if it meant, taking my boots off and running down in my fuzzy socks.

I had successfully made my way partially down the hill when I felt my phone buzzing from deep inside my purse. Apparently Bobby was 10 minutes away. Pleasantly surprised I made it slowly and successfully to the supermarket to see a black Audi parked with the hazards flickering across the market. I walked around to the passenger side knocking on the glass window. Bobby swiftly turned to his right, unlocking the door. "Hello," I said entering the car and reaching my hand out to shake his. "Kalispera," he replied leaning forward to kiss me on both cheeks, then apologizing for his lateness. He looked exactly as I remembered; the collar of his black overcoat turned up high against his chiseled jaw, his hair gelled in place, and his eyes full of mystery. He took a quick look at me, put the car in drive, and drove off quickly.

*

The small bar was quaint and cozy. The exterior was decked out in tiny white Christmas style lights, and there were a few high tables and chairs filled with patrons smoking and drinking. It was a sight you'd never see in the bitter Chicago winter. Inside the bar the smoke was thick and hazy, and there stood Theron behind the decks of a pioneer turntable adjacent to a mid sized bar. His red football cap covered a large part of his face and I waited patiently for him to look up. Soon enough he spotted me, calling me over flashing his familiar jovial smile. "I'm sorry I'm late Theron," kissing him hello on both cheeks. "Oh I know it's not you Bridget, Bobby has timing issues," he answered laughingly. I took my place on the stool across the DJ booth, while Bobby eventually joined me after greeting the bar's staff. I sipped on a vodka cranberry while Bobby stuck to his juice. I swayed to the music and had some light conversation with Bobby when he turned to me suddenly, "so what do you think of me Bridget?" Surprised, I stumbled on choosing a few words. "Ah, I don't know you Bobby, and I don't like to judge people, especially those I just barely met," I replied a little flushed and off guard. "Well just try," he said starring deeply into my eyes. "I think you're very open minded Bridget, and pretty, well you certainly like to make an impression on people," pointing towards my bust region. *The nerve!* "I'm not trying to impress anyone Bobby," I scolded in an annoyed tone. "I don't mean it in that way Bridget, perhaps it's my English. I meant you are impressive in general." "Are your eyes green?" he said leaning in starring closely at me. "Wow, they're so deep, and beautiful, like emeralds."

I had to admit I was taken back by his compliment and sudden interest; it was even a little embarrassing, something I wasn't used to back home. In fact it was rare for a guy to hand out a sincere compliment altogether. Bobby's line of questioning continued for the next little while, his attention not staggering from me for a single minute, and before I knew it Theron's set was up and it was time to go. Eager for some fresh air I excused myself waiting outside until they finally exited. "After hours Bridget?" Theron asked putting his arm around me. "It's my turn to drink and have fun now," he said in a playful tone. "Umm I was gonna call it a night actually," I said glancing at my watch and patting the collar of my faux fur. "Oh come on it's like a 5 minute walk," he responded. "You're in Greece – this is what we live for," he continued, "and I know you don't have anything like this in Chicago, beside we won't stay too late. Bobby will take you back home afterwards." His argument was convincing enough for me to saddle up and walk along side the guys on the cracked pavement for a few blocks. A few narrow streets later, and a slight turn, a partially lit street revealed a large crowd standing around a dimly lit sign that read *Le Bug*. The scene brought me back to my club days in Chicago, and the interior was just as I suspected. There was something infectious about the dry ice, loud music, and go-go dancers; a love-hate relationship I had clashed with for years. Making our way to the DJ booth was quite the task. We were literally swatting sweaty, high bodies and ducking to avoid getting wacked from flailing arms and burning cigarettes. Theron led the way and I walked closely behind Bobby. I could barely see through the dense smoke and began to feel uneasy when a hand reached behind to grab mine. Bobby pulled me close to him and led me through the overcrowded club. "Are you alright?" he asked attentively.

"Yes, thanks, I'm fine," relieved Bobby sensed my uneasiness and surprised he had cared enough to pull me into safety. I suppose it was a European trait – protecting women in their group. Mikey hadn't gotten to that part yet, or perhaps skipped it, but nevertheless Bobby and Theron took good care of me, and I relished every moment of it.

The DJ was cute. He wore his headphones across his head letting his blonde locks run lose under the black leather. Apparently he was Athens' best. He played a variety of techno and deep house. Admittedly more amusing to watch than to listen to, pouring vodka into his mouth straight from the bottle, and handing out shots to friends and fans close by. I was happy to be the recipient of a few drinks, chatting up a few of Theron's friends, and dancing alongside Bobby. I wasn't sure if it was dancing or light grinding but Bobby had strategically placed his body against the side of the DJ booth facing me, perhaps shielding me from the crowd, or just keeping me close to him. I felt his arms pulling me close periodically, each time swarming out of his reach, yet returning close to his safe haven. The sweat from my heavy heap of hair had drenched my set of tank tops and the nape of my neck, causing me to sporadically lift the heavy locks above my shoulders for a few seconds. As I lowered my arms my elbow grazed the arm of a woman trying to make her way through the crowd into the DJ booth. Her fuzzy dark curls brushed the side of my face as she swiftly turned to me – her wide hips pushing through excessively tight blue jeans that masked her husky pear-shaped body. From what I could translate out of her dark set lips, she was wailing something about me, or to me, heaven only knew, but the Greek words I could make out were 'smile, nice, keep on moving…' My face must have been flushed, as Bobby turned to me immediately asking me what was up. "I think that girl has an issue with me, look at her she's totally gawking at me!" I called out loudly into Bobby's right ear. "Are you sure you didn't misunderstand Bridget? She seems to be friends with the DJ. She was probably just giving you a compliment. This is after-hours. It's about love and peace here" he said laughingly. "Where I come from, brawls and cat-fights in nightclubs are common Bobby and this is the way they start," I explained matter-of-factly biting into a hangnail on my right thumb. "Nothing's gonna happen to you here Bridget." When Bobby spoke, I didn't have to ponder about anything. I was slowly letting my guard down, surrendering my defenses. He was sure of himself and the situation, he was a man, and I felt safe with him. He pulled me close hugging me, my nose rubbing the side of his neck, which by the way smelled surprisingly amazing. I had never stood so close to him, his arms felt hard and developed, and I wondered what his body looked like under his cream v-neck sweater. The DJ slowed down the track and the lights were lightly cast above us. I could barely make out Bobby's face through the clouds of smoke before the haze began to clear revealing his eyes coming closer to mine. I felt his chest close, strong, and broad, waiting to catch me; but a moment later he took a deep breath and stepped away, lowering his arms to the base of my back and leaning his head on my shoulder.

I couldn't believe it, but he was vulnerable; shy almost. I comforted him, moving my hands up and down his spin, than hugging him, holding him close to me, but he pulled away once more. *Could Bobby Siteros be afraid? Shy? Lost or even wounded by a women? Oh snap out of it Bridget, you don't know a real man from a whole in the ground!* That's it, it was time to remove myself from Bobby's arms, but as soon as I tried to loosen my self from his grip, he grabbed me close and kissed me softly. His kiss was powerful, similar to his presence, and completely unfamiliar. *Oh God, what are you doing with Theron's best friend, and a guy you don't know – don't even like for that matter?!* My so-called feelings however, all vanished when I leaned in and reciprocated his commanding kiss. After several minutes of tasting Bobby's lips and caressing his firm chest, he surprisingly pulled away, standing inches from my face, starring through me. He was unsure of something; conceivably it was me, and my apparent inexperience, rigid shell, or perhaps himself.

Oh Bobby, what the fuck are you thinking, and who the fuck are you anyways?! I wanted to know him, draw him closer. I raised my chin and opened my mouth, provoking him to come closer, *and he did,* I couldn't believe it worked. He came nearer, kissing me again, this time jarring my mouth open with his tongue. I pulled him closer, bringing my arms up around the back of his neck and up and down his back. I kissed him back softly, than without realizing it, passionately. He pulled me in even tighter, and this time I could feel his erection against me. Did I have all this power? I was shocked yet psyched with my influence over a man, a man like Bobby no less. We grew more intense with each kiss; stopping for air from time to time, but Bobby, came back each time with more intensity, barely leaving me from his reach. His only words were 'you kiss pretty' which he whispered to me in Greek in between breaths of smoky air. I smiled but was admittedly embarrassed at the newly found attention. I pulled away feeling the eyes of one thousand partygoers plastered on me, two of them belonging to Theron.

"Having a good time Bridget?!" Theron had suddenly appeared five inches from my flushed face. Bobby stood still unaffected. "Yes Theron, thank you for bringing me here, everything is alright." My face felt like a bushel of extra spicy hot peppers, and Theron's face spoke volumes of confusion, but I was too high and unconcerned with the rest of the world to pay attention to anyone else. The kissing exhibit continued with Bobby pulling me closer each time, but not before I pulled away to catch my breath, and take a look at the crowd. I wasn't sure if he was claiming his territory or trying to numb my lips, but he lured me in time and time again with passionate kisses. What felt like hours later, I finally managed to pull myself away, grabbing some water and much needed oxygen. "Are you alright Bridget?" Bobby asked tenderly placing his fingers on my face. "I know it's hot in here, if you need air, or just to get outta here, let me know, it's your call," he continued patting my hair, keeping his eyes on mine. "Yes, Bobby I'm tired."

"Theron get your things, were outta here," he yelled signaling for the jackets. His command was exhilarating. When he spoke people listened and although I didn't know why, I didn't care. We began to make our way through the sweaty bodies once again, and this time Bobby held my hand tightly. Theron led the path to the crowded exit, stopping to greet friends along the way. The same doormen waited to greet us upon our exit. This time, I received a nod as well, I didn't know if I was being acknowledged because Bobby held my hand, and me close to him, but I enjoyed it nonetheless.

The Athens air felt brisk and perfect. Breathing in the winter Mediterranean atmosphere was exhilarating and unfamiliar. It didn't puncture your lungs or freeze your throat; it was welcomingly smooth and inviting. We walked together towards Bobby's car, Theron reaching it first, waiting by the back door as we approached. "Sit in the passenger seat," he said pointing to the front. I turned around to look at Bobby before walking around to the other side when he paused and grabbed me by the turned up collar on my faux fur coat. He pulled me close to him, right to his lips, than kissed me hard. I kissed him back softly, now accustomed to his aggressiveness. I didn't contest Bobby, question his affection, or my reaction for that matter; instead I decided to go with the flow, and leave it up in the Mediterranean air.

13

Bobby held my hand for most of the car ride, letting go to shift gears and light his old Holburn tobacco. After dropping off Theron at a friend's place he headed straight for Mikey's apartment, this time remembering most of the road on his own. "We're almost there, a couple more right turns up the hilltop and we're good," I explained. Bobby listened carefully, and followed my instructions but said little to nothing, the entire ride. I didn't pretend to understand European men, Bobby, or men in general for that matter, so I decided to reciprocate Bobby's silence. By the time we had reached Mikey's neighborhood, the sun had risen over Athens revealing the aging buildings and soiled streets, much of which filled with graffiti and piled garbage. Needless to say the city was much less appealing in the daylight; the mysterious sexiness vanished and replaced with the serenity of a religious Sunday morning.

I was happy to arrive at Mikey's and call it a night. My contact lenses were suctioned to my eyes like a toilet plunger and I was eager to rip off my smoky clothes and snuggle under the duvet. As soon as the car stopped I un-clicked the partially broken seatbelt and Bobby did the same. We reached for each other without speaking. He kissed me furiously and I reciprocated placing my hands on his neck and along his exposed chest. "Is your cousin home?" he asked. "Yes, he is. Goodnight Bobby," I answered in a rush. "No," he said pulling me in close to him, "I don't want to lose this feeling," his eyes fierce firmly planted on mine. I was indeed flattered at Bobby's intense attention, but was admittedly a little uneasy. He was an experienced European man, and I was nowhere near what he was accustom to. "I want to change and remove my contact lenses, I mean I need to go to sleep Bobby," I stuttered. *Could I sound any more boring or pathetic?* I knew by his smirk he was about to make an American joke, but instead he insisted I go grab a few things and come back down. "No," I replied. "Ok then, let's go," he countered pulling the car back into drive and rolling down the hillside. "Ah, what do you mean? Where are we going? I'm... I'm not sleeping with you Bobby. I'll see you again." I desperately wanted to see him again and I knew leaving with him now would not help that plea. It was a trap I wasn't willing to fall into, but before I could escape from his grasp, he had made up his mind. "Yes you will see me again

Bridget, you'll see me again soon, but I'm not sleeping without you tonight" he said putting the car in first gear and driving off.

*

"This isn't the best part of town Bridget so keep your purse close," *Great, just what I needed to hear for my paranoid psyche.* "It will do just fine though for a clean room close by, and I need to drive Theron to the airport in a few hours," Bobby explained as he held my hand, interlocking his fingers in mine as leading the way. About 25 minutes after we had left Mikey's, Bobby had pulled up in front of a motel somewhere outside the downtown Athens core. I had no idea where we were, but I imagined I somewhat fit in, with my three quarter faux fur, over the knee boots, and smeared eyeliner on a Sunday morning. I might as well have been Julia Roberts in Pretty Woman; only we weren't walking into the Beverly Wilshire. Instead I was starring at the dirty, checkered floor of a seedy motel on the outskirts of town.

Embarrassed beyond belief, I stood a few feet behind Bobby as he spoke to the front desk clerk arranging for a room for a few hours. He was direct and took control like a pro. I didn't want to think about how many times he'd done this before, or how he arranged the stay or the price. It was Greece, it was the Mediterranean, and I needed to live for the moment, even if I wasn't sure if I was proud or mortified with my decisions.

"Room 207 Bridget – we can take the stairs," Bobby commanded confidently showing me a gold keychain with the room number stamped on it. We walked slowly up two short flights of stairs to find a room of decent size that stunk of moths and strong cleaning products. The bed sheets were off white, and made from some type of synthetic woven fabric, and the room felt ice cold. Thus far, I had noticed Europe and central heating didn't have a good relationship. Bed bugs, and a pissed stained mattress ran through my head, but I didn't mention a thing to Bobby. I wasn't about to let him think I was a wuss, and be the focal point of another bad American joke- I was the daughter of a Greek Goddess after all, and it was time to unleash my inhibitions.

Bobby called downstairs to order some water and seemed to have a good command of the situation, so I said nothing, and only tried desperately not to think about his past experiences here. My thoughts became more meaningless as he began to get undressed. He sat on the bed in his sweater and black Calvin Klein boxers; I lied beside him in my jeans and layered tank tops. *Is this what one-night stands were like? I felt like a clueless prude. I am not sleeping with this guy – ok we have chemistry but I'm so not in his league – I mean I haven't even waxed!* Endless thoughts buzzed through my tired head, each more outrageous than the next, before Bobby leaned over and kissed me interrupting the stream of excuses I had conjured of why *not to be here.* His kiss made everything better and more intense at the same time. Before I knew it, I had lifted his arms in the air and was removing his sweater. His chest was built perfectly, separated and muscular with light hair dispersed in between, a very pleasant surprise. He kissed me throwing me on my back, pulling my hair tight back and looking into my eyes. His words were easy to translate, "you're perfect" he said, and kissed me soft and long, using his hands to remove my sticky jeans from my sweaty legs. *Ugly panties* were all I could think of. *They are decent Bridge! There is nothing wrong with light grey Brazilian panties and a plain nude bra.* Bobby's warm hands lifting my tank tops interrupted my thoughts, but his actions were in turn interrupted after the second layer.

"There's more?!" he asked confused while letting out a faint chuckle. His expression may have actually been cure if I wasn't mortified. "Uh, the third tank doesn't count it's technically lingerie." The third layer of clothing was a cotton white lace tank that was suctioned to my body for the last few years. I barely ever left home without it. It kept my tummy safe from cold air and painful aches, a symptom of IBS I had no intention of telling Bobby about. I can't say I was comfortable in my mismatched bra and panties but Bobby didn't seem to notice much less care about the fashion faux pas. The kissing was endless and the time frozen. Bobby's arm muscles budged as he held me closer, almost in a headlock at times; he was like nothing I had ever experienced, sensual and powerful. "I can't believe I feel so close to someone so fast," he said softly looking at the disco ball hanging from the purple ceiling. He felt good, and right, even though it was going against everything I had ever imagined 'right' to be. Thoughts of past relations fled through my head, more so how wrong they were. This was right – and it didn't matter that I barely knew him, Bobby and I were connected; there were no mixed signals, and most importantly *he was no Mr. Big*. My daydreaming was once against interrupted, but this time it was with a small blue packet that read DUREX on it. It must be the European equivalent to Trojan condoms I thought, my limited experience leaving me pondering. In fact I had never even bought a pack of condoms or looked at the drugstore display.

Bobby tore open the shiny blue package using his canines and placed it on his erection. Panicking I pushed him lightly on his chest, "umm Bobby, I was serious when I said I wasn't going to sleep with you. I mean I said I wanted to sleep with you and I meant it, but I'm not having sex with you." My naïve-ness sounded even worse aloud. Afraid he'd kick me out of the room for not giving him what he was apparently accustomed to, I was pleasantly relieved when he muttered "Ok," with a faint smile, holding me close and leaving the condom on.

The next hour or so felt more like a wrestling match then an attempt at lovemaking. Bobby consistently tugged at the little articles of clothing I had left on my body, trying to touch me any way he could. It was animalistic, and although it was full of passion and excitement, and what I had always wanted, it was way too much, way too soon. There was no way my green demeanor was going to allow me to turn this into *a night in Paris* in a number of hours. After some foreplay and more tugging, Bobby had finally tired himself out enough to fall asleep. Leaning to his side he turned towards the room's door, allowing my backside to rest against him. I could only assume this is what spooning was; something I had heard great things about but never experienced, *and it exceeded all my expectations.*

*

We had slept for an hour, tops. It was one of those sweet naps that left you confused and happy upon awakening. Bobby's phone went off periodically, a bird chirping noise echoing in between notifying him of a text message. I had opened my eyes for a few minutes when I felt Bobby reaching for his mobile. "Theron," he said in a deep sultry voice. "What?" I answered half asleep. "Hey baby," he said kissing me on the cheek. "Theron's sending me text messages - he wants to make sure I don't forget to take him to the airport," he chuckled as he said it, laying his phone down on the nightstand. Considering his track record with time, I knew it was the continuation of the 'inside joke' Theron had eluded to at the bar. "This has never happened to me before" he said pointing to his now deflated erection, and finally pulling off the clear Durex that enclosed it. "What?" I asked inquisitively. "I've been kissing you for 4 hours," he continued. I turned to face him, smiling than blushing. "I told you I wasn't going to sleep with you Bobby, and you know in the US we say there's always a first time for everything." He laughed a deep sexy laugh, and propped himself up, reaching for his clothes. I followed putting on my layers of tank tops, skinny jeans, than grabbed my battery-drained blackberry. I pointed to the now momentous disco ball hanging from the ceiling wondering if the camera had any juice left at all. The flash went off and the blackberry went completely black. "Ready Bridget?" Bobby asked turning towards me.

"Yes I'm ready," I replied before placing the mobile in my pocket.

Bobby leaned into me placing a soft kiss on my swollen lips. I grabbed his hand walking towards the exit, and shut the door to room 207.

14

The third time round uphill, Bobby seem to find his way back to Mikey's apartment quickly and efficiently. After changing gears and lifting the emergency break of the Audi, he kissed me goodbye a few times and told me to be careful. "Na prosexeis," it was a typical endearing Greek phrase I had grown up with. "Ok Bobby, I will, kisses," and just like, I began falling into the seat of a Mediterranean Goddess, perhaps the driver's seat. Bobby drove off in a hurry and I could sense a little urgency under his otherwise calm demeanor.

The apartment was quiet. Mikey must have been out for the afternoon. I ripped off my sweaty, smoke drenched clothes and headed for a hot shower. I scrubbed over every inch of my skin and tossed my tangled mane under the running water until a unanimous smell of eucalyptus and fresh flowers inundated the tiny green tiled bathroom. By the time I had dried off I could smell something delicious coming from the kitchen. Mikey must have been cooking up a storm for a late Sunday afternoon lunch with his friends. I wrapped myself in a towel and tiptoed to my room quickly throwing on my favorite sweats and sinking under the feather filled duvet. The scrumptious smell of homemade food and even the afternoon light weren't strong enough to keep me awake. Thoughts of warm kisses and manly arms propelled a smile across my face; I closed my eyes and fell fast asleep.

*

The morning sun was brighter than usual. *Where was I, and what time was it?* I looked around the pale violet room squinting towards the light peering through the fuchsia curtains. Of course, I was in Mary-Anne's room, in Mikey's apartment; *get a grip Bridge.* I leaned over the bed and grabbed my charging blackberry. 8:35 am Monday. It was a rarity for me to have slept all the way through Sunday and the night to follow, without even waking to pee. More like a record for me; my body must be in some kind of shock. I grabbed my phone to have a second glance, no text messages. I secretly hoped there'd be one waiting, but I wasn't about to get my hopes up and follow the pattern that had doomed me for years. It was one night, albeit one amazing night, but that could have possibly been it. I mean, I was just an American girl with a very un-Mediterranean outlook on life; one who didn't own matching lingerie, could barely drink, or order the right entrée. Bobby Siteros could surely have any hot-blooded European man-eater that knew how to handle her man. He was attracted to me for one night – it must have been the bust hugging tank tops and tight jeans, but now it was over. *This is why you don't sleep with men on the first or second date Bridge – and yes, sleep and no sex still counts!* After my inner pep talk had subsided, and I had awoken my senses with a strong cappuccino, I loaded up my black Mac book to check for emails. There were several emails from the usual suspects accompanied by interesting subject lines:

Leonidas Papadopoulos: Commercial Revisions

Vivian: Are you socializing at least?!

Oliver: I Want to see the first edit!

Bobby Siteros Wicked Games

My heart raced. Bobby had sent me an email just after 5 am. I scrolled the track-pad over all the emails clicking only on Bobby's.

Let me see you dance

I love to watch you dance

Take you down another level

Get you dancing with the devil

Take a shot of this

But I'm warning you…

He had written out the words of the song Wicked Games by *The Weeknd* and had attached the 'a capella' version, two versions actually. Surprised and exited I played both versions and saved them in I-tunes. He was charming and romantic after all, and different, *and he liked me.* I flushed and finished my cappuccino thinking of a witty response.

Why weren't you sleeping at 5 am ☺?

Kisses, Bridget.

After replying to the rest of my emails, I threw on a long oatmeal sweater and pair of leggings and headed towards the metro. I had a fairly long metro ride followed by a quick trip on the suburban railway, where Leo would be picking me up on route to his home studio in "Taylor's Port," a seaside town almost 40 km from the center of Athens.

Leo was punctual as always, waiting for me in his beat up white Suzuki. He waved me over and I happily ran into the passenger seat, "thanks for picking me up Leo." "No problem Bridget, in fact there's no other way for you to get here without a car," he said chuckling in a soft boyish laugh. Leo was incredibly kind and caring, I could tell he was a loyal boyfriend and would make for a caring father. "I think your going to really like it here Bridget. Taylor's Port is known for its beaches, and traditional Greek food; we call them *tavernas*. If we ever finish editing I'll show you around. It's always buzzing here, thousands of Athenians have built their country-houses here and there are usually large crowds on weekends and holidays." "Sounds great Leo," I responded elated to see another beautiful part of Athens. Taylor's Port was indeed picturesque. Small fishing boats sat on the water like a painted portrait, kids ran around by the shore, mothers and strollers walked slowly and finally fishermen sat by the port's edge waiting for their catch.

"It's exquisite Leo, and you get to live here!"

"That and tranquility is exactly why I moved here two years ago; actually to be close to my ex-partner as well. He had a home here, and as our tech business was taking off we needed to get things done quickly and Athens is quite the jungle to get around in, so I moved out here. He helped me get find my place here and get settled." I could sense sorrow, frustration, and disappointment in his voice. I wanted to console him, to tell him not all people were money hungry whoremongers, but the only thing I could think to say was "I understand Leo, but you did salvage something beautiful, look what you come home to everyday." He seemed to shrug it off and about 15 minutes later we had arrived at his townhouse. His home studio was the main floor of a three-storey detached town house facing the water.

The walls were filled with 1980's album covers and the shelves were overflowing with beta tapes and old records. "I've got all the equipment I need right here," he said removing a yellow bed sheet to reveal two flat screen computers and a baby grand. "All the magic is made right here," he said flashing a somber stare and gentle smile. "I have no doubt," I smiled giving him a high five breaking his serious tone before we settled into editing.

The hours flew by quickly. Leo was pleasant to work with, calm and well mannered, he smoked his homegrown tobacco furiously, while I offered editing instructions and musical input; we were a good team and managed to complete a first edit for all the commercial spots. "We need to open a window Leo." "Oh shit, I'm sorry Bridget, I forgot you're not a smoker." "Well definitely not a European smoker," I said chuckling softly. "But I do kinda feel like a walking ashtray since I've been in Greece." "It's a part of our culture," he said racing for the window hovering over the baby grand, "I forget it's such taboo in America. There, that should do it," he said, cranking open a few windows. "I'll be taking you to the suburban railway in a few anyways Bridget, remember there's no transportation out here." I had almost forgotten that Taylor's Port was pretty much secluded and I would be relying on Leo to get me around. "That's awesome of you, thank you Leo" I replied, grateful that a practical stranger, a man I barely knew, was taking such good care of me. "I'll be right back" he said heading for the kitchen. As I looked through my laptop for any new emails, my blackberry began to buzz and make beeping noises. I had an incoming text message.

Bobby: How is it going in editing beautiful? The director better be treating you well. Kisses, Bobby.

I wasn't sure what power Bobby held over me, but he made my face light up, and my stomach fill with butterflies. I imagined his kiss on my lips and smiled. "Anyone special?" Leo asked re-entering the studio with a bowl of fresh cut fruit. "I noticed you didn't eat much today. The fruit here is full of vitamins, try some," he said placing the bowl on the wooden table. Leo was definitely well trained – as a boyfriend. I wasn't sure if it was from the woman he currently lived with, a past relationship, or his mother, but he was like a well-trained soldier, a faithful boyfriend, and caring fatherly figure.

"You read my mind Leo, I indeed am in need of vitamins! I was just thinking of what I'd cook tonight." "I bet Bridget; was it thoughts of boiled chicken breast and mixed greens that brought that larger than life smile to your face?!" Shocked at his perceptiveness, I turned three awkward shades of red. "Well at least I know I'm working with one heck of a smart Director Leo!" " Just be careful," he said sternly. The guys here are different. I have a sister, and I used to tell her the same thing, and she's not a naïve, sweet, pretty American," he said covering up the piano keyboard with a clean bath towel. "Well that's quite a compliment coming from you Monsieur Director!" I replied trying to make a joke out of the 'dating European men' subject. "Ok I get, it, I won't pry, just promise to be careful, you remember the stories I told you about my ex-partner; people aren't always what they seem here. Come on, let's go, your carriage awaits you Madame."

I grabbed some fruit and nuts to go, and stuffed my blackberry in my jacket pocket, zipping it up securely. The train station was fiercely chilly after nightfall. The ride from Leo's place out of the port took longer than expected and I had 20 minutes to wait before the next train would be arriving. I paced up and down the platform, wrapping my lengthy lavender scarf around my neck, trying to warm up the rest of my body. Just as I reached over to adjust the scarf's tassels, I felt my pocket vibrate then beep again. Another text message was arriving.

Bobby: Are you OK baby? Tell me when you're home. I worry you're out there alone. Be safe baby, my baby ☺.

In my hurry to leave Leo's I had forgotten to reply to Bobby's first text. I was impressed he had followed up with another message and hit reply to send him a response.

Athens Bridget: The director was a perfect gentleman. I wish the ride home was quicker and warmer, but otherwise I am fine. And yes I will text you when I'm home. Filia.

*

Over an hour and a half later, I was back in Mikey's apartment removing my boots from my tired feet; enthused about tossing my smoky clothes into the hamper. I dove under the covers in my tank top and panties, logged into I-tunes, grabbed my blackberry and began typing out a message for Bobby.

Athens Bridget: I am under my covers Bobby. Is that safe enough? Kisses Bridget.

Bobby: Well that depends on two things Bridget. Who's covers you're under, and who's under there with you.

His wit made me smile and helped overlook his cocky demeanor. I lay on my back removing the tight elastic band that had held my ponytail up all day, slowly placing my fingers through my hair, rubbing my sore scalp. My skin felt warm and smooth under the duvet. I felt different, lighter, sexier, and more liberated than I could have ever imagined. I conquered. There *was* truth to the Mediterranean mysteries and myths. As I began to drift off my phone began to buzz and ring loudly; it was Bobby.

"Hi Bobby," I said answering in a low soft voice. "Hi," he replied with a long pause, "I just wanted to make sure you were alright." "You mean you wanted to ensure no one was smuggling me under the blankets?" He laughed in true Bobby Siteros style, low and sexy. "Sure that too." He paused for a moment than spoke softly, "so would you like to go to the cinema tomorrow? We could go eat or catch a movie, I know you like movies." "Sure tomorrow works for me Bobby." "Ok great, I'll give you a call after work, goodnight and sweet dreams,"

94

"kisses Bobby" I replied before clicking the end button. Bobby's vulnerability was a pleasant surprise. I decided not to stop and think about why he was being so sweet and whether all men were like that when they wanted something. Consequently it was just then, and there, that I decided no one needed to know about Bobby. I would be keeping Bobby Siteros all to myself. There would be no consulting with Vivian or Lea or even Mikey for that matter; no one was going to rain on my parade. I had heard enough lectures on dating and warnings about Mediterranean men to last me a lifetime, and decided it was best to keep matters of the heart just about there – close to mine.

15

I didn't know if my ears had become increasingly sensitivity since arriving in Athens, but the sound of Skype ringing in the early morning felt like a jackhammer pounding away on my skull. I had forgotten to log off my laptop and my Skype account for that matter, and it seemed to be a freefall for my fellow American girlfriends to have an overdue catch up session. After lifting my tired eyelids, I scrolled down through my missed calls to see a couple group conferences from Lea and Vivian. Just as I began to type a response the Skype icon began bopping up and down again. I hit the green receiver to see Vivian and Lea huddled over the screen of a large PC. "Well it's about time, Bridge!" "Good morning to you too girls," I responded in a raspy voice. "Remember I'm 8 hours ahead here." "Turn on your camera, Bridge!" they rang out with outmost enthusiasm. Happy to appease them, I leaned over to tap on the camera button nearly rolling right off the bed.

"Wow you really are half asleep," "oh stop it, Vivian, she looks awesome!" "Why thank you Lea – a nice compliment considering I'm in my morning glory, make-up-less and in bed and all." "You have a great glow Bridge, and you look like you've slimmed down" she replied with a mischievous smile. "It's the Mediterranean girls. There's definitely something to those myths. Mikey says it's in the air. I personally think it's the food and all the climbing for those of us who are carless in this rocky city." "Climbing? Ever think of taking a cab Bridge?" Vivian replied peering at me closely through her glasses. I dreaded what she'd ask next. "I don't know, you seem to have a bit of a glow too Bridget," she said with an intrigued look on her face. "I wouldn't say it's a full blown glow Viv, but I do see a tinge of brilliance," added Lea, starring closely into the camera. I laughed until I developed a stitch in my side, meanwhile Lea finally interjected, beginning her inquisition. I managed to fill them in on all the filming in Paros, Oliver's family, including the near death of his grandfather, the Greek ambulance, and the race to the airport.

"How's Leo the director?" Lea asked. "Is he hot?!" added Vivian, her glasses slipping down the sharp bridge of her nose, "is he responsible for your new flush?" "Leo is a perfect gentleman girls. He's a real artist, and very talented, I'm lucky to have him. Anyone else would have walked off set dealing with Oliver. He's also practically engaged *and* not my type." "Well have you met anyone else? Lea continued in what I could tell was a mound of hope. "Come on, you need to have some fun out there or Oliver will drive you mad!" she added in furry. "Well he's not staying much longer Lea. He travels back and forth for the business, so he will leave me in peace to finish the editing, thank God. To answer your question, yes I've met people and keeping my options open. Don't worry you girls will be the first to know."

I pondered about spilling the beans about Bobby but though better of it; it was way too soon to launch that investigation. "You totally like someone Bridget, I can see it in your face, I hope he's hot" Lea said smiling, "and sweet of course– you deserve sweet." "Well, we'll be right here waiting when you decide to spill Bridge! Youssef is waiting for me, I've gotta run." "Ok sending love Viv," "love Bridge!"

After Vivian's departure I chatted with Lea a little longer, telling her a bit about the nightlife, food and my experience with the locals. I desperately wanted to tell her about Bobby, eventually alluding to the type of men I'd met, when filling her in on Theron. Although her line of questioning was a lot lighter than Vivian's I decided it wasn't the right time to open up that discussion. I supposed I feared hearing an abundance of what I considered senseless warnings, *and nothing would put a damper on my date tonight.* I knew I'd hear an earful about not having Googled him, or cyber-stalked his social media accounts, and I wasn't prepared to answer any questions about *why I hadn't.* Bobby and I had a pure and organic chemistry; something I barely understood myself, maybe it was something only made in the movies, I didn't know and I didn't care. Moreover, trying to explain it to anyone, would only launch an inquiry, and taint my new passion, and so I left it at that, and promised I'd email more often.

*

I spent the day working on additional script changes for Oliver. He had grown increasingly annoying with odd requests after he had seen the first edits Leo and I were so proud of. Nevertheless, they were his herbal tea concoctions and I wasn't about to have a war on my hands so I did the extra work.

The day had turned into night and I hadn't heard from Bobby, so I decided to borrow Mikey's cookbook and make some semi-authentic Greek Food. A short while into my expedition my phone began to buzz and beep. Bobby I thought, reaching for my blackberry with a smile.

Mikey: I've gotta work an overnighter Bridget – I'll see you tomorrow around 9 or 10 am.

Surprisingly, I'd be home alone tonight after all. I continued making my string bean and vegetable tomato sauce medley, all the while thinking of Bobby and what I'd wear tonight. Just as I was finishing the dish my phone rang, but this time there was no familiar name attached to the screen, instead it was replaced with a long local numbers starting with +30.

"Hello?"

"Hi Bridget," a soft deep voice responded on the other end of the line. After a few moments of silence, Bobby spoke, "you seem surprised it's me Bridget." "I just didn't recognize the number." "Well save it in your contact list than" he answered with confidence. "I thought I did, my phone's old who knows..." "Perhaps," he replied in a low voice, "but the system here isn't that greatest, especially for semi-permanent SIM cards and newcomers." Bobby's tone was serious, as always, for all I knew he was referring to something a lot more intense than phone lines, but once again, I decided to discard it.

Apparently Bobby had finished up late from work and was able to come over in a couple of hours. "Well we can start here and see what's playing at the local theatre. Mikey is working overnight," I blurted out without much thought. Pleased with that answer, Bobby sent me his kisses and said he'd call me when he was close by, "or lost," I added in. I was giddy and excited to see him, and the next few hours were witness to that. I changed my outfit about seven times, fidgeting with my make up and blown out mane incessantly. He was coming to the apartment so I didn't want to be in heels or anything too sexy. Cute and casual would do the trick, so I settled on a pair of black yoga pants and a bright yellow t-shirt that read *blondes have more fun.*

*

Bobby was late. I had eaten, changed my outfit numerous times than back again, and touched up my makeup until every lash was painted, and eyes were circled in thick black liner. I wondered if he had fallen asleep. A text wouldn't hurt I thought, maybe a call would be better. I hesitantly scrolled down my address book clicking on Bobby's name. The ring tone sounded off for several times with no answer. Disappointed I began to write a text message.

Athens Bridget: Hey Bobby, if you're tired or fell asleep please let me know. B.

Could I have been wrong about him? I longed for my girlfriends. I should have told them about him this morning; I had no clue what I was doing and longed for their comfort. One night of passion may be nothing out here. As I contemplated removing my makeup and slipping into my PJ's, a familiar number appeared on my phone as it began to ring.

"Hello"

"Hey Bridget. I'm sorry I'm running late, Athens is crazy with traffic this time of night. If it's too late and you'd prefer I didn't come please tell me now, I can turn around and go back home." I felt like an idiot, an inexperienced idiot at that. "No, no Bobby, I don't have an early morning tomorrow. I just thought maybe you had fallen asleep." "No," he said chuckling. "See you soon." He must have realized I was a real amateur by now. Would a European woman do that? I wasn't sure if I should be baking cookies or slipping into black nylons and garters, but I opted to stay in my urban casual outfit and watch a rerun of *Sex and the City* until he called.

Two episodes later, I was beginning to doze off, when my blackberry rang. Bobby had arrived unfashionably late and the outer door was locked, so I through on my bootie slippers and ran down the steps to open the door. Bobby stood looking at me through the large glass door, dressed in his black overcoat, blue jeans, and boots. *Oh God, I was under-dressed,* and the expression on his face suggested the same. "I thought you'd be coming in some type of athletic uniform" I said, "I am in uniform," he answered, kissing my lips gently.

The elevator was definitely tight quarters; in fact I don't ever riding with anyone else. While it barely fit the two of us, Bobby remained well mannered, in his usual serious demeanor. I didn't know if it was from his upbringing or his disposition with women, but the cocky, abrasive, and what I thought was an egotistical manner, was long gone. "Is tropical mix ok?" I yelled out from inside the kitchen. "Yes it's fine Bridget," he replied politely. As I poured him a glass of juice he began to ask me about my personal life, past relationships, lovers and experiences. Needless to say he seemed quite shocked at my amateur record. He repeated what he had told me the night we met at the Cheetah Club. The details pertaining to his past three relationships and only real girlfriends, including his recent split from his long-term girlfriend. "Why didn't you get married?" I asked interrupting him in one of his stories. "Because I didn't want to marry that woman!" he responded abruptly. His animated expressions made me laugh. Bobby eventually joined me in laughter and leaned in to kiss me, his body weight pushing me back onto the leather sofa. He caressed my breasts over my t-shirt and I wanted to kiss him more, deeper and with more passion when he stopped suddenly. "I should go, it's late," he gasped standing up to catch his breath. *He should go? After a bloody juice and a few short kisses?! God it must be this outfit!* "You barely just got here Bobby. You don't have to go, you can sleep over. Mikey is working on over night shift." My words felt rushed; desperate almost, I was clinging to Bobby for every breath, and was far from ready to let go. Barely comprehending my own thoughts or words, I watched Bobby slip his boots off, grab his tobacco, and head for my bedroom. My body was moving faster than I could think and I had no clue what I was getting myself into, but I did know one thing, I didn't want Bobby to leave me.

"It's this one," I said pointing to Mary-Anne's room, then to the bathroom, "and there's the bathroom in case you need to go." "Yes good idea," he said. Thank goodness! I had a few minutes to rip off my yoga pants and t-shirt looking for a semi- cute pair of panties and matching tank. I opted for a baby pink ruffled pair of panties I had picked up on a girls weekend in Vegas and a black spaghetti strap tank top to match. I was placing night cream on my flushed face when Bobby re-entered the room.

"Um, it's night moisturizer, do you want some?" I asked looking at him with embarrassment.

"No thanks," he replied with a sultry chuckle reaching for my side of the bed.

"Uh Bobby that's my side, that's where I sleep," I said shyly unready to give up my newly found comfort zone.

"Oh really? Because that's my side too," he responded in a deep alluring tone.

"Well than, I guess you're going to have to wrestle me for it Siteros."

"Oh I love a challenge Bridget, but this is gonna be an easy win" he said picking me up and throwing me on the opposite side of the bed. Shocked and breathless I said nothing as Bobby placed his body on top of mine, kissing my face and lips tenderly. He threw the duvet covers off and placed the cotton sheet above us. "I love these" he said pulling down my panties. His hands caressed my body, as he reached for the hem of tank top lifting it over my head and unclasping my bra buckle. *God, I should have worn a better bra. You don't know what you're doing Bridget!* But it was too late I was thinking no more. "Do you have…" Bobby said softly. "Yes," reaching for my Legally Blonde make up case pulling out a small blue Trojan packet. As I pulled the plastic square out from the case, a long string of condoms remained attached. There I was in a bed with Bobby Siteros holding up a long string of lubricated Trojan condoms. Bobby looked up, laughing uncontrollably. "If I didn't know better, I'd think you were some kind of porn star," he said chuckling away. "Now why do you have all those Bridget?" Considering he wasn't exactly aware of my inadequate sexual history, I assumed he really did think I was in the porn business. "I've been single for a while Bobby, I guess I was just…keeping… you know waiting for…" I could barely get the words out. Turning away I ripped a packet off the trail

102

end and handed it to Bobby. He opened it and placed it on with ease, saying nothing at all. "Please take it easy on me," I whispered, hoping he'd disregard my anxiousness. Ignoring my request Bobby kissed me hard, with passion. He kissed my breasts and held them tight, then moved his hands closer to my leg lifting it sliding allowing himself to climb on top and inside of me. The motion was painful, and for the first few minutes I wanted it to stop, but he didn't flinch, Bobby was all over me, his heavy body comforting me like a blanket. "Turn over," he growled helping flip me onto my stomach. "Lift yourself up slightly," he said pulling my legs up and slamming into me from behind. It was easier to take the pain this way, but at the same time, cold, and impersonal. A few moments later I flipped myself onto my back and found my groove. Bobby slammed into me again and again until he succumbed inside me. I could feel his body heat beating again my chest, as he lay his head down on my bosom. "Go to the bathroom first baby then come back to bed," he said ripping the condom off and discarding it in the wastebasket. He never asked how I felt, if I was satisfied, hurt or happy; and I didn't breath a word. Instead, I did as I was told and returned to Bobby's arms where he laid waiting on my side of the bed. There was no feeling in the world like that of my face against his bare chest. He kissed my forehead and held me close. "Goodnight baby." "Goodnight Bobby," I whispered placing my hand on his naked body.

16

I was sore the next morning. I had woken before Bobby, no surprise to me; as I rarely ever slept in, and I was quickly learning, Bobby loved his sleep. I turned and reached for my blackberry, it was just after 8 in the morning. Mikey would be coming between 9 and 10 am, so I had to use my time wisely and get us out of there before he arrived. I looked over at Bobby, lying sound asleep on my favorite bedside corner. His eyelashes fluttered erratically, and I almost felt guilty waking him from his deep sleep. It was difficult to contain myself around Bobby; an emotion admittedly, I was not accustomed to. In fact nothing I had felt in the Mediterranean was like anything familiar to me. I had decided, perhaps subconsciously but decided nonetheless, that I was indeed a new person. As I lay beside Bobby, I placed myself back into my Parisian fantasy, this time imagining myself in a quaint apartment in the trendy French district of Etienne Marcel. A Parisian actress, I had just been seduced by my director, and lay in the aftermath of a long series of lovemaking. I was a self-sufficient sex kitten who hated the word no. My morning daydream soon turned into confidence as I leaned over to touch Bobby until he awoke with an erection. "Turn," he whispered helping flip me onto my right side. I dug my nails into his thighs, holding on for dear life as he slammed into me again and again finally finishing inside the Durex he had slipped on as he awoke. We laughed when it was over, slept a bit more, cuddled, and told stories; well Bobby spoke and I listened attentively.

"What time is your cousin going to be home?" Bobby asked in his sexy morning voice. "Soon, we need to get up and go," I answered with a sense of urgency. As I finished my sentence and arose from under the covers, I could hear a key turning in the door. "What was that?" Bobby asked calmly turning to stare at me with his big brown eyes. "Oh shit, he's home early!" I whispered. Having placed the key in the opposite side of the door the night before (a standard for European doors), Mikey was stranded until I unlocked from the apartment's interior. Before I could throw on my glasses or a pair of sweats, he began ringing the doorbell relentlessly. "Coming Mikey!" I yelled in my most

'I'm not having a heart attack' voice. "Bobby, please don't move, just wait here," I said, slipping his beige sweater over my head. "Ok Bridge, but you've got the sweater on backwards," he said calmly. "Well no time to fix that now Bobby" I said racing to the door. Mikey was standing in his co-pilot's uniform, holding a pillow and looking rather exhausted.

"Good morning cousin," he said in his usual sweet tone.

"Good morning Mikey, I'm sorry for the delay, I couldn't find my glasses."

"I was ready to nod off, I'm half asleep," he answered. Perfect, I thought, he should go right to bed, and it'll be easy for me to slip out with Bobby.

"I'll be quiet and leave soon so you can catch up on your sleep," I replied. "Oh I'm way to wired to sleep," he said walking towards the kitchen. "I'm going to be in the kitchen cooking for the next little while Bridge, I need to eat first." *Oh my, I was screwed. What kind of girl would Mikey take me for now?! 'Mikey please meet Bobby, the guy I met at a club a week ago, I invited him over to your place, drank your wine and let him have his way with me in your sister's bedroom!' Snap out of it! Just because you've been stuck on the 16th floor of a Chicago high rise in your ice cream coned PJ's doesn't mean the rest of the world is sharing your painfully dreary life! I mean Mikey is probably used to this...*

As my mind ran wild I slipped back into the bedroom to update Bobby. Somewhere between the Parisian actress fantasy and my Chicago flashback, I had decided it'd be best to sneak out of the apartment while Mikey was in the bathroom; only Bobby didn't find my solution quite as fitting. "What?" he said starring at me. "Is this an American fraternity thing Bridget? You know if we run out like a pair of cheap thieves I can't use the washroom so we can't go for breakfast, I'm going home." Although he seemed annoyed, it was Bobby's direct no-nonsense approach that got me moving. "Ok give me a moment," I said getting dressed and shutting the door behind me. I exited the room feeling anxious, knowing I needed to come clean. "Mikey!" I called out into the kitchen, "I need to tell you something." He peaked his head out from inside the refrigerator looking at me with compassion. "I know Bridget," he said composed as always. "The tobacco and the car keys in the living room gave it away." God he was good. *Mental note: do not to try and slide anything by Mikey… ever.*

"So what do you want me to do?" he asked. "Well he needs to freshen up, once he's done, I'll bring him out to meet you. Just promise no inquisition, ok?" "I'm not promising anything, Bridget. Is this the guy from the Cheetah club? Theron's friend?" he responded without hesitation. "Yes," I answered shyly. Mikey appeared to take it well. He continued cooking in the kitchen while I brought Bobby up to speed.

The introduction and conversation was surprisingly smooth and pleasant, and manly. They swapped a few army stories, remarks on politics, and shared some tobacco before smoking a few cigarettes. Mikey was a Godsend, and although I was relieved, I felt much like a tart waiting for her John on the street corner. After it was all said and done, Bobby and I headed for brunch on the terrace of a posh mall on the city's outskirts. Malls were rare in Athens, and this one was beautiful, extraordinary actually. Employees in black suits and white gloves opened the shiny glass doors to the award-winning shopping center. We rode the escalator to the third level dedicated to the European version of a food court. We settled into the terrace of a corner restaurant, laughing and fritting over spinach pies and fresh orange juice for the next hour. I surprised Bobby by paying for the bill when he slipped away to use the restroom; something I didn't know was against womanly conduct in Europe. "Thank you, but don't ever pay again Bridget," he said politely. "It was a nice gesture, but if a man is a man he pays," he said sternly kissing me softly on the lips and holding my hand down the escalator.

Thirty minutes later, he dropped me back off at Mikey's before heading to work. "Bridget, before you go, I wanted to ask you something," he said rolling some tobacco in his parked Audi. "Theron is spinning in his hometown this weekend and I wanted to go. Have you heard of Samos? It's a beautiful island - let me know if you'd like to come so I can book the airline tickets and room." Unprepared for what he had asked, I starred at him waiting for the punch line. Bobby wanted to take me along on a 'boys' weekend to a Greek island, or perhaps on a romantic getaway? Either he was joking or Mediterranean men progressed quickly and smoothly. "Bridget, are you interested?" He said pulling on my loose ponytail. "Let me know ok baby." I nodded all the while bewildered and kissed him goodbye.

107

Mikey's apartment was tranquil. I undressed and threw myself into a hot shower, scrubbing away last night's passion all the while dumbfounded at Bobby's weekend proposal. I wondered if it was just a nice gesture or if Bobby really wanted to spend a weekend with me on a beautiful Greek island. By early evening I had managed to forget about the proposal for a while, focusing on some editing and new Mediterranean recipes. The sun had barely fallen when I received a text message.

Bobby: Hi Baby, let me know if you can come to Samos, I'll need to book the tickets soon. ☺

Gushing, I tucked away the phone message and checked in with Leo, ensuring I'd be ok to be absent for the weekend. Needless to say we had a lot of work ahead of us since Oliver was making the completion of the promo spots quite challenging, but Leo gave me the ok to take the weekend off. I could sense Bobby's contentment after replying to his invitation. He didn't seem surprised however, perhaps he did this for women often and it wasn't a big deal to him, *but it was to me.* Bobby's response was short and to the point:

Bobby: Send me your full name and birth date so I can book your ticket, kisses.

I sent along my info and ran to my room to look at my clothes. I needed outfits for three days and two nights. *Oh no, I had to go shopping.*

*

Shopping in Athens was definitely different than in the US. Most stores were independently owned, excluding the international retail chains

108

that could be found in nearly every district. It was a good thing Zara and H&M were available on nearly every shopping block. Not to mention the prominent European comparisons like Bershka and Pull & Bear. Elegant and understated, topped with a great shoe or jacket would do the trick for my trip. Unfortunately I hadn't planned on looking anything but grunge-chic on my filming expedition, and I had brought limited attractive shoes with me; so that's where I'd begin.

I knew which shoe stores to hit based on my window-shopping during long walks and jogs throughout the city center. Surprisingly the local brands were not cheap, and the Euro wasn't on its way down any time soon. I knew I really couldn't afford to be shopping for much of anything, but needed to look and feel confident for this trip. A superb pair of spiked stilettos would do the trick. My eyes scanned the large glass window at *Kalogeros* Shoe Shop. There were dozens upon dozens of stilettos showcased on small clear platforms facing the large store windows. Pumps, platforms, sandals, wedges, boots, closed toe, open toe, lace ups, spikes, and not a ballet flat in sight. European women sure knew how to pour on the sexy.

I had rarely if ever, seen such a variation of stilettos in all heights and colors imaginable. There, as I stood in awe of a whole new world, I spotted them. A pair of 6 inch, salmon colored, closed toe stilettos finished off with metal spikes lined along the back of the heel. They were the perfect accessories for my weekend outfits. My dream pumps were 195 Euro and way over my budget, leaving no room on my credit card to buy anything else until my next paycheck. Oh well, I thought, I was half way around the world and wasn't about to let my past inhibitions get in the way of my new found excitement; so, onto the credit card they went. I left the city square shortly after, on route to the metro, walking down the cobblestone streets taking in smells of roasted chestnuts and burning corn. Inhaling the brisk air, I felt giddy and optimistic for the first time in years.

*

"Can you sit on this end of the suitcase Mikey? It should close if we balance out our weight!" "Are you sure you need all this for two days Bridget?" Mikey answered wiping the sweat from his brow. "It's two nights and three days actually, and yes, I've been on too many trips unprepared and most importantly without selection. Besides that, I have a meeting with a local production company who wants to see me before I leave for the airport so that's another outfit change!" "Ok you're the boss, Bridget, and by the way those are some sexy high heels I saw in there, killers actually." "Really, Mikey?" replying with a laugh and a devious smile, "that's exactly what I was going for, man-killer."

*

The next few hours as well as the following morning went by quickly. I was much more focused on my meeting with the local production company, rather than the getaway weekend. They were well known distributors of Hollywood films in foreign territories, and a friend of Leo's had seen my work and connected me with a distribution company who needed a foreign sales rep, who apparently had a background just like me. The company was situated in a beautiful coastal suburb and heavily guarded with several layers of security from the tall white gates to the President's office. Mr. Abadi, a wealthy Middle-Eastern businessman turned producer, ran the company, and looked to be in his late fifties. He stood about 5 foot 5 inches tall with thinning grey hair, and square tinted glasses. His office resembled what I assumed the Middle Eastern version of the oval office looked like in the 1960's. Getting to him required bypassing two receptionists, a VP of sales, and his personal assistant. To top it off the gaudy office was controlled by a doorbell-like buzzer the President manually controlled from under his desk.

"I hear you produce commercials and films here Miss Lane," Mr. Abadi said to me in a thick Middle-Eastern accent. "Well I do a variety of things in entertainment Sir, but I…" "No, no let me speak," he said cutting me off in mid-sentence. Mr. Abadi had a distinct way of controlling conversations or interviews *if this was one,* barely allowing me to speak while bombarding me with a variety of questions. The conversation *or inquisition* went on for over an hour, ending with a hardy handshake and "we'll be in touch." I wasn't sure what exactly he wanted from me, or what I could provide for him, or even how the meeting had gone for that matter, so I shrugged it off and left it up to chance. The truth was I was much more interested in preparing myself to meet Bobby down the street than landing another commercial gig.

I powdered by nose, and adjusted my lace up heels under my high-waisted jeans, throwing on my supple leather jacket over my blouse for an edgier look. Bobby was surprisingly on time, pulling up as I turned the street corner, immediately exiting the car. He placed my suitcase in the trunk of his Audi and leaned in to kiss me gently on the lips. I filled him in on my odd meeting during the ride to the airport. He was surprisingly interested and supportive in my encounter with Mr. Abadi. "Follow up with him Bridget, it sounds like a great company," Bobby said grazing my hand. "Maybe this is where you're supposed to be," he added. I blushed fantasizing what it would be like to live in the Mediterranean and work for a prominent international company, and most importantly not have to hustle to make ends meet. Bobby always knew what to say to keep me interested. He must have had a lot of practice, or maybe it was a script; *but how could it be?* How many American former PR girls slash aspiring movie producers had he met in Athens? He interrupted my peculiar thoughts, by grasping my hand, then lifting it to his mouth for a few kisses. I decided this was no time to think; after all I was on vacation, and going to spend the weekend with Bobby.

*

The plane's landing to the short flight was soft, and the passengers rose quickly, scrimmaging to gather their overhead luggage and head towards the rear exit of the small plane.

"It's ok, you can look hunny you're single," I proceeded with a furrowed brow and devious smile. Catching Bobby checking out a flight attendant may have struck a jealous chord in me, but it didn't last. *"Oh am I?"* he replied at my sarcasm, grabbing me by the waist and landing a few kisses on my lips and neck. It was a nice save on Bobby's part. His words were sweet, but I preferred the gesture. If I hadn't already, it was there and then, in between the isle of the small jet plane that I recognized I needed him, his attention, and care, and perhaps love, and I was prepared to fight for it if I had to. The reality was I still

111

hadn't determined what we were, but the truth was as long as Bobby made me feel this good, I really didn't care.

17

The airport on the Island of Samos resembled the size of Mikey's apartment. The staff was friendly and the smell of the sea cast a spell on all things close by. Theron was waiting for us in a battered up Chevy pickup truck reminiscent of the one used by Oliver in Paros. "So what do you think Bridge? You're finally seeing my hometown!" Theron inquired enthusiastically. "It's quaint and lovely Theron, just as I imagined," and indeed it was, just as Theron, sweet and charming, and full of promise. "My girlfriend is home now but you'll meet her at dinner. We'll eat at a traditional tavern later tonight ok?" "Sounds perfect Theron," I conquered losing myself in his trademark bear hug.

Fifteen minutes later he had dropped Bobby and I off at a quaint hotel by the island's port. The lobby resembled the motel Bobby and I had first been to in Athens, perhaps a little larger but complete with the plastic plants and a bizarre concierge to match. The hotel's clerk was a short stocky woman with a mousey brown blunt cut and bangs covering the upper part of her eyelids. A Greek version of Anna Winters flashed into mind as she began to speak. "One room, two persons, two nights, I have this correct?" she said in her Greek accent. "Yes ma'am that's right," I answered. "You pay on way out, now you go to floor five, room 502," she said handing over a heavy gold padlock with a single silver key dangling from it. The elevator was another experience altogether. It barely fit the two of us, much less my over-packed suitcase and Bobby's 20-pound carryon. A couple elevator rides later we were settling into the damp room on the fifth floor's corner. Bobby immediately began putting away his shampoo wrapped neatly in plastic bags, while I shuffled through my luggage for a comfy evening outfit to change into. I wondered if Bobby had packed his own things; they were meticulously put together, all wrapped in pristine plastic zip lock bags. Although I had wanted to really get to know him better this weekend, I decided it wasn't a great time to approach Bobby with personal questions, and a deep meaningful conversation. In fact, I rarely felt that it was. It seems Bobby was regularly in deep thought, almost melancholy at times, and approaching him felt almost disruptive. Instead I continued sorting through cute under clothing, limiting my usual analytics and removing most thoughts from my head, *most except for sex of course.*

Bobby sure took his time in the bathroom. He must have been in there for 35 minutes when I heard his voice from behind the thin wood door. "I forgot my shaving cream!" he yelled out, "you can use my shower gel," I replied softly from behind the bathroom door. "Oh yeah, good idea thank you Bridget." He always seemed to be well mannered, and even though I hadn't figured out if it was genuine or not, I suspected it was accredited to a close family and even closer mother, something Mikey had mentioned to me about Mediterranean families. After stifling through my lingerie bag, I slipped into a pair black lace panties and white lace camisole and brushed out my mane out so it fell long and soft over my overflowing bust. Needless to say the cami was old and tattered and at least a size to small, barely being held together at the seams by the skinny white spaghetti straps, but it was my favorite, and I'd choose it over a brand new Victoria's Secret cami any day.

I slid into the flower sheets, moving away the navy blue comforter, and reaching for my blackberry off the nightstand. Of course Oliver had sent me a number of messages demanding to see more recent edits of the videos. Naturally I was not humored by his aggressive, tactless style, especially during the weekend, but decided I was not going to be bothered by his ridiculousness, not this weekend. As I began to type a witty response Bobby appeared from the bathroom, a white towel hanging form his hips, shaking the access water from his hair. He walked towards the wooden dresser checking himself out in the mirror, when his eyes glanced into another reflection in the far side of the square mirror.

"You working Bridget? All ok?" "Sure," I blushed, putting down my blackberry, "if you accept that the client is not sane, than all is ok." He smiled, walking towards the bed. "Well if you want me to speak to him I will," he said sternly. Bobby didn't mess around when it came to business. He looked straight at me, from top to bottom, leaned in, and kissed me. His kiss was harder than usual, and I pulled him closer, grabbing him by both shoulders causing him to collapse onto me. His build was impeccable. His shoulders round and muscular, his biceps bulging as he pressed his hands into the mattress springs. I traced my hands up and down his arms, onto his chest and kissed his neck, burying my nose in his smell, a mixture of fresh rain and D&G cologne. He was gorgeous and I couldn't wait to melt into him, returning my lips to his, never wanting to remove them. His hand slid down my right side, pulling down my lace panties then pulling open his towel, letting it fall naturally from his hips. "You're so wet" he whispered, placing his hands in and out of me, then before I could think to respond, his entire body was moving in and of me, slowly yet intensely. "Don't stop, Bobby, whatever you do don't stop," my heart was racing. Bobby cupped my breasts with his hands, than kissed them firmly, moving his lips, and tongue towards my neck than back to my mouth. I wanted this to last forever, the intensity, the emotion, and the climax. It was a combination of the most extreme sensations I had ever felt, and just then he crashed into me one last time, yelling out, before collapsing on top of me. His forehead was wet with a furry of sweat beads, falling heavy against my bare breasts. I watched as Bobby's head bopped up and down against my heavy beating chest; his face was peaceful and I was elated that I might have been the cause of his calmness. Bobby fidgeted to peel him self away, "lay here" I said interrupting the movement, "don't get up," and so he didn't, and I watched him fall fast asleep in my arms.

*

While Bobby slept, motionless, my phone went off relentlessly. Oliver called incestuously, and then followed up with text messages when I didn't answer. Bobby's phone began to go off as well. Between his tweeting texts and my classical ringtone it felt like a weekend at the bazaar after a while. While I was left without a moment of shut-eye, Bobby seemed to be able to sleep through a storm and waking him up was a harder task than I thought. When I finally did, he was disoriented as if he'd been asleep for days. I completed my makeup – including wing tipped black eyeliner and a sparkly golden eyelid. I slipped into a pair of black pleather leggings and a white loose tank top. I figured my faux fur and new spiked stilettos would add some spice to the simple outfit. Bobby looked up at me, starring into my eyes, "I'll go get ready," he said. I touched up my make-up as I waited. When he re-entered the room I was in my fur and heels, and there was no doubt about it, I was

115

fishing for a compliment opening and closing my coat to reveal the low cut tank top. "Let me check you out," he said looking at me from head to toe. "Yes, I approve," he said. "A compliment would do," I replied stubbornly. "You're gorgeous and you know it," he said staring directly into my eyes. Shocked yet elated I leaned in for a kiss. "No kissing with that lip gloss" he said in a stern voice. "Before you know it, I'll be covered in some berry gloss that will end up smeared on my face all night." *Now that was a trained boyfriend comment, if I'd ever heard one.* I smiled at him, wondering what exactly he'd gone through with his past girlfriends. Starring into his eyes, I grazing his nose with my fingertips then headed for the door.

*

The tavern was a 15-minute walk from the hotel. Theron was sitting at a table with a few guys and one female, presumably his girlfriend.

"Welcome" called out Theron from across the room holding up a glass of wine. "Join us while there is still food!" "You better be joking!" called out Bobby, "I'm starving!" he added. "Bridget?" Theron asked looking at me with a wide smile, "you hungry too?" "Yes" I answered, feeling quite famished. "There is plenty of food, and we will order more. Come and meet everyone now" he said running off a slew of names while pointing to the crowd of people across the wooden table. He walked over to a young woman at the midst of the table, "and this is Hermia Bridget." "Harika," I said leaning over to shake her hand; the only person I physically introduced myself too. "Nice to meet you too," she replied in a soft tone. "Pretty name as well," I added. "It's the feminine form of Greek Hermes, meaning *of the earth,* " she said proudly. That was a great way to describe Theron's girlfriend. She stood about 5 foot 6 inches tall with big brown eyes and the same color hair to match. Her smile was nothing short of brilliant, and her lips, beautiful, and large, covered in bright red lipstick. While she probably carried about 20 extra pounds on her pear shaped frame, they were spread out evenly, producing voluptuous curves in all the right places. "I've heard so much about you," I said, "oh," she responded surprised. "Theron and I have known each other since grade school" I said re-assuring her we were childhood buddies and nothing more, but Hermia seemed quite disinterested, maintaining a very serious disposition. She was a grade school teacher who was less inclined to join me in any type of conversation. Something I had learned was normal for local women. Needless to say, dinner was more of the same. Conversations that surrounded local politics and economics and not much about anything I was well versed on. Young adults my age were not like the twenty or thirty something year olds in Chicago; they were ancient thinkers who carried out their parent's political and economic views over the dinner table, not to mention their traditional family values; of course complimentary to the way they ran their love lives – free love, free sex, free spirits.

Meanwhile Theron had cracked a couple of comments about our appetite to which Bobby laughed, earning him a swift kick under the table.

"If you kept your legs to yourself, no one would have been the wiser Bridget – look now everyone's noticed" Bobby said laughingly. I felt the blood rushing to my head onto my beat red face. I guess it was universal - when men got together they became high school boys again.

"Did you like the food Bridget?" Theron asked as we gathered our jackets. "Yes it was delicious, thanks for having me," anything would have been at that point in the night, but the Samian food and wine was actually really tasty, and I knew it was important for Theron to hear that from me. I recalled how big they were on homemade liquor too, Theron had explained 'no' wasn't an option here. It was actually offensive to reject a drink, which explained why I was barely walking a straight line on the way to the nightclub.

*

The venue was a small indoor space situated by the main port appropriately named *By the Sea,* with a cute courtyard encompassing it, complete with glass windows and doors. DJ Elektra was already warming up the decks for Theron as she'd be playing alongside him throughout the night. She was tall and thick framed, with short fringe bangs and thick-rimmed glasses. The tips of her hair were dyed blue, and I thought we just might hit it off. I was right – Electra's energy was just that, electric. She was full of life and zest and wasn't afraid to speak to a 'foreign girl'. She had played alongside Theron for years and was

117

quite a confident performer. We chatted in between sets and she kept me company while Bobby worked the room. He conversed with whom I could only assume were old friends, and checked out the remainder of the occupants; every breathing female to be exact; something I had yet to see from Bobby. I watched as he roamed the room like an experienced predator on the hunt, while I remained muzzled in a corner, wincing from the pain of my throbbing feet.

Conversely, Hermia stood by her man, close by the DJ booth for most of the night, sipping on mix cocktails and rolling homegrown tobacco. She looked my way and smiled from time to time, but that was about it, except for one instant, when she turned to me. "Those girls are all on Ecstasy," she said pointing to a group of three girls huddled by the DJ booth. "We know them here on the island, they are local college girls, who take 'E' and come here looking to take something back to their dorms." I looked over to see Bobby standing near the crowd of girls. I watched motionless as he approached the group. *What the fuck was he doing?* The girl closest to him was a short brunette with a few extra pounds around her stocky body. Her bust was enormous; the cheap tank top she wore, barely leaving anything to the imagination. I looked in confusion as Bobby walked towards her, staring at her intensely, allowing her to place her hands on his chest, up and down. *What the fuck was going on?!* I looked at Hermia who returned a calming glare. "They're just club whores," she said, "they are known here Bridget, nothing to worry about." As I listened to her words wondering what would transpire next, Bobby turned away from the girl slowly and walked towards me. *Was this what Bobby was about? An attention-seeking womanizer, who needed affirmation from every woman in the room that he was attractive and wanted?*

"What was that about Bobby?" I yelled out over the roaring sound system, "Oh crazy college girls, totally hitting on me" he replied as charismatically as I'd ever seen him. *What was he saying?! I witnessed that entire escapade - he was the instigator!* "But you...I saw you approach her!" I rang out in disbelief. *What the fuck was going on here? I know what I saw!* "Let's go Bridget, are you tired? You must be," he said grabbing my arm. I don't know if it was the alcohol, my aching head or feet, but I allowed Bobby to pull me away, and followed him out of the club all the while bewildered and speechless.

The walk back to the hotel was cold and felt longer than the one earlier to dinner. My studded spiked heels made the bottoms of my feet burn and pound with every step I took; in fact walking on hot coals may have been more comforting. "You alright Bridget?" Bobby asked placing his arm in mine to help with the trek back. "Yes, just tired and a bit cold" I answered. It was a complete lie, albeit a white one, but one nonetheless. Bobby's unforeseen behavior had me troubled but there was no way I was going to get into that now. A few minutes later we were back at the hotel, but much to my dismay the room wasn't much warmer than the island streets. "Can you put the heat on Bobby, I'm freezing," "aren't you from some cold, windy city?!" he responded mocking me with a smirk. "Yes but we use central heating there," I replied sharply.

As I leaned towards the nightstand to turn off the antique lamp, the evening's occurrences swam in my head. The reality was I really didn't know who Bobby was, or what ghosts he had in his closet, and I was no step closer to figuring it out. Bobby lay on his back, handsome as always, his waffle shirt dragging on his chest perfectly; but with my emotions ajar and my body sore, I didn't want to make love to him. "Turn to the side," he said softly, "I just want to hold you." Perhaps he had read my mind, or felt the same way, but that's all he had to say, to seize my thoughts, and force me to fall fast asleep in his arms.

18

The sounds of the unconventional thermostat changing positions had awoken me about 10:30 am the next morning. Bobby was sound asleep crouched in the fetal position on the left side of the bed. I covered him fully with the blanket and made my way to the bathroom. My throat was sore and I felt congested; I couldn't believe it, I had woken up with the flu. I threw on my sweats after massaging some tinted moisturizer on my face and polishing my lashes with a light coat of mascara. I had the perfect remedy in mind to help me recover.

"May I have a herbal tea with a lot of honey please?" I asked, willing to beg for some homegrown comfort for my raw throat. "Of course Ms. Lane." As it turns out the hotel's front desk manager also ran the breakfast bar. "Any particular flavor or mountain herb?" she asked politely. "Anything herbal, preferably not grown on the island of Paros," I answered sneezing in between. There was no way I was letting Oliver enter my thought process on my day off, at the very least for this weekend.

I sat in the breakfast area sipping tea and reading the International Herald catching up on world news. There was no text or call from Bobby, a sure sign he was still sound asleep. After a couple cups of strong tea and loads of honey, I returned to the room where Bobby was as I suspected, sleeping away, only to my dismay he was tossing and turning in discomfort. I crouched beside him, caressing his shoulder "hey it's ok," I said. He grabbed my hand, pulling me towards him, and kissing me softly. It was as if he was dreaming and I was his protagonist who had just entered the room. I kissed him back, pulling the sheets away from his body allowing me to get underneath. He pulled my sweat pants down and my sweatshirt up over my head, caressing me everywhere with his strong hands. His fingers entered inside me, jabbing me, with force and rage this time. I fought back pinning his arms against the bed, then kissing his chest, he moaned with pleasure as I moved down close to his stomach, kissing his belly button, as he moaned softly. I don't know if it was the island air, the herbs, or honey but I suddenly lost control of any inhibitions, and sank my face lower towards Bobby's erection. I was confident and in control, while Bobby moaned almost immobilized, excluding his groin which thrust up and down with the motions of my mouth. I tossed my mane behind my shoulders, letting it fall softly towards my tailbone, while I got into a comfy four legged position.

I went to work; my lips grazing his erection as he began panting and giving me directions; "all in now," he growled, pushing my head down close to his sex, and so I did, and he moaned loudly. "It's perfect," he groaned, grabbing a condom from the nightstand. He placed it on carefully and grabbed me by the back of my hair, then lifted me up positioning me on top of him. Wet with desire, I motioned my body up and down, then in circles, leaning forward allowing my breasts to graze

his chest, then his mouth. His hands caressed my rear end, his fingers slipping in and out of me from behind, then gripping my buttocks tightly and flipping me onto my back, all the while managing to stay inside me. Bobby was in control now, pumping hard, in and out of me, than pulling out unexpectedly to kiss me everywhere. "Please Bobby, I need you now, please," I was panting for more of him. Then before I could open my eyes Bobby was pushing himself in and out of my body again, while I began thrusting my body to meet his. "Open up baby," he said caressing my thighs, then bringing his tongue inside my mouth, to meet mine. My body began to tremble, an unfamiliar, insatiable feeling, "that's a girl" he said "now while you're trembling, I will do you hard and you will cum," and so he did, and so I did, and we finished together.

Without words I lay panting on the bed with a racing heartbeat. "Oh my," I said still in shock from the morning's events. "Good morning," he said in a low groggy voice, before rolling over and heading for the bathroom. I realized at that moment I had no idea who Bobby was. I might as well have been his escort, but I was lured in too deep to care now. A half hour later he returned from the bathroom, all fresh clean-shaven. "Your turn," he said putting the final touches on his perfectly gelled hair. Bobby was a completely different person after sex. I could have been a 4-foot bear or a Victoria's Secret supermodel, but I don't think he'd have noticed the difference; it's as if all his senses were turned off.

*

I was pleased to meet up with Theron and Hermia in the town square for a walk, coffee and eventually lunch. I figured hanging out with another couple would solidify our "togetherness," something Bobby never spoke about, and *I figured* was not worthy of a discussion. We were obviously together, whether we discussed it or not. I mean he acted like a boyfriend, he brought me on a weekend getaway, he paid for me, and took care of me, so I had decided we were together it was as simple as that. I did however think about Bobby and Theron's behavior from time to time and wondered if they had shared some sorted past experiences. In fact I was sure they had, but deflected it to another part of my brain where I wanted it to stay buried.

"I don't know how I will make it out tonight guys, my throat and sinuses are getting worse," I proclaimed blowing my nose into a scrunched up tissue. "Hermia isn't coming out tonight either Bridget, so we can have a boys night" Theron responded. The words alone triggered a bad feeling, there was something about the two of them being bestees that didn't sit right with me. "We'll see," I said walking towards the hotel entrance.

By the time I had entered the damp room, my sinuses were completely clogged and I had a persisting dry cough. "You should stay in and rest tonight Bridget," Bobby said with concern. "We'll go out for a drink and I won't be out too late." Late in the Mediterranean had another meaning, as I had learned early on. "Sure Bobby," I responded gritting my teeth. "I'll bring you back something to eat – what's you're favorite?" he asked in an endearing tone. "In all of Greece, its Spinach pie," I replied with ease. "Done," he said followed by a wink. I lay down as Bobby prepared for a night out. He was meticulous as ever, every hair was in its perfect place, his cologne evenly spread on his body, and his collar turned up high on his coat. I couldn't believe he was being so scrupulous about a boys' night out, and even worse, I couldn't believe I was in this predicament.

After Bobby left I fell asleep for a few hours. I wanted to be fast asleep when he returned so he wouldn't see the disappointment in my eyes, but between the deafening thermostat and my clogged nasals it was impossible. By the time 4 am rolled around my eyes were ajar and watery and the sounds of keys fussing at the door awoke me completely. "You're awake?" Bobby said softly as he entered the room. "I guess…" I responded groggy and congested. "I brought you Spinach pie," he responded, placing a brown oil stained paper bag on the dresser then leaning down to kiss me on the cheek. "So did you miss me?" I asked, "did *you miss me* Bridget?" he inquired, his hazelnut eyes beaming into mine. "I'm not telling you," I whispered, "me neither," he said kissing me passionately before turning me to my side and spooning me.

Hours later I lay awake tossing and turning. I didn't know what it was about this hotel, but sleep was not part of the all-inclusive features. It was all I could do from waking Bobby to ask him how he could sleep so soundly over all of the ruckus. Leaning towards his side of the bed I noticed bright orange earplugs placed delicately in his ears, while his Samsung Galaxy played sounds of rain on the nightstand. Wow, he had some routine, either that or he'd come fully prepared. As I sat awake struggling to breathe, I wondered how many times Bobby Siteros had fallen asleep to sounds of rain, *with someone else.*

19

"I can squeeze in just give me like a foot of space!" I called out. Wearing high heels in an over packed pick up truck may not have been the best choice for the ride to the airport. They didn't exactly allow me to straighten my legs, and neither did the four bodies in the front of Theron's pick up truck; all a result of Bobby's late awakening. Apparently cabs were an anomaly on this island. They were few and far between and the local call in service had a waiting list. "Thanks so much for doing this Theron." "We don't use those words in these parts Bridget. There is no 'thank you' amongst family and those whom we call friends; and when a Greek calls you his friend you might as well be family. It is not this American notion of friendship, it is blood," he concluded with passion. "I noticed Theron," I replied trying to sound grateful and deviate from my present annoyance. A result of waiting for Bobby in a dark room, then the hotel lobby for longer than I cared to remember, and now this glorious ride; having all put a dent in my romantic island weekend. The truth was I knew it was more than that, but I had decided to block out Bobby's odd behavior as well as the emotionless afternoon sex.

"I like that." I was in the midst of getting dressed and wearing a long navy blue T-shirt that looked more like a dress with a pair of pumps when Bobby had awoken. "Come here, and keep those heels on," he instructed ripping open a Durex from the nightstand and putting it on his erection. He waited until I approached the bed then positioned me on all fours, pulling down my lace panties, failing to remove them fully, leaving them hovering around my ankles as usual. He was in no mood for foreplay, not even a kiss. He caressed me where my panties had been, then began ramming into me, pulling me by the back of my hair relentlessly until he came. It was uncharacteristically raw, and I said nothing to him before heading to the bathroom. I had heard of couples having rough sex from time to time, even that it was normal not to always make love, but it was all-new to me. I felt way too much like an apparatus to admit I received any pleasure from it, but would never admit it aloud, for fear all lovemaking, and more importantly all the attention would be forever gone. I yearned for him now, for his fulfillment, but the scariest part was I had lost complete control of what I was doing…

Luckily Theron snapped me out of deep reminiscence when he continued his afternoon sermon "you know, to us, Bridget, family is God's gift, it is not something chosen, therefore you must treat it as such." Theron's hometown demeanor was sweet and refreshing, and on any other day I would have embraced his wise words, but not today. "Expectations Bridget," I could hear Vivian's voice right now… "expectations will eventually lead to disappointment, so just don't have any."

*

We arrived at the Samos airport in plenty of time, and I was starving from the lack of breakfast and the wait time for Bobby to get up and ready. "Hungry Bridget?" Theron asked. "Starved actually, but I'll wait 'til we're in Athens, I don't want to get anything from here," I replied sharply. Bobby hadn't mentioned anything about food, which only annoyed me more, and now he was over at the far side of the main check in area speaking with a female airline crewmember. "I asked him for a favor Bridget, I hope you don't mind," Theron said leaning into me. "Who? Bobby? Mind? What was the favor Theron? And I hope it didn't entail a date with one of those crew members." "You always had a great sense of humor Bridge! Of course not, one of my college buddies is moving to Athens and he needs someone to carry a couple bags over." "Uh I can't do that Theron, I don't know what's in them." "First of all, this is not *Bridget Jones Diary part II*, we aren't in Thailand and that's not a strange guy, it's my College buddy, and secondly, Bobby's going to do it. He's speaking to them now." "First of all, that number one had like three parts to it, and as far as your second point goes, I could still be an accomplice as we're travelling together." Theron chuckled, his belly bouncing slightly as he grabbed my face kissing me on the cheek and putting his arm around me. "You're one in a million Bridge, don't ever change." "I'm still not carrying any bags over, and how do you know about *Bridget Jones Diary*?" I replied laughingly. "Because you were either watching it, or discussing some integral part of it, whenever we Skyped. Come on, let's go," he said keeping his arm around me.

The ladies at the baggage drop off were configuring the excess bags and of course flirting with Bobby, who seemed happy to reciprocate. I might as well have been Greek spinach pie at this point, boiled and smacked between layers of phyllo dough, buried and forgotten. What seemed like an eternity later, we were all checked in and ready to board. Bobby finally gave me a recap of what Theron had requested of him. "I wouldn't do it," I said, in my best 'valley girl' voice. "They're Theron's friends, that's mean," he replied looking down at me with an intense stare. My rhetoric with Bobby was most definitely loaded; twisted in emotion, angst, and disappointment. All of which were of course oblivious to him. *Think like a man Goddamit Bridget – don't ruin this. Mean? Oh and I suppose ignoring me while flirting with those airline attendants was perfectly acceptable?!* "It wasn't my intention to be mean or unhelpful Bobby, you just never know these days…who's got what in their luggage." "Americans!" he replied letting out a deep breath. "For the last time, it was Theron's friend." I immediately dropped it after that, there was no point to the conversation, and the luggage carrier wasn't even at the heart of the matter, I had realized he loved watching me squirm. "Excuse me Miss, do you need something before take off? I noticed you hit the service button," a young pretty flight attendant asked hovering over me, her eyes glancing periodically at Bobby. "I let go of Bobby's hand and reached for the Adavan pill bottle in my coat pocket. "Just some water please, I think I'm going to be sick."

*

The plane ride back was full of turbulence and I was on edge the entire time. Bobby on the other hand, showed little emotion. He was focused on getting back to Athens and his work, and I couldn't wait to get into Mikey's apartment and burry myself under the covers. The flight only made my flu symptoms worse. By the time we landed my nasal passage way was completely clogged, and my ears were ringing. Bobby was sympathetic to my discomfort bringing me to the airport's pharmacy. Taking charge he spoke to the pharmacist on my behalf explaining my symptoms to her. She handed him a little bottle and explained how to use it, along with some over the counter tablets. "This is medicated nasal spray Bridget, and the tablets are to fight the flu symptoms. Every 6 hours as required, ok?" Bobby had an authoritative caregiver's

127

manner that was unbeatable. I felt safe and in his realm of thought again. Maybe Bobby wasn't moody, flirtatious, or selfish maybe I just didn't understand him, or men at all, for that matter.

*

I started to feel better on the car ride home. I had picked up some well-needed chocolate from my favorite Greek patisserie, after spotting the familiar sign in the airport. Perikli's was a family owned bakery with recipes over 100 years old and I had discovered it around the corner from Mikey's apartment. Bobby confirmed it was the best in its class and picked up a box for his mom while treating me to an assortment of chocolate covered oranges and dates.

I hadn't gotten used to Bobby always treating me but had learned it was the way Mediterranean men operated and took care of their women, so I conquered politely after offering to buy my own of course. Either way, I couldn't wait to devour the sweet confections, packing my mouth with chocolate was a sure way of avoiding any conversations about Bobby's behavior.

"I'm going to park on the side of the apartment and grab your luggage," Bobby said, pulling up the emergency break. I stepped out of the car without hesitation and headed for the outer door of the apartment. Bobby carried up my luggage to the lift "you got it from here Bridget?" he asked waiting with me for the elevator to arrive. "Sure Bobby thanks. Did you have fun this weekend?" "Yes," he replied without hesitation, pulling me close for a short tight-lipped kiss. "Ill call you tomorrow, get some rest." "You too Bobby, goodnight. Glad you had a good time." "I told you I did Bridget" he snapped back. I must have really felt 'off' bringing that up again, perhaps it was the daze from the Adavan, or maybe I just needed to feel more secure. Regardless, Bobby drove off in a hurry, and I made it to the second floor and into Mary-Anne's room without thinking about it twice.

"Bridget is that you?!" called out Mikey, I could hear a couple familiar voices coming from the living room, "get in here and tell us about your trip!" "Sure cuz," I replied in the most upbeat voice I could muster; "I just need to wash up and change and I'll be right out." I wanted to speak to Mikey about the weekend and get some well-needed advice, but I woke up some seven hours later on a bumpy pile of clothing, immobile in my uncomfortable airplane outfit. I was congested and soar, and needless to say, more dazed and confused then ever.

20

Sleeping in tight jeans was utterly painful. But the pain in my throat and head was undeniably worse. My body ached, like it had been tossed and pounded for hours on end. It must have taken me two hours to get into my morning routine and start sorting through my emails. Oliver of course had sent several, which I read and forwarded to Leo; and Vivian and Lea along with my mom had requested updates on my work and love life. Lastly there was a message from Uncle Dmitri, a welcome surprise. We hadn't spoken since I arrived in Athens, and between my whirlwind experience filming and spending all my spare time with Bobby I had forgotten to let him know that I was alright. I decided to respond to his email first:

Uncle D! I'm so sorry I haven't been in touch since I arrived in Greece. The filming went great and now I am in editing. I can't wait to show you the final product. Leo has been really great, I'm so glad you connected us. Let's Skype when you have some time! Love Bridget.

I spent the next few hours, doing some work and cleaning up my mess in Mikey's apartment. I had decided against discussing my weekend with Mikey or anyone else for that matter. Bobby and I had something special and I knew if I began complaining about the little things I found odd, everyone around me would be forthcoming with their opinions, which would just put a damper on my newly found excitement.

Later that night I decided to whip up a batch of my famous brownies. Bobby hadn't brought up baking again since our first encounter, so I thought it was about time to surprise him. Partway through the mixing my blackberry went off. It was Uncle Dimitri. He had received my email and wanted to let me know his son, my cousin Niko was in Athens with his girlfriend and wanted to meet up. It was perfect timing as I wanted to fill up my days and nights as much as possible to avoid missing home, and the universe was answering my call. Excited, I whisked up the rest of the batter and poured it into a pan than into the oven, and ran to my room to ransack through my closet and find the perfect outfit. "Something smells amazing in here!" "Mikey you're here, perfect just in time. It's my famous brownies, and I need your help!" "Sure what's up?" he said biting into an apple. "Niko is in town, Uncle Dimitri's son, with his girlfriend, they want to meet up, but I have no clue where to go." "I know, Niko got in touch, we will meet up at an Indie concert later tonight. However, as far as starters go, I haven't been living downtown long enough to discover any places that are eclectic enough for your taste. Have you thought of asking Bobby?" "No, I mean Uncle D just let me know a short while ago." "Ask him, that'll be your best bet." I sent Bobby a text message knowing he'd love coming up with a solution for me. He responded right away, stating I should go to his cousin's lounge in a chic part of town. "One of my cousin's owns a great place called *Colors*. I'll set it up for you, and meet you there later in the evening for a drink." It was all settled. Bobby was at his best when taking control, and of course seemed intrigued with the thought of me needing him.

*

After trying on a couple of outfits I settled on a short-sleeved burgundy dress complete with tassels I had purchased from an unknown vintage shop in South Chicago. I paired it up with skin colored fishnet stockings and my spiked pumps.

"Jesus Christ, you look hot Bridget!"

"Really Mikey, it's not too much with the nylons and all?"

"No, you look great, and I'm impressed at how quickly you've gotten into the Mediterranean dress code. Top that off with your fur and Bobby will be salivating."

I blushed and disappeared into Mary-Anne's room to complete my makeup. I paid extra attention to accentuating my eyes; knowing Bobby had a thing for them. I coated each eyelash and blushed my cheeks with just enough bronzer, finally dabbing my lips with cherry gloss before heading for the door. "Be careful tonight!" shouted out Mikey, "you look dangerous." His words had me running back into my room and sorting through the top drawer of my vanity. I grabbed two Durex packages and placed them in the zipper pocket of my night clutch. "You're right Mikey, Athens is a dangerous city, but I'll be careful.

*

A half hour later I had arrived at Colors. It was quite the eclectic upscale lounge, and what I could only assume was an archetypal Mediterranean hotspot. It was only half full making it very easy to spot Nikos and his girlfriend. To my surprise, he had barely changed since my childhood visit. "Niko!" I called out. "Bridget, my beautiful cousin!" he said, putting down his cigarette and walking briskly towards me. He hugged me than paused kissing me on both cheeks. "Welcome, Bridget, welcome! We are so happy to have you here" he said with enthusiasm. I was overwhelmed with Niko's warmth, something that was generally very prevalent in Greece. "Well my dear Nikos, you look quite handsome yourself, in fact you've barely changed since you were 12; maybe except for the facial hair and height." Niko stood over 6 feet tall, in a very thin frame, and had a full head of long dark hair he pulled back in a low ponytail.

"Bridget this is Melina, my girlfriend." "Harika," she smiled softly reaching her arm to shake mine. "Lovely to meet you as well Melina." "Melina is an art student at the University of Athens, we travel back and forth," Niko explained holding her close. "How romantic," I replied smiling. Melina, a petite brunette who reminded me of Christina Ricci, was as sweet as Greek honey, ironically the origins of her name. "Well art is my major," she explained, "but I'm also studying anthropology, the psychology of man and the political and economic theories that have lead to the demise of the cradle of civilization," she went on. All to which I responded, "wow, how deep." Although completely mind blowing when I had first arrived in Greece, Melina's speech was pretty consistent with what I had heard from many Athenians; for them it was time for a revolution, but for me, it was a Friday night out, and I couldn't wait for Bobby to join us.

A couple vodka soda's later we had discussed modern art, fundamentalism and some family history. "We need to head out soon Bridget," Niko said waving over the waitress, "we're going to head out to the big Indie concert in town." "Oh yes, Mikey mentioned he is going as well." "Yes we're going to meet up, and I don't want to miss him. Is your friend coming soon?" "I'm sure he is, he has a bit of a time management issue." "Well if he's from here it's innate, don't take it personally cousin," he laughed. Just as I looked towards the clock to check the time, Bobby was entering the front door. He was in his black overcoat; his hair gelled back in its usual perfection, his eyes carrying the customary serious stare. "He's here, I'll go get him," I said, getting up and squeezing through the two small tables next to us.

Spotting me, he sent over a leisurely wave, a simple hand gesture that made me melt. His command over me astounding, and although I didn't understand how it had become so intense, I missed him. Feeling weak in the knees I walked over, unresistingly planting a small kiss on his lips. "I'm going to say hello to my cousin at the bar and I'll join you guys in a minute," he said coolly.

A few moments later Bobby joined our table, and after introducing him to Niko and Melina he had jumped right into the political discussion. I was happy to sip on another drink and watch as they discussed current events and Bobby's business. "Bridget I'd love to stay, you guys are great company and all, but we really need to get to the concert." "Totally cool Niko, we'll be getting going soon as well."

After a short fight about the bill, Niko and Melina left, Bobby paid, and we exchanged some chitchat about what we'd do next. "Let's get to the car and see where the night takes us," Bobby suggested, as full of passion as I had seen him since we met.

He greeted his cousin goodbye and introduced me to the owner, of course another cousin, a well-known former model, and club owner in town. "Where are you from he asked?" looking at me from head to toe and back again. George was a handsome 50 something year old Clooney type, except for the shoulder length feathered hair. "Chicago," I replied shyly. "I figured the U.S.," he said. "Seems all you girls work out there, must be the lifestyle," he said pointing to my body in my fitted maroon dress. I couldn't remember the last time I had received a compliment on my body, or the last time I had worked out for that matter; but the best part was I had never even thought it about since leaving Chicago. "Hope to see you here again," he said. Feeling confident, I thanked him and kissed him on both cheeks. Bobby shook his hand firmly and followed me out the door. The walk to the car park was challenging in spiked heels. The streets were not exactly cobblestoned but more like cracked and broken, with large abstractions running through the sidewalks. It seemed they were made for anything but walking in high heels. A few blocks later we had reached the parking lot, Bobby waving down the attendant and handing him over the ticket. "What?" I said brashly, as I caught Bobby starred harshly into my eyes. "Nothing, just looking." he replied opening the passenger side of the car.

"What shall we do?" I asked as we drove out of the lot. Bobby suggested a few spots, dessert, wine bars, after hours, none of which faintly interested me. Then he looked down at my fishnet nylons and suggested something else. "We could always go to a hotel room," he said "you know, have a nightcap there." Perfect, I thought, just what I wanted, but I wasn't about to let on. "So what made you change your mind Bobby? Was it the nylons?" I asked watching his eyes follow mine down to the thighs and back up again. "Aa…" he said stuttering, "the nylons, heels, dress, I'd say it was a combo Bridget." "So where to then Bobby?" "You'll see, put your seatbelt on," he commanded speeding off into the Athens night.

*

It was 12:30 am when Bobby stopped the car outside the Athens Plaza near the downtown core. "We should be ok to park here for a few hours," he said, clicking the alarm on his car and heading for the canteen across the road. "Do you want anything?" he asked running across the street. "Just water, I guess." "They'll have water there," he replied. After buying a couple of snacks and placing a small blue box in his pocket, he locked my arm into his and led me across the street towards the hotel.

The Athens Plaza was well lit, and buzzing with people – I guess no one in Athens slept except for the American visitors. "Good evening," Bobby said acknowledging the staff and greeting the front desk clerk. "We'll need a room for a few hours." "Regular or a suite?" replied the clerk. "A suite," Bobby replied after a few moments, pulling out a wad of cash from his pocket and throwing it on the counter. He filled out the necessary form and was handed a key. Bobby handled himself like a

135

pro, or perhaps like someone who rented rooms often, but I paid little attention, I was too caught up by the moment, and enamored by the new excitement in my life.

The suite was on the 5th floor with double French doors opening the room to a large balcony facing the Acropolis. The Parthenon was lit, and sparkled amongst the dark night and ballooned full moon; the sight was magnificent. "The Parthenon is to the left, and the Lycabettus Mountain is towards the right," Bobby explained as he stepped onto the balcony. He had removed his dark overcoat and was standing in a black V-neck sweater, revealing the top of his built chest and collarbones. "It's beautiful Bobby." It was a little chilly in my tiny dress, but beautiful none-the-less. "Lets go inside," he said, tapping my left arm. I was convinced he just wasn't very affectionate, in fact I had realized the only time he ever was, was our first night together. I could have taken it as disinterest but instead coughed it up to his pre-occupation. *I knew he was into me; he had to be, why else would he be spending time with me, and bring me here? I was sure he wanted only me.* I needed little more from him to get me inside the pretty suite. I sat by the bedside and begin removing my stilettos.

"Did I tell you to remove those Bridget?" "Um no, I just…" "Keep them on" he said in a stern voice, "and come over here." I walked around the bed to the other side, feeling powerful and wanted. Bobby stood with a wide smirk on his face before grabbing my face and kissing me hard, jarring my mouth open with his tongue. I wanted him bad, and held onto him by his biceps. He pushed me down until I fell onto the bed; he followed on top, kissing me without hesitation, caressing my breasts over my dress. "Can I rip these?" he whispered, pulling on my fishnet pantyhose; and then without warning he tore a gapping hole at the crotch seem, and thrust his fingers through it. Bobby kissed me hard, caressing me until I was dripping everywhere. Then once again entered me without warning, propelling his body with force, over and over again, and then lifting my legs up in the air, in the uncomfortable V position that he loved. "That hurts," I said softly, "but I like it, I get so deep," he moaned. I endured the pain, and discomfort, until I couldn't take it anymore, forcing my legs down and turning to my side. Bobby continued to penetrate me with my dress waist high and fishnets and spiked heels in place. He turned me onto my stomach, then on all fours, and lastly onto my back again where he came after his familiar announcement and final thrust. Rolling over and removing the latex from his dwindled erection, he threw it in the wastebasket, "you can go to the bathroom first Bridget," he said in his emotionless after-sex manner. It was raw and unsentimental, but it was Bobby, and I never thought to ask why he was so cold, I just went with it.

*

After taking turns showering Bobby returned in a fluffy hotel robe. I was under the covers but Bobby had no desire to join me. "I'm comfy here," he said, pointing to the outer comforter and his robe. "You can lie here," he said, pointing to the robe and his chest. I tried but it was uncomfortable. Bobby was distant and although sweet in his gestures, different from how I remembered him. As my mind soared, I began to question his motives, but he stopped me in my tracks. "I know you must hear this a lot, but you have very beautiful eyes Bridget," he whispered softly starring deeply into my eyes. The truth was I didn't, in fact I only ever heard it from *him*, and I wanted to let him know, I didn't need compliments from anyone. I was fine with just thinking I was mediocre, something unthinkable to Mediterranean women. "I don't need compliments..." I couldn't finish the sentence before Bobby interrupted "you should just say thank you, you're a woman, you should like compliments." I didn't bother trying to explain what I meant, this time I thought I'd be better left lost in translation. In fact, months after my first encounter with Bobby, I had realized much of what I perceived about him may have been simply a matter of misinterpretation. I tried nestling onto the thick robe that covered his chest, but before I knew it, our time was up. We scurried around the room gathering our things, and I cleaned up as much as I could, "you want a job here?" he asked looking up at me, "leave all that to housekeeping," he commanded sternly. The truth was I felt bad leaving a mess just for a few hours, and was embarrassed by the condom wrapper and used latex, especially since I would be entering the now brightly lit lobby in a fur coat and fishnet stockings.

*

Bobby starred into the unforgiving sunlight of day, squinting his honey brown eyes, "I forgot how ugly Athens was during the day," he said in disgust, "I'm never in this part of town, I'm always working." "I bet Bobby, but I supposed it could be worse, the south side of Chicago ain't pretty either, after all, every city has its' East LA," I sighed admiring the character of such an antiquity of the capital city. "It's what Bridget?!" he asked baffled in his thick accent. "It's bad part of town," I said laughingly, giving his cheek a soft squeeze.

A short car ride and a small kiss later Bobby had dropped me off at Mikey's. I was happy to change out of my sexy evening get-up and wipe what was left of my makeup off my face. As I tucked my Chicago jersey into my PJ bottoms and sunk under the covers, I checked my blackberry before turning it to silent. There were no goodbye texts from Bobby, no sweet dreams, and no longing sentiments of any kind. Even though I was not accustomed to it, I wanted it *from him* nonetheless. Perhaps I needed something back that never existed at all. As I pondered what Bobby Siteros was thinking, and what he wanted, I realized I really didn't know the man I was sleeping with, *at all.*

21

I spent the next few weeks going to and from Leo's home studio in Taylor's Port trying to perfect the promo videos. I had assumed Oliver would have eventually come around, but that wasn't the case. Leo and I were at our wits end, not to mention, the commercial crew who was awaiting payment. I had begun missing home and friends, as I was starting to spend a lot of time either in transit or home alone. Mikey worked long and odd hours and spent his days off with his girlfriend in her beach house on the other side of the city. Oliver was back in Chicago sending off our work to any half credible wanna be producer, who would send Leo and I new scripts and editing directions. He'd be returning to Athens in a few days and I couldn't wait to wrap up the project and get paid. In the interim, I had sent Lea and Vivian a list of additional clothing and toiletries I needed and couldn't afford to buy. Luckily, Oliver had agreed to add them to his luggage, even though Vivian was not happy about having to see him when dropping them off. "He's a bonafide pervert Bridget," she had said in a Skype conversation following her meeting with Oliver. "This I know oh too well Viv, but I'm stuck, and I can't afford to buy the same things in Euros it makes no sense." "How much longer are you going to stay there, Bridge? I mean Spring is approaching!" "You're all alone there and ... uh are you all alone actually? Bridget have you met someone? Is this why you're staying?" Vivian urged inquisitively. I was in dier need of telling someone about Bobby. Bouncing a few things off a girl would help, besides I couldn't keep my feelings wrapped up inside anymore. "Ok here it goes, I'm dating someone, but it's no big deal." "Dating someone?! No big deal?!" To no surprise, Vivian's line of questioning was intense; inquiring about every last sorted detail would be her new pet project. I however, gave her the Cole's notes version and enough information to keep her at bay, and of course relieve some of my anxiety.

"So the Calvin Klein boxers I packed were for the mystery man?!" she asked playfully. "Well they could be for Mikey," I giggled. "Nice try Bridge," her sarcastically reply quickly beaming me back to reality. I had a man, a man I yearned for, a man who was keeping me in Athens, and a man I longed to see in Calvin Klein boxer briefs no less.

"I just hope it's all worth it in the end, Oliver gives me the creeps, be careful when you pick up your things," a sound warning from Vivian. "I'm meeting him at the airport when he arrives Viv – it's fine," I concluded reassuring her, and myself I'd be safe. In fact Oliver had insisted I meet him there, something I didn't mind, since it was just a metro ride away, that and Bobby would be picking me up from there, and we'd be spending the night together. I was too excited to have Vivian's inquisition ruin a rare night with Bobby. "I'll be careful Viv, thanks for sending my things." "Well, I hope you wrap up soon, and have fun with this mystery man in the meantime," she added supportively. I felt no need to reveal Bobby's name or any other info for that matter. I knew she'd be on Google and every social network in a heartbeat, and I'd be hearing regularly from her and Lea about it. There was just no way anyone was going to taint my new excitement.

*

I spent a good hour perfecting my hair and makeup in the mirror, than arranging the perfect outfit to wear to the airport. I settled on my blue jeggings, the tightest pants I could find, and my black over the knee leather boots along with a long white blouse, and leather jacket to top it off. I wanted to appear cool and casual, even though I was dying to see Bobby. We had corresponded in the last few weeks, phone, text, Skype; Bobby was cool and collected as usual, but it wasn't nearly enough of what I needed. The metro ride was quick and easy and I had arrived in ample time to meet Oliver and load up my empty luggage before meeting up with Bobby.

Unfortunately, for me, I had forgotten to check the flight status before I had left Mikey's, a rule I knew oh to well from my PR days. Apparently the O'Hare airport was backed up and Oliver's flight would be delayed. The waiting was incredibly tedious, and there was absolutely nothing to do, *except of course to wait*. No one to speak to, to email or text, all of which seemed like foreshadowing of things to come if I didn't get things wrapped up soon. Two hours went by before Oliver arrived. I had never been so thrilled to see that sour butterball in my life. He was angry, which I anticipated, but handed over all the things Vivian had packed without any issues. Luckily he was too distraught to discuss business, and even offered me a ride home in his rental car. I happily declined, knowing Bobby would arrive any moment.

*

Another thirty minutes later in the Athens International airport, and no Bobby. Distraught and exhausted by this time, I decided to swallow my pride, along with all of my excitement and send him a text message.

Athens Bridget: Bobby, Oliver came and left. Are you going to make it or should I just leave?!

A few moments later my blackberry began to buzz.

Bobby: Grab a coffee or something baby, I'm going to be late.

Disappointed and emotionally a wreck, I through my blackberry into my bag, and contemplated what to do. There was no one to speak to, hang out with, or call for a coffee. Bobby had consumed my new world, and I hadn't made a single friend in Athens, he had become my only refuge.

"Every refuge has its price Bridget, if you're not happy go home." Luckily I had managed to track down someone close by who actually cared about me, and would listen to me. "Thanks for the advice Uncle D, but I can't leave until I hand Oliver the final promo spots, even worse, I can't leave until I pay this crew, I could never leave them all hanging." "Alright hunny, well just know I'm here for you. You're not desperate and alone, these circumstances are just temporary, you'll be home again soon." *Home? What the heck was I going to do back home?!* Going back into that monotonous lifestyle was frightening. I was a changed woman, with a lover and new inhibitions; I could not go back there! As I contemplated Uncle D's words and my fate, my mobile began buzzing in my ear. "Uncle D I need to go, thanks for the chat, I'll let you know what happens." "Alright my darling be careful." I

141

glanced down at the screen at the familiar number; after 2 hours, Bobby was calling.

"Hello."

"Hey baby, I'm almost there, meet me outside and we'll park together." Infuriated and confused, I listened to Bobby's easygoing and unapologetic voice. I wanted to tell him I hated him, and never wanted to see him again, but instead I politely agreed to meet him outside, all the while wondering if Bobby cared about anyone else except himself.

I gathered my large red suitcase and walked across the arrivals area waiting for the black Audi to pull up. Bobby pulled up a few minutes later, getting out of the car to place the suitcase in the trunk. He looked the same as always, dressed in his black overcoat and blue jeans. "You're not going to believe what I had to go through to get here," he began. "There was no water to shower, no...." "Bobby I've been waiting for over two hours, you really have no defense." My rage however, was overcome by the sight of Bobby and I was too hungry and tired to discuss anything, much less argue with the man I longed so bad to see. "Perhaps we should just stop now Bobby, let's change the subject," exhaling deeply. Bobby smiled pulling my scarf up past my nose laughing then lowering it quickly to kiss me softly, and just like that, I had let him off the hook easier than I ever imagined.

*

We parked in the airport's designated departures region, and walked through the gate until we reached the food court. Bobby held my hand the entire way, interlocking my fingers softly, producing butterflies throughout my empty stomach. It was a small gesture he had rarely exhibited, almost never actually, and just like that, I had forgotten the prior four hours. The food was stale and tasteless, a first since I'd been in Greece. "What do you expect in the airport at midnight," Bobby said as he chewed. "Mousaka?" I answered giggling. I was not going to let this night go to shit, I had spent way to much time preparing and anticipating a great night cap to let it fade into nothingness. Bobby had sensed my angst as he joked about cutting the night short a couple of times. I couldn't understand him. It seemed almost like a task to him; something he felt he was obligated to do and even though he couldn't wait to get me into bed the moment he met me, it seemed now he couldn't care less. We finished up quickly, and went for a walk through the half empty terminal, Bobby showing me some of the technology he had installed. It was certainly impressive, and I wanted Bobby to know I thought so; I was just so exhausted from the day and night's events that I could barely stand any longer. "You're beat," he said in typical commanding Siteros style, "let's go." "Thanks, I've had a long day," I replied, a warm feeling beginning to beat again inside me. By the time we had walked to the car and began driving away from the airport, I was feeling great about Bobby again. He made me smile and laugh, just like when he was first trying to win me over, *and he cared about me, I knew it.* "So where should we go?" he asked. "I feel comfortable at the Athens Plaza," I expressed softly, "and it's close to home." "The Hilton's the best in the city," he replied. It was also 250 Euros a night, something I had checked out a few nights before. "You can pay for that night," he said laughing, "I'll pay for the Athens Plaza tonight."

*

The hotel had the usual number of guests bussing through the lobby and sifting in and out of the dining room. By this time, I had gotten used to the speech with the front desk clerk; Bobby paying the room all upfront in cash, and grabbing the hotel key while I waited a few feet to the side. I had even gotten comfortable with the idea that was written all over the staff's faces; an American mistress to the Greek business man; I may have even felt a little flattered. The room was nice, outfitted with a large bed equivalent to an American King size, and a sliding glass door leading out to a modest balcony. I couldn't wait to get into bed and snuggle with Bobby under the covers.

I changed into in a low cut black tank top and boxers while Bobby remained in his clothes, unzipping the case to his laptop computer and placing it on his lap. *What was I thinking?! Snuggling?* Like that had *ever* happened. Each time I saw Bobby it was as if I had forgotten what the last time was like. "I'm writing some emails to some Chinese manufacturers. Maybe you can help me perfect my English," he suggested in his archetypal business demeanor. "Sure," I answered feeling more like throwing the laptop on the ground. "They don't seem to understand the parts I need to order, my ex-partner used to take care of all the emailing." He looked distraught, and in deeper thought than usual, and even though I was beat, for the next hour I reluctantly became his secretary.

*

"There, you should be all good now Bobby," I said slamming the laptop shut and snuggling in close. "Oh no you don't Bridget, you're not going to fall asleep and let me watch an American film alone." I propped up, "sorry I didn't realize you wanted to watch a movie, I just felt comfortable for a moment," I replied in disappointment. As I leaned back to my side of the bed, my tank top scooped far beyond my bra, exposing a blue satin demi cup and front closure. Bobby looked at my bust pouring out of the bra and came closer kissing the top of my chest and pulling up the bra to caress and kiss my overflowing bosom.

"There's a front opening you know," the words fluttering from my lips softly. "I don't care," he answered, revealing a low moan and pulling at my boxers to reveal a mesh blue thong laced in pink trim. Bobby grabbed me with animalistic passion kissing me hard and removing his clothes with his free hand. His body fell heavy against mine and his lips met mine once again, but this time they never left. I tried to get him to change from the missionary position, but he wouldn't budge, he wanted to remain on top of me, and that would be the end of it. He grabbed my panties with his right hand and lifted my right leg up letting them fall around my ankle. His fingers slipped in and out of me while his mouth stayed suckled interchanging between both breasts. I caressed him as best as I could reach, removing his tight boxers, allowing him to enter me. His thrusts were rough and I held onto his back pulling him in even further. It was animalistic passion, hard and impersonal, and I didn't want it to stop.

"I want to finish all over you," he said, slipping out of me and placing me on top of him. I had learned to love giving Bobby oral sex and he expressed his admiration with vicious groans every chance he got. I grabbed onto his thighs, digging my nails into them as he grabbed the back of my head pushing me down forcefully, and just then he began to haul away, and I didn't understand why he pulled me off of him until he came –all over me. Shocked and annoyed I ran into the bathroom and into the shower. As I lathered up, I thought about how disrespectful Bobby was, and now after seeing him use me like a toy, I was sure it was not love making for him. I scrubbed my face and body trying to erase any trace of Bobby left on me.

After feeling somewhat content with my hygiene I re-entered the room to find Bobby on his laptop. His lack of emotion never ceased to amaze me. Infuriated I wanted to tell him off, but I knew there would be a logical explanation to all the crazy thoughts swimming in my head.

"You didn't have to blow your stuff all over me you know, my face is off limits you know!" I shouted out, my temperature rising. "What?" he answered laughingly. "I'm just comfortable with you Bridget, it wasn't meant to be disrespectful, I can't always control myself at that time." Bobby's nonchalant demeanor always seemed to discount the events at hand, once again leaving me pondering about myself. Perhaps I was a prude after all – or just not the Mediterranean sex Goddess Bobby was accustom to. "Bridget, let me tell you something, I know this is coming from insecurity and perhaps limited experience, but you're very good at sex. Now please don't let this go to your head, you know I'm not big on compliments, but that's the truth." And there it was, the quick line from Bobby Siteros that had managed to turn the tables around once again. "Come lie here Bridget, you must be beat. Bring some of that chocolate we picked up at the airport too." I smiled, knowing my favorite chocolate would give me the little pick- me-up I needed. I sat beside him in bed starring at his computer screen until my eyelids got the better of me, collapsing in front of my tired hazy eyes; the soft words of a Greek love song were the last thing I remember hearing.

22

I woke up to find Bobby in the fetal position several feet away from me on the far right side of the bed. As if that didn't make me feel isolated enough, I don't think we had touched once during the night. I yearned to touch him, to wake him, to feel his body wrapped around mine, but instead decided to pack up my things and shower and change while he slept. When I returned into the room, Bobby was up. "Hey, morning," I said softly, unclear weather I was happy or not to see him. "Hey Bridge, we should let room service know they can bring up the breakfast buffet." "Ok, you can go ahead, I'm just cleaning up my things." A half hour later we had both taken back to the bed when the hotel room doorbell rang. "Can you get it Bridget it'll be room service." "Um… I'm not dressed Bobby." "Fine I'll go," he said mouthing something on the way to the door, which after translation I figured out it meant, "I hope it's not a woman." Annoyed at his words, I pondered if Bobby was indeed that insecure, not wanting a woman to see him without his perfectly gelled hair or matching attire. "Come and get it while it's fresh," he said sitting down in front of the buffet spread. Taking a pan across the table I decided I didn't like anything the hotel offered except for some freshly squeezed orange juice. "It's all included, eat up Bridget." "I don't really like it, I'm not a big morning eater, it's ok," I responded a little annoyed there was nothing I could devour. "Starving yourself won't get you a flat tummy or slimmer thighs Bridget, you need to change your diet and of course workout." Bobby's response might as well been a series of bullets shattering through my ego. A part of me wanted to roll up in a ball and cry; the other part, reach for a breakfast roll and throw it at his inflated head, then tell him to fuck off and leave the room. I took a deep breath and settled on a milder approach. "So you obviously don't like my body Bobby, why haven't you mentioned this before?" He looked up at me in between his bites of bagels and scrambled eggs, "I didn't say I didn't like your body Bridget, if I didn't think you were attractive I wouldn't have approached you. All I'm saying is that you have a good frame, and great structure to work with, so if you got rid of some of the fat, you would look amazing." I wasn't sure if I should be saying thank you or reaching for the butter knife this time. He continued as he chewed on sausage "I have a tummy too; in the summer season I get my abs back." I chalked up Bobby's approach to brutal European bluntness and a shitty self-outlook, and proceeded to ignore the conversation turning to my luggage and re-folding my clothes. Bobby's approach was utterly brash- did he actually care about me? Or was this a lame attempt to distance himself from me? I convinced myself it was a cultural issue – *I mean what American man in his right man would dare say that to a woman?!* This was a case for Lea and Vivian, but it would be hours or perhaps days before I could connect with them, and they would surely be ready to persecute Bobby; it was a lose-lose situation. I clenched my teeth and looked up over the breakfast table, "you know Bobby, I'm totally cool with myself, it took a lot of years, but I am." Little did he know I spent my adolescents clearing up acne, removing braces and glasses and shedding a lot of baby fat. "I'm just telling you something that would help you Bridget," he said in his typical composed manner. Unready to face the reality of what Bobby had said, I turned away and focused on organizing my newly found clothing and accessories, all unnoticed by Bobby. When he was satisfied with his breakfast he poured himself some coffee, read the sports section of the paper and joined me on the partially soiled bed where I continued to disappoint myself with several *desperately seeking Bobby* acts.

*

I was happy to finally be home late the next afternoon. I could hear Mikey's voice coming from the living room; he must have had some company, something I was happy about. He and his friends were usually full of compliments and were generally nice guys, and I was in no mood to hear any more criticism about my imperfections; especially because further to Bobby's criticism came rejection. My last hopeless attempt at gaining his attention at the hotel had began with a full body massage that turned into filatio, which I then attempted to turn into sex at which time Bobby refused, apparently due to a full belly of breakfast. "I can't Bridget," he had said, "I just ate and you can't work out after you eat, I'll get cramps and vomit." It was settled, there was no need to speak to Lea or Vivian about *this situation* after all. In fact I could hear one of Vivian's famed mantras now; "women use sex to get love, and men use love to get sex, never believe a man." There it was in one simple sentence, *the truth*. Bobby either cared only about himself or someone else who I didn't know about, whichever the case, neither was letting him move on. I had made him a priority, and he hadn't even made me an option. Was I so desperate for attention I was using sex to gain his love? *If deep down inside, I knew this, then what the fuck was I doing?* I sat under the hot shower pondering just that, and more specifically, why I had become so addicted to someone that didn't give a damn about me.

23

"Next time please place yourself in the front of the class Miss. I'll be able to guide you a lot better." I nodded acknowledging the yoga instructor's comments. Fedon looked to be in his late twenties; he was strikingly sexy with short dark hair and bright blue eyes, with perfectly waxed eyebrows sitting above them. He was built like an Adonis of course, and even though I wasn't sure if he was gay or not, I had simply decided he was, showing up to yoga classes in messy up-do's, unpolished nails and my college sorority sweats; something typically unseen in Athens. The women in the Athens hot yoga classes were immaculate; their hair sprayed to perfection, matching yoga attire and exceptionally firm bodies. Needless to say I was much more comfortable in the back row, and so I slipped to the edge of the heated room allowing my mind wonder, I pondered about the last few weeks.

*

The weeks following my last encounter with Bobby had gone by fairly quickly, yet agonizingly. Leo and I worked on production revisions while consistently arguing with Oliver until he departed for Chicago once more. It was becoming apparent that Oliver came and left at his leisure, complaining about our work each time, and I was going absolutely nowhere. I had become a permanent fixture in a strange city and for the most part all alone. Bobby and I corresponded over text and email whenever he initiated contact, or I sent a whiny message in my most vulnerable state – on my period or in bed trying to fall asleep. In any case when he did reach out his concern was work rather than me; typically relating to a translation for his Chinese partners.

In the meantime, I continued my *Athens Hot Yoga* classes, took up smoking hash with Mikey, not to mention long walks on deserted beaches and desolate marinas. I decided if I was going to live to see the day of the final Herbal Tea campaign I would have to expand my horizons, and have something else to think about other than Bobby and my painful work. The weekends were the most excruciating, specifically Sundays, which were a family day in the religious state. As mostly everything public in the ancient city (excluding eateries) was closed, I had invested in some back-to-back Yoga classes to stay busy, *and amongst the living.*

"I see that you have good mobility and endurance Miss, but you need to practice your postures," Fedon continued as I checked out his sculpted abs. The major challenge wasn't quite the posture technique, but understanding what the heck was going on. The language barrier was increasingly harder to crack when I was in the downward dog position, so I spent most classes twisting and turning to catch a glimpse of the instructor or experienced yogis.

After hours in a suffocating hot room, I returned to Mikey's apartment famished and exhausted, just the way I liked it. Content knowing Mikey was home hanging out with his girlfriend in his bedroom, I decided to start up my laptop in the living room checking emails while I waited for yesterday's leftovers to heat up. At sight of the familiar home-screen, the Skype icon began to bounce up and down. I had a few messages from Lea and Vivian, a new edit from Leo, and one last surprising message, *from Jack*. I read through the customary messages leaving Jack's for last.

Unwilling or perhaps unable to answer any of the girls' questions, I skipped over them, downloaded Leo's latest edit, than clicked on Jack's message:

Jack: Bridget, I haven't heard from you since you landed in Athens. How is the commercial going and are you alright? J.N.

Short and to the point, that was Jack. I thought about what I would say over some re-heated noodles and veggies.

Bridget: J, did I thank you for taking me around London? I'm sorry if not, I loved it. I'm still in editing for the commercials, Athens is a unique place; I'll fill you in when you can talk sometime. Luv Bridget.

I sent off the Skype message and worked away at my bowl of noodles, when the Skype icon bounced up again:

Jack: I can talk, JN.

I was shocked. For one because Jack wasn't slammed with work and was able to talk and secondly that he was interested in what I was doing in Athens, especially after his chilly disposition in London. I stuffed the remaining noodles down my throat and proceeded to call him.

"Hello Bridget." "Jack!" I answered with intense enthusiasm. I missed the sound of a friendly voice, the voice of someone who cared about me. "Are you doing alright Bridget? What happened with the commercials?" I proceeded to fill Jack in on the story in its entirety, from the filming on Paros, to Oliver's crazy family dynamic, his atrocious disposition, and the current ghastly situation. His response was very Jack-like, direct, and simple. "Let me see your contract; please tell me you have a contract and this clown signed it." My response seemed to deflate the atmosphere; even thousands of miles away I could tell I was an utter disappointment to him. "Jesus Bridget, how do you expect to fight this guy with nothing in writing?!" "Well I have emails!" I said defensively. "That's not enough. Alright I'm sorry for scolding you but you needed to hear it," he responded sternly. "I don't disagree with you Jack, but at this point, I need your help, and more importantly a friend, I'm all alone out here." Jack was all business at this point; my dramatic situation might as well have been his new development project. "First thing's first Bridget, finish all the work with the requested changes, then send me an outline of everything you've done. Once your work is done, I will take care of invoicing this guy from my offshore company and have him pay me. I'll take care of pursing payment and wiring you the money for you, and your production crew. Just leave that all to me" he concluded confidently and reassuringly as only he could. I was dumbfounded with Jack's efficient plan, his kindness, and determination with helping me. "I don't know what to say. Thank you, Jack. I don't know what I'd do without you." "You don't have to thank me Bridget, I just want you to get paid – and your crew as well. You've travelled half way around the world, done a great job, and should be paid, period – let's get you paid and outta there. This isn't good for you." The words echoed in my ears like burning sirens. *Leave? Where would I go?* The thought of returning to my Chicago apartment was inconceivable to me now. *I was a new woman, and knew I couldn't go back to my old life. What about Bobby? Was it all over?*

"Bridget are you there?" Jack had turned on his camera, and I could see him rocking back and forth in his beloved leather chair. "Yes Jack, I'm sorry I was just in a daze I guess."

After devising a secure plan to extract payment, Jack and I reminisced for an hour or so while I ate, than ate some more, and he laughed at my *après-hot-yoga* appetite. We spoke about the past, how we met, how long we'd been friends, and even why we never dated. I alluded to timing and inexperience, and the fact that I was a new woman now, but Jack seemed to become quite disinterested with that topic of conversation. "You don't need to explain Bridge, that was years ago and we've both moved on," he responded in a hurry to move the conversation along. *Moved on? He's moved on?! With who? Jack wanted me to know he had a new love and was only helping me out of pity.* His words crashed into me like ten-foot waves, only I was no longer standing dumbfounded on a deserted stretch of beach; I had been carried away into an unforgiving sea.

24

Jack didn't love me after all. He had given up on me and was only helping me out of sympathy. I yearned for a hit of my favored drug, Bobby, even if it was for just a few moments of pleasure. Jack and I said our goodbyes and I promised I'd be in touch when I wrapped up the project. As I logged off my computer feeling confident yet confused about going back home, my blackberry tweeted the familiar sound of a text message. To my excitement, Bobby had sent me a message, but much to my dismay, it was not to say hello, he missed me, or wanted to see me.

Bobby: Hi Bridget, how are you? The Chinese manufacturers wrote me another email. Can you translate it for me write a response according to the points we previously discussed about the machinery? I'm eager to install my new lighting technology, similar to that I did for the airport vendors' years ago. Cheers ☺.

I read the text message over a few times, until I was compelled with an assortment of emotions. Disappointment, anger, and loathing ran through me at a furious pace, almost until my entire body was burning up. I threw the blackberry onto the carpet and took a deep breath. The text had triggered an abundance of thoughts, and I began drifting away...

How the hell did you get here Bridget?! I thought of the night in the Toronto hotel, Vivian, Lea, and Oliver walking through the lobby. Meetings at Oliver's office about the Herbal Tea campaign, discussions with Leo, the Athens airport, Paros, Leo again, and then ... Leo, oh my God. I grabbed my blackberry dialing Leo's number frantically. The familiar long beep was nauseating; *pick up, please pick-up*. "Yes, hello," a soft voice answered. "Leo, thank God you're there, it's Bridget. I need to talk to you about something. Actually, just ask you something." "Sure, of course Bridget, are you alright? You seem flustered," he replied with his usual fatherly concern. "Yes," I said softly, "I just need to ...umm... remember the business you had with your ex-partner. Vending machines, lights, state of the art lights from China, and..."

"Yes, yes, Bridget," he interrupted "that was years ago, what are you getting at?" "Your partner, what was his name?" I asked anxiously, my stomach rumbling of anxiousness and frantic panic. "Why, Bridget, have you met him?" "I don't know Leo, just answer... please!" I urged panicking, "I just need to know his name please, just say the name Leo!" I was almost shrieking now, my pitch scratching the base of my throat. "Bobby, it's Bobby Siteros," he said as softly as I'd ever heard him. As soon as the words travelled through the airwaves into my eardrums, my sweaty palms gave way, and my blackberry slipped through my fingers onto the fuzzy red carpet. I stood facing the glare of the Lycabettus Mountain through the sliding glass door; the same image I had once admired standing next to Bobby. "Bridget"! Leo's voice echoed from the fallen blackberry. "Bridget, are you there? Answer me, I can tell by your silence he's gotten to you." I starred at the black mobile contemplating crushing it to bits, smashing any evidence of ever hearing the truth. Instead my mouth went dry and knees grew weak, eventually giving way for me to fall to the ground, my head slowly hitting the bright red carpet last, right next to my once beloved device. "Bridget?!" Leo yelled again. "I'm here Leo," I whispered into the phone. "Thank God, I thought you had past out or something. Please don't tell me you're in love with him Bridget. If you've slept with him, fine, but otherwise stay away. He is a liar and a womanizer – you know the rest. He is not for you, not for a girl like you I mean..." his voice now tender and compassionate.

I laid on the carpet motionless as Leo continued, "he is a gigolo, he sees women as shoes, like all those pretty shoes you have lined up in your closet, the ones you buy for no apparent reason except you want them, and of course because you can have them," he continued now more authoritative than I'd ever heard him, and I could bare no more. I had been played for a fool – I was nothing but a muse. "I've met him, Leo, yes," I murmured. "Oh God Bridget, of all the men in Athens... did he take you to Samos? Actually forget it, I know the answer. Listen to me carefully, stay away from him, you're just another pretty pair of shoes in the store window, nothing more...I know this sounds harsh but..." "Thanks, I have to go," I whispered clicking the red button in his mid-sentence. Unable to hear any more, I tossed the mobile as far as I could. Everything was a lie. *Why did Leo mention Samos?* Of all the men, in the world, I encountered the worst of them; and now I'd had an affair with a semi-professional gigolo; one whom I'd become co-dependent on, no less.

I don't know how long I was lying on the floor, but I eventually found myself in the shower cranking up the hot water as much as I could tolerate, letting it smolder my skin. I closed my eyes, allowing my hair, and body to become drenched. For a moment, I was back home, in my Chicago apartment getting ready for a night out. It was safe and warm and Vivian was waiting for me in the living room. Life was easy, uncomplicated, tedious, *but safe,* and there was no Bobby within reach. Then in an instant, the hot water turned ice cold, awakening me from my reverie. Gasping, I opened my eyes looking up at the nozzle. I turned the showerhead away from my body quickly to face the small white exhaust fan I had never noticed in the shower's corner. The fan was a tarnished shade of pearl with partially scratched letters along the bottom. I rubbed the cold water from my eyes to read the word spread across the bottom, SITEROS. *"What the fuck?! Get out of my head, 'get out! You liar! You pig! You fucking bastard!"* I yelled aloud, sobbing and grabbing the fan with both hands than tearing it from the tiles. I held it close, starring at it, before smashing it against the wall, the bathtub, and any concrete surface I could find. I continued to whip it around until it broke into dozens of pieces and my icy hands were bloody, filled with several cuts from the jagged edges. My legs collapsed beneath me, my knees crushing my fall as I sat kneeling in the bath, sobbing, allowing the ice-cold water to freeze my skin. I don't know how or when I got up from the shower or bathroom floor, but somehow I did, and headed for the kitchen.

Wrapped in a bloody towel I grabbed the large wine bottle sitting on the counter, and filled Mikey's beer mug with as much wine as I could fit inside. I drank, and drank, and cleaned up the bloody mess, eventually throwing the towels into the washing machine. I took in as much wine as my belly could endure before retiring to my room, curling up into the fetal position waiting for sleep to take me away.

Everything will be better in the morning Bridget darling. I could hear my mother's voice now, her warm hug and reassurance that everything would be alright - *as long as I went to bed.* I closed my eyes tight, avoiding crying myself to sleep, and held on to my soaked pillow to stop the violet room from spinning. Soon enough I had drifted off and didn't hear another noise that night, not a set of keys or creaking door, loud voice, or incessantly ringing blackberry.

25

Bobby held me tight. His bulging biceps created a pillow for my head when his chest was not available. "I love your eyes, you're so beautiful, I can't believe I feel so close to someone so quickly," he said kissing me softly. "Don't go anywhere," he whispered softly in my ear. "Bobby, there's a reason I came here..." "Of course there is baby – you belong here, with me..." "Don't go Bobby, stay just a little longer..." "I'm not going anywhere baby, and neither are you Bridget." "Knock on wood," he said hitting the bedside table with his knuckles. He knocked over and over again, as I clenched to him tightly, my nails digging in his skin. The sound of his knuckles echoed against the dense wood, growing louder and louder with each motion...

"Bridget are you alright?! Can I come in, it's me Mikey." I gasped at the loud voice, causing me to jump up from my sleep, confused about my dream, and my whereabouts. I pried my eyes open, allowing the light hitting me directly in the face. "I'm ok Mikey, I just need to get dressed," I replied groggy and confused. I stood from the warmth of my bed slowly realizing I was still in a bloody towel under the comforter. God, I felt sick, and sore for that matter. Peering over the assortment of cuts and bruises on my body, I threw on my sweats and glasses and headed for the kitchen.

"So What's up Mikey?" I said in my most convincing 'I'm not hung-over voice.' "I was worried I haven't seen you in a couple of days. Not to mention the bathroom fan is in shambles and there is blood splattered all over the washing machine." His response was characteristically methodical, parental, and filled with genuine concern. "I'm so sorry Mikey, I'll pay for the fan, and clean up whatever I need to," my voice cracking with self-pity and exhaustion.

"That's not the point Bridge, *why* is the point. What the fuck is happening to you, and when's the last time you ate?! You've lost weight and are starting to look gaunt."

"I'm good, totally fine, I'm just going through a bit of a stressful time."

"So you smashed the fan, cut your hand, stopped eating, and took up drinking, all because you're fine?"

"Ok Mikey when you put it that way it sounds really bad. The fan was an accident."

I continued my stream of lies until Mikey was somewhat satisfied with the information and seemed a tad less concerned about my sanity. He was exhausted after a couple of all nighters at work and was beginning to doze off at the kitchen table.

After a short lecture he headed for bed and I was left alone in the kitchen with a head that felt like the size of my Chicago apartment, the walls heavy and caving in. I ransacked through Mikey's drawers until I found the Greek equivalent to Advil and popped a couple of pills washing them down with some cold milk. I prepared a much-needed cappuccino and headed to the living room to recall my laptop, blackberry, and work notes I had left sprawled are over the living room. My recovered notes were mostly scribbles of some voice over lines, a few mantras, and think bubbles that didn't make nearly as much sense in broad daylight. My laptop was as I had left it, the cover upright, with the screen's wallpaper clearly visible in the morning's sunlight, a satin grey tie, and black mask.

I grabbed the cozy brown blanket off the armchair and curled up on the love seat. Pulling the blanket over my soar shoulders I felt something poking me in the base of my back; reaching in, I recovered the obstruction from the crevice of the couch, *my blackberry.* I held it admiring its dilapidated state, and realizing how insignificant it had become to me now. Just a few months prior I had hung on to every tweet, ring, and message it delivered; a portal to my elation, and now it had become the bearer of bad news, or no news at all.

I clicked the home button to check the time but the device was completely dead. Ordinarily I would have been running for the charger to bring it back to life, but now I couldn't care less. I threw it onto the ottoman and began checking my emails. My inbox was flooded with messages and I proceeded to skim through them, answering a few lines to appease each sender. Relieved my absence had gone virtually unnoticed, I threw myself into my work, focusing on one goal: *getting the commercials finished and moving on.*

The day soon turned to another lonely night, then day again, until a few days had come and gone. I remained inside Mikey's apartment, working, eating, and nursing my way back to reality. Unready to face anyone, even myself for that matter, I avoided my mobile, social networks and any human contact, even hiding in my room when Mikey had friends over. My hibernation had paid off work wise. Although Oliver and I were no longer on speaking terms, Leo and I had finished all the videos, and he was now dealing with the malicious butterball. A gesture I knew he offered in my fragile state, but of course never let on. The tumultuous relationship that had brought me to Greece was now severed *for good*. I was surprised at how low a thirty something year old miserable excuse for a man would stoop to avoid payment. The arguments had led to some profound name-calling and an exceedingly harsh exchange of words, and considering my state of mind Oliver heard a hell of a blasting. I took Jack up on his offer, had him invoice Oliver from his offshore account, and had Leo handle the rest. It was time to let go of the fragile girl who was co-dependant and lost, and regain control... *of me*.

A few days later I decided to rejoin the land of the living. I showered, blew out my hair nice and straight, and dressed in a pretty skirt and blouse. I recharged my blackberry and headed for the metro. There was something to be said about the outside world when you've been away from it for a while. The smell of the air, the look on people's faces, even the speed of the cars whizzing by; it all felt fresh and new, and different. As I headed down the steps of the red metro line, my blackberry began to vibrate and beep continuously. I had almost forgotten it was charged and in my purse. I reached to the bottom of my bag to see a screen full of messages; missed calls, and text messages. As I scrolled through the messages, a familiar number began to ring in my hand.

"Hello," I answered in an indifferent tone, no longer feeling connected to my once loyal device. "Bridget?" "Yes," I responded inquisitively. "Hi its Bobby, how are you?"

My heart sank. Weeks had past and all I got was 'how are you?' It was a clear sign I never meant a thing to him. Endless amounts of mixed emotions pumped through my body. Anything I would say would be laced with anguish, and I prayed I wouldn't break down. *Keep it together Bridget*!

"I'm good thank you, just busy with work. I'm getting paid soon and I'll be leaving." *Way to blurt that out Bridget*. I wanted to shock him, to hurt him, to leave him hanging as he had left me. "Is that why you haven't answered any of my calls or messages?" he asked in a calculated tone. "I haven't received any work emails if that's what you mean Bobby." "I've been calling you for the last few days," he went on. "Oh my phone? Oh, I almost forgot I had one," I said under my breath. "My phone's been, umm... it's been out of order." "Your blackberry's been out of order for a week?" he responded frustrated. Unprepared for his line of questioning, I tried avoiding the topic altogether. "I've been so busy trying to wrap up this project," I continued, "I haven't been able to translate what you need or..." "Forget about that Bridget" he interrupted, "I can do it on my own. When are you leaving?" "Soon, as soon as I can," I responded. "Well that sounds kinda dramatic to me Bridget." "It must be your imagination," I replied exuding some attitude. "I feel like I've had this conversation before Bridget," his tone no longer empathetic. "And why would you care when I'm leaving and how I'm doing Bobby?" "What?" he responded almost enraged. It was the first time I had heard Bobby sound so annoyed. I could no longer control myself, and decided to turn back up the escalator for better reception. "Listen Bobby," I began, "it's obvious you don't care about me, I mean that's quite clear now. You call me for work, and work alone, not to ask how I am, after all this time, and certainly not to see me! I assume you used me for whatever purpose and..." "I used you for what? Sex? Work?" he interrupted yelling this time. "I hate that term Bridget! I have never *used* anyone in my life - including that ungrateful ex-partner of mine, who ironically threw the term around the day we fought – that disloyal bastard!" "Oh I've heard all about your past partnership Bobby, and in some detail," I responded coyly. "What, how?" he replied in a puzzled and inquisitive tone. "Oh yes," I continued "I've heard you're quite the ladies man too Bobby. You really know how to fool them, and reel them in, don't you?! Oh and your business tactics are just deplorable! Taking advantage of a starving artist trying to make a living..." "Hold it right there lady! You've obviously been speaking to someone who has misinformed you! To backtrack for a moment Bridget, you are not, and never were my girlfriend – you are far from being my girlfriend!" His words were harsh, cruel almost, like sharp knives twisting through my heart. I had been quite the fool, an inexperienced American girl who barely knew how to float, yet swimming in a sea of sharks. I wanted to curl up on the street and sob, but as I looked down at the cold cement, the sight of my bruised knees and bloody hand brought me back to reality. *It's over Bridget! You've cried enough it's time to pick yourself up.*

"Oh really Bobby?" I responded angrily. "That's quite clear now, but you most certainly painted a different picture when we were 'dating'. Or maybe it's my fault, I'm sorry I guess there are different rules in the Mediterranean. I assumed we were actually dating over the several months we spent together... you remember don't you? The lunches, dinners, bars, trips, and endless nights in hotel rooms? Surely you remember those Bobby?! I sure remember your demands; 'stilettos on' were always a must, ring a bell? So how were all the others? Just as good? How long have you taken me for a fool?!"

"Bridget stop!" he yelled out. "No!" I replied now breathless; *he was wicked, cruel, and he needed to know it.* "Ironic you chose to send me the lyrics to Wicked Games Bobby... Did you take notes?!" "What? Look Bridget" he said sternly, "I don't want to hurt you, you're a great girl, but I was in a relationship for so many years and it didn't end well, and I don't want..." "Stop, just stop right there. I've heard enough," I interrupted. "You've clearly misled me and now back peddling." I expected a fight, some type of lover's quarrel or admittance that he had fallen for me and was just confused, but he would have no part of it. "You're acting like a disgruntled girlfriend over nothing Bridget! We barely had anything; it was nothing!"

His words penetrated me like bullets, each one hurling through a different part of my wounded soul. I grew more disoriented with every word he said. I actually thought I'd faint on the cobblestoned streets from the lack of blood rushing to my head. *Oh no you don't Bridget. You will not let this selfish man pull you back into darkness.*

"You know what Bobby, since you have admitted you were never exclusive or *even with me* for that matter, and you've made it clear I meant nothing to you after all this time, I'd say that makes you're a fucking philandering, asshole!" I had decided Bobby Siteros was a lost and tortured man with an ugly soul looking for retribution and glory to swathe his sorted past.

"What did you say?" he answered in a daunting voice. I decided to ignore him, continuing my rant, excited with my new self-confidence.

"I suppose if I took a peek into your social media networks I'd find you surfing for girls; sending likes, hearts, making plans, while I was waiting for you, cooking, catering to you like a fool!"

"Yes, I have female friends on the Internet I go out with; I suppose you've been researching," he added coyly.

The truth was I hadn't. Against my better judgment, and of course Vivian and Lea's, I had neglected to ever enter his name into cyber world afraid would contaminate anything we ever had. None of that, however mattered anymore, his voice said it all. Bobby had been living his life, having careless fun with other women while I waited at Mikey's pondering what the fuck I had done wrong. The thought of Bobby in a seedy motel with attention seeking skanky women made my stomach turn. *But I would not let him make me feel cheap!*

"So how many were there than? And where did I fit in!?"

 "Bridget, that's enough," he said sternly. "I would like to see you before you leave. We can go to my house in Taylor's Port."

"Oh that won't be necessary, I've been there, several times actually."

"What, how?"

"Not your house specifically, but the Port. My director lives and works from there, that's where I've been doing all my editing."

"What's his name?" he asked lowering his tone.

"I told you the day we met Bobby, but considering I've been so insignificant to you, I suppose you remember nothing."

"Just tell me his name Goddamit," he yelled out. I stood bewildered at his ingeniousness derogatory tone. It must be coming from the guilt.

"My director is Leonidas Papadopoulos." The other end of the line was silent. "He told me you were his partner Bobby, no need to worry I know about it all."

After a few more moments of silence he replied by asking me an assortment of questions.

"How long ago did this happen Bridget?"

"Obviously not very long ago Bobby. So how many were there?! You forgot to answer the first time I asked!" I yelled out now running down the escalator deciding to head back to the Metro's platform.

"What?!" he shouted back "speak up, you're breaking up."

"Forget it, I have to go," I answered back as the speedy silver metro approached the platform. "I'm losing reception…" he called out, "Bridget, wait don't hang up…" but before I knew it the metro had arrived, the line cut, and the phone went dead. Tossing the mobile back into my purse I imagined the hurtful exchange would be the last words I'd ever hear from Bobby Siteros; until of course I called him from the Central Athens police station later that night.

26

"He had square, almost cube like silver framed glasses and beady brown eyes. Oh and an orange T-shirt and jeans, and I think his phone was a Nokia…" Officer Stefanos Diakos sat across the long metal table taking notes, his legs crossed, his yellow stained fingers removing the Marlboro Reds from his mouth, incidentally blowing most of the smoke in my direction. "I guess there are no laws about second hand smoke in these parts," I murmured. "What?" he answered in his thick accent displaying a face of confusion, adding another cigarette butt to the jam-packed ashtray. "So let me get this straight," he said in a decipherable Greek accent, "this man, with the beady brown eyes and orange t-shirt, followed you throughout the metro station, then proceeded to videotape you as you rode up the escalator." "Actually to be more precise Officer, the pervert had placed the video camera up my skirt and was recording my panties as I rode the escalator and who knows when else!" "It happens," Officer Diakos replied in low-key fashion crossing his legs. "He could be a crazy pervert part of an illegal porn team or even worse prostitution ring connected to hard drugs and the mafia!"

"You have quite the imagination Miss Lane; I can't file a report, but we will keep an eye out for him, or others, especially at the metro stations. You should call someone to come and pick you up, just so you feel safe tonight. It's more psychological warfare then anything else." "That makes sense Officer, but it's just… my cousin is at work pulling another all-nighter and I don't…" "Perhaps you have a distant relative, or a friend, anyone?" he interrupted. As I sat in the uncomfortable metal chair trying to decide what to do, my blackberry tweeted from inside my purse:

Bobby: Bridget are you alright? I just finished work. We should speak.

I didn't want to admit it, but I was stuck somewhere in between love and loathe, and was relieved to hear from him, especially now. I began to type a reply:

Athens Bridget: Bobby are you able to come and get me, I'm at the central Athens police station.

Moments later, my blackberry began to ring. "Yes, hello," I whispered brining the device up to my ear. "Tell me you're alright?" Bobby blurted authoritatively. "Yes, I'm fine, the officer just thought I'd be better off if someone picked me up and took me home, and Mikey is working overnight…" "I'll be there in 20 minutes" he replied in my mid-sentence "and stay inside the building Bridget," he added sternly. His voice was firm, and I wasn't sure if he was annoyed from the previous altercation or my current mess. All the same, he was concerned with my safety, a common trait known to locals, especially to foreigners, they called it 'filoksenia,' being hospitable was the closest interpretation Mikey had offered. Nevertheless, it was something I no longer misinterpreted for Bobby's love or friendship.

*

Bobby was pretty prompt in picking me up and taking me to Mikey's. The mood was tense, unquestionably different than any past encounters. He even looked different. His hair now longer, reached the base of his neck; curling at the bottom and his face displayed a full-grown beard. He looked strikingly handsome in casual attire, jeans, and a t-shit, and although I had no intention of ever seeing him again, I wanted to leap into his arms the moment I did. That quickly changed however, once I was in the familiar passenger seat of his Audi.

"You're cold Bridget," Bobby said glancing over at me at a red light. "Yes," I answered sneezing uncontrollably. The night had turned quite chilly, and my skirt and blouse had become an inadequate source of warmth. "There may be a tissue in there," he responded solemn as ever, pointing to the open glove compartment box. The small space was overflowing with receipts and paperwork, and I began to shift everything around in search of a tissue. I know longer felt comfortable prying through Bobby's private space, if I ever had, that is. I was not

168

his girlfriend, something he had made exceptionally clear; in fact I had no place in his life, except for the helpless rescue call.

I reached in for what felt like a small tissue box, and pulled out a familiar rectangular blue package. Durex condoms. "Nice," I exhaled with a disappointing sigh. "Always ready for a rainy day, huh Bobby?" I felt the blood rush to my head, while the urge to swat him right in the face grew more intense. "They're mine. I mean ours; from the last time at the hotel remember? We got into an argument, and only used one. Open the box, there are two left in there." I remembered that night distinctively, but it was Bobby that was mistaken, or utterly lying. We hadn't fought; in fact it was good old fashion rejection. I opened the box, a sick feeling lurking in my stomach. *What would it matter now anyhow?* A box of condoms was a few measly Euros and sold on every street corner; and nothing Bobby could say, would take back what I had discovered from Leo; I threw the blue box back into the glove box, *fuck it, what was done, was done.* I turned towards the driver's seat, my emotions bouncing up and down on the yo-yo string Bobby was pulling with a sole finger.

"So you met Leo," he said in a playful voice. "No I didn't *just meet him* actually, we've been working together since before I arrived in Athens. He's been my director, my editor, my friend" I replied matter-of-factly. "Ha-ha," he laughed sarcastically, "oh so you think, Bridget, Leo is not a bad guy, but his interest is within himself and his priorities, let me assure you. He's you're director because you're his client, your editor because he can't afford one, and your friend because you're paying him. That, and he may be trying to sleep with you; that fool, never did have any game. Sadly I know him oh too well. Did he tell you we spent the night in jail together?" His coyness was annoying and almost alarming. He was one cold hearted, sarcastic son of a bitch.

"Sure did, I've heard it all, the women, the partying, the lies, and of course the dissolution of the company." "The women?" Bobby responded with an ironic giggle. "Leo couldn't get laid if his life depended on it." "Bobby, I know about all the women, *and your* women, the cheating, the one night stands, the control issues and..." "Oh is that what he told you?" he sneered cutting me off in mid sentence. I had obviously hit a nerve Bobby wanted to address. "Guys do stupid things when they're young Bridget, and there are a large

169

amount of women that make them selves readily available for that to happen." "Oh I'm sure about that Bobby, no need to go into detail." "Simmer down there Bridget," he responded sternly. "As far as cheating goes, you know I've had three relationships, but there were a lot of breakups and make-ups in between, and yes other women, who, well I didn't date but I suppose you could say, had fun with. However, when I'm with someone, I'm with someone; I've already told you, I don't throw around the word girlfriend."

Oh God make it stop! I couldn't wait for him to close his cocky mouth and shut up! It was settled, he was the king of manipulation. "Well you sure throw around enough 'my baby', 'my love', 'kisses' and other crap to mislead innocent parties Bobby," I mumbled. Although I thought I had whispered the words under a deep breath, *I had clearly not.*

"What did you say?!" he snapped. "I can hear your words under your breath Bridget!" "Well I didn't realize I said that aloud Bobby," I answered rolling my eyes at him as he turned away. It was a childish habit – well that and sticking my tongue out in annoyance that had brought back a rush of passionate memories from the last seven months.

I couldn't remember the last time I had had a good laugh, and I desperately needed its healing powers. I wanted to laugh, cry and scream out at once; and it was at that instant that I realized I was more fucked up then ever. I wasn't in love, but I loved this drug, the rush, the excitement, the climax, and of course the high. My body tingled just thinking about it. The aftermath of course was always destructive, but I didn't want to think about it, just this once, I wanted to breath and let go, even if it meant putting my guard down with Bobby, just for a moment.

*

Bobby parked the car without asking me if he could come upstairs, and proceeded to escort me inside the apartment. It wasn't nothing like before, I didn't run to the kitchen to make him something to eat, offer him brownies or even water. "I need to take a shower," he said without hesitation starring into my eyes, "there's plenty of hot water, go ahead," I answered. Maybe fighting is what Greek men did to get grounded; I had no clue what was going on or what I was feeling, but for the first

170

time since I had met Bobby Siteros I didn't care. Did going with the flow ever hurt anyone anyways? Visions of desperate addicts feeding off toxic substances came to mind. *Perhaps one last hit would give me the closure I needed to move on?*

I sifted through my dresser drawer while Bobby took his time showering, something I remembered fondly. Not knowing exactly what I was looking for, I stopped cold at the site of my unworn Victoria Secret pink nighty. It was sheer lace, and very short. I held it up to the light looking at its sheer 'provocateur-ness', pondering. I made my way to the kitchen looking for a shot of anything that would take the edge off; vodka it was. Returning to my adopted room, I pushed my skirt to my ankles, than pulled my shirt over my head. Standing in my bra and panties, I turned to the mirror, admiring my new shape, before unclasping my bra and tossing it aside, than slipping the nighty over my head. I reached for my stiletto salmon pumps, slowly placing my feet into them, recalling the pain they had inflicted during my trip to Samos. *This was crazy. What the fuck was I thinking?!* I panicked making my way back to my closet sorting through clothes to cover the revealing short gown.

"Shouldn't you be waiting at the door in matching fishnets and an overcoat?" Bobby's voice was sarcastic to say the least. He had entered the room looking just the way he used to when we were together; wet slicked hair, a towel wrapped around his soiled body and a fierce look in his honey brown eyes. *You can do this Bridget. You're a grown woman for Christ's sake.* "Never satisfied with me are you Bobby?" "I didn't say that Bridget. There you go reading into things too much, you're body looks great," he said taking a step forward. "Your entitled to your opinion," I said taking a step back. "I never said I didn't want you Bridget," he whispered grabbing me from the back of my hair, jolting my head back. "Let go of me!" I said sternly pulling his grip from my head and finally my face.

"What happened to your there?" he said pointing to the cuts and bruises on my right hand. "Oh these," I replied shyly, almost forgetting about my furious outrage. "The washroom fan, it wasn't working so I..." "so you decided to beat it up?" he added with a furrowed brow.

171

"Something like that, I didn't know your family made those too," I murmured changing the subject swiftly. "My dad had a stake in that business years ago, way before he got into anything else. Bridget, I… I'm sorry if I hurt you," he said, bringing my wounded hand towards his beard. "Don't, just don't, and stop looking at me like that." "Like what?!" he answered starring deeper at me. "You know that look, stop looking at me so hard in the eyes. It's different now," I responded almost in rage. "The game's over, there ain't no love here," I responded turning away from his suffocation.

"Look at me!" he urged grabbing my arm turning me swiftly towards him.

"I liked you, I wanted you, I still do, but it was just too much too fast, you were running, and I was…" "Stop it, I'm not going to listen to this! It's not fair!" I yelled, frantic to get out of his breath, his reach. "I was no where near running, you chased me remember?!" I continued, not stomping in my salmon pumps; and your, your disgusting sorted past! You were not real! You know very well you fucked with my head Bobby!" "Bridget, I would have never gone out with you if I didn't like you, or felt something. My past, however, it didn't end well …" "Stop Bobby! Enough! Shut the fuck up! I don't want to hear anymore about your fucking ex-girlfriend and how she fucked you up – because obviously she did! And no more about how much you liked me ok? It's done!"

I turned away from him wanting to run out of the room when he pulled me back with force and kissed me hard. "What are you doing?!" I yelled pushing him back. "I hate you!" I shrieked pulling away again trying to leave his embrace this time smacking him on the chest. "You used to love that spot," he said pointing to the red mark I had left on his skin. "I don't love you Bobby, I never did," I replied starring right into those eyes that had fooled me so well, and hurt me so bad. Revealing a smirk-like smile he lifted his hand to my face, the back of his fingers caressing my warm cheek, then yanked my hair back with his other hand. I yearned to spit in his face, slap him again, and run, but instead I stood motionless. "Come here baby," he said pulling me closer to him, and it was at that very moment that I gave in.

Bobby kissed me furiously and I in turn kissed him back, swirling my tongue in and around his mouth, touching his face, holding his head in my hands passionately. Leaning towards me he grabbed me by the behind lifting me in mid air allowing me to straddle him before throwing me on the unmade bed. He dropped atop of me fully erect and reached into his jean pocket, pulling out the tiny package that had infuriated me less than a half hour earlier. Bobby didn't waste any time moving my skimpy panty to one side, pushing his fingers inside me. I didn't say a word this time. I wanted him to take off my clothes, just this once, *take them all off,* and feel his bare body against mine, but he continued to push away different parts of my nighty to kiss my breasts, feel my body, and then penetrate me. He was thrusting into me over and over again keeping me pinned on my back. I opened my legs as wide as I could to feel him, for what I knew would be the last time. "Let me move," I called out. "No," he replied swiftly, kissing me hard in between deep breaths. Apparently, Bobby wanted me to remain in the missionary position, while he pounded into me over and over again, kissing me harder each time, his lips only leaving mine to kiss my breasts, then coming back to my mouth. There would be no room for words tonight; it felt like the end of a beautiful war, only there would be no apparent victor.

Bobby's touch persisted to be fierce, and excluding what I knew was the passion in his eyes, he was completely emotionless. Those warm brown eyes that never could hide anything, and had put me in this predicament in the first place. When he came, he was quick and quiet, and I needed him to stay inside me, just for an instant. "Stay," I whispered, as he dropped his sweaty forehead on my chest, "just for a moment longer," "no," he replied coldly "it's not a good idea," pulling out carefully. He propped himself up off the bed, glanced at me, then headed for the bathroom.

I decided not to watch Bobby walk away; instead I repositioned the frayed nighty over my body and turned my back to the door, starring at the beautiful city view. The lights twinkled brightly, and I watched them dwindle through the glass as I curled into a ball holding myself under the comforter, never once moving, or looking back.

27

"You are a paid woman Bridget!" Jack's voice rang through my laptop speaker like an early morning fire truck siren. "The money arrived this morning safe and sound in my Swiss account – the entire amount. I'll have it wired to you by end of day." There was no messing around when it came to Jack and business, in fact his efficiency had become an unfamiliar gesture in these parts. "I can't thank you enough Jack! You really are a life saver," I replied in the most upbeat tone I had heard myself in weeks. "You don't have to thank me Bridget, just please never ever do business without a contract again, promise me." It was the least of the promises I needed to make to Jack. I wanted to tell him what a good a friend he was, a wonderful person, and how much more I appreciated him now, now that I had met the vindictive alter ego of man. "I promise Jack," I muttered softly recalling the last few months of my life.

Almost 7 months had passed since I had arrived in the Mediterranean, but it felt more like years. I was forever a changed woman, mentally, physically, and emotionally, having at the very least, attained *some* self-recognition, regardless of how painful it was. I could no longer attribute my horrible choices in men to lack of experience and being chosen by unfit partners; *I knew I had chosen them.* Men like Bobby, who made the task of loving him, increasingly difficult, and of course would never love me back, had one thing in common; they were all emotionally unavailable. I chose to date men that could not genuinely love me, and by the time I had realized why, it was far too late. I had avoided real love, to avoid real loss. It was a horrific cycle that this time, had resulted in addiction, an addiction to affection, attention, or perhaps the incessant pursuit. Now leaving Athens on the brink of summer, I had closed the longest chapter of my life, and was ready to begin a new one.

"I'll be flying out British Airways Jack. There is a layover, and ..." "I will be there to pick you up," he interrupted, "send me all the flight info, we are going to have a proper evening out this time." I had expected nothing more from Jack, and was genuinely excited about his proposal. "That would be great Jack, but I know you're so busy and...." "I don't want any further discussion about this Bridget, I will be there," he said sternly. I knew better than to continue the conversation, and I really did want to see Jack and thank him for everything he'd done for me, even though the thought of him and his *'new person'* was less than comforting. Elated, I thanked him again, promising to send my flight info, and ended the Skype call to continue my packing.

I must have spent the entire last month getting ready for this day; one month to the day, since I last saw Bobby, and un-coincidentally that I booked my ticket home. I spent every day since then, tossing out, and giving away anything that held a memory of the last seven months. I wrapped up my beloved faux fur marking the clear bag it sat in with MaryAnne's name, then sat on the edge the stripped mattress holding my salmon spiked pumps in my hands.

Vivian's advice was one thing, but seeing it through, well that required an entirely different effort. As I pondered what to do with the memorable stilettos, images of Bobby raced through my mind, caused a burning sensation throughout my body starting with my head. I was leaving Athens tomorrow and it was time to leave the first part of the year just where it belonged, buried in a pile of ashes I wished I could throw in the bottomless sea that surrounded me.

At times I pondered leaving the beauty of the Mediterranean in the brink of summer. Perhaps staying with Uncle Dmitri would be fun, but he was off to Italy for a series of performances in *San Remo*, and waiting around alone was not an option for me. Uncle Dmitri had suggested renting a house on a island and waiting for Vivian and Lea to join me while he toured, but the isolation of the past 7 months had gotten to me, and I had absolutely no intention of spending another dreadful moment alone.

I had begun to suffer from severe headaches and panic attacks, which had even landed me in a Greek emergency room on a few occasions. I had passed through nurses, doctors and even neurologists, who all found my unanimous diagnosis quite boring, *chronic anxiety*.

I recalled the Doctor's words clearly. "You know Miss Lane, people here are dying, and you're visiting us once a week with a headache, take some Zanex and have a drink, this is Greece after all, you are much to stringent with yourself."

They sure were quite quick to prescribe anti-anxiety antidotes, but I was weary about taking anything that would alter my natural state *again*. I had gone through a short sprint of that in College, but had since learned to control my anxiety, *or so I thought*. Jack, who was incidentally the only person I spoke to about the last month's issues, had talked me through my anxiety and out of taking any pills. *Well for the most part anyway*. The nights leading up to my departure were either sleepless or filled with nightmares, so I made a few exceptions; without some shut-eye I'd never be able to get myself together to leave.

Mary-Anne's photos and wall decor were barely visible to me now; the room had its own memories; a few of them passed through my mind as I reached for the glass of water and Zanex from the vacant dresser. I sat on the undressed mattress starring at the ceiling. The walls once coated in laughter, lust, and new beginnings, were now drenched in pain, tears and hurtful endings. I popped the pill into my mouth and took a few gulps of water, before dropping the salmon pumps onto the floor. "The pain will fade with the memories," Jack had said after one of my anxiety attacks. Little did he know the pain ran much deeper than the headaches and the memories embedded in my mind. Closing my eyes I reached for the light switch I had kicked off in passion on so many occasions, carefully grasping it, and flipping it off for one last time.

28

"One way to Chicago via London Miss?" "Yes, that's correct," I answered to the *Mrs. Doubtfire look-a-like* British Airways rep checking me in. "You're a little over the luggage allowance dear, but I'll let it slide, just this once," she smiled. "Thank you Ma'am, it's the jeans, they get me every time." "Frequent flyer I see dear?" "Used to be. PR girl, well I was, the jeans they're like a kilo a piece." "That's right dear, and now?" "Now?" I responded puzzled. "Did you give up the PR for a family, what are you doing now dear?" The blood must have rushed to my face causing me to blush, because Mrs. Doubtfire's eyes softened and treaded down to me gently. Keeping my eyes on my luggage I took a deep breath before answering; "I guess, chasing rainbows Ma'am." She smiled, pushing up her glasses on the wide bridge of her nose, before looking down at the computer. "Aisle seat ok dear?" "Yes, that's perfect," I responded in delight, hoping she'd taken a liking to me, and placed me around a few vacant seats for some excess leg room.

"You know, it only comes after the rain Miss Lane, usually heavy down pours." I looked past her thick librarian glasses, into her baby blue eyes, retrieving my passport. "The rainbow dear. It appears after some tumultuous conditions, but it does come." *Mrs. Doubtfire* smiled handing over my boarding pass, "Gate C dear, the gate is open, safe travels." I walked away bewildered recalling the past seven months, and conceivably the series of foreshadowing events I had endured.

I walked briskly, pulling my carry on luggage with one arm, and pulling up my belt-less jeggings with the other. I spotted Gate C and waited at the back of a short line to hand over my boarding pass and enter the private seating area. The customs agent was in my eyes view; there were a few passengers in front of me, the first of which holding up the line with an apparent expired passport. "I'm in a rush!" called out a rather large woman dressed in a velour pink tracksuit. "Yeah we all are lady - it's an airport!" called out another traveler. My attention was swayed from the small altercation breaking out at the boarding Gate, by the sound of a familiar voice. "The lighting won't work there, it needs to be on a flat non-reflective surface." The conversation was between a young dark haired man who was conversing with a group of engineers and what looked like an airport executive in the far East side of the terminal. He was in a white hooded sweatshirt and jeans, with multi-colored sneakers and wore a yellow lanyard around his neck. A quarter turn and gasp later, I had confirmed *it was Bobby*. There he was, the friend, the lover, the manipulator, the liar. Close enough to run too, and far enough to hide from. I was torn between calling out his name, and hiding behind a soda vendor. Luckily, my two-inch mary-jane's had made the decision for me. Firmly screwed to the ground below me, they made sure I wasn't going anywhere. From the looks of it Bobby was doing well. I admired his tenacity; he was surely the youngest in the bunch and taking the lead. That was Bobby in his finest hour, where he knew exactly what he wanted, and made it happen.

"Hello Miss, you're holding up the line, we need to get everyone onto the mini bus on the tarmac. Are you ready to board or do you need some more time?" The customs agent looked at me reaching out his hand for my boarding pass and identification. "Uh um I don't know just a minute," I answered pondering if I should I run to him for one last hug, and one last goodbye. "*You're not my girlfriend Bridget - it was nothing…*" A variety of memories raced through my head, causing it to start to throb and burn again. "*The rainbow only appears after tumultuous times dear…heavy rainfalls.*" *Goddamit why me?! Why now?! Why couldn't you just fucking love me Bobby?!* I began to choke on my tears as I moved away from the line. *No!* It was too late and I was never going to see any light running back into the rain.

"Miss, I need to get these passengers through, are you ready now, or would you like to wait?" I starred into the officer's piercing eyes pondering my own fate. "No!" I replied with a gasp, "I don't want to stay I'm ready to go," handing over the boarding pass and my passport.

"Are you coming back Miss? One-way?"

"One-way Sir."

He grabbed my passport and looked at his screen; "seventh of January, until …wow," he said stamping a blank page of my passport, and handing it back with a smile. "I see you've been with us for seven months to the day. How was your stay Miss Lane?" I grabbed my passport and inhaled a deep breath before turning to face the awaiting bus, "rainy Officer."

29

I had only been here once before, but Heathrow Airport felt familiar and bizarrely comfortable. I scoured the terminal for Jack, wired from the events leading up to my departure and the sleepless flight. Collecting my luggage and going through British customs was quicker than I imagined so I figured I was early. I propped my unmatched pair of suitcases against the emergency exit, and reached into my Puma bag scrambling for my aged blackberry. The cracker wrappers and lollypop sticks created a fort for the device, but I eventually found it. Pushing away the crumbs from the screen, I held the power button, waiting for the mobile to light up. "You know you really should get an I-phone, it does everything for you." I looked up to see two navy blue eyes starring back at me, "Jack!"

He looked just he had seven months earlier, perhaps with a little more color in his cheeks. He was in a dark suit this time, and from the looks of it, it was Hugo Boss complete with a silver tie, and tailored to fit his slim physique. I jumped up to hug him, partially taking him by surprise nearly throwing him off balance. "It's so good to see you Jack, a friendly face, I mean." "You too Bridget, looks like the Mediterranean agrees with you, you look amazing. Your hair is longer, and lighter too, I guess you've been hitting the beach, that would explain your glow as well." I forgot how meticulous Jack was, and how attentive. I blushed at the series of compliments, forgetting what it felt like to feel adored by someone. "Thanks Jack! I attempted some hot Athens Yoga classes." "Well you definitely look a lot better than you sounded," he continued. "I was worried there for a while." "I'm ok Jack, better now; that chapter is closed." "Glad to hear it," he said putting his arm around me. "Well let's get you out on the town and enjoying some of London."

*

We walked to the fourth floor of the parking garage where Jack led me to a two-door, black BMW with tinted windows. I stood by the passenger's side while Jack loaded my luggage into the trunk all the while thankful he hadn't arrived in an Audi. "Bridge?" "Yeah Jack," I answered inquisitively, are you planning on driving?" "Oh God, why what's wrong?" I answered in panic "don't they drive on the other side of the road here?! I won't be able to complete right turns…" "Precisely my thoughts," he said chuckling, "than you might want to get around to the other side, the driver's side is opposite here too." I peered inside the tinted windows to see a large black leather steering wheel staring back at me, "oops," I said blushing.

Part of me still couldn't believe this was my old friend Jack, the Jack that asked me out, time and time again, the Jack that was my friend unconditionally, and the Jack that was no longer available. He looked incredibly handsome, not to mention powerful, behind the wheel of a sports car, but I had no intention of ever letting him know I thought so. He had moved on, and I was no home-wrecker, besides that, he had obviously lost any romantic interest in me, and was merely coming to the aid of a hopeless friend. "Bridget, stop thinking about whatever it is you're thinking. It's over now. You're safe, everything will be ok," he said laying his hand over top mine for a split second. Little did he know, I felt perfectly safe with him, and it wasn't Athens I was thinking about at all. "Deal," I replied with a smile. "How far is your flat?" "We're almost there," he said as serious as ever, ripping the sports car into the next gear, passing over a few lanes.

A few moments later he was pulling up into a mid-town area with a row of town houses and low-rise apartments. "That's me," he said, pointing, to the building furthest on the right side of a long block. It was a boutique style condominium with perfectly placed pot lights and flowers surrounding the freshly cutgrass and a neatly paved walkway. Jack pulled up and placed the hazards on, jumping out quickly to grab my bags. "Follow me Bridget. I'm going to take you upstairs, then park underground," he explained.

Jack's apartment was on the 9th floor, and was the quintessential bachelor pad. A one-bedroom chic and stylish flat furnished mostly in black leather furniture, and a huge flat screen TV acting as living room's center- piece. "Make yourself at home I'll be right back," he said grabbing the bags from my hand and placing them on the ground before running out the front door. *Did he just caress my hand?* It felt like he caressed my hand purposely as he grabbed my bags...*Snap out of it girl, he is a gentleman, and he is taken!*

I walked slowly through the apartment; the walls were bare except for a few minimalistic paintings and Jack's framed degrees showcased on the pale blue walls. His MBA from the University of London, along with his undergraduate degree from the London school of economics and political science hung in wooden frames above the fireplace in the den. There were no pictures with friends, girlfriends, or family. I didn't expect to see any sentimental portraits, but secretly hoped I'd find a photo or two of his significant other. The kitchen was chrome silver, the refrigerator, stove, and microwave perfectly matching, and there wasn't a dish in the sink or utensil on display. I opened the refrigerator to find it pretty empty except for the classic evidence of a take-out guru, ketchup, mustard, mayo, salad dressing, *and some vodka.*

"Hungry Bridge?" Jack had returned and I hadn't noticed him standing in the front door. "Oh you startled me, I didn't hear you come in," I said closing the refrigerator door. "Food would be good. I was kinda fidgety on the plane – didn't eat or sleep much." "Dinner out it is then, and yes you look like you could use a good meal." "I wasn't eating much in Athens..." It was the sound of my own voice that brought me back to reality. Bobby had fucked with my head, he was a master manipulator who had convinced me I needed fixing, but the truth was he was the broken one after all. Jack stood starring at me as I fidgeted with my handbag, uncomfortable with the thoughts in my own head. "Yes that's obvious Bridget," "what is?" "That you weren't eating much in Athens." "Oh yes, that. Well, I was stressed and..." Stumbling on what I wanted to reveal, I decided to keep my love affair with Bobby undisclosed. "Bridget you're always beautiful you don't need to diet," he added clutching my face with his hands and kissing me on the cheek. *Oh my.* I felt my body tingling starting with my toes; "Jack, I, I...I want to treat dessert," I said smiling broadly, "you need to take me somewhere with a lot of chocolate." *Desert? Chocolate? Jesus Bridget is that the best you could do?!*

"Deal," Jack said chuckling. "I wouldn't mind changing either Jack." My jeggings and mary-janes had done the trick for the flight, but weren't exactly the look I was striving for, for my London debut. "Take your time, I've got some work to do, use my bedroom and let me know when you're ready to go," he said, his calm disposition putting me at ease. I opened the heavy dark wood door to Jack's bedroom, bringing the larger suitcase of the two with me. The walls were a pale green, the large chrome framed bed was perfectly constructed, and covered in a silver & black pinstriped duvet with a combination of different sized black and grey satin pillows. It looked more like a showroom than a bachelor pad, or perhaps what a bachelor pad actually looked like. I giggled with my own naive outlook, thinking how much the bedding reminded me of one of Jack's power suits.

I opened the tattered red suitcase and rummaged through the mess of clothes and shoes until I pulled out a rolled up black dress. I held it up high allowing it to unravel and eventually drop to the ground. It was a floor length black cotton dress with cut outs placed strategically on both sides, finished off with a long gold zipper in the back; a current fashion trend I had only previously dreamed of wearing. I had noticed the dress in a boutique's window and had bought it to attend an evening out with Bobby. I envisioned us sipping wine on the rooftop of the Acropolis museum, my hair blowing in the wind, the hem of the black dress dragging against the concrete. We'd be rubbing elbows with European movie moguls, as I pitched my beloved film ideas with great passion *for the hundredth time*. The night however never came, and just like many things in Athens the fantasy had quietly subsided and eventually disappeared.

Stop! Get out of my head! Thoughts of Bobby made my head start to pound again. Snap out of it Bridget! I looked into the full-length mirror behind Jack's door, holding the dress against my frame; this dress was just too pretty to waste. Once I got back home, I knew I'd be back in my Victoria's Secret sweats and UGGS, and would have no use for this beautiful dress. I shook off my momentary stoop of self-pity and placed the dress over my head, twisting it forward to firmly seal the gold zipper. Luckily the straps were adjustable, allowing me to configure my abundant bust in just the right places. I slipped on my black pumps, and loosened the elastic from my ponytail, allowing my highlighted blonde locks to fall way down the base of my back. I massaged some moisturizer into my sun kissed face, and topped off my mascara with a fresh coat, then grabbed my favorite night clutch. For the first time in over 7 months, I felt no pressure to be perfect, suck it in, take an hour perfecting my makeup or drink obsessively to mentally prepare myself; and ironically I felt better than ever. I tossed my clothes into the suitcase, slammed it shut and exited the bedroom.

"Ready Jack," I announced, entering the den. He had his back turned towards me and was typing away an email, his suit jacket hanging perfectly from the back of his leather chair. "Great Bridge, I'll be right there," he replied rocking slightly back in forth in his chair; a trait I remembered fondly during our Skype conversations. I grabbed some lip balm from my purse as I was waiting, and dug my finger in to scoop up a small dollop, pressing it against my pink lips. "I made reservations at…" he started as he turned around. "Yes, where Jack?" "What?" he answered looking straight at me, his eyes wide and deep blue. "You were just saying you made reservations but didn't say where." "Yeah… I was saying…I'm sorry Bridget, I was a little taken back by umm…" "Oh no, it's the dress, you hate it, it's all wrong isn't it? I had bought it for a special occasion but I…" "No, no, that's not what I meant, not at all. You just, I mean, you went in looking like… and now you… you look incredible Bridge – gorgeous actually." Taken back by Jack's reaction, I felt the blood rushing to my face, and my hands starting to tingle. "Really, it's ok?" "It's perfect" he said coming closer, his smell a combination of spice and bark and primrose, manly and strong.

"Listen," *yes Jack, take me in your arms and tell me how you feel…* "I can see you're in deep thought," he continued *little do you know Jack!* "The dress may hold some memories for you, perhaps some hurt, but you're in a new place, you need to dust it off and leave it all where it belongs, in the past. That chapter is closed, and you're ok now. You were supposed to wear this dress *here, tonight* – nowhere else but here, and now."

I don't know how he did it, but he always knew the exact right thing to say. *I love you Jack.* I wanted to leap into his arms and tell him that, and hug him until he peeled me away, but my fantasy went sour when he gave me a quick wink and tap on the chin. He might as well have been a proud baseball coach at this point, sending me back into the dugout after a motivating pep talk. "Let's go I've made reservations at the most famous Italian place in town," he commanded grabbing his pristine suit jacket from the chair, "you *are* hungry Bridget?" "*Starved,*" I replied with a grin.

185

30

Apparently *Cipriani's* was an infamous Italian restaurant with several international locations. Jack was quite cultured about food and wine, carefully explaining the legacy of the restaurant and cuisine. The restaurant was located in the heart of Mayfair, a few steps away from the most elegant shopping I had ever seen. The atmosphere was elegant yet electric, and the bar had a diverse variety of visitors and Londoners, quite the international clientele.

"Do you like it?" asked Jack. "Like it? Closer to love Jack." London was far off from the Mediterranean style taverns I had experienced in the last seven months. "The menu is pretty traditional Italian, it originated in Venice," he continued, it's a hot spot for celebs too. "Oh that would explain the photographers lurking around outside, I thought maybe they were for us," I added with a giggle. "Well they could very well someday be for you Bridget, just keep focusing on your dreams and one day they will become reality, don't let anyone steer you off-course."

There he went again, telling me exactly what I needed to hear. It was almost torture having someone so great and so inaccessible around me. Jack ordered a three-course meal for us both, and a great bottle of Italian wine. We ate and drank and laughed for what felt like hours. "We can't leave without some dessert Bridge, hope you saved some room." The truth was I couldn't eat another bite, but the thought of leaving Jack made me incredibly sad. "Of course," I answered, you know how much I love…" "Yup, chocolate, its already on it's way – triple layer chocolate cake, dig in," he said smiling, showing off his beautiful pearly teeth. Jack called over the waiter after we had finished dessert and polished off the bottle of wine, handing over his credit card. "I hope its not too expensive Jack, I don't want you spending your money on me." "It's nothing Bridget, it's a company expense." That was Jack, he sure knew how to take the wind out of my sails. *What the heck was I complaining about?! He wasn't leading me on, or playing games, what did I want to hear, lies?* We were friends, and he had just paid for a very expensive dinner and I should be more very thankful. "Thank you Jack, dinner was wonderful," I said standing up from the table. As I made it to my feet, the room began to spin and I lost my footing, just barely catching myself by hanging on to the chair. *Oh my goodness, I was drunk.*

"You're very welcome Bridge, are you ready?" "Oh yes," I said with a chuckle. "What's so funny, you alright?" "Um Jack, I don't drink, I mean, I usually don't drink, I have a very low tolerance," I added laughingly. "Bridget are you bloody drunk?" "Why yes Sir, I'm afraid I am," I replied chuckling in a British accent. "Oh my word, I know that face, and that 'Sir' bit oh too well Bridget Lane." "Oops," I responded laughing away. "This should be interesting" he said holding me up, "let's go, the night is young." "Where to Mr. Nichols?" "I think we have some time to hit Soho perhaps a pub, although in your state…" "In my state, dancing would be much more appropriate," I said grabbing his hand and leading him towards the exit.

*

Apparently, the closest and coolest nightclub in Mayfair was a place called *Babble*, and according to Jack, quite appropriate for me tonight considering I had become quite the motor mouth. Babble was on the edge of Berkeley Square, and a known hotspot for Saturday night club-goers. "I think you're going to like it Bridget, it has a long list of exotic wines," he added with a sarcastic smile. *Man there's nothing sexier than that sarcastic smile!* "Very funny Jack," I responded careful not to disclose any emotion as we bypassed the line-up. "Did you grease the doorman or something?" "Not exactly, I entertain clients here quite a bit." *So you do have a wild side after all Jack Nichols…let's see what else I'll find out tonight!* The club looked like a modern version of something found in Scarface; multi-colored neon lights over high rise glass tables, complete with waitresses in solid gold dresses and short blonde wigs. I imagined myself in a long green satin gown, a short blonde bob with bangs, dancing to 1980's disco music; Jack aspiring to dance alongside me, amongst a group of hording fans, pursuing me until I was his. My fantasy however was quickly interrupted with a few pushes and shoves from the crowd. Perhaps I wasn't Michelle Pfeiffer, but regardless *I was a new me.*

"I'll grab a table Bridge, follow me," Jack ordered politely placing his hand on the base of my back. We sat in a corner table, outfitted with white leather couches and sparkling Mastiqua water. "It's water made from Mastika." "Mastika?" I answered confused. "Oh I thought you may have heard about it in Greece, "it's a resin gathered from trees that only grown in the Mediterranean, – it has some unique health properties, used in ancient times - it's pretty amazing." *You're pretty amazing Jack.* His intellect and caring demeanor was quite refreshing. I guess this is what boyfriends should be like, but what did I know. "It's better for you than purified water, here try some," he offered. "Are you trying to sober me up?" "Well you do have a plane to catch at some point," he responded with raised eyebrows. "I'll be fine Jack," I said grabbing the glass and gulping down some of the water. He was afraid of something, but what was it? *Just what are you hiding Jack Nichols?*

My thoughts were interrupted by the sight of an oncoming waitress carrying a sparkling platinum tray with a bottle of wine, and two glasses. "I thought we should stick to the same if that's alright," Jack said pouring some wine into the glasses. It was perfect; and I expected nothing more than that from Jack. I smiled saying nothing. "Cheers," he said, holding up his glass, to …" "To London!" I interrupted, "to making this night last forever!" I gulped as much as my stomach could withstand before grabbing Jack by the arm. "Let's dance!" Surprisingly Jack didn't hesitate much, that or my strength had severely increased under the influence of Italian wine. The dance floor was packed with a mix of who I assumed, were well-dressed Londoners and European visitors swaying to the sounds of soulful music pouring over the speakers; it was the perfect blend of rhythm and blues and Motown. I danced in what I felt was slow motion, holding my wine glass in one hand and my studded clutch in the other. The dry ice obstructed my vision from time to time, but the neon lights always led the way back to the table, the wine, *and of course Jack.*

What felt like a lifetime later, I had lost any concept of time, and eventually location and setting, the only thing I knew was that I was free, and finally happy. Before I knew it, the bottle of wine was empty and Jack was escorting me to the ladies room. "It's almost closing time Bridge," Jack called out as I went for a final round on the dance floor. "Are you ok to walk to the cab?" he asked with a concerned look. I wondered what he'd say if I said 'no'. Considering I was intoxicated and in five inch heels, I'd have no choice but to do just that. "How

189

about a piggy back ride?" I replied with a smirk. There was something to be said about good old-fashioned liquid confidence. Before I knew it I had wrapped my legs around the front of Jack's body and was hanging onto his tie with both hands, balancing my head on his right shoulder. "You know people are much heavier when drunk," I said slurring the words out as best I could. "People or you?" Jack replied chuckling. "Ok we're getting into the cab now, watch your head," he added with concern, carefully placing me into the back seat of the black taxi.

I must have dozed off during the taxi ride back to Jack's because the street, elevator, and apartment entry were all a blur. I did however feel my head hitting the cold satin pillow, and the warmth of the duvet against my body. Everything was spinning; the ceiling light, the dresser, and the square room could easily have been converted into a Rubik's cube. My eyes were partially open, enough to see a faint shadow of a man in a suit leaning over me. His cool satin tie grazed the side of my face as he kissed my forehead, and turned off the light, right before my eyelids fell heavy and everything went dark.

31

There was no radiant light to wake me up in London. No salacious sun peering through fuchsia curtains; or warm glow to kiss my body; just the ringing of a horrific hangover beating on my heavy head. Actually everything was soar, my head, my body, and oh, my feet. I could barely lift my head off of the cold pillow beneath me. *Where was I?* I looked around the room, squinting my eyes to try and make out somewhat of a comprehensible image. I patted my hand over the night table until I found my tortoise shell framed glasses; quickly placing them over my tired eyes to see several suits hanging in a man's closet across the bed. *Oh yes, I was in Jack's apartment in London. Thank God.* I unrolled the covers so find myself in the black dress I had bought from the overpriced Greek boutique. *Oh right, I was in London visiting Jack on my way home, and wore the dress last night.* It was all coming back to me now. My black pumps were tossed in the corner of the bedroom alongside my favorite leopard night bag. I cracked open the bedroom door to see Jack asleep on his black leather sofa. He was partially dressed in his suit and I could see his feet and one leg peering out from beyond the crochet blanket. As I crept up closer, I noticed the blanket had shifted from his body exposing his bare chest and bulging biceps. Oh my, Jack was hiding that body under suits all these years?! It wasn't possible; perhaps he had recently hit the gym with his new lady friend. Whatever the case, he looked like Clark Kent resting after a battle as his alter ego– a much more handsome version actually. I tiptoed closer to raise the blanket under his chin, than headed for the shower.

I recalled bits and pieces of last night's events as the water poured down on me, waking me up, one warm minute at a time. Oddly enough I wasn't terribly mortified about any particular untamed act of craziness – either that or I had limited recollection of the night. Feeling partially awake I packed my luggage and threw on a pair of torn jeans and a cropped blush pink t- shirt. When I was all packed up and ready to go, I made my way to the kitchen in search of coffee. My hair hung long and wet, dripping fresh drops of water down my back, and onto the wooden floor as I searched through the cupboards for any source of caffeine.

To no great surprise, Jack's shelves were perfectly organized and labeled, reminiscent of Mikey's apartment; what was it with single handsome bachelors? I could learn a thing or two from them. "Upper right cabinet behind the tea, I bought your favorite Cappuccino," a groggy voice spoke out from under the blanket. "Jack you're up, I hope I didn't wake you." "Nope, you didn't I need coffee too." "Coming right up. You still drink Espresso?" I asked looking further in to the cabinet. "Yes, you remember?" he asked propping himself up on the couch exposing his sculpted chest. "Yup, not that common for American guys," I replied burying my flushed face back into the cabinet. "How come you got my fav Cappuccino?" "Cause I know you like it," he countered nonchalantly. It must be his girlfriend's; the box was open after all. *Don't let it get to your head Bridget, you're catching a plane today and will be on the other side of the Atlantic by Chicago nightfall.*

"What time's your flight?" Jack inquired standing tall revealing his half naked body. "Umm like, 4 pm I think," I said stuttering and turning around. "Great, plenty of time for coffee, breakfast, and a mini tour on route to the airport. I'll jump in the shower, gimme 20 minutes." As soon as he had turned away, I leaned back twisting my head to catch a quick glimpse. His back was sculpted and broad, ending in a perfect V-shaped waist. His pants hung perfectly on his hips revealing the upper elastic of his Hugo Boss boxers. He was sexy, smart, caring *and my friend...* I could barely come to grip with the apparent facts.

Taking a deep breath I began fiddling around in the kitchen making coffee and bagels. Jack reappeared about a half hour later, freshly showered wearing a navy blue v-neck t-shirt and jeans. He was barefoot and smelled of musk and some type of cedar wood shower gel – he was quite the sight for sore eyes, and my heart sank just thinking about leaving. "Are you all packed – passport and all?" he asked swinging his legs around the bar stool to take a seat. "Yup, I'm all good," I replied feeling a cobweb of sorts developing in my throat. "Do you know which terminal?" he mumbled amidst a mouth full of bagel. "Nope, let me get my ticket," I replied scurrying to my travel bag. "The bagels are good Bridge," "not that making a bagel and cream cheese is tough Jack, but I have come a long way from burnt toast," "that I know oh too well," he responded laughing taking another bite.

"Ok, so it looks like I'm departing from Terminal 2 @ 4 pm – 14 hundred hours."

"Terminal 2, alright, but what was the last part you mentioned about the time?"

"Oh the departure time 4 pm – or 14 hundred hours as you say in Europe!" I replied in my mocked British accent. "Let me see that ticket please Bridget," he asked in a serious tone.

"Oh my, Bridget, you don't know how to read military time do you?" "Sure I do Jack, 14 hundred hours is 4 pm."

"Oh God Bridge where did you learn that? I'm assuming they don't teach military time in American schools."

"From working in Athens of course," I replied with confidence. "Well were you usually late?" he asked chuckling. "Ok Jack, what's the deal? I'm sure I've screwed up somewhere – you're looking pale – now fess up!"

"Bridget," he began, clearing his throat, "14 hundred hours is not 4 pm – it is 2 pm." "Oh my God – run Jack, we gotta go – oh shit – I can't believe I did this!" My heart pounded as I ran for the bedroom tossing my over packed luggage into the den. "Jack, if I don't catch this flight I'm screwed. "Bridget calm down," he urged calmly grabbing my arm softly. "We're never gonna make it." "Come on Jack, let's go!" "Bridget stop, it's pointless," he continued coolly, "I'm afraid you've missed your flight." I froze dropping my handbag to the floor placing my face in my hands. "Are you sure Jack?" I looked up at him with whimpering eyes, looking for a sign that it was some kind of joke. "Yes Bridget." "Jack that ticket is not changeable, that psycho client of mine booked it, and now I'll need to buy a whole new one, and I'm broke." "What happened to the money you made from the commercial?" "I used the down payment to live off of the entire time I was in Athens, and the remaining payment was for the crew, director and expenses. I'm screwed. I really screwed up this time Jack. More than any other time I've called you crying." "Hush Bridget," there is a solution to every problem and we'll find it," he said putting his arms around me to hug me. I turned to him, placing my head on his chest, and my arms around his waist. I had managed to cause yet another catastrophe; and it was at the heap of this moronic mess, that I felt the most comfort I had experienced in the past seven months.

32

Jack insisted I stay put until I figured out exactly what I'd do next. I wouldn't accept his offer to buy me a ticket home, and since my credit cards were racked up, my only option was to borrow the fare from Lea or Vivian or earn the money in London. "You could produce some commercials here Bridge, or do some PR or something – I don't know much about your line of business, but you do have an EU passport, and you can work here." "You mean like, live here, and move here?" I was dumbfounded by Jack's suggestion. "Well, I meant stay until you save up the money to buy a flight home. You can have my bedroom and I'll sleep on the couch." *I wonder what your girlfriend will think of that.* "I could never have that Jack. I'll take the couch. "We'll see Bridget, but on second thought, finding a gig here quick will be quite difficult especially this time of year. You could always help me out at the office, that way you can earn your ticket home fair and square," he suggested, taking a bite out of an apple. Not wanting to put Lea or Vivian in a difficult position, or tell my either parent about this disaster, I decided Jack's proposition was the best solution. "As long as I get the couch you've got yourself a deal Mr. Nichols," I said extending out my hand. He took a moment to stare at it, then shook it firmly smiling, "ok deal Bridget."

*

London was light years ahead of Athens. Not to mention triple in price. I thought the Euro was bad, but the pound was a bloody nightmare. I could barely afford a pack of gum. There were high rises everywhere, digital signage, blocks and blocks of brilliant boutiques and popular theatre districts in the west end and central London featuring long-running musicals. Not that I'd be able to attend much of anything, but it filled my artistic heart just daydreaming about it. So daydream I did, that plus window-shopping and people watching, had become my new hobby. Jack provided me with a metro pass for the underground, and my first few days consisted of trying to find my way to his office with as little detours as possible. The London underground was no Athens two-line metro system; that was for certain. The city was massive, and always seemed full of global visitors. As the weeks flew by, I began to feel more and more like a Londoner. I was barely getting lost on the underground, chatting up new faces in places I frequented, well ok, Jack's office, the supermarket & corner coffee house; and for the most part, was actually happy. Jack pretty much worked late every night, or had late dinner meetings, so I found myself alone most evenings, but unlike my experience in Athens, didn't really feel lonely. I credited it to the electricity of the city, a new lifestyle, *and Jack*. Even thoughts of the last several months had begun to subside. I spoke to Vivian, Lea, and my mother, often on Skype, and there was an overwhelming positive consensus; I was safe and sound with Jack in London. Mom knew all about Jack; the shoulder he lent me after every failed attempt at dating, creative endeavor, and nutty adventure gone wrong. Of course after each story, she had insisted he was the one I should be dating; little did I know she might have been on to something after all. Ironically enough, dating was the furthest thing on my mind since arriving in London. I hadn't focused on much else asides from assisting Jack with his work, and looking for additional PR gigs; of course that included saving money for my ticket home, even though it no longer felt urgent, thanks to Jack's hospitality.

Excluding long conversations with a woman named Robin, Jack's personal life was pretty dormant, or at least something he wanted me to know nothing about. I suspected Robin was the lady in his life, but he never really mentioned her, except for a few dinners and other outings she accompanied him on. Perhaps it wasn't that serious after all; what ever it was, Jack seemed content with his life, and showed no inkling in pursuing me.

*

It was Friday night, and Jack had arrived home at a decent hour. I wondered if he wanted to perhaps eat out, or ask me to head out to the theatre. "I've got a dinner thing with Robin tonight, so I'll be eating out Bridge, no need to save me anything, I'll be late," Jack called out from inside the bathroom. "Sure thing Jack," I responded masking my disappointment. He had just exited the bathroom in a sharp grey suit and salmon colored tie; he must be taking her to the ballet, or maybe to the theatre followed by a fancy dinner. Whoever she was, she was lucky. I hadn't seen anymore London nightlife since my drunken stupor the night before I missed my flight, and I suppose I didn't deserve any more of Jack's generosity. I decided to curl up on the couch in my pink sweats and have a three-way Skype call with Vivian and Lea.

"Maybe we should come for a visit?" Vivian suggested after hearing what London had to offer, "yes I would love to get away from Gio and my parents for a bit," added Lea. "Really, you guys could do that?" I responded in great pleasure. "Yes, it's vacation time after all for us corporate girls, and you've been alone way too long Bridge. Hopefully you can come up with the rest of money for your ticket home and we all fly back to Chicago together." Lea's plan was great, perfect actually, but I couldn't figure out why the thought of leaving London left an achy feeling in my stomach. Nevertheless I couldn't wait for the girls to arrive, and finally hit the London nightlife.

*

It was just after 1 am when I logged off my computer and crawled into the black couch that had become my bed, when I heard the sound of keys at the door. Jack was home. He entered the den quietly as always dodging my tossed shoes, careful not to wake me. He was speaking on the phone softly, but I was able to make out a few phrases. "Great to see you Robin... Alright tomorrow... not a problem... of course I'll make it happen, it's a deal." *It's a deal?! Jack was using the same line he used on me! I guess I'm not that special after-all!* He must have been more smitten then he was letting on. Annoyed, I decided to block out the rest of the flirtatious conversation scrambling for my I-pod and headphones. Stretching to reach my headphones, I nearly went rolling off the couch and crashing into the coffee table. *That was close.* The last thing I wanted Jack to think was that I was awake and eves dropping. I placed the headphones into my ears turning my I-pod on full blast, avoiding the rest of his conversation. *Men, they are all just the bloody same.*

33

"Bridget!" I turned towards the shrieks, coming from the arrivals gate to see Vivian and Lea running towards me hauling their luggage sets through the Heathrow airport. "Vivian! Lea!" I had never been happier to see my best friends than this very moment. "Good God girl you look amazing!" Vivian yelled out, pushing up her large round frames towards the bridge of her nose. "Bridget I'd never know you from a European glamour puss – you're gorgeous!" "Thanks Lea, you look great too." I blushed forgetting how much I had changed since I had left Chicago. "Do ice cream jammies, high pony-tails and scrunchies mean anything to you anymore Bridget?" "Well maybe on Sundays Vivian, now get over here and squeeze me!" I replied laughingly, barely recalling the dull unfulfilled days and nights, in our colorless condo, staring at the snowy city through the large living room window. Unbelievably it was less than a year ago. I looked down at my over the knee boots, skinny jeans, and partially sheer top, I was a new me, and the past just seemed like a faint memory now. "Is it true what they say Bridge? Mediterranean women don't even diet, it's just the climate, the lifestyle, and… the men?!" asked an intrigued Lea. "Well not that I'm a pro at any of the above girls, especially in the male department, but it'd definitely say it's nothing like the American lifestyle I led." "Led?" asked Lea. "You mean you're officially a European Goddess now?" Vivian added striking a pose. "You guys must be jetlagged or something – I'm simply comparing the lifestyles and putting the facts out there. You know, there's no cut-off time to eat here, ruthless fitness regiment, or heinous look for smoking some tobacco. There's just something in the air that makes you go with the flow and not over-think things too much."

I suppose I should have credited my parents for the warning, in fact I was still dumbfounded about their accuracy, but instead I referred to Mikey. "Mikey told me about it when I first got to Athens, but I didn't understand it until I experienced it…" "Experienced what exactly?" inquired Lea with a puzzled look, "*the Mediterranean paradox* girls, it really does exist." "Well we'll take your word for it Bridget – so have you met any hot guys since you came to London?" "Vivian! She just got over a traumatic experience with that prick Bobby, she needs time to heal," scolded Lea. "How are you doing with that by the way, and more importantly how's your head?" I knew the girls' inquisition would have eventually begun, but didn't expect to hear Lea's mama nature come out so quickly. "I'm good – better at the very least," I responded reassuringly. "I needed to get away from him, that whole situation, I'm feeling much better now. Jack has been a Godsend." "How does he look? Same as when we first met him Italy?" asked Lea chomping on some bubble gum. "Uh not exactly…"I responded stuttering on my words. "Let me guess," Vivian interjected, "pasty white, exceedingly thin, drinks like a fish when not working obsessively, wealthy, and has a few women going on at all times." "Vivian! Jack would never be that guy. He was always a perfect gentleman," resounded Lea. The thought of Jack, perhaps even the sound of his name made me smile, and apparently made the blood rush swiftly to my face. "Are you blushing Bridget?" asked Vivian walking right up to my nose. "No," I defended abruptly. "Ah yes I think you are – either that, or a pound of pink blush fell on your face this morning before leaving for the airport." "Vivian stop. Would you let her breathe please," interrupted Lea smacking her bubble gum. "Ok fine, but Bridge you gotta tell us, how is Jack?" Vivian waited for a response while configuring her matching luggage in a neat row. "He's… well, he's…." I grabbed one of the luggage pieces and a handbag and headed for the Heathrow Express. "We need to get downtown girls, and there's a train coming in a few minutes – we shouldn't miss this one. Come on time to hustle!" I scolded.

A few moments later we had handed over our tickets to the train attendant and squeezed into the first cargo. "Ok we're on board Bridge, so stop dodging the questions. We get it, you're procrastinating," Vivian said sarcastically. "I just hope your hesitation doesn't involve that idiot Bobby! If I ever see him…actually better yet I'd rather not see him, just get me a lock of his hair, I'd love to put some black magic on that S.O.B" Vivian continued on her rant. "No Vivian, and when did you start practicing black magic?!" I countered frustrated with the interrogation.

Since settling in London, I had proceeded to fill the girls in on every last detail I had endured in the past seven months, most of which was received by a jaw dropping *what the fuck were you thinking Bridget!* As therapeutic as it was, spilling the beans on my Mediterranean experience, and what I thought was destined love, radiated an abundance of self-awareness, and some tough love from the girls, particularly from Vivian.

"I've barely thought of him guys, in fact, he's pretty much non-existent to me now. He used me for what he needed at the time and when he was done he left," I concluded. "Well, when you put it that way Bridge… Good lord, are you listening to what you're saying?!" Lea asked perturbed with my words. "You're ok with that?" she added. "Just think about it girls, we all do it; we meet someone, and want them for something; love, affection, attention, maybe prosperity, and when we're fulfilled, we simply continue living the life we had before, with or without them, whatever suits us best."

"Did you get that from *Before Sunset* Bridget?" asked an intrigued Vivian, "it sounds like something Celine would say." "It's just such a pessimistic view," added Lea, "and not like you at all – you are an eternal optimist, especially when it comes to love." "Well maybe I'm just more grown up now girls. I just realize everyone wants something, I was what Bobby *thought* he wanted, I fulfilled my purpose, and when he was ok, he moved on, without me. Maybe it was to heal him from his ex, or prove to Theron or to himself, he could do it. Whatever the case, when he was satisfied, he let me go, he was just harsher about it. I was not his victim, I know that now. I needed him too, and he was there for me, only I was in it for the long haul and he wasn't. I got damaged and he moved on, I just don't recover as quickly, or maybe ever. I mean are we ever the same exact person after something significant ends? I know I'm not, and I'll never be, and I think it would be a shame and a waste of an experience if I was."

My speech had surprised even myself, but I'd never felt more liberated. "You have a point Bridget – some good points actually, but… and yes there is a but," continued Vivian, "you were his blonde American Princess, he took care of you, then disappeared and didn't even contact you to see if you're alright, and you were all alone. Not a call or a text even - that just makes him an asshole," she concluded with vigor. "Sure he may very well have been an asshole to me, but he might be a Prince to another girl, the one he loves. I'm just not what he needs, and I know now, he is not what I need either, or will ever need again." "I agree with Vivian for a change," Lea said, "you were his blonde…" "Well maybe I was just the wrong shade," I interrupted with vigor.

201

The girls' words evoked a sick sentiment in my stomach I had long forgotten. "And that rough sex," Lea continued, "for goodness sake you weren't some two-bit hooker!" Taken back by her words, I looked up in her soft brown eyes looking for comfort.

"The moral of the story is that we need to plaster up that damage with a hot guy," she concluded pushing back the hair away from my face and radiating a soft smile. "You mean – get over someone by getting under someone else?!" added Vivian. "No Vivian! She's not a call girl for goodness sake!"

"Enough with the call girl references guys please!" I said adjusting my boots over my knees.

"Oh lighten up Lea! Bridget, I'll I'm saying is you need a distraction!" "So how's Jack then? You never did answer." Vivian was relentless, removing her glasses to clean them with one of Youssef's monogrammed handkerchiefs. "What?" she said looking up. "He was crying when I left, and I took it as a memento."

A warm feeling surged through me as the train slowed down. "Our stop's coming up girls, get up – grab the bags," I directed. *'Paddington station, arriving at Paddington Station.'* The doors slid open as we scrambled with the luggage making our way onto the platform. "Well Bridget?" Lea said struggling with her bags. "Well what?!" I responded in my best dumb-founded manner. "You've managed to avoid any talk of Jack the entire ride, so what's the deal?" she asked adjusting her unity scarf. "Well girls, you can ask him yourself he's standing right over there," I said pointing over to the escalators. Jack was standing in a tailored grey suit and white button down, leaning against a large pillar; he held his I-phone then glanced at the large watch sitting on his wrist. "Oh my - that's Jack?" gasped an open mouthed Vivian. "I'm speechless – he's… he's James Bond!" "He sure has come a long way since that Italian vacation. You've definitely been holding back Bridge," Lea added fidgeting with her ponytail. "Well ladies," I began, as I led them towards Jack gesturing a brief wave, "you wanna know how Jack is…? *He's fucking amazing; and he's taken.*"

34

"Technically I introduced you guys; I mean if I hadn't been dating his cousin…you gotta admit I am the bearer of good news for this trio!" Lea exclaimed gushing with pride. "Oh shush Lea! It's not like you got her an investor deal with that Martin character! You had a summer fling with an Italian hottie who had a cute cousin – they were bound to meet!" Vivian replied with a wink my way.

Jack had dropped us off at a quaint Fish & Chips eatery close to home so we could catch up while he went back to the office and would be meeting us later on if he had time. If he didn't have plans with Robin that is. "Let's just get the elephant out of the room shall we," Vivian said sipping on her diet coke. "What elephant would that be?" I asked puzzled. "So, he's totally gorgeous, a perfect gentlemen and treats your friends like gold." "Oh that elephant," I replied nodding my head with raised eyebrows. "But he has a girlfriend, you're sure?" Lea asked with inquisitively. "Yeah Lea, I mean he said he's moved on - that we've both moved on - and after hearing that, I never brought it up again. I wished he'd stabbed be through the bloody Skype icon during that conversation. Anyhow being here with him in the flesh, he's made it crystal clear, *we're buddies.*" "Just hold on there Bridget – and stop the sulking. Have you actually seen this girl?" "No I haven't, nor do I ever want to Vivian. I'd rather she remained a figment of my imagination. Once I see her, she'll become real." "Do you think she's a model or an actress? Hence the low profile dating?" Lea added. "Oh way to add salt on her wounds Lea! Pass me the ketchup would ya', I'm ready to lick these frites off the plate; all diets are off while I'm on vacation."

I was always in awe of Vivian's confidence, perhaps more so now than ever. "I don't know much guys, but whoever she is, they definitely spend a lot of time together," I added skeptically sipping on some Pellegrino. "How about sleepovers?" Vivian asked pushing another fork full of frites in her mouth. "None at Jack's, thank God, that would be mortifying!" I replied cringing at the very thought. "Well there's only one thing to do," Lea said looking at Vivian then over at me. "It's the only thing that ever worked on Gio. Good old fashion jealousy. You need to make him jealous Bridge." "Jealous with what?" I asked perplexed. "Leave that to us, we're hitting London tonight."

"Suck it in Viv! Lea grab the left side and I'll zip," I directed stretching the black spandex fabric as much as it allowed. "We have success! Now that is one booty hugging pencil skirt!" "Tell me about it Bridge, Youssef loves it." Lea zipped up her low-rise jeans, threw on a crop sweater and platform sandals, while I decided on black leather shorts and a knit blush pink sweater. "Now that's Mediterranean hot Bridge!" "Really you think Lea? Like Italian chick?" I asked. "Hell yes!" "Just top it off with the highest stilettos you own girl!" Vivian called out from the marble bathroom. The hotel room at the *Park Towers Hotel in Knights Bridge* was nothing like what I had experienced with Bobby in Athens. There was no odd concierge, smelly bed sheets, or half lit disco ball hanging from a cracked ceiling. Instead the posh suite, courtesy of Youssef's business partner, belonged to an upper scale hotel in a trendy neighborhood, fully loaded with affluent guests and wardrobes to match. "What are you thinking about Bridge?" Lea asked poking me gently, "you seem a million miles away." "Nothing," I said placing my hands in the pockets of my leather shorts. There was no point to ever discuss Athens, Bobby, or any futile events of the last seven months, *ever again.* "Did you tell Jack where we were headed tonight?" Vivian asked interrupting my thoughts. "No Viv, it's senseless really. He knows I'm staying with you guys at the hotel for the week and I'm sure he's happy to have his place back to himself. Let's change the subject, shall we?!" I tucked away my morning sweats, and any lingering reflections, and headed for the door. "Didn't we say we're going to party tonight?! Let's get outta here ladies!"

By midnight we had hit a few hotspots in downtown London. Our last stop was a hotspot I had heard about from the interns in Jack's office. It was an up scale Hookah lounge complete with white and orange cabana booths, flavored Turkish tobacco, and Hookah pipes on the table tops; ironically it was very reminiscent of the Mediterranean.

"Those guys have been eyeing us since we got here," Vivian said pointing to two guys in fitted suits standing by the bar. "Oh my they're coming over here, they probably saw you pointing Vivian!" "This is not a bad thing Lea, Bridget needs to flirt and have some fun." "Don't play off like you won't be inhaling the one on the right Vivian," Lea said adjusting her crop top. "Need I not remind you that we are in London ladies, it's time to have some fun," Vivian responded standing to smooth out her skin tight pencil skirt. Watching Vivian was always entertaining, this time it was blind sighting, and leaving me completely oblivious to one half of the dynamic suited-duo.

"So what's your name?" an unfamiliar voice called out before taking a seat to my left. "Oh you startled me," I said looking past his black and white checkered suit jacket, red vest, and white button down. "Bridget, I'm Bridget," I said reaching out my hand to shake his. His soft hands featured manicured nails and perfectly cut cuticles. "Nice to meet you Bridget, I'm Faaris." His accent was nothing like Jack's, it was slightly British, with a foreign twist.

"Unique name," I said looking into his pale green eyes, taking the last sip of my Vodka soda. Faaris was a 35 year-old doctor; a GP as he put it, from the UAE who had studied in France, was trilingual and extremely flirtatious. "Let's grab a drink, what are you drinking?" he asked, "tequila, short glass, no ice – Patron if possible," I answered without flinching.

"Wow a woman that knows what she wants." *Little did he know I only recently learned what I shouldn't want.* He returned a moment later with two drinks handing one to me. "Here you go Bridget, I got the same, sounded good." "It is Doc, but just sip it, tequila is much better that way," I said confidently. "You're kinda cute Bridget," he said downing the drink; *so much goes for my advice.* "Thanks Faaris," I said in my infamous sarcastic tone. "I mean you're beautiful you just had a cute smirk on your face. Speaking of your face, you've got great collagen." "Are you implying I've had Botox Doc? I'm not your patient you know." "Yes I'm aware of that Bridget, and excessive collagen would actually imply fillers not Botox, and it's a compliment, you look great," he said staring at my bust.

The audacity! Ok Bridget, you've had enough practice now, you can play his game back. "Would you like to question the authenticity of something else Doctor?!" "Yes... I mean, no... I'm sorry, but your body is distracting, and that's not a line. Perhaps you don't know how attractive you are," he said waving over the bartender for another drink. *Now that was a line. I was no different than any other girl on this British rooftop – or was I?* "Perhaps I just don't trust strange men," I said getting close to his face, "and you have every right not too Bridget, so we shouldn't be strangers for very long." The doctor's confidence made his distracting suit less noticeable and his demeanor much sexier. "We're going to go grab a bite to eat, you and your friends are welcome to join us," he said taking a sip of his new drink. "Sorry but the girls are beat," I answered without hesitation, "ok then give me your number and I'll ring you," he said handing me his I-phone. He sure didn't miss a beat; he was either a persistent brat or a type A pro, whichever it was, it didn't stop me from typing in my name and number before rounding up the girls.

"So where we going to eat?" called out Vivian. "We're going back to the hotel remember?!" I said kicking Vivian over her ankle booties. "Oh yeah I forgot," she said fidgeting with her hair. "You're welcome to join us ladies, I'm in a two seater, but we'll arrange something," Faaris added in – of course conveniently mentioning he drove a two-seater – code for what I knew was a luxurious sports car that lured in type A gold-diggers. "We're good Faaris, thanks again," I said kissing him on both cheeks and shaking his friend's hand sternly.

After saying our goodbyes we hailed a taxi and were back on route to the hotel in no time. "Vivian! I could almost kill you over that comment. I was trying to avoid that guy at all costs!" "But why Bridget? Why would you want to do that?! You need to meet new people, and date! How many single, good looking, successful men are there left?!" "Plenty Vivian." "Are you thinking about Jack, Bridge? because yes Jack is great, but like you said he's taken, and even he thinks you should date." "What? What did you just say Vivian? How would you know something like that?!" "Because Bridget, he suggested we come here, he called me on Skype one afternoon. He was worried about you." Vivian's words hit me like what I assumed Mike Tyson punch would feel like. *I was mortified, even my loyal friend Jack thought I was pathetic.* "Vivian, Jack wants me to date other guys?!" "Not exactly," Lea replied intervening half asleep. "Glad you could join us Lea, now I suggest you spill it." "Ok hang on," she said sitting up. "Vivian's being evasive. Jack called us, yes, because he was worried and thought you could use your friends. He didn't say anything about dating. On the other hand," she continued, "I agree with Vivian, you do need to date. First of all you need to redeem yourself, and your self worth after that idiot Bobby. Secondly, you need to know there are other guys out there just as great as Jack." I wished I was drunk, too intoxicated to comprehend what my friends were saying, but it was the truth. I needed to move on, and perhaps a date with a handsome arrogant, doctor would do the trick. "Ok, if he calls, I'll go out with him." "Enough guy talk! Last one out pays the cabbie!" Vivian said racing out of the cab, dashing for the hotel's from entrance. Lea and I looked at each other as a simultaneous laughter broke out in the cab. "Oh bloody hell!" the driver said swerving toward me and Lea. "This usually only happens with drunken college kids. Well, which one of you are getting out to inform her this is not your hotel ladies?!"

35

The shopping in London was amongst the best I had ever seen, not that I had become a connoisseur, but I knew a good thing when it came along, relative to fashion at least. "We need to hit Harrod's before it closes girls," I said directing the girls to the next block over. "Slow down Vivian, you don't want to end up in the wrong place again." "Thanks Lea, hopefully it won't take you twenty minutes to come find me like last night." "Well Vivian, if you hadn't insisted you were in the right hotel, and had the bell man practically carry you up the stairs, we could have fetched you a little sooner, not to mention paid half the cab fair!" "How much did you have to drink anyway?" I asked laughingly. "Not much at all, which leads me to believe one of those Arabian Knights you met must have spiked my drink!" "Hilariously entertaining as always Vivian, but no one spiked your drink, and Faaris is no Knight in shining armor – not with that cockiness!" "Well you'll never know unless you date him," Vivian said opening her clear mushroom shaped umbrella catching the drizzles of rain. "Close that thing would ya! We look like American tourists!" "Well we are Lea!" "Girls stop it, we need to hit Harrod's before it closes, and I don't want you to leave London without seeing it."

Sometime after my lecture, and a few purchases at Top Shop my blackberry began to buzz. I had received a text message from a number I didn't recognize. "Is it Jack, Bridge?" asked Lea, "no it's a text message from the guy…" "It's the Arabian Knight isn't it?!" called out Vivian from behind the curtain of the change room. "What do you have super sonic sensibility or something Viv?!" "When it comes to certain subjects, yes in fact I do." "Well don't dilly dally Bridget, what's he saying?" "The usual girls, nothing romantic don't worry. He's saying hello, and he would like to go out to dinner…" "Well are you going to go?" Vivian interrupted before I could get out the full message. "Of course not," I responded. "It's your last night in London. Faaris lives here, and at the rate I'm making, and spending money, I'll have a chance to see him another time." "Just promise us one date before you leave London," Lea said turning to me practically sulking. "Sure Lea, I promise," I said pinching her right cheek. Her last words resonated more than anything else we had discussed, *before you leave London…* I had almost forgotten why I was still here; saving money to leave was the furthest thing from my mind, but it was reality.

*

We decided to spend our last night together in London at the hotel's restaurant, and had invited Jack to join, but he declined, claiming he had scheduled plans he could not break, *with Robin*. I had barely thought about Jack and Robin since the girls had arrived, especially since Jack was the one who suggested they come, a clear sign he had no problem with me dating any other men. "You don't know that's what it means," Lea urged, sipping on some Pinot Grigio. "Forget Jack for now, she needs to focus on Faaris," Vivian interrupted in between her bites of Sirloin steak and gulps of red wine. "If Jack didn't care about you he wouldn't have asked us to come Bridge!" "I'm not saying he doesn't care Lea, but it's obvious he's given up on me romantically. There is no passion, or an ounce of jealousy, and like my mom says *where there ain't no jealousy, there ain't no love.*" "Since when do you take your mother's advice?" scowled Lea. "Well the truth is girls, since the time I was in her birthplace and natural mating ground she's been bang on! Now I know that she actually understands men." "She's really got a point there," added Vivian. "I'm all about the jealousy with Youssef, I watch that savage like a hawk, if his eyes aren't on me when other men are around we've got an issue. Now back to the Knight. I believe we have already made a pact; in our absence, you will go out with him - at least once," Vivian urged reaching for a small grey box from her purse. "Here this should help," she said sliding the gift box across the table towards me with a broad grin.

"What's this?" I asked perplexed, "I'm in no mood for parting gifts." "Alright, then allow me to do the honors," Lea responded reaching over tearing the box open from the taped edges. "Since you don't seem to take our advice, maybe you'll take his," she said holding up a pink hard covered book featuring a man dressed in suspenders, a bow tie, and a wide smile. *Get the Guy: Learn Secrets of the Male Mind to Find the Man You Want and the Love You Deserve.* "Matthew Hussey is all the rage here Bridge! Vivian discovered it at Harrods!" *Oh my, was I that much of a mess, that my two best friends thought I needed self-help books?!* "I know what you're thinking Bridge - for the record it's not a

210

self-help book!" Vivian said resting her hand on my slouched shoulder. "He's Britain's Steve Harvey," she continued. *Oh yes, the 'Think Like a Man guy…' the American love aficionado my mother thought would reset my brain to think like – well anyone but me.*

"You should both know I didn't get past page five…" "well besides the fact that that's highly evident," Vivian interrupted, "additional advice from a British hottie who knows men couldn't hurt!"

Although the girls' preaching was passionate I could bare to hear little more. No book would help me find my way back into Jack's heart, and enticing a simulated Arabian Knight was the least of my worries. "Forget everything for now girls –it's time to make a toast," I said raising my glass. "Let's cheers to us, to London, to…" "to love, to finding and holding on to love," Lea interrupted. "Alright, if we must! Cheers to us!" I added; the sound of our clinging glasses solidifying our toast. "What would I do without you girls?!" "Go on a date with a hot doctor and send us the juicy details for starters," replied Vivian. The girls laughed as a variety of angst surged through me. I knew they meant well, but the thought of another painful diversion caused my head to ache.

"Damn I'm out of battery, Bridge grab a photo of us, we need to document our last night!" "Good idea Viv, Lea concurred leaning in for a photo. I grabbed my blackberry fidgeting for the camera icon when a variety of photos began to pop up on the screen. "Come on Bridge, what's the hold up? Is it another message form the sexy doc?"

"No Vivian, it looks like a disco ball and some tacky curtains," Lea replied peering over my shoulder.

There it was in dim lighting, the faint colors of room 207 that had once seemed so brilliant. It was the first time I had seen the photo, forgetting I had actually taken it.

"Oh, Mikey and I had gone to a second hand shop, and I just couldn't resist." I hoped my lie would satisfy the girls, and my momentary nostalgia. "Seems like precisely opposite your taste Bridge." "Sure Lea," I nodded recalling the grungy room, lingering smell, and buried memory.

"Yeah well sometimes you gotta remind yourself of what you don't like in order to discover what you do," Vivian added. Her words were

211

unknowingly profound. I was going to be alone again soon, and knew the girls were right, Jack had moved on, and I needed to as well. "Ok girls, a hot date with the Doc it is, consider it done; now smile!" I said pointing up my phone and hitting delete.

36

I managed to stay quite busy after the girls' departure. I was catching up on work I had neglected at Jack's office, and Faaris was giving me some much-needed attention. Albeit it was via cyberspace, but I figured Skype calls were the best way to go until I felt ready to date again. He was intelligent and attentive, and great to look at, and when I misplaced his cocky references and egotistical remarks, I liked him, or at the very least was intrigued.

He definitely had a unique flare, and tried quite hard to impress me, which was endearing, except when it came to material processions. There were his two sports cars, lavish condo, designer clothes, shoes, even his socks, oh and who could forget numerous amounts of luxury colognes. He even insisted on displaying his couture shower gels over Skype, leaving the camera on while he showered. It was almost nauseating, and I detested it to say the least, but his smart, sexy demeanor seemed to get the better of me. Much to my dismay, I was determined to find out whether his intentions were genuine or not, *and frankly I had nothing to lose.*

*

It was Saturday night and Jack had gone out, leaving me home alone. I decided to send Faaris a text message and perhaps try a first date; if he answered we could catch a movie or grab a coffee. I had only managed to spell his name when I accidentally hit the send button. Seconds later, my blackberry was buzzing. He had just returned home from errands and had barely slept from too much partying the night before, so we decided to check out the new Woody Allen film. I had 30 minutes to get dressed, make-up and all, and jump onto the tube in time to catch the previews. Faaris lived right next to the Empire Theatres so we decided to meet by the main entrance an hour later. I brushed out my mane and through on some tinted moisturizer with 2 coats of mascara followed by some pink blush. I decided on a quick and cozy theatre outfit; black leggings, my high top wedge sneakers along with a low cut V-neck knitted sweater. *There, that would do the trick, cute and cozy;* I patted on some cherry lip-gloss, and ran out the door. By the time I had reached the theatre I had a few messages from Faaris asking me about my whereabouts.

"We've missed the previews and start of the movie," he said on the other end of the phone. "I know, it took me longer than expected to get here." "My place is right down the street, walk over and we'll meet," he commanded before ending the call. Looking forward to seeing him again, I walked over briskly and a few minutes later had arrived at what looked like a new condo development in the heart of London. The lobby was quite posh, complete with white leather couches and a variety of intricate artwork and sculptures hanging on the walls and throughout the busy lobby; a far cry from the world I was accustomed too, even after moving in with Jack. "May I help you Miss?" asked a sharply dressed concierge. "Sure I'm here to see, Faaris." "Alright Miss, Faaris who?" he asked with an awkward look on his face. "Oh, ah, I actually don't know his last name," I said feeling my face turn beat red. "On second thought, I'll send him a message."

I walked back through the revolving doors feeling more like Julia Roberts in thigh high plastic boots, than an American lost in London. I felt a familiar, esteem killing nemesis penetrate my body as I waited for Faaris. Thankfully he made his way down to the lobby quickly. He looked different than I remembered. He was wearing a blue shirt unbuttoned way past his chest, black jeans, and brown dress shoes with bright red laces. His belt buckle was classic Gucci, and although he looked like he was trying exceptionally hard to prove something, I had to admit, he looked awfully sexy. I waved at him from beyond the lobby door trying to maintain my composure, knowing the girls would have gotten a kick out of seeing the *Arabian Knight* arrive in a semi suit to go to the movies.

"Do you want to go for Sushi?" he asked somewhat excited, "I already ate, remember, we decided on a casual movie?" I said pointing to my outfit. "I know, I know" he said "but I'm just beat from a late night and we've missed the start - let's just go up to my place, watch a movie there and order in." Faaris' proposition seemed perfect, I was tired, casual, and preferred subdued environments over busy nightclubs & restaurants any day. Without thinking it through, *at all*, I agreed, and before I knew it we were standing in the lift on route to the 44th floor; or as Faaris referred to it, his humble penthouse. "Your hair is curly," he said, staring at me, "I remember it straight from the night we met," he added placing his fingers through a few ringlets. "That's correct, I straightened it," I replied wondering what his next critical observation would be. Perhaps he was more accustomed to skinny blond Brits or voluptuous Emirate brunettes – *who knew, and who cared.* "It's sexy, long and beautiful," he said staring at me continuously. He took a step closer grabbing my hands, oh God he was going to examine my nails, my unpolished, un-manicured nails. "You have cold hands, are you anemic?" he inquired. *Did this guy ever remove his stethoscope?* "I was waiting for you outside and it's 10 degrees Celsius. I'd say it's not that clinical doc." "Oh, yes, that may be it, too, but you may want to try a multi-vitamin none the less."

*

Faaris' flat was several thousand square feet. It was one large floor with giant empty spaces, large pieces of art placed on perfectly wallpapered surfaces, and sporadic pieces of red leather furniture. It looked more like a showroom than a home. "Is the wallpaper velvet?" I asked, touching the soft black surface. "Partially Bridget, I had an interior designer put it all together for me." While Faaris had the 'perfect' answer for just about everything, my walls, and sarcasm, were at an all time high, and I couldn't help but entertain myself. *You mean one of your fuck buddies, a frequent sleepover buddy, or the hostess you bang on weekends who moonlights as an interior designer!*

"Do you like it Bridget?"

"What?" I answered popping out of my colorful daze.

"The apartment, the décor?" he said taking out two short glasses.

"Sure, what's not to like about leather, velvet & opulence!"

"What can I say, I like nice things," he said pouring some Grey Goose Vodka in a sterling silver shaker.

"Vodka soda right?" he asked placing the shaken liquor in a short square glass. "I hope its alright I added some light cranberry juice to sweeten it up." He placed a leather coaster on the table before handing me the drink. "Now how in the world would you know that Faaris? I do believe we were drinking Tequila together, than again it is a common ladies drink and I'm sure you entertain her quite a bit," I added sarcastically. "You were drinking it before we met, before the Tequila," he said taking a sip of his drink. Dumfounded and embarrassed I chose to take the vow of silence. "I'm observant when I'm interested in something," he continued, pouring himself another short glass of whiskey. My momentary shock had subsided. *Who did this guy think he was?! Light cranberry Juice?! He obviously had chicks in here on a regular.* "So you studied in France?" I asked searching for holes in his story. "Yes, I completed Med school there than went back to Dubai for my internship. My father is a gynecologist there, so I fulfilled my internship in his office." He was ridiculously impressive and becoming more attractive as the night went on. He didn't ask me much about anything, except for one thing, *if I had a boyfriend.* "Well I did, at least I though I did, while I was working in Athens, but I left, it wasn't good for me." My rambling didn't seem to phase him, maybe he was accustomed to dealing with emotionally unstable thirty year-olds, or was just tuning women out in general; whatever the case he didn't flinch. "What about you?" I asked. "I had a girlfriend for a couple of years, but she didn't know what she wanted...and" "and now?" I interrupted anxiously. "Now I'm single," he replied just as I expected, cocky and confident. "So how many women are you actually dating then?" I pondered with a smile. "One, or two... I have a couple of women I see. You know go to the gym with, have dinner with, and then we fuck," he blurted taking another sip of Whiskey. "Oh I see," I muttered startled with his direct approach. "Well what do you want with me then?" I asked crossing my arms across my chest. Faaris smiled and poured himself some more Whiskey, once again unfazed. "We need to watch a movie in the other room," he said matter-of-factly pointing to the guest room across our view. The room was equipped with a large screen TV and rather large bed outfitted with tall brass bedposts, a satin blue duvet, and layers upon layers of gold and bronze colored pillows of every size; not to mention harem styled curtains. With the exclusion of a canapé hanging above the bed and hand woven Persian rugs, I'd say his guest room was straight out of The Royal Mirage, Dubai. "The internet connection doesn't carry well into this room. The bed is quite large and outfitted like a couch, come follow me," he directed without hesitation.

"So what's her name?" I said walking closer to the guest room.

"Who are you referring to Bridget?"

216

"Why your interior designer of course."

"Nobody you'd know hunny, a friend of my sister's from Montreal, Canada," he replied nonchalantly.

You mean your Francophone sex buddy who fly's in to see you on the weekends, and has watched Sex and the City part II, one to many times!

"Since you work in show biz, you choose the movie," he commanded handing me the remote.

"I'm still trying to make one actually, my dream feature film."

"You're very talented," he said caressing my face and placing his drink down on the nightstand. *Talented?! He's known me for 5 minutes!* I ignored his attempt at buttering me up, focusing on his beautiful eyes. He was maddeningly sexy up close, and smelled amazing; no surprise considering he owned most of the men's fragrances in major British department stores. "Lets get comfortable," he suggested staring into my eyes and then disappearing, his head now heading for the ground. *What the?!* Before I knew it I was over Faaris' shoulder, my backside in mid air, my bust pinned against his right shoulder and my head hanging a few inches above the ground. "You've got some long hair there Bridget – it's sweeping the floor." "That may be a sign for you to put me down Faaris!" "Your wish is my command beautiful," and just like that, I was being flung forward onto the slippery blue duvet.

"You know there may have been an easier way to get me sit down," I said breathing heavily. "Maybe, but it seems I've got you lying on my bed now, so it was successful." "Not for long doc," I said sitting up and recovering the remote control. "Does this stuff actually work on women?" "What stuff?" he asked looking at me perplexed. "You know, the Simon Cowell shirt, the penthouse, fireman lift, I mean I could go on…" "No, no I think I got it," he responded with a chuckle. *I was waiting for him to secretly turn on a stereo system and play Your Sex is on Fire to top off his routine when he answered, 'yes."* "Yes?" I asked. "Yes, *all this,* does usually work on women." "Somehow I'm not surprised," I said grabbing the remote from his hands. "Come on let's watch something, I haven't seen a good flick in a long time."

We snuggled watching the movie until Faaris' body gave way, and he fell fast asleep; his left arm still lodged under my body. I tried closing

217

my eyes but of course there would be none of that – I would stay alert as ever, listening to the voice of Denzel Washington and the sounds of Faaris' illustrious snoring. Apparently turning up the TV's volume to muffle the noise, (a tactic I used on Vivian to sound her off), wasn't successful, but it did however awake Faaris a little while later.

"Come here," he mumbled half asleep, tapping his bare chest with his fingertips. His chest was a masterpiece. It was smooth and muscular and the color of caramel. He stroked my hair softly, then ran his hands up and down my body. Faaris was exceptionally passionate and sexual. He grabbed me by the back of the head and pushed my face onto his, kissing me with passion. I moved my hands against his chest, kissing him back and swirling my tongue in and around his mouth. I didn't love him, care about him, or even know him, but I wanted him, at the least just for tonight. *Perhaps I'd be my first real one nightstand?!* It was like entering an alternate universe, perhaps how men thought of sex. Faaris lifted up my sweater, tearing off my bra and kissing me passionately; he was aggressive and immobilizing. He caressed me everywhere, and although I tried to reciprocate I felt stone cold. "I want to fuck you on the kitchen counter," he whispered in my ear. The truth was I wanted Faaris to make love to me, hard and long, feel his intensity inside me, kiss him everywhere, climax and be done. I needed to feel the passion, then get dressed, and leave him without a word. Contrary to my fantasy however, I knew I'd never be able to just walk away, and by the looks of it, this was what Faaris was accustomed to, and I wasn't about to be another notch on his belt.

"I should go, it's getting late," I said attempting to peel myself out of his warm arms. "Just sleep here," he responded, continuing to kiss me, his lips making me tingle allover. "You've got tentacles like an octopus," I said trying to unravel myself from under his wound limbs. Unaffected by my words, Faaris eventually allowed me to get out from his reach, out of the guest room, and into the kitchen.

"The doorman will get you a cab Bridget, they are usually lined up outside here anyhow," he said standing in the kitchen in his tight boxers, pointing to the glass that surrounded the entire west side of the flat. "Let me show you," he continued, bending down and picking me up with his now trademark fireman lift. "Faaris!" I called out laughing "put me down." *How many over the shoulder lifts does this guy have in his routine?!* Faaris hadn't gotten what he wanted, but he was still being sweet, something I wasn't quite accustomed to at this stage. *Could the Arabian Knight actually like me? Quite doubtful Bridget! Snap out of it, this is how he gets women to fall for him!*

After softly placing me back onto the hardwood floor, I gave him a small kiss and made my way to the shiny elevators in the hallway. "Send me a message when you're home safe Bridget," he whispered sticking his head out of the heavy door to his flat. "I don't want to wake you, go to bed you're beat," "I'll wait up," he called back, and with the sound of the lift a door shut. *Charming bastard!* Who ever Faaris was, he was relentless, at the very least, I had to give him that.

*

The ride home was quick; the British cab drivers sure stepped it up a notch after midnight, I only wished the meter had slowed down, *immensely*. Paying in pounds was a nightmare, and made it progressively difficult to save the money I needed for my airplane fare back home. I wasn't going to let money, or *lack of it*, ruin my feeling tonight; I was being courted by a handsome, successful, single doctor, and hadn't thought of Bobby *or Jack for that matter* all night long.

I tiptoed into the apartment not wanting to awake Jack or answer any questions about my whereabouts. If he asked I'd say I was out with some of the interns in the office, or girls I met out shopping. *Why was I so paranoid? He didn't care about me in that way!* After changing into my boxers and tank top I scanned the apartment for any sign of Jack. His bedroom door was ajar, so I pushed it open to find an unmade bed, but no Jack. He never left his bed unmade; he must have been in a big rush and left before I returned home. I closed the door and retired to the leather sofa.

Having just returned from a date with a handsome, sexy, successful man who wanted me, maybe just for the night, but wanted me nonetheless, I had no right to moan and groan about Jack being elsewhere, or with another woman. The truth was the thought of Jack with someone else in his bed made me feel sick to my stomach and empty inside. I could never say the words aloud, but it was in fact reality. I grabbed my blackberry and sent a message to Faaris.

London Bridget: I am home safe Octopus man.

I switched off my phone and pulled the covers over my eyes waiting to hear the apartment door swing open, Jack stumbling on a pair of my sneakers, than asking if I was awake. I waited and waited, but the door never swung open, and Jack never came home.

37

I wasn't sure if it was because I had fallen asleep with a combination of angst from Jack's apparent absence or butterflies from my new crush, but I had awoken much later than usual, and with an awful stomachache. The London fog sure didn't make it easy to get up in the mornings either. To top it off, there was still no sign of Jack, and at this point I was convinced he had eloped and was going to barge in wearing a lei around his neck and a shiny silver ring on his finger. Perhaps going to Hawaii for a wedding and honeymoon over the weekend was a little excessive, but I knew Jack wouldn't spare any expense for his new love.

By the time the sun had gone down, my incestuous imagination had run wild; this time Jack would be calling to tell me he was moving to Waikiki, or at least staying there with his new wife for the duration of the summer. Not having a single call, text or Skype message to answer, I managed to cook, bake, and tidy up as much as I could, and was looking forward to a good night's sleep and getting into the office bright and early the next morning. As I laid in the fetal position trying to consol my persistently aching belly, my blackberry began to buzz. I had received a text message from the love doctor himself.

Faaris: What about cooking for me sometime?

The arrogance! Not even a greeting – a hello beautiful, or how are you?! I grabbed my phone in furry and answered immediately.

London Bridget: Evening doc, it's much too soon for that. Cookies maybe, for starters.

Faaris: ☺ ☺ ☺ when?

London Bridget: I suppose when you're done with your numbers one and two.

A few moments later the familiar buzz sound went off.

Faaris: No massage, no food and no sex, and you want me to get rid of one and two?

Well at least it was clear, the Arabian Knight was a fraud, a sex-seeking womanizer. I thought about ignoring the text but figured I should humor him, and his game.

London Bridget: Doc, I'm sorry to disappoint you, but I'm either number one or I'm zero, I don't exist.

There, that should shut him up. But the phone continued to buzz. Of course he wouldn't accept defeat this easily, he was a seasoned player after all.

Faaris: You can be my one and a half ☺

He was infuriating, and I wasn't about to let his sex appeal and charm get the better of me.

London Bridget: Doc if you wanna eat, just eat, then let's eat. I'll be in your area tomorrow night.

A minute later the familiar buzz sound went off again, but this time it'd be for the last time.

Faaris: Sorry but I'm working an all-nighter at the hospital.

There it was, the refined player's version of rejection, 'put out or get out.' I should know this by heart by now. Enraged that I had almost allowed myself to fall for yet another manipulator, I decided to pick up the phone and dial his number. I didn't know what I was going to say; perhaps I'd get rid of some built up frustration or tell him I wished he contracted a vicious STD from one of the women in his harem! Regardless, I never got the chance. He of course declined the call. I had lost all my power, and failed at yet another attempt at love. *Damn Vivian and her bright ideas; and of course those leather shorts.*

As the apartment filled with the melodies of *London Grammar*, I returned to the familiar fetal position anticipating my new realization would at the very least, alleviate a little anxiety, and some of the pain in my stomach, but it unfortunately did neither.

*

"Hunny it's times like these that we must turn to a shrewd man for words of wisdom." I knew my mother was a firecracker and telling her about my latest disappointment may not have been one of my finest ideas, but I wasn't ready to discuss it with the girls and needed to vent. "Ok Mom let's hear it." I was awaiting a yoga proverb or perhaps something clever she had learned from my Granddad.

"Dear, listen to me carefully, there are three things in life that cannot be long hidden: the sun, the moon and the truth." We have Buddha to thank for those words darling. You see, sooner or later Dr. Faaris' true colors would have exposed. The universe did you a favor allowing you to discover this now, before you fell for this manipulator or God forbid developed a relationship with him. You don't want to end up like your friend Lea darling, so many years in deep, she just can't get away from that young man." "Mother! Lea loves Giovanni! And besides he isn't a manipulator – or a … I don't know, but he's different, he loves Lea." "Alright dear, simmer down. I'm just glad you figured out this Doctor person so quickly; a bruised ego will disappear quick enough darling, unlike a broken heart. Now tell me how is Jack?" "He's great Mom." "Now's there's an unfortunate ship that sailed …" "Uh thanks Mom, everything's great, gotta go, love you!" I hung up Skype before my mother could get into the *Jack situation again*. One more discussion about 'the one that got away' or my horrible choices, and I'd be pushed over the edge today.

*

Monday's at Jack's office were always busy. After hanging up with Mom, I had decided to leave early and speak to Jack about my paycheck and perhaps leaving London at the end of the month. I still felt a little queasy, conceivably it was uneasy nerves from the occurrences of the last couple of days, but whatever the reason, I felt increasingly nauseated and decided to skip breakfast and catch the early train. Jack was uncharacteristically late. Not having seen him in his apartment the last few days was worrying enough, but now he was a no-show at the office as well. I had tried calling his mobile but it was off and I didn't bother leaving a voicemail. "What time do you expect

Jack in Dolores?" "Well I'm not sure my dear," she replied in her posh British accent. Dolores was Jack's personal assistant and a sweet fifty something year old, with short black and grey hair and oversized bifocals; she had a mild manner and killer sixth sense. I could see why Jack relied on her so much. She was always a few steps ahead of him, and knew him particularly well.

"Well do you know where he is at least?" "Yes dear, he's on a retreat with Robin. I do expect him in today." *Of course he was with Robin.* My heart sank. Out of my body it went, down the river and into the lowest point of the dark sea; now unfortunately familiar territory for me. Possibly the worst part being that it was all my fault. I was out frolicking with a man who's only desire was to sleep with me, leaving the door wide open for Robin to come in and swoop Jack away for good.

"Is everything alright my dear? You're looking… well a little green!" "I've barely slept Dolores. I haven't been feeling well the last few days, and it's just gotten worse. It's my stomach, I think I'm going to throw up." "Oh dear, was it something you ate possibly?" "No I've barely been eating, oh my, I think I'm going to be sick." "Oh dear! Bridget! Oh my! Someone call the paramedics she's collapsed!" And that was the last thing I remember before waking up in the emergency room.

*

"Orderly, lift on the count of three, one two, go. Get her on the gurney, we're heading for surgery." *Surgery?! Oh my God, what's happening to me?! I could see several hospital staff dressed in scrubs hovering around me, fastening an oxygen mask to my face.* "Miss Lane, can you hear me, I'm Dr. Bodkin. You're appendix burst, we're wheeling you in to emergency surgery. Node if you understand me." I nodded furiously scared as hell, and satiated with pain. I tried to look around for a familiar face but the pale walls and sharp corners moved too quickly past me; then came the loud bangs of the swinging doors. "Let's move doctors! Get the anesthesia going now. Bridget when you wake up you'll be feeling much better. I want you to count backwards from one hundred." The doctor's words became more and more faint, his image blurry, and as my eyes began to shut all I could think of was, *where the fuck was Jack.*

38

The recovery room felt like I was awakening in the Hotel de Glace. The beds were snow banks and the tabletops were sculpted blocks of ice. *Was it normal to wake up in a subzero temperature? Where was I anyways?* I lifted my right arm up and pinched my left hand as hard as I could. "Ouch!" "You're alright Bridget, don't try to move yet, we removed your appendix before they ruptured," a soft voice called out. Oh yes, my aching stomach, my appendix... I dozed off again. This time the air was warm, salty, and moist. Palm trees swayed in the breeze, white cube-like homes were piled up on hilltops in the distance, and fishing boats swayed along the shore. The wind was tangled in my messy hair, as I stood on the sandy beach starring at large yachts sailing on the stretch of sea. "Come on hunny, let's go for a dip the water is beautiful," a familiar voice called out from the distance. A strong hand reached out, placing mine in his. "But I feel cold," I replied squinting up at his face through the overwhelming sunrays. "No baby, it's time, come on, it's time ..."

"Time to wake up Bridget! Wake up Bridget..." I awoke to the sight of two bright blue eyes staring down at me, my hand remaining in his, just as in my dream. "Jack you're here," I muttered, "of course I'm here Bridget," he replied patting my hair with his free hand. "How are you feeling?" "Fine, never better," I joked, "confused actually." Jack smiled his world famous smile, "well you sure know how to make a guy worry," he responded holding on to my hand tightly. "I was feeling sick, I couldn't find you." "You might want to check your email from time to time Bridget. I emailed you days ago. I was away on a business retreat." "I use a blackberry a decade old remember?! My British SIM card doesn't allow me to sync my email." "Well that's what laptops are for," he replied in his charming tone. "I assume you sent it to my work email. I haven't checked that for days." I thought about my weekend with the so-called Arabian Knight – his penthouse, guest room, and the customary disappointment; it was settled, I was a walking disaster.

"I arrived just after you collapsed," Jack began. "Dolores was frantic, I called the paramedics and rode with you here." "You did?" I asked in confusion. "I don't remember seeing you." "Dr. Bodkin is a old College buddy, I called him as soon as we arrived. You were quite out of it." "Jack, I don't know what to say, I was so scared, thank you."

"You don't have to thank me Bridget," he said leaning down and kissing my forehead. I wanted to get up and hug him but I couldn't move; my stomach muscles felt like I had done a thousand sit-ups. "I want to get up." "Oh no you don't" he snarled quickly. "In fact the Doctor has relayed strict orders to me." "Well it's not fair if you're friends, he'll obviously take your side." "First of all this isn't a game young lady and secondly, Dr. Bodkin was called away and sent in Dr. Maniker *who is not my friend,* so I'd say were at even strength."

"Who's that?" I responded trying to place together blank spots in my memory. "Just another physician, a colleague of Dr. Bodkin, he's new, but good, don't worry. I've got a lot of catching up to do at the office; I'll be back to fetch you this evening. Eat all your food, *including the Jell-O* and do what the nurses say, please, no feisty stuff." "Sure Jack, I promise," I agreed wincing in pain. It hurt way too much to move so I knew I'd be bound to my word; I smiled and waved and couldn't wait for Jack to return.

*

I spent the next few hours in and out of heavy sleep; continuing to dream lucidly. The next time I opened my eyes a nurse was standing over me, "your blood pressure is great Miss Lane. Your temperature is improving as well." "My temperature?" "Yes you've had quite a high fever since recovery. You were burning up earlier so Mr. Nichols had you moved into this private room. He's been calling regularly checking up on you." "Jack?" "Yes, Bridget. The Doctor will be in soon to examine you. If your fever drops Dr. Maniker will release you. If not, you'll have to spend the night. I've been keeping Mr. Nichols a breast of the situation, he'll know when to come collect you," she said with a smile. "Thank you Nurse. May I ask you for a favor?" "Yes, Miss Lane, what is it?" "Can I have a mirror?" "Let me get your bag and see what it contains." "My bag?" "Yes, I believe Mr. Nichols had his assistant drop it off earlier, Dolores if I recall correctly." "Wow, yes!" I replied gratefully. My heart filled just at the thought of Jack; now he was looking after me and even though I was detained to a bed, and immobilized I felt like the luckiest girl alive. He was amazing, just like

Penelope had said about Javier, he was her *'amazing'* and Jack was mine, and it had only taken me six years to see it.

I opened my dilapidated Puma bag to find a change of clothes, including my favorite Chicago Blackhawks T-shirt, a hairbrush, some makeup, and my glasses. Jack must know me better than I thought I don't think I could have packed a better hospital bag myself. I decided I'd try to make myself look decent for my release later this evening. Moving around wasn't easy but I managed to change into the fitted t-shirt, and pair of stretch yoga pants. I brushed out my hair placing it in a high ponytail and positioned my glasses high on the bridge of my nose. I had some energy left over so I decided to put on some mascara and blush. I felt my forehead and decided my fever had subsided and I was ready to try and move around. I swung my legs over to the left side of the bed reaching for my shoes.

"Excuse me, but where do you think you're going Miss Lane?" a voice called out from just a few feet away. Having my back turned towards the window I couldn't see a face, but the voice sounded oddly familiar. "You must be the new Doctor," I replied still facing the wall, I'm just grabbing my shoes, I feel a lot better." "I believe that's for me to decide Bridget." I turned around as swiftly as my body allowed me, to see the Doctor standing by the door; there he was in a white overcoat and stethoscope around his neck, Dr. Faaris Maniker.

39

"You're Dr. Maniker?" "In the flesh Bridget - ironic isn't it?" "Ah I could think of a few other words for it, *for you actually*," I whispered under my breath. "What was that Bridget?" "Nothing just rambling, still a little woozy you know." "Exactly why you shouldn't be moving about! Oh nice glasses," he said checking me out up and down. "Looking pretty hot Bridget." *I had just had surgery and he was still being a womanizer. It was unbelievable.* "I hope you're referring to the fever Doctor." "No, you're good actually, the fever has subsided. I meant you look really sexy in those glasses. Cute and sexy all around; and in good health might I add young lady. I'll be signing your release forms." "Thanks," I replied gritting my teeth then placing a cardigan sweater over my t-shirt. I must have been mad thinking sleeping with this guy. Sexy and charming and all, he was a womanizer with no compassion, or respect for women for that matter. "You should be fine in a few days, just take it easy, no heavy lifting, excessive moving around and so forth. Have someone take care of you. I can send someone over if you're all alone here." "That won't be necessary I'll be fine," I replied sharply. "Is that guy taking care of you, your roommate?" "I can take care of myself Faaris. I don't need anything, save your energy for your numbers one and two." "Come on don't be grumpy Bridget," he replied chuckling annoyingly. "You are a feisty one, I'll give you that much." *The audacity! I wanted to tighten that stethoscope around his neck nice and snug and show him feisty.* "Considering I've lived with excruciating pain for the past few days, collapsed from a rupturing appendix, am recovering from major surgery and speaking to someone who doesn't pick up the phone when he doesn't get what he wants, I'd say I'm in pretty good spirits Doc."

"Bridget why are you up?! Everything alright in here Doctor?" Of course as any superhero would, Jack had arrived in perfect time. "Yes, Mr. Nichols, Ms. Lane is recovering nicely, you'll be free to take her home as soon as I complete the paperwork." "Thank you Doctor," Jack said reaching out his hand to shake his. "The nurse will be in to have you sign the discharge papers shortly. Remember to take it easy Ms. Lane." "Of course Doctor, I'm not planning on being the subject of any fireman lifts for a long while." Faaris turned and headed for the door, a broad smile apparent on his face as he turned for the hallway.

"Thank you for coming Jack, and for packing my things." "Come on Bridget, no need to say thanks, we're in this together," he said helping me off the bed and onto my feet. *In this together? Did he love me or not?!* This was torture, but as long as Jack was with me he wasn't with Robin, and I was going to make the best of it. "You know Dolores, fine details are her specialty. Did she pack everything you need?" For the first time I felt Jack was covering something up. There's no way Dolores would have unknowingly packed my favorite hockey t-shirt, or yoga leggings or glasses…. "She did a great job yes, I wouldn't expect anything less." "Great I'm glad Bridge. An orderly will be on his way with a wheelchair, and no, I'm not even contemplating letting you walk; I'll be waiting at emergency with the car," he said sternly kissing me on the forehand.

A few moments later the orderly arrived assembling my things and helping me get into the wheelchair. "Excuse me orderly, I need to speak to someone in registration about insurance or bill payment. I think I have travelers insurance, or my Visa does… I'm just not sure how it works here; can you get someone to help me? "Straight away Miss Lane," he said pushing me through the bare hallways around the short corridor.

The attendant at the registration desk was a cheery older gentleman who was eager to be of assistance. "It seems there is nothing on your account Miss Lane, the bill was settled this evening, and a home care nurse was added to ensure you don't have to commute to and from the hospital." "Well who did that?!" I asked, blushing and twiddling my fingers. There was only one person who had only always put me first, a noble superhero, who once loved me, and was now content with being my roommate. *"Mr. Nichols,"* we said in chorus.

"I want to pay you back Jack." There needs to be a limit to your generosity. Bridget you're in no state to discuss this." "I don't feel right about it Jack." "It's fine Bridge, I can afford it." "That's not the point. I'll work at your office until I save the money to pay you back." "Bridge you'll have to take up permanent residency to get that done." "Don't mock me Jack, you know how competitive I can be," I said crouching over in the front seat of his BMW. "Yes I do know that characteristic quite well, now relax and enjoy the view," he said speeding off past Big Ben, and afar from a newlywed couple taking photos.

*

"Your sleeping in my bed and I'm not having the slightest discussion about this Bridget." "Ok Jack, but I don't want..." "What is it? And don't tell me you prefer that stiff leather sofa. You need comfort and rest." "I meant I don't want you to go." "I'm not going anywhere," he said with a sigh, "we're trading quarters, I'm taking the couch." "What if I need something, will you be able to hear me?" "Alright tell me what's wrong, what are you afraid of? Next time I go on a trip I'll send you a text message, better yet I'll call you. You don't have to worry you'll never be alone again," he said hugging me gently and kissing my forehead. His words were comforting, perhaps just what I needed to hear. I retired to his room nursing my newly acquired stitches, searching for a clean pair of boxers and tank top. Jack's bed was incredibly comfortable and quite the upgrade from the rigid couch. Unable to stretch for the stereo remote, I hit any button I could reach on the shiny black converter. Orchestrated sounds of violins and piano keys soared through the speakers, then a Jazzy voice joined; *'I put a spell on you...I put a spell on you, because you're mine...'* Thoughts of the past weekend floated in my head, my sarcastic exchange with Faaris, visions of Jack's unmade bed, his midday rendezvous, his weekend retreat, the ambulance, the hospital, Dr. Maniker... *Oh make it stop!* I slammed the remote and buried my face into the merciful fluffy pillow.

*

Jack was particularly attentive during the week to follow. He called to check on me daily, arranging the nurse's visits and even leaving the office at a decent hour, claiming he preferred to work in the comfort of home – something he had earlier mentioned he detested. "Dolores and the interns miss you Bridge; they sent your favorite chocolates," he said one Friday afternoon after arriving home early. "How did you...I mean, how did they find these here?" Chocolate covered dates and orange wedges are sold all over the world Bridget, besides you had mentioned it once in the office, and they found the Greek sweet shop you love, its just opened in London." Jack was sure quick to shoot down any prospect that could remotely signify any feelings for me. Perhaps Robin had him on a tight leash. Whatever the case, I immersed myself in the moment, looking down at the shiny box, fearing the chocolates would bring back memories of Athens, the airport excursions, even late rendezvous with Bobby.

"They're perfect Jack," I said undoing the shiny red bow to reveal a variety of beautifully aligned sweets. The past and its memories lingered in my mind; I knew my mom would be disappointed in me if I admitted it. She always said the only thing alive was the present, and the moment something was over it was dead and gone, including relationships; "all discarded lovers should be given a second chance, but with somebody else Bridget." The words of Mae West rang clearly in my head. "You know they're not a pair of Louboutins," Jack said staring at me in confusion. "No Jack, they're way better," I said popping a piece of chocolate into my mouth.

40

"Stretch Miss Lane, big inhale through the nose, exhale through the nose, now push further until your head touches the floor." It was in this position in every class that I questioned why the heck I put myself through this! I could barely squeeze out a breath through my nostrils and was sweating buckets. It was an uncontrollable rainfall pouring down my burning face, while my caboose was in the air trying to stabilize my head to the ground. One would think I would have become accustomed to hot yoga in the last six weeks, but that wasn't the case. Some 90 minutes since I entered the room baring 50 degrees Celsius, I was laying in shavasana; the dead pose; and quite representative of how I felt. "Namaste," called out Jean, the former prima ballerina turned yoga warden that ran the class. At the sounds of her words, I ran for air and a cold shower. The birthday gift from Jack was thoughtful, my only gift actually, and I was going to show him I appreciated it by going to as many classes as my body permitted. The package of classes at the *London Hot Yoga Studio* may have been a hint I needed to get out more, or a sign that he wanted me either dead or partially debilitated, but I'd be going nonetheless.

"How was class Bridget?" Jack asked as I walked limping through the apartment door. "Oh just great, getting more flexible every day," I said reaching for the ice pack in the freezer. My body ached, and I thanked heavens Jack had his back turned to me enthralled in his large desktop computer. "I really want you to take back your bedroom. I mean I've inconvenienced you enough Jack. I'm feeling good – the hot yoga is really helping," I said stuffing some crackers down my throat while using my other hand to hold the icepack over my throbbing knee. "We'll see about that Bridget, depends on what the nurse says." The nurse's weekly visits were almost up, but of course Jack wanted to ensure I was all healed and ok to partake in activities excluding death-defying yoga. I had been working from home, and had saved a bit of money considering I was barely leaving Jack's flat. Then of course there was online shopping, Vivian's brainy suggestion to keep me occupied, simultaneously hindering me from having collected all the money I needed to pay back Jack.

Nonetheless, Jack was not complaining and seemed to enjoy having me around during the last little while; he even started to try my cooking. We stayed up together watching late night movies and trash TV, which usually ending in me falling asleep on his shoulder and him carrying me to bed and tucking me in before retiring to the sofa. As of late we had discussed the production scene in London, and he offered to help me find some work when I was feeling up to it. I wondered when he'd ask me to move out, but it never came up, *well Jack never brought it up*, but I was always waiting for the bomb to drop; there was no way I'd ever be able to pay back Jack and live in London on my own. In possibly the best news yet, words of Robin were scarcely mentioned around the flat. Perhaps he had realized she wasn't the one for him after all, or that flaunting her in my face would only lead to awkwardness. Dolores would have much better insight on their relationship status but working from home gave me little access to her, or the interns for that matter, who I had grown to rely on for the office gossip.

"Bridget, I'm jumping in the shower," Jack called out from inside the bathroom, I'm expecting Robin shortly – we're heading out. Grab the buzzer and door would 'ya." *What?! Expecting Robin?! Get the door?!* I looked like a freight truck had run me over, twice, and my body had just been recovered from the Thames River! My face was beat red, with yesterday's mascara running under my eyes, my hair was wet & sweaty, and I was limping in pink leotards and a ripped t-shirt.

Once again, my thoughts had gotten the best of me; Jack was simply sparing my feelings by not bringing Robin around more. Whatever the case, I couldn't meet Jack's girlfriend looking like this! With no access to the bathroom and a wobbly right knee, I hobbled over to the kitchen sink sticking my hair and face under the tap until it was drenched. I rolled up my pink leggings and removed my t-shirt remaining in a semi sheer white tank top with a peek-a-boo sports bra. There, I'd look like a sex kitten, or a JLO back up dancer; it was the best I could do on such short notice.

I could hear the water beating down furiously in the shower; the steam was peeping out from under the door, and slight echoes of Jack's voice hummed *bohemian rhapsody*. It was a rarity to catch Jack let loose, and I had discovered singing in the shower was one of his stress coping mechanisms', it must be an important night. He sure was taking his time, perhaps he was thinking of taking the next step with Robin, maybe he's ask her to move in with him, or possibly even marry him?! He must have arranged a romantic dinner, somewhere upscale with items on the menu I couldn't pronounce. He'd slip the ring into a glass of Cristal Champaign, then take her for a walk in central London, stopping by Big Ben to take photos! Urgh! All the speculating was starting to drive me mad! I had to find out if he was really going to propose; I needed evidence! I found myself looking through Jack's desk, dresser drawers, a couple cooking pots and even digging my hand into the soil of the roses I had planted, but I uncovered nothing.

If I were Jack, where would I hide a ring box? I would be very sensible, yet clever, away from my roommate, and close to me. As I pondered, I sat on the black leather couch to rest my leg, moving Jack's work clothes aside. I picked up his shirt then his pants to fold them, when a small black box fell out, tumbling on the floor. *Oh my good Lord, my ludicrous suspicious were right on after all. Jack really was going to propose. I had lost him forever.* I picked up the velvet box slowly and held it in my hand, starring down at it miserably. *Do I dare open it?* I placed my left hand over top the soft box and slowly pried it open. The sight was astonishing; just like something out of the movies. A cushion cut, baby pink diamond placed on a studded white gold band. If there was one thing I knew, it was celebrity jewels. It was easily over five carrots. As I starred at the remarkable diamond, the entrance buzzer ran multiple times. *Oh no!* I quickly shut the box and placed it back in Jack's pants, leaving them just as they were on the couch. Distraught, I hopped over to push the talk button on the white box hanging by the door. "Yes," I said holding back the button, and my tears. "Jack? Oh Bridget that must be you," it's Mrs. Arthur from 201. I've forgotten my keys, do you mind kindly buzzing me in dear?" "Sure Mrs. Arthur, just hang on a second," I said pressing down the 'open' button. "Oh are you coming in as well?" I could hear Mrs. Arthur speaking to someone else – but the response was muffled. It sounded like a few people were conversing, but the sounds of Mrs. Arthur's grocery bags were concealing the rest of the noise. *Oh good heavens, was she coming up now?!* "Mrs. Arthur, Mrs. Arthur, are you still there – can you hear me? I called out in a panic." "Yes, yes dear, I hear you, I am still assembling my groceries." "Who else came through the door, I mean what did they look like?" I asked anxiously. "Well, there was a tall man, in a suit, you know dear the Kevin Spacey type, he said he was meeting a business associate." Kevin Spacey? I guess Mrs. Arthur got out more than me. "Oh and there was a tall red head. Looked like that actress with the perturbing bust line – now what was her name… you know from that American TV series – *Madmen* I believe, oh yes Christina Hendricks dear. I think she was voted sexiest woman alive. I tell ya, she's some hot tamale!" "Ok, ok! Mrs. Arthur I get it! I mean got it, thank you!" *Christina Hendricks? Sexiest woman alive? Figures Jack had chosen a staggering rock.* He was dating ginger hotness and I was a hot mess. As I contemplated my dreadful fate, I heard the shower seize. Perhaps Jack would answer the door after all, perfect, I'd hide in the closet until ginger was gone!

As I looked towards the bathroom waiting for the brass handle to turn and the door to swing open, I heard several knocks coming from the front door. *Oh my, Jack please come out!* "Would you mind getting that Bridget, I still have to shave." *Shave? Urgh!* "Ah I think you looked fine earlier Jack, I mean the clean shaven look is really overrated." A few seconds later Jack appeared in front of the bathroom door dripping wet, his dark hair slicked back, a dull blue towel hanging from his hips. Considering I was hobbling on one leg, toppling over was becoming pretty probable. "So you think the scruff looks good Bridge?" "Definitely," I said nodding my head furiously. "Cool, I'll leave it then, I'll just work on gelling my hair," he said closing the door again "be a doll and grab the front door would 'ya Bridge." Well that *backfired! Me and my big mouth! Now Jack would look even sexier and I'd still have to face my fate!* "Sure thing Jack," I murmured limping towards the front door. *Here goes nothing,* and so with a deep breath, I reached for the handle and pulled the door inward waiting to greet my nemesis; but what I found standing before me wasn't at all what I expected.

41

"Can I help you?" I asked starring at the unfamiliar man at the door. "Yes, is Jack in? I'm meeting him here." "Yes he is he's just getting ready." "Do you have a quick meeting, he mentioned he has plans with Robin." "You must be Bridget, very pleased to meet you, I'm Robin."

Robin? Jack's Robin? I stood motionless at the door; eyes wide open, and mouth ajar. If Robin was a man, and here now, then all the other meetings, rendezvous were business meetings weren't with a woman, they were with him?!

"It's nice to meet you too Robin," I reciprocated extending my hand to meet his. "Please come in, I'm sorry to keep you out there. I was just expecting...well someone else." "That's quite alright Bridget, I'm sure Jack didn't want to bore you with business details at the end of the day. I'm more of a silent partner, investment end and such." "I see," I answered in complete bewilderment. "I have residencies throughout Europe so Jack usually visits me on business retreats, it's easier that way, but I happen to be in London visiting my daughter, so I thought I'd be a splendid time to catch up. He tells me you're helping out in the office, but really work in entertainment." I continued to gulp stiffly, the blood rushing like burning firewood to my face. "Are you on camera? I can see a little Jane Fonda look going on here." "No," I said blushing at my disastrous outfit. "I... I just finished a hot yoga class. I've never done anything in front of the camera." "Well you should, Jack tells me you're a real fireball, and now that I've seen you, I can see it for myself! My daughter produces local television shows here in London – ring her up and set up a meeting – that is of course of you plan on staying in London." "Well, I, I haven't really thought past..."

"I see you've gotten acquainted," Jack said exciting his bedroom in a sharp blue suit, silver button down and matching pocket square. "You look great Jack," I said rolling up my leotards to avoid them from falling further down my leg. "Thanks Bridge, what happened to your eyes?" "My eyes?" I said, looking into the toaster to see a raccoon like reflection. "Oh nothing, nothing at all," I said wiping the black smudges with a tissue. Jack appeared a few minutes later and greeted Robin with a stern handshake and half hug, then got into some small talk about business. They were heading out to meet some other investors and weren't sure what time they'd return. "Don't wait up Bridge," Jack called out. "Pleasure to finally meet you Bridget cheerio dear," added Robin. "Pleasure's all mine Robin!" I replied shutting the door behind them and sinking onto the hardwood floor.

Exhausted yet somewhat comforted with this newly found information, I was happy to have some alone time, take a long bath, and think. An hour later I was feeling and looking, more like the old Bridget. I had blow-dried my hair straight and even put on a fresh coat of makeup, and felt rejuvenated. I decided to throw on a pair of jeans and a sweater and take a walk into town. I replayed the last couple months in my head. *What did it all mean? Robin was not his lover; he was his business partner, and a man no less! And then there was the ring…what was that about?* Did Jack have a girlfriend I didn't know about, or was he holding the ring for a friend? Who knew, but I couldn't wait to hear what the girls thought of this mind- blowing news.

*

The air in London was different tonight. The pain in my knee had subsided for the most part, so I decided to keep walking and eventually headed to a retro cinema. Paying a couple pounds, I entered the theatre to watch a classic Woody Allen film, *'Match Point,'* the perfect love, lust, and murder mystery. I was munching on buttered popcorn and gawking over the movie I had seen so many times in my tattered PJ's when I recalled the violent, nasty murder scene that made me cringe; talk about a love affair gone wrong. I decided to sneak out just as Jonathan Rhys Meyers was loading up to shoot the unsuspecting neighbor and his disgruntled pregnant lover, the beautiful aspiring actress played by Scarlett Johansson.

"You never could watch horror films Bridget," my mother said on the end of the phone. "Yes I'm well aware of that mother, I forgot about that part and now I'm afraid to get back on the tube." "Well are you expecting to run into any disgruntled lovers on the London tube dear?" she said chuckling ever so slightly. "Very funny mother!" I wanted to tell her what I had discovered about Jack but it was pointless. If Robin didn't exist as I imagined, then there must be another, either way it didn't change my relationship status with him.

An hour later I had reached my final destination via the underground and was walking swiftly down the wide blocks, incessantly popping my head over my shoulder. I entered the apartment to find it dark except for one corner, where Jack was sitting, rocking back and forth on his leather chair in front of the computer. "Bridget," he said with concern as I entered the room, "I want to talk to you." *Oh God, he knew I looked through his things, he was kicking me out. Play it cool Bridget.*

"Sure Jack how was your meeting?" I replied as calmly as possible. "Fine, I've been worried about you – I couldn't reach you." "My mom called me from Chicago and killed my battery – antique blackberry remember?" "Yes," he replied smiling. "So you finally met Robin," "yes," I murmured, embarrassed to admit what I had really been thinking. "He's been helping me out with one project in particular I've been meaning to speak to you about." "Oh yeah? He told me his daughter works in TV, I'll give her a call on Monday," I added exhausted. "Great, but I wasn't referring to that. Come here I'll show you," he said getting up from his cushioned chair. "Jack I need to speak to you, I have to get something off my chest. I just, I can't do this anymore." "Can't do what Bridget?" *This! Living with you, working for you, wanting you, wanting you to love me* – but the words just wouldn't come out.

Jack was getting dangerously close to my face. "Just forget it, I'm beat and rambling." "Bridget," he said standing so close I could feel his breath over my skin. "Something's are more easily shown than said, come here." Jack had grabbed my hand and placed it in his, he hadn't done that since we met in Florence. *He was about to break some bad news, he was going to move in with his girlfriend, and I was going to have to leave!*

"Open the door to the bedroom," he said sternly. Puzzled I walked slowly towards the door twisting the handle until it opened enough for me to see an abundance of flickering lights shining straight into my eyes. There were countless tiny flames sitting upon hundreds of candles. *Oh my, he was setting something up for tonight?! What was he looking for, my approval?!*

"Oh God Jack, I think I'm going to be sick," I said running to the bathroom; sweating, with a rapidly beating pulse, and equally pulsating heart, I dove for the toilet and locked the door behind me.

"Bridget are you ok in there? You've been in there for quite a while!" *Yes! and I am never coming out!* 'I just need a few days Jack, to figure things out, and I'll be out of your hair!" "Bridge can I come in please?" he asked after a faint knock. I was being ridiculous, a grown woman lying on the bathroom floor. I pulled myself together and entered the living room to find Jack sitting on the couch, his arms crossed.

"Bridget I think you've misunderstood…." "Jack please stop; I know about the girl… I mean I thought it was Robin… ok maybe it was a little farfetched, but all the signs were there, then I met him, and he's … your business partner, *and a man*, but that still doesn't explain the mid afternoon siesta – which you never take…the unmade bed, which you always make, the long nights, weekend dates, and now the candles and…"

"Good heavens Bridget stop and take a breath! Let me talk would you!" I nodded furiously, admitting it sounded like a good idea considering I'd been on a tangent for the last while.

Jack pushed the frizzy hair away from my face and looked into my eyes. "Yes I took a nap, a siesta as you put it, that afternoon, because I was tired; no I didn't make my bed because I was running late, and the seminars and retreats were with my business partner Robin; yes a man, a married man, with a daughter & two grandkids. I wanted him to help me with a special project because he also invests in a diamond emporium." "What, why..?" I interrupted. "Shush, not your turn yet," he continued. "You should also know I insisted on home care because I did not want you to have to deal with that Dr. Maniker character at the hospital ever again. Yes, I know about that. He's not good for you Bridget." "Oh," I said clenching my teeth and swallowing deeply. "How long have we known one another Bridget"? *Was this a trick question?* "Around six years," I replied. "Actually six years to this day Bridget. Do you know how many days there are in six years?" "No," I don't" I replied confused. *Where was he going with this?!*

"Well I do, there are 2190," he pointed out pulling me off the couch. He took my hand again, this time walking me over to his bedroom and opening the door wide to reveal the incredible spectacle once more. There must have been thousands of pink and red petals dispersed amongst the glowing candles. "Bridget," he said his nose grazing mine, his hand touching my face. "You drive me mad, always have." "Oh God, I'm sorry Jack…" "And I have loved you every day since I met

you; as many rose petals and lit flames as there are in this room, 2190."
Oh my God, was this really happening?! "I want to give you something but it comes with conditions - one big one really." "What is it Jack?" I responded feeling weak in the knees. Slipping his hand into the front pocket of his slacks, he removed the black velvet box I had discovered earlier. He held it close to his chest, than opened it exceptionally slowly revealing the beautiful pink diamond ring.

"I want to know if you will accept this ring, but on one condition." "What is it Jack?" "That you will drive me mad forever." My heart beat quickly as the blood rushed to my face, and tears filled my eyes. "Jack, that is the easiest question I've ever had to answer. Of course I will drive you mad forever, I love you Jack." "I've always loved you Bridget," he said placing the stunning rock on my finger, then kissing me softly. I wanted him to kiss me forever. "This feels like a dream," I said pulling away. "Oh my beautiful, Bridget," he said starring into my eyes, "but it is." "What?!" I asked muddled in confusion. "What do you mean Jack?" "*It is a dream.*" "What?!" I replied again anxiously. "You're dreaming, Bridget." "Wake-up Bridget, you're dreaming." *What?! Where was I? What was happening?!*

I opened my eyes to see bare faint beige walls, an I.V., and a nurse standing over me.

42

My belly was sore, and my mouth was dry. "You were dreaming Miss Lane, I thought it best to wake you, you seemed agitated." "Where am I?" I asked the nurse confused. "You're in London Mercy Hospital, you're appendix burst and the ambulance brought you in." "Oh yes with Jack." "No actually Mr. Nichols' assistant Dolores brought you in. Mr. Nichols arrived later on." "I see, and Dr. Bodkin, he said it all went ok?" "That must have been some dream Ms. Lane," the nurse said taking my stats. "Well?!" I asked starring up at her in confusion. "Dr. Bodkin is working with Doctors without borders in the Philippines. The doctor will be in to see you now," she said walking away. "How's my favorite patient?!" The curtain swung open to reveal Dr. Faaris Maniker standing before me with a smug grin on his face.

*

"Feeling better Bridget?" Faaris asked, looking through my chart. "Sure, I guess. I'm sore, thirsty..." "Suck on these ice cubes," he said handing me a white Styrofoam cup. "Everything looks good, Dr. Maylor is one of our finest surgeons. Good thing he was on duty when you were brought in. I'll be taking care of you from here forward." "Oh great," I said sarcastically. "I told you I was on call that night Bridget, it was the truth." "No doubt Doc," thanks. "When will I be discharged?" "In a hurry to get somewhere? Doctor's humor!" He said chuckling. You should be alright to leave tonight so long as you have someone looking after you." "Oh...I guess I don't after all." "I thought Mr. Nichols may be the lucky candidate," he said smiling. "He's putting me up while I'm in London, I'm helping him out at the office too. Why do you care anyways Faaris? It's not like you have a lack of women waiting to make your bed or pick up your socks!" "Feisty as ever – even after surgery, gotta love that," he said shaking his head. "Well if you need anything while you're still in London, you can always give me a call. I do rounds here on the weekends, and you'll need some after care." "Thanks," I said looking up at him over the rim of my glasses. *I can't believe I was in my vulnerable state and at the helm of Faaris – the make belief Arabian Knight!* "Cute glasses by the way," he said winking as he turned to leave. "Goodbye Doc, it's been a blast," I muttered turning my back to him to grab my clothes.

Who would have thought putting on socks would have been such a difficult task, but apparently for me, it was. "Need some help Bridget?" a familiar voice called out from beyond the curtain. "That better be you Jack!" "In the flesh, boy I can't leave you alone for a second can I?" he said walking over to help me pull up a pair pale pink socks. He was dressed in his weekend attire, his favorite sweats, and sneakers – mine too for that matter.

"The Doctor says you'll be as good as new in no time. Do you want to come here for aftercare?" "NO!" I blurted out even before he could get out the sentence. "Alright, not a problem, I'll set up a nurse for the apartment if need be." "Gosh I had the weirdest dream Jack." "When you were under?" "Yes, I suppose, I don't remember much before that." "It's normal, I'm sure, do you remember any of it?" "Yes, but I'll save it for a rainy Sunday afternoon," I said pulling my boots over my black leggings. "Thanks for bringing me some clothes Jack – you did bring them didn't you?" He sat looking at me, but not as he usually did, he was different. "Yes, well sort of, I sent Dolores." "Cool, thanks," I said placing my jacket over my shoulders. "Here let me help you with that" "thanks" I said, thankful to have Jack by my side. "You bet Bridge, I was worried about you," he added softly, helping me place my arms snuggly into the sockets. "How was your retreat thing?" "Fine, kinda boring actually, would have rather been at home playing a game of Chess with you actually."

Now that was a first. Jack looked genuinely concerned about me. "You know I'm ok right Jack?" "Yes, but I just... I mean you're here all alone and I should have been there for you." Still deciphering my vivid dream from reality, I had a profusion of questions. 'Let's get outta here pretty lady," and just like that, Jack whisked me in his arms and placed me gently in a wheelchair.

"So what did you decide about homecare Miss Lane?" asked Graham the sweet orderly who had been looking after me since I arrived.

"I would recommend the patient coming in."

"Dr. Maniker, I didn't see you there," Jack replied swiftly, a fierce look in his eyes.

"On second thought, I'm going to take some time off and make sure Bridget heals alright. We'll give you a call if need be Doc, thank you," Jack said extending out his arm to shake Faaris' hand. *Amen.* I smiled and waved goodbye to the staff avoiding eye contact with Faaris; "take good care Bridget," he called out as Jack wheeled me towards the exit. "Bet you're glad to be outta *that place* Bridge," "oh you have no idea Jack."

*

"You feel like some ice-cream Bridge?" "Ah, is that a trick question?" "I see, you still believe chocolate is the cure for everything?!" he said stopping off at my favorite ice cream shop on the way home. He had grabbed a variety of ice cream treats, handing me over a bag of cool desserts in the car. He was being as caring as I'd ever seen, reminiscent of when we first met in Florence, even more so than what I had dreamt.

Jack remained attentive for days and even weeks to follow. However unlike my dream, he didn't attend weekend retreats, spend a wealth of time with Robin, or buy me a hot yoga package for my birthday. Instead Jack planned a dinner to celebrate my special day, at a cozy restaurant next to China town.

"Wow you look beautiful Bridget." "Really you like it Jack?" "Yes," he said confidently. I wore a gold baby-doll dress, with a built in bronze bra and satin straps that met in a soft bow at the base of my neck. Jack was in his usual tailored suit, but more casual, omitting the tie, with a few extra buttons left open on his shirt; he looked incredibly handsome, and was classically unconcerned with himself, or how good he looked; putting forth all his attention towards me. It was quite the change since before my hospitalization.

"Everything alright Jack?" I asked after he had poured me some more wine. "Of course," I'm just thankful you're alright Bridge." "I'm fine, you don't need to worry; and I will pay you back for the hospital bill."

245

He looked up at me before lifting his knife to cut through his thick steak. "If it keeps you longer in London, fine," he said chewing on a piece of steak. Not anticipating his answer, I felt the blood rush to the face and my palms begin to sweat; Jack had shown no remote interest in me staying put since I had arrived in Europe, *what exactly did he mean?!* "Let's go for a walk," he said after we finished dinner and shared a chocolate dessert. I don't know if Jack was making up for lost time, but he had swapped his usual tranquil demeanor for a talkative, upbeat, spontaneous one. "You know you were under for a while Bridget, and I had the chance to think about a lot of things. You were also mumbling quite a bit." *Oh no! What had I said? What had he heard?!* "Well I can't defend myself there" I said blushing. I had gotten quite used to Jack looking and smelling, perfect, amazing and unattainable, and tonight, just like any other night I was going to fight off any feelings for him. We were walking past Piccadilly Square when he stopped and took me by the arm.

"Listen, Bridge, I don't want you going out with any scum bags here." I was taken back by his blunt remark. Jack had never spoken to me so frankly. "You were saying something about Faaris in your dream, you were distraught. I could sense the tension in your voice. I know something happened, and I don't want to know what, but I know a womanizer when I see one, he's not the guy for you; and I'm not going to stand by and watch you relive another heartbreak from yet another jerk. You deserve much better."

The words struck deep into my core. *Just what had I exposed about the last few months, and what had I said about Faaris in my dream?!* Suddenly thoughts of Bobby, Faaris, and even Jack's evasiveness ran through my head, and before I knew it, warm tears were clogging up my eyes. *Don't cry Bridget, whatever you do don't cry!* "Well I guess it's me then Jack, I'm just not good enough for the good guys right? Is that what you mean?" I screeched. "That is not what I said Bridget! I'm saying a guy like that…how can I put this - he uses a formula, it's a numbers game for him, and he can just slip any girl into play. He's looking out for number one, himself, and no one else. Guys like that have no intention of wanting to get know you. Frankly if I ever see him again I'm going to swat him in the…" "I see," I interrupted whirling in pain from the reality of his words. "I suppose I made the same mistake with Bobby? Well, I guess I should have known better but it sure felt right when he was chasing me and tossing me around like a yo-yo while he figured out whether or not he was going to keep me!" I continued my rant now sobbing uncontrollably. "You want me to avoid scum?! Well I sure got that memo late. Oh and Faaris?! I guess I should have seen that one coming too, but the Doc sure had a great game plan!"

"Bridget Lane!" Jack snapped trying to grab my arm, but I slipped away and continued my rant. "I'd say it's a pretty wicked game you guys play Jack! Yes! I'm including you! You haven't shown the slightest interest in anything about me since I got here, excluding my near death of course! I'll get my things together and go as soon as I can. You and your girlfriend need some time together after all!" A last sob, and swift quarter turn, and I was running for the closest tube station.

"Bridget wait!" Jack called out turning to follow me. As if I didn't feel bad enough…I had consistently chosen to date horrible men that used me for their selfish purposes, and now it was my own fault too! I continued running, catching the tube just in time, and reaching the apartment block moments later. I ran down the final blocks to Jack's flat in my strappy gold sandals distraught at how ridiculous I felt. I unlocked the door, to find the space quiet and dark. I grabbed my suitcases and began throwing my clothes, shoes, and accessories in as quickly as possible. If Jack wanted to be here, he would have been, but he too, like all the others, had given up on me. I dug my blackberry out of my purse checking for messages, hoping someone had remembered my birthday. Asides from the girls in Chicago, there was one other text message:

Theron: Happy Birthday Bridget, kisses, Theron.

I suppose Theron's message should have brought me some joy, but it didn't. Incidentally it was a reminder of what our relationship had become; a cold obligatory birthday message, over text. I wiped away my tears and threw the phone into my bag. We hadn't corresponded since his last gig in Athens, and part of me was saddened at what I now knew, was the loss of a friendship. Although we never discussed it, dating Bobby had driven a permanent wedge between us. I felt as if my heart was breaking all over again. Throwing on a black suit jacket over my gold dress, I grabbed my luggage, and headed out the front door.

The hallway was empty, and I walked down the cushiony carpet reaching the elevators, for what I knew was the last time.

*

I managed to make it to the main intersection where I tried to wave down several passing taxis; finally stopping one. After tossing my luggage into the trunk, the driver settled inside and began driving away. "Where are you headed tonight all dressed up ma'am?" I had forgotten I was still in my gold dress, strappy heels with watered down mascara running under my eyes. "I don't know," I whispered pondering what in the world I was going to do.

As the words slipped through my chapped lips a bright red double-decker bus filled with tourists drove past us. The passengers' faces were pressed up against the windows on the lower level, and groups of loud tourists cheered from the upper deck. A neon sign flickered on the side of the large bus that read 'WE DO AIRPORT PICK-UPS TOO!' *I guess that would be my sign. It was time to go.* I closed my eyes and took a deep breath. "Have you decided where to, Miss?" "Yes. The closest airport, please sir."

*

It was ironic how different the Heathrow airport looked when I was using it as an escape route. It wasn't welcoming or cheerful. It was quiet and grey, with an array of passengers asleep on chairs, and floors; the late night cleaning crew was busy waxing floors and gathering garbage. I walked directly to the closest open ticketing counter dragging my luggage along the freshly waxed floors. "I need a ticket to the United States, Chicago please, one-way."

Apparently the price of a one way was *way more* than a round trip; something I suppose I should have known had I been monitoring prices and saving money for my trip home. "I don't care," I said "about the price, I mean" handing over several credit cards. "Put a little on each until you reach the total please." "Will do ma'am," replied the ticketing agent, "but the next flight isn't until the morning." "Great," I

248

said shrugging my shoulders, and feeling desensitized to any further disappointment.

I had already spent a full night in the airport and wasn't worried the slightest about spending another one alone.

While I was waiting for the news about the ticket I decided to send a message to Vivian and Lea, letting them know I was coming home. Surprisingly Vivian wasn't trying to convince me to send Jack a cookie-o-gram or surprise him in Agent Provocateur lingerie, "if he loves you he will come after you, he will know where to find you," she said. I decided to delete her message once I had read it and not respond. It was done; I was a disaster, a walking bloody disaster and the longer I stayed in London the worse I would get.

An hour later I was still waiting for the sales attendant to come up with a solution for me. I must have fallen into a light sleep when I heard a distant voice calling me. "Excuse me, Ms. Lane, I think I have something for you," the ticketing agent rang out while waving me over. Exhausted from the night's events, I could barely keep my eyes open. I leaned down to grab my luggage, hooking the handles around my wrist, staring down at my perfectly painted toenails, *oh my how I'd changed*. As I staggered to my feet, a hand reached out to help me, his eyes waiting to meet mine.

"Jack? Why are you here? Just go, I'm going home." "Oh no you don't Bridget," he replied in the most serious tone I'd heard yet. "You had your turn and now I'm going to have mine. You didn't let me get a word in edgewise, is that fair?" "No, I suppose not," I answered shamefully. "How did you know I was here anyways?" "Vivian called me. I was worried sick you know." "Oh yes, I'm sure of it, that's why you raced home to find me?" "No, I was giving you time to cool off, and frankly I needed a drink after that tangent. You were really out of line Bridget." "What?!" I said placing my hands on my hips. "You heard me," he continued in a vengeance. "I was just trying to keep you safe; and by no means was I telling you to leave or that you are at fault for dating men that are no good for you. Those guys were all jerks, and I wanted you to know it was time to stop letting that happen. Further to that, there is no secret girlfriend you were referring too; you have quite the vivid imagination Bridget. You know how I felt about you;

249

and you made it clear how *you* felt. I was trying to be respectful of your choices, but I can't stand by and watch you date scumbags when I know you deserve better, *the best actually*."

I stood admiring Jack's flawless face as he wiped the smudged mascara from under my tired eyes. "Bridget Elizabeth Lane, you can really drive a sane man mad – absolutely crazy actually." "So I've heard," I said softly. After a deep breath Jack reached down grabbing me by the waist and lifting me in the air, "and don't ever change." I was motionless, and partially stunned. *Oh God please don't let this be another dream.* I leaned my head on his shoulder and held on tight; I'd never felt safer, Jack was my comfort, my friend, my love. I wanted to tell him to never let go, but I didn't deserve his love. "You can hold on as long as you want Bridge, because I'm never letting go," he whispered. My entire body tingled, while my feet dangled in mid air. Jack pulled away for a second looking at me in the face, and then kissed me softly. I pressed my lips against his, tasting my own salty tears. Soft, and tender and tingly, it was the most beautiful kiss I had ever experienced. I was floating for what felt like hours, kissing Jack in a timeless bubble.

"Just tell me it's not a dream, there are no rose petals, candles or giant pink diamonds are there?" "What?" he answered puzzled; "I think we should get through at least one non-drunken date first, don't you, Bridge?" His words brought a broad smile to my blushed face, and before I could respond the ticketing agent sounded loudly from over the counter.

"Miss Lane, excuse me, but we've found you a ticket. It leaves in a few hours, boarding will occur shortly." I looked up at Jack, waiting for a reaction. It was the moment of truth. He looked down at me than towards the attendant, picking up my luggage and walking over to the counter. *Oh God,* Jack had changed his mind; he was sending me home, I guess I was just too much trouble to handle after all. Mortified, I watched *as* Jack reached the counter, speaking to the attendant before putting down my luggage. It was the longest minute of my life, and I had no clue how it would end. Moments later she handed Jack my credit cards with a smile. "Thank you for looking, but it turns out we won't be needing that ticket after all Ma'am.

43

A year later...

"We're live in 3-2-1. Audience applause now!" "Bridget you're on!"

"Looks like the royal family is expecting yet again! It's two more for William and Kate; yes they're expecting twins, while wedding bells are ringing for Prince Harry and Cressida Bonas. Hello everyone, and welcome to your weekend edition of *London Lane.*"

"She sure has a calling for this Jack." "Tell me about it Matthew. I'm just glad Robin set up the meeting with Iris and she saw it in her as well," Jack said tapping the fair-haired, smiling Brit on the back. "Well you'd be blind not to Jack– the apple didn't fall far from the tree you know," Robin added with a chuckle.

"So what'd you guys think?" I said walking off set towards the three awaiting men.

I had met Robin's daughter Iris, a month or so after my birthday, and she had concluded I was much better suited to work in front of the camera rather than behind. The creative team at *Garden Flower Productions* had developed an entertainment show based on an '*American girl in London*' appropriately named after my feisty Irish surname, and the city that had brought me hope, love, *and of course Jack*. A few months later, thanks to some magic from Robin, Iris, and Jack, I was hosting the trendy entertainment show, which of course centered around my views on *everything London*.

"You were great, you're always great," Jack said kissing me and holding me in his embrace – a place I forthrightly was happy to never leave.

"Would you stop adjusting that bow tie, Matt?!" I said looking up from Jack's torso. "Your segment's not until next week remember!" "Well as you're fully aware, I'm still single Bridget – we're not all as lucky as Nichols over here – although I must take some of the credit for that," he smiled grasping Jack's shoulder. "Well perhaps your appearance on Bridget's show next week will add a boost that profile, Hussey!" Jack responded placing his childhood friend in a boyish headlock.

251

"Was great to see you gentlemen but we gotta run, Bridget's friends are coming in from Chicago and we're picking them up from the airport." Jack extended his hand to give Robin a hearty handshake, and Matthew a half hug, while I waved goodbye to the crew of the Channel 2 studio in central London.

Jack stopped to shake the hands of a couple execs as we passed them by the exit. "Oh dammit, Jack I forgot my gift for the girls, I'll meet you in the car." "Ok hunny, wiggle quickly," he said softly tapping my lips with his before removing his hand from my behind.

I walked briskly into the studio, my legs constricted in my white knee length pencil skirt, in search of my surprise for my two best friends.

"Is this what you're looking for?" a soft voice called out from behind my desk.

Joanna, an ambitious intern was holding up a large paper bag with two small gift boxes inside. "Yes love, thanks so much. How you doing by the way, you alright Jojo? You don't seem as chipper as usual," I inquired slouching to look into her eyes. "I guess - it's a personal thing – you know boys," she responded quietly, her freckle filled face and large puppy brown eyes looking up at me with despair.

"I see, well you're in luck, that just so happens to be my specialty. Shoot kiddo." "I'm just upset because I liked a guy in my English Lit class, he's captain of the rugby team, super popular and all. He asked me out last weekend but after we went out once he never called me ever again."

"I see. Well, let me ask you this. Did he try to sleep with you?"

"Yes ma'am."

"And did you?" I asked crossing my arms over my knit sweater. "No, I couldn't, I mean I barely know him, I don't love him." Taking a deep breath, I placed her hand in mine and stroked her bright red ponytail. "You remind me a lot of myself. The only thing I can tell you is that you did the right thing. You may not see it now, but you will eventually; and it will come around the same time you begin to understand that 'intercourse is one thing, but intimacy is everything'.

"Wow, pretty heavy words."

"Sure are kiddo, not my own, borrowed from a great book, but I've learned from them none the less."

She opened her arms for a big embrace, to which I reciprocated, holding her in tight. "Thank you, for the words of wisdom."

"You bet; see you on Monday Jojo."

"See you Monday Mrs. Nichols."

44

"What is it Bridget?!" Vivian held up the large silver box softly tugging at the black velvet bow holding it together. "Well open up the box and find out Viv! On second thought wait 'til Lea returns from the lou, you should open them up together." "The lou! My you've become quite the Brit Mrs. Nichols." "Well considering she married her British Prince, I'd say she's pretty much an unofficial royal Vivian!" Lea added sitting swiftly back into her spot on the fluffy rug. "Only a city hall quickie wedding just won't do, girls, but not to worry it's what were here to take care of!" Lea had happily taken on the role of the wedding planner and I was content to let go of the reigns, except for a few surprises of course.

"Well since you've both convinced me to have a fairy tale wedding, you're going to have to accept the gifts," I said pointing to the beautifully wrapped boxes. "If it's Stella Mc Cartney I'm visiting on a monthly basis!" The thought of designer labels brought make memories of my Chicago apartment, month-to-month struggles, discarded ice cream coned PJ's and a mundane lifestyle that was now a distant memory.

"What are we supposed to do with these?" Vivian asked looking perplexed at the object lying in red tissue paper. "Well take it out of the tissue" Lea said holding hers up. "You wear it on your head Viv! Didn't you watch the royal wedding?! "Yes girls, you shall be wearing fascinators at my regal wedding" I said in an animated British accent. "I thought it was some kind of lamp shade," Vivian said placing the olive colored accessory on the crown of her head. "Move it forward," I said coming closer to adjust it, the décor should be facing outward and forward." "Well if you want me to wear antlers at your wedding – than so be it," Vivian said walking around balancing the fascinator proudly. "Oh shush Viv! If it's good enough for Posh Spice…so be it!" "Oh my, we are going to look like Beatrice and Eugenie, the daughters of the Duchess of York" Vivian said in her best sarcastic tone. "Well I'm not insisting on matching gowns girls, wear what you like girls." "Thank goodness you haven't turned into a Bridezilla!" "Now that would be pointless ladies, I have married the man of my dreams, and only have things to be grateful for," I replied shifting the large pink diamond on my right ring finger. "You never did tell us why you eloped. Good God you're not pregnant are you?!" shrieked Vivian repositioning her glasses. I smiled placing a large pillow under my t-shirt. "Hmm, looks pretty good don't you think girls?! I'm kidding, just kidding," I chuckled throwing the fluffy purple pillow at them. "I lost a bet. I'm sorry it's not more exciting," I concluded opening a bag of sea-salt bake rolls. "You got married because you lost a bet?" Lea asked perplexed. " I expected something much more romantic from Jack; but since it worked, can you share the formula? Will it work on Giovanni?!" "Or Youssef for that matter?" added Vivian crunching on a few cheese Doritos. "Judging from my track record, I think you can guess the answer to that one girls. Ok get comfy, this is how it all went down…"

*

Jack and I had been dating for a few months. When he travelled for work he brought me along, we explored new cities together, and were virtually inseparable. In my alone time, I practiced reading the teleprompter off computer programs Jack had downloaded for me, for my new television gig. Although we had gotten quite close, Jack continued to keep some of his walls up. He would bury himself in his work and some nights the closest I could get to him was his assistant Dolores. Then one rainy night I had returned home from the Channel 2 studio to find a dark apartment filled with hundreds of candles and rose petals.

"So what do you think Bridge?" "Wow you really add a new meaning *to making girls dreams come true Jack!*" "Well I think that would be one girl from here forward," he said walking to towards me in blue jeans and a black v-neck t-shirt; he smelled his usual delicious manly scent of cedar wood and musk. "Your soaked," he said, shifting my wet hair from my face. He grabbed my bag throwing it to the ground, than finally removed my drenched jacket, tossing it on the couch. Sounds of Steven Tyler and Aerosmith were streaming over the speakers; *I'm losing my mind girl, cause I'm going crazy…I need your love, hunny… crazy, crazy, crazy for you baby…*

"Quite appropriate, don't you think?" he said, pulling me close. I was virtually speechless. "Dance with me baby." I walked into Jack's arms, my wet dress pressing against his chest. "I'm sorry I couldn't get to you sooner," he whispered in my ear. I held onto his body tightly, warm tears dripping from my eyes. Jack grasped me from around the waist lifting me up to reach his lips, than kissed me softly. My lips, my face, then my neck, his face nestled perfectly on my chest; I wrapped my legs around his waist, resting my body on his. Making love to Jack was like nothing I had ever experienced; it was so intense, it made my heart hurt. "I had bought the ring before your dream you know." "What?" I said, looking up in disbelief. "A cushion cut pink diamond. You may have more talents than you're aware of Bridget." "I love you but I don't believe you Jack," I said unwrapping my legs from his body and standing up tall.

"You wanna make a bet?" "Name it," I said crossing my arms smugly.

"If I show you the pink diamond, with a date of proof, you have to marry me..."

"Hmmm let me think about that - sure I'll marry you Jack, some day." "Tomorrow," he said staring at me fiercely. "If I show you a pink diamond ring right now, with proof of a date, than you marry me tomorrow."

Without breathing space for an answer Jack disappeared and returned moments later with a small black velvet box. "Go ahead open it up," he insisted handing me the box. I held it trembling, than opened it slowly to reveal a giant pink rock set on a white gold band. "Oh my God, it's even more beautiful than the one I dreamt of Jack." "Take a look inside," he said sternly holding the ring up to me. A tiny white piece of paper that read 'authentication' sat at the bottom of the box. The script was in Italian and I couldn't make out all the words except for two, *Florentia, Italia* followed by a date, and the year, almost seven years prior. "What does this mean Jack?" "It means you are marrying me tomorrow," he responded placing the pink diamond ring on my left ring finger. "You bought this ring in Italy, when we met in Florence?!" "When you know *you know* Bridget," he said placing both hands on my face and kissing me passionately. "Now all you need to do is buy a dress," he whispered lifting me up above the ground again, sweeping me off my feet yet again.

"Wow Bridge! and just like that you married him the next day?" inquired a wide-eyed Lea. "Pretty much; *I guess when you know, you know*," I responded smiling and grazing the shiny pink diamond sitting on my ring finger. He gave Dolores his credit card and told her to take me shopping to find whatever I needed, and the rest as they say, is history girls. But tomorrow will be different, you all are here, Mom and Dad, even Uncle Dmitri & Mikey are flying in from Greece." "To tomorrow!" we rang out in unison clinging our champagne flutes. "Until tomorrow world!"

45

"Is the rain really bad luck for the bride Lea?" "Oh don't be silly Bridge, the odds of it raining on any given day in London are quite high, and secondly you're already living with, and married to your prince charming, nothing is going to change that," she said caressing the needle lace sleeves on my wedding gown. "My mom always said when it rains the bride is crying," I replied anxiously. "Your mom also uses a lot of ancient Greek proverbs that aren't applicable nowadays, so get a grip, you're makeup will smudge," Vivian interrupted entering the room fascinator first. I stood up to grab a tissue, having looked at myself in the full-length mirror for the first time. I had chosen a long sleeve mermaid style satin & lace dress, with a nude and lace back fit with a hundred tiny satin buttons running from the base of my neck all the way down my tailbone. The Spanish veil to match ran to the floor and sat on the crown of my golden blonde hair. "You're absolutely stunning!" a voice whispered from beyond the dressing room, "Dad! "I'm so glad you made it." "Aren't we all," added in my mother as she entered the church's back room. "Considering I'm going to have each one of you on either side of me in a few minutes, I'd say it's best not to quarrel; particularly in front of Jack's parents, they are rather posh, and British, and very conservative! If they heard your Irish and Greek fireworks they may ask Jack to stay clear!" I urged at them both fluttering my thick lash extensions furiously. "Dear you really need to be more proud of your heritage, embrace the passion!" my mother went on adjusting her large hat. "I gotta back the yogi up on this one Bridget, now that's something you can't buy darling."

"Yes, alright, I get it Dad, and I love you but this is not the time, please!

Apparently raising my voice had silenced my overzealous parents; my mother smiled hooking her left arm in my right; my father reciprocated on my left side, positioning the long Spanish veil over my face. After turning to them both, I looked dead ahead and placed one foot in front of the other, slowly making my way down the isle. The heels of my rhinestone-encrusted heels sunk into the deep red carpet with each step, which to my dismay was followed by a lucid flashback. Visions of Mikey's living room floor, the shaggy red rugs, beaming mountains in the background, and my distressed body lying on the floor; the floor I thought I'd never get up off of.

I inhaled deeply focusing at the magnificent sight ahead. The candles burned brightly illuminating my way past the gazing attendees, down the isle, than finally Jack, who stood waiting for me at the end of it all. He wore a charcoal colored three piece tailored suit, with a white necktie, tears filling his deep blue eyes as I walked towards him. Finally reaching him amongst the brightly lit altar, the flashbacks and preceding memories subsided. My father placed my hand in his, whispering something into his ear, than let me go.

Mom and dad behaved except for a few sharp tongue daggers, and Vivian and Lea each sported their fascinators alongside matching dresses in the front row. Mother had opted for a large yellow hat and dress, evidently inspired by the Queen in the latest royal wedding. She had consistently reminded me that Prince Phillip was part Greek and I had committed to a traditional Greek Orthodox wedding to appease her. She had coincidentally renamed Jack, Jacob, or Jacoba in Greek. Thankfully we had bypassed a full Greek Orthodox baptism for him, the church allowing us to marry given he was christened under the Christian faith.

"*Jacoba*" the priest said turning to him, "the Eastern Orthodox Church joins two believers into one. The Orthodox ceremony is steeped in ritual and symbolism. It is a Sacrament - and unlike other religions, has not been truncated or altered throughout the history of time. Are you ready young man?" He looked flushed, turning to me than the priest; I hoped he wouldn't pass out; I had heard of this happening to grooms under immense pressure.

"I've been ready for seven years father," and with his sweet words the priest began to chant loudly. The lengthy ceremony was under way; there was the exchange of rings, the lighting of the candles, the crowning, the readings from the Bible, the drinking of the common cup, the ceremonial walk, and lastly, the proclamation of husband & wife. It was the deepest and most meaningful experience I had ever lived, and I was utterly grateful my mother had insisted on it. "From here forward," the priest said linking our hands together with vigor, "there is no 'I', no 'me', only 'we.' Congratulations Jacoba and Elisavet, 'Na zisete eftychismeni' (live happily)," he said blessing us. I turned to Jack, a tear running down my cheek; he quickly dried it using his fingertip than lifted my hand to kiss it. "You may not kiss your bride in the Greek Orthodox Church," the priest urged looking at us both, "but you may look at each other well, and admire the beauty you see today in one another acknowledging its temporary wonder, for it is the first thing to fade. May God be with you."

We turned to see our family and friends standing and clapping lightly. Walking back up that same isle, *married*, felt completely different; I stopped to hug my parents, than Vivian, Lea, Uncle Dmitri, and Mikey. "Ready to go Bridge?" Jack asked turning to me then facing the large open wooden doors of the church. "That's Mrs. Nichols now," I replied grabbing his hand walking slowing towards the exit.

The rain had stopped and I had never seen the sun shine so brightly in London. We walked through the doors and down the steps of the church into a shower of white rice clusters and cheers. "Look here!" "Over here!" different voices called out for a picture. "Here guys," called out Lea, "in front of the rainbow, its perfect!" I stopped cold holding up the hem of my dress, my thoughts taking me back to the Athens airport. *"It comes after the most tumultuous of rainfalls dear, but it does come..."* and there it was, just as she had said, the most magnificent multicolored arc I'd ever seen. "Beautiful phenomenon isn't it Bridge," Jack said squinting at the bright colors piercing his eyes. "Only if you knew Jack, only if you knew."

*

By the time the reception was over, Jack and I were exhausted and ready for a getaway. My parents had asked me not to make any travel plans, so I assumed their gift was some type of honeymoon, and I of course had no say in whatever it was they were planning.

"So open it up Mrs. Nichols, let's find out where we're going tomorrow," Jack said pulling me down beside him on the hotel's fluffy king size bed. "Please let it be somewhere sandy and hot!" I squealed

261

opening up the large white envelope to disclose two smaller manila envelopes. I unfastened the smaller of the two, first; it held a wedding card embellished with a big red heart on the cover and a handwritten note in the interior.

"To my (only) and dearest daughter, your father and I have been saving this gift for a long time, before you were even born. We hereby give to you, and your new husband, a villa located on the beautiful island of Skopelos. You will find tickets to the island, as well as a deed to the house in the other envelope. Enjoy your new home, and make sure to fill it with memories, they are the only things that last forever. Love and light, Mom."

Dad had characteristically added in 'and dad' after Mom's note. "Jack they're giving us a house...a villa actually." "What?! where?!" "Well the note says:

"P.S., Skopelos is a small Greek island in the northwest Aegean Sea. It is the closest inhabited island to the beautiful island of Skiathos where my family is from and your father and I first met. It's a magical place, Google it dear. Mom."

As I had suspected, the other envelope yielded the flight reservations, "and here are the tickets to get there Jack," I said handing him the envelope over the cushiony bed. "Wow, well, I guess we'll be flying to paradise tomorrow Bridge." "*Guess* is right Jack, it is my parents *after all.*"

EPILOGUE

"Ladies and gentlemen this is your Captain speaking, Yiorgos Giannakis, we will be starting our decent into Athens in approximately 25 minutes, please prepare for landing." "We're here Bridge," Jack whispered caressing my face over his shoulder. Jack's navy blue eyes matched the blue sky behind the airplane's window, and waking up to them, made everything good, feel better.

"Is it a long layover Bridge?" Jack asked placing his arms through his suit jacket. "No just a couple of hours," I responded, adjusting his loosened tie and kissing him softly. Apparently there was no way of getting to the villa on the island of Skopelos by plane. We would be flying into Skiathos, the nearest island with an airport, than have to take a ferryboat to Skopelos. Our first stopover however, would be the Athens international airport. "Ladies and gentlemen, welcome to Eleftherios Venizelos Airport. The temperature is 28 degrees Celsius, partly sunny and cloudy, accompanied by light winds. On behalf of British Airways, we hope you enjoy your stay in Greece."

The airport was just as I remembered, and although I had feared the familiar surroundings may have triggered painful memories, I was pleasantly surprised to feel nothing at all, with Jack by my side the past was dead and buried. "I need to grab my favorite food while we're here Jack; there's nothing like Greek Spinach pie – you gotta try this," I said handing him my bags. "I'll be waiting for you right here Bridge," he said kissing me softly, *music to my ears*.

The smell of cooked feta cheese made my stomach growl as I stood in line of the local café I had once adored. Looking down I noticed the laces on my booties coming undone; bending down to tie them up something caught the corner of my eye. It was a bright beer hologram flashing in the center of the airport's floor. Oh yes, the infamous I-floor. "Wow! That's so cool!" a redheaded little boy called out. "Oh there's a lot more to see kid, I can alter this entire image just by stepping on it!" Evidently one of the concept designers had taken interest in the youngster, that or he was just enthused to show off his brilliant holographic design. "This was all my concept kiddo, I also imported the machines in the waiting lounge," he went on in his heavy accent. My stomach filled with knots at the sound of the unpleasantly proverbial speech. With too many people in front of me and a racing pulse I decided to exit the line picking up my pace back to Jack. I swerved past groups of people, and lingering family members trying to organize their passports. "Pardon me please!" I said trying to get around a group of airport workers hovering around in grey-t-shirts, the latter of which was taking up the small space I needed to squeeze through to get back to Jack. He looked slender enough for me to squeeze by so I made an effort to slide by him as discretely as possible. Just as I was aligned with the back of his airport t-shirt, a few inches away from his long dark hair, he shifted closing the gap between me, and my awaiting husband. Just great, my heart was beating even faster, and my head was beginning to ache. "Excuse me please, I really need to get through!" At the sound of my voice the airport employee reached for the nape of his neck, fiddling with his hair, then clearing his throat, and turning to face me directly. His bright yellow lanyard hung loosely on his chest disclosing an Athens airport security pass, and confirming his identity. "Hello Bridget." *Bobby.*

###

ABOUT THE AUTHOR

Christina Vlahos started her career in show business at the age of 22 when she began working at MGM/UA in Toronto. She has since worked as a publicist and communications specialist for various talent, entertainment, and production companies in North America and Europe. Christina later moved into production where she currently resides both behind, and in front of the camera, working as a creative producer, writer, and television presenter. As a teenager she wrote poetry and dreamed of writing a novel. It wasn't until 2013 however, that she re-picked up a pen, keeping a journal upon the advice of her Uncle while producing a commercial in Greece. It was those journal entries that eventually inspired the story *Wicked Games*.

Christina is currently working on the sequel, WICKED ISLAND.

Friend me on Facebook: facebook.com/wickedgamesthebook

Follow me on Twitter: twitter.com/cristinavlahos

Follow me on Instagram: griega22

Made in the USA
Charleston, SC
12 August 2015